MW00437025

The RIFLEMEN OF THE OHIO

BY JOSEPH A. ALTSHELER

CHAPTER I

THE EYE OF THE FLEET

The fleet of boats and canoes bearing supplies for the far east turned from the Mississippi into the wide mouth of the Ohio, and it seemed, for a time, that they had come into a larger river instead of a tributary. The splendid stream, called by the Indians "The Beautiful River," flowed silently, a huge flood between high banks, and there was not one among the voyagers who did not feel instinctively the depths beneath him.

A single impulse caused every paddle and oar to lie at rest a few moments, and, while they swung gently with the slow current just beyond the point where one merged into the other, they looked at the two mighty rivers, the Mississippi, coming from the vast unknown depths of the northwest, rising no man knew where, and the Ohio, trailing its easy length a thousand miles through thick forests haunted by the most warlike tribes of North America. The smaller river—small only by comparison—bore the greater dangers, and they knew it.

It was the fleet of Adam Colfax, and the five who had gone to New Orleans and who had come back, triumphing over so many dangers in the coming and the going, were still with him. Henry Ware, Paul Cotter, and Shif'less Sol Hyde sat in the foremost boat, and the one just behind them contained Silent Tom Ross and Long Jim Hart. After the great battle on the Lower Mississippi in which they defeated the Indians and desperadoes under Alvarez, the voyage had remained peaceful as they pulled up to the Ohio.

"It's our own river again, Henry," said Paul. Both felt a sort of proprietary interest in the Ohio.

"It's so, and I'm glad to look on it again," replied Henry, "but the Shawnees, the Miamis, the Wyandots, and others will never let us by without a fight."

He spoke with gravity. But a boy in years, the many stern scenes through which he had passed and his natural instinct for the wilderness made him see far. He was thinking of the thousand miles, every one with its dangers, that they must travel before they could unload their supplies at Pittsburgh for the struggling colonists.

No concern of the future troubled the soul of Long Jim Hart. He was once more in the region that he loved. He looked at one river and then at the other, and his eyes glowed.

"Ain't it fine, Henry?" he said. "These two pow'ful big streams! Back uv them the firm, solid country that you kin tread on without the fear uv breakin' through, an' then the cool steadyin' airs that are blowin' on our faces!"

3

"Yes, it is fine, Jim!" said Henry with emphasis.

He, too, ceased to think, for the moment, of the future, and paid more attention to the meeting of the rivers. The Ohio, at that point, although the tributary, was wider than the Mississippi, and for some distance up its stream was deeper. Its banks, sloping and high, were clothed in dense forest and underbrush to the water's edge. Nothing broke this expanse of dark green. It was lone and desolate, save for the wild fowl that circled over it before they darted toward the water. The note of everything was size, silence, and majesty.

"We begin the second stage of our great journey," said Adam Colfax to Henry.

Then the leader raised his hand as a signal, hundreds of oars and paddles struck the water, the fleet leaped into life again, and boats and canoes, driven by strong arms, swung forward against the slow current of the Ohio. Some rower in a leading boat struck up a wild song of love and war, mostly war, and others joined, the chorus swelling to twenty, fifty, then a hundred voices. It was a haunting air, and forest and water gave back the volume of sound in far, weird echoes.

But fleet and song merely heightened the effect of the wilderness. Nobody saw them. Nobody heard them. Desolation was always before them, and, as they passed, closed in again behind them. But the men themselves felt neither lonely nor afraid. Used to victory over hardship and danger, their spirits rose high as they began the ascent of the second river, the last half of their journey.

Adam Colfax, stern New England man that he was, felt the glow, and Paul, the imaginative boy, felt it, too.

"I don't see how such an expedition as this can fail to get through to Pittsburgh," he said.

"I'd like to go on jest ez we're goin' all the time," said Shif'less Sol with lazy content. "I could curl up under a rail and lay thar fur a thousand miles. Jest think what a rest that would be, Paul!"

Henry Ware said nothing. The Mississippi had now dropped out of sight, and before them stretched only the river that hugged the Dark and Bloody Ground in its curves. He knew too much to trust to solitude and silence. He never ceased to search the forests and thickets on either shore with his trained eyes. He looked for little things, a bough or a bush that might bend slightly against the gentle wind that was blowing, or the faintest glimpse of a feather on a far hill, but he saw nothing that was not in perfect accord with nature. The boughs and the bushes bent as they should bend. If his eye found a feather it was on the back of the scarlet tanager or the blue jay. Before him flowed the river, a sheet of molten gold in the sun, current meeting boat. All was as it should be.

But Henry continued to watch. He, more than any other, was the eye of the fleet, will and use helping the gift of nature, and, as he knew, they had come to depend upon him. He was doing the work expected of him as well as the work that he loved, and he meant that he should not fail.

The song, mellow, haunting, and full of echoes, went on, now rising in volume, then falling to a softer note, and then swelling again. They finished the last verse and bar, and began a new one, tuned to the stroke of oar and paddle, and the fleet went forward swiftly, smoothly, apparently in a world that contained only peace.

Jim Hart turned his face to the cooling airs that began to blow a little stronger. Paul was rapt far away among the rosy clouds of the future. Shif'less Sol, who held neither oar nor paddle, closed his eyes and leaned luxuriously against a mast, but Henry sat immovable, watching, always watching.

The hours, one by one, dropped behind them. The sun swung toward the zenith and stood poised in the center of the skies, a vast globe of reddish gold in a circling sea of blue. The light from the high heavens was so brilliant that Henry could see small objects on either shore, although they were in the center of a stream, a mile wide. He saw nothing that did not belong there, but still he watched.

"Noon!" called Adam Colfax. "And we'll land and eat!"

Rowers and paddlers must have food and plenty of it, and there was a joyous shout as the leader turned the prow of his boat toward a cove in the northern shore.

"See anything that looks hostile in there, Henry?" asked Adam Colfax.

He spoke rather lightly. Despite his cautious nature and long experience, he had begun to believe that the danger was small. His was a powerful party. The Northern Indians would hear of the great defeat sustained by their Southern brethren, and would avoid a foe whom they could not conquer. He looked for an easy and quiet journey up the Ohio.

"I don't see anything but the ground and the trees," replied Henry, smiling, but continuing, nevertheless, to search the forest with those wonderfully keen eyes of his.

"Perhaps we can find game, too," added Adam Colfax. "We need fresh supplies, and a country deserted like this should be swarming with deer and buffalo."

"Perhaps," said Henry.

When their boat touched the bank, Henry and Shif'less Sol sprang ashore, and slid silently into the forest. There they made a wide curve about the cove that had served as a landing, but found no signs of life except the tracks of game. After a while they sat down on a log and listened, but heard nothing save the usual sounds of the forest.

"What do you think of it, Sol?" asked Henry.

"O' course, Henry," replied the shiftless one judiciously, "we've got to expect trouble sometime or other, but I ain't lookin' fur it yet awhile. We can't have no dealin's with it till it comes."

Henry shook his head. He believed that the instinct of Shif'less Sol, usually so

5

alert, was now sleeping. They were sitting in the very thickest of the forest, and he looked up at the roof of green leaves, here so dense that only slim triangles of blue sky showed between. The leaves stirred a little. There was a flash of flame against the green, but it was only a scarlet tanager that shot past, then a flash of blue, but it was only a blue jay. Around them, clustering close to the trees, was the dense undergrowth, and they could not see twenty yards away.

The faint, idle breeze died of languor. The bushes stood up straight. The leaves hung motionless. The forest, which was always to Henry a live thing, seemed no longer to breathe. A leaf could have been heard had it fallen. Then out of that deadly stillness came a sudden note, a strange, wild song that Henry alone heard. He looked up, but he saw no bird, no singer of the woods. Yet the leaves were rippling. The wind had risen again, and it was playing upon the leaves in a mystic, solemn way, calling words that he knew or seemed to know. He glanced at Shif'less Sol, but his comrade heard only the wind, raising his head a little higher that its cool breath might fan his face.

To Henry, always attuned to the wilderness and its spirit, this sudden voice out of the ominous silence was full of meaning. He started at the first trill. It was not a vain and idle song. A strange shiver ran down his spine, and the hair on his head felt alive.

The great youth raised his head. The shiver was still in his spine. All his nerves and muscles were tense and drawn. The wind still sang on the leaves, but it was a warning note to Henry, and he understood. He sat rigid and alert, in the attitude of one who is ready to spring, and his eyes, as he looked up as if to seek the invisible hand among the green leaves, were full of fire and meaning.

Chance made the shiftless one glance at his comrade, and he was startled.

"What is it, Henry?" he asked.

"I was hearing something."

"I hear nothin' but the wind."

"I hear that—and much more."

Shif'less Sol glanced again at his comrade, but Henry's face said nothing, and the shiftless one was not a man to ask many questions. He was silent, and Henry listened attentively to the melodious breath of the wind, so gay, so light to one whose spirit was attuned only to the obvious, but so full of warning to him. He looked up, but he could see nothing. Nevertheless, the penetrating note came forth, never ceasing, drumming incessantly upon the boy's brain.

"I think we'd better go back to the camp, Sol," he said presently.

"So do I," said Shif'less Sol, "an' report that thar's nothin' to be found."

Henry made no reply as they plunged into the green thicket, treading soundlessly on soft moccasins and moving with such skill that leaves and boughs failed to rustle as they passed. But the note of the wind among the leaves pursued the boy. He heard it long after the glade in which they had sat was lost to sight, fainter and fainter, but full of warning, and then only an echo, but a warning still.

The feelings color what the eyes see. Shif'less Sol beheld only a splendid green forest that contained nothing but game for their hunting, deer, bear, buffalo, wild turkey, and other things good, but Henry saw over all the green an ominous, reddish tint. Game might be in those woods—no doubt it was swarming there—but he felt another presence, far more deadly than bear or panther.

The boy saw a small object on the ground, almost hidden in the grass, and, without slackening his speed, he stooped and picked it up so silently and deftly that Shif'less Sol, who was a little in advance, neither saw nor heard him.

It was the feather of an eagle, one that might have dropped from the wing of some soaring bird, but the quick eye of the boy saw that the quill had been cut with a knife, as the feather of a goose used to be sharpened for a pen.

He suppressed the sharp exclamation that rose to his lips, and thrust the feather into the bosom of his buckskin hunting shirt. The last echo of the warning note came to him and then died away in the forest.

They were at the camp fifteen minutes later, and the eyes of Shif'less Sol beamed at the joyous sight. In all their long journey they had found no more pleasant anchorage, a sheltered cove of the Ohio, and firm ground, clear of undergrowth, sloping gently to the water's edge. The boats were tied in a great curve about the beach, and nearly all the men were ashore, glad to feel once more the freedom of the land. Some still sung the wild songs they had picked up in the West Indies or on the Spanish Main, others were feeding fires that crackled merrily and that flung great bands of red flame against the glowing yellow curtain of the sunlight. Pleasant odors arose from pots and kettles. The air of frolic was pervasive. The whole company was like so many boys with leave to play.

Henry left Shif'less Sol and approached Adam Colfax, who was sitting alone on the exposed root of a big tree.

"You found nothing, of course?" said Adam Colfax, who shared the easy feelings of his men.

"I found this," replied the boy, drawing the eagle feather from his breast.

"What is that? Merely the feather of some wild bird."

"The feather of an eagle."

"I fancy that many an eagle drops a feather now and then in this wilderness."

"This feather was dropped last from the head of an Indian warrior."

"How do you know it?"

"See, the quill has been trimmed off a little with a knife. It was part of a decoration."

"It may have fallen many weeks ago."

"It could not be so. The plumage everywhere is smooth and even. It has been lying on the ground only a little while. Otherwise it would be bedraggled by the rain or be roughened by the wind blowing it about among the bushes."

"Then the feather indicates the presence of hostile Indians?" said Adam Colfax thoughtfully. "I know by your manner that you think so."

"I am sure of it," said Henry with great emphasis.

"You're right, no doubt. You always are. But look how strong our force is, men tried in toil and battle, and they are many! What have we to fear?"

He looked over his light-hearted host, and his blue eyes, usually so cold, kindled with warmth. One might search the world over, and not find a hardier band. Truly, what had he to fear?

Henry saw that the leader was not convinced, and he was not one to waste words. After all, what did he have to offer but a stray feather, carried by the wind?

"Dismiss your fears, my boy," said Adam Colfax cheerfully. "Think about something else. I want to send out a hunting party this afternoon. Will you lead it?"

"Of course," said Henry loyally. "I'll be ready whenever the others are."

"In a half hour or so," said Adam Colfax with satisfaction. "I knew you wouldn't fail."

Henry went to the fire, by the side of which his four comrades sat eating their noonday meal, and took his place with them. He said not a word after his brief salute, and Paul presently noticed his silence and look of preoccupation.

"What is the matter, Henry?" he asked.

"I'm going with a little party this afternoon," replied Henry, "to hunt for buffalo and deer. Mr. Colfax wishes me to do it. He thinks we need fresh supplies, and I've agreed to help. I want you boys to promise, if I don't come back, that you'll go on with the fleet."

Paul sat up, rigid with astonishment. Shif'less Sol turned a lazy but curious eye on the boy.

"Now, what under the sun do you mean, Henry?" he asked. "I've heard you talk a good many times, but never like that before. Not comin' back? Is this the Henry Ware that we've knowed so long?"

Henry laughed, despite himself.

"I'm just the same," he said, "and I do feel, Sol, that I'm not coming back from this hunt. I don't mean that I'll never come back, but it will be a long time. So I want you fellows to go on with the fleet and help it all you can."

"Henry, you're plum' foolish," said taciturn Tom Ross. "Are you out uv your head?"

Henry laughed again.

"It does sound foolish," he admitted, "and I don't understand why I think I'm not coming back. I just feel it."

"I notice that them things mostly come contrariwise," said Shif'less Sol. "When I know that I'm goin' to hev hard luck it's gen'ally good. We'll look for you, Henry, at sundown."

But Paul, youthful and imaginative, was impressed, and he regarded Henry with silent sympathy.

CHAPTER II

THE WYANDOT CHIEF

Henry rose quickly from the noonday refreshment and, with a nod to his comrades, entered the forest at the head of the little band of hunters. Shif'less Sol and Tom Ross would have gone, too, but Adam Colfax wanted them to keep watch about the camp, and they were too loyal to insist upon having their own way when it was opposed to that of the leader.

Five men were with Henry, fairly good hunters on the whole, but more at home in the far south than in the woods of the Ohio. One, a big fellow named Larkin, had an undue pride in his skill, and another, a Frenchman, Pierre Cazotte, was a brave fellow, but uncommonly reckless. The remaining three were not of marked individuality.

Henry examined them all with swift glances, and decided at once that Larkin and Cazotte, full of overweening confidence, would want their way, but he said nothing, merely leading the band into the mass of dense green foliage that rimmed the camp around. He looked back but once, and saw his four faithful comrades sitting by the fire, it seemed to him, in an attitude of dejection. Then he went forward swiftly, and in another minute the forest shut out camp fire and comrades.

"What's your notion, Henry?" asked Larkin. "Have you seen signs of deer or buffalo near?"

"Both," replied Henry. "There are good springs and little open places in the woods not more than a couple of miles away. We're pretty sure to find deer there."

"Why not buffalo?" exclaimed Larkin. "I've shot more deer than I could ever count, but I've never killed a buffalo. It's the first time that I've been in this part of the country."

"Nor have I," said Cazotte. "We have many people to feed, and ze buffalo ees beeg. Ze deer ees too leetle for all ze mouths back there."

9

"Right you are, Frenchy," exclaimed Larkin jovially. "We'll pass the deer by an' go for buffalo if we have to travel six or seven miles further. What this gang wants is buffalo, an' buffalo it will have."

"I don't think we ought to go very far from the camp," said Henry. "These woods from here to the lakes are the hunting grounds of the most warlike tribes, and bands may be near us now."

Larkin laughed again his big jovial laugh.

"You're thinkin' a lot about Indians," he said, "You're brave—everybody knows it —but a fellow can put his mind on 'em so hard that he can see 'em where they ain't."

Henry laughed, too. He knew no offense was intended, but he was confirmed in his belief that Larkin meant to have his own way. He saw, too, that Cazotte and the others were ready to back him up. But he would not yield without a protest.

"It's true, I am thinking a lot about Indians," he said earnestly, "and I think I have cause to do so. They're here in these woods now. I'm sure of it, and they know of the presence of our fleet. We ought to be very cautious."

Larkin laughed again, and his laugh contained the slightest touch of irony.

"I'll wager there ain't an Indian within fifty miles," he exclaimed, "an' if there was one he wouldn't keep us from our buffalo, would he, Pierre, old fellow?"

He slapped the Frenchman on the back, and Cazotte returned the laugh.

"Not a hundred Indians could keep us from heem," he replied. "I taste the steaks of that mighty buffalo now. Ah, they so good!"

Henry flushed through his tan. He did not like even that slight touch of irony. He had held in mind a tiny prairie not more than two miles away where they were almost absolutely sure to find deer feeding, but he abandoned the idea and thought of another and larger prairie, of which he and Shif'less Sol had caught a glimpse three or four miles further on. It was quite likely that buffalo would be found grazing there.

"Very well," he said, "if you're bound to have it that way I'll lead you. Come."

He led swiftly to the northeast, and Larkin, Cazotte, and the others, already tasting their hunting triumph, followed. The undergrowth thinned, but the trees grew larger, spreading away like a magnificent park—maples, oak, beech, hickory and elm. Henry was glad to see the bushes disappear, but for the second time that day the sound that made the chill run down his spine came to his ear, the warning note of the wind among the leaves. It soon passed, and he did not hear it again.

The open woods ceased, and the bushes began once more, thicker than ever. They were compelled to go much more slowly, and Henry, risking another laugh at himself, told them to make as little noise as possible.

"Anyway, if Indians are about they'll hear us shootin' our buffaloes," said Larkin.

"So we needn't mind a little snappin' an' cracklin' of the bushes."

"It's a good plan in the woods never to make any noise, when you can help it," said Henry.

The others heeded him for a few moments, but soon relapsed into their slovenly ways. It sounded to Henry's sensitive ear as if an army were passing. But he would not speak again of the need of caution, knowing how soon another warning would be disregarded. Meanwhile he kept a wary watch in behalf of his careless comrades, searching the thickets with eye and ear, and trying to guard them from their own neglect.

Another mile passed, the third since they had left the camp, and they came to a little brook. As Henry crossed it he distinctly saw the impression of a moccasined foot in the soft soil of the bank. It could not be more than an hour old.

"Look there!" he said to Larkin and Cazotte. "See the proof of what I have told you. An Indian has passed here this very afternoon."

Larkin glanced at the trace in the soft earth and shook his head dubiously.

"Do you call that the footprint of a man?" he asked. "It may be, but I can't make it out. It might have been put there by some animal."

Henry frowned. These men would not be convinced. But he said nothing more and continued to lead the way. Before him lay a stretch of thick wood with matted undergrowth, and beyond this, as he had discovered when scouting with Shif'less Sol in the morning, was the prairie on which they might find the buffalo.

This thicket opened and received them, the bushes closing up behind them in such compact order that nothing could be seen ten yards away. But Henry's eyes caught the glimpse of something to their right. It was the feather of an eagle, the second that he had seen that day, but it was thrust upright, and it adorned the head of a living warrior.

"Down! Down at once!" he cried, and, seizing the careless Larkin, he fairly hurled him to the earth. At the same instant a dozen rifles crackled among the bushes. The light-hearted Frenchman fell stone dead, a bullet through his head, and two more men were wounded. A bullet had grazed Larkin's shoulder, burning like the sting of a hornet, and, wild with pain and anger, he sprang again to his feet.

Henry had felt all along that the party was in his care, and he was resolved to save Larkin from his own folly. He also sprang up, seized the big man and dragged him down a second time. But as he sank into the concealment of the bushes he felt a blow upon the side of his head. It was like the light tap of a hammer, and for a second or two he thought nothing of it. Then his knees grew weak and his sight dim, and he knew that he was hit badly.

"Run, run!" he cried to Larkin. "The way by which we came is yet open and we may escape! It's the only chance!"

Larkin glanced back. He had been foolish, but he was no coward.

11

"You're hit and we won't leave you!" he exclaimed.

"Go on! go on!" cried Henry, summoning up his energy with a great effort of the will. "I'll look out for myself! Run!"

His tone was so compelling that Larkin and the others sprang up and made at top speed for the camp, the bullets whistling about them as they went. Henry tried to follow, but that extraordinary weakness in his knees increased, and it was growing quite dark. He had risen to his feet, but he sank down despite every effort of the will, and he saw a dim world whirling about him. A dozen dusky figures shot out of the obscurity. One raised a tomahawk aloft, but another stopped the arm in its descent.

He was conscious that the dusky figures stood about him in a ring, looking at him intently. But he was fast growing dizzier, and his eyelids were uncommonly heavy. He gave back their looks with defiance, and then he sank to the ground, unconscious.

Henry revived in a half hour. Some one had thrown water on his face, and he found himself sitting up, but with his hands tied securely behind his back. His head ached terribly, and he felt that his hair was thick with blood. But he knew at once that it was only a glancing wound, and that the effects, caused by the impact of the bullet upon the skull, were passing.

He was a prisoner, but all his alertness and powers were returning. He was not one ever to give up hope, and a single glance was enough to tell him the whole situation. A half dozen warriors stood about him, eight or ten more were returning, evidently from a chase, and one bore a ghastly trophy at his belt. Then three had escaped! It was perhaps more than he had hoped. He knew that another hideous decoration was in the belt of some warrior near him, but he closed his eyes to it, nor would he look at the body of the fallen Frenchman.

"You come with us," said a warrior in fairly good English.

Henry looked at the speaker and recognized at once a chief, a young man of uncommon appearance, great in stature and with a fierce and lofty countenance, like that of the ancient Roman, sometimes found in the North American Indian. He was a truly impressive figure, his head clean-shaven except for the defiant scalp lock which stood aloft intertwined with small eagle feathers, a gorgeous red blanket from some Canadian trading post thrown carelessly about his shoulders after the fashion of a toga, a fine long-barreled Kentucky rifle lying in the hollow of his arm, and a tomahawk and knife at his belt.

Henry felt instinctively that he was in the presence of a great man, a great chief of the woods. He recognized here a spirit akin to his own, and for a full minute the two, boy and man, gazed intently at each other. Then the chief turned away with a slight laugh. He made no sound, but the prisoner knew from the motion of his lips that he laughed.

Henry looked again at the group of warriors, and now it was an examining glance. They were not Shawnees or Miamis, but certain features of paint and dress showed him that they were Wyandots, a small tribe, but the bravest that white men ever faced on the North American Continent. It became an axiom in the Ohio Valley that a Wyandot might be killed in battle, but he could not be taken prisoner. Thirteen Wyandot chiefs were in the allied Indian army that was beaten by Wayne at the Fallen Timbers; the bodies of twelve were found on the field.

Henry fully understood the character of the Wyandots, their great enterprise and desperate courage, and he knew that their presence here, west of their own country, portended some great movement. His eyes came back to the chief, who repeated his statement or rather command:

"You go with us!"

"I have no other choice," replied the youth with a tinge of irony. Then he added, with some curiosity: "You are a chief, I see that. Will you tell me your name?"

"I am called White Lightning in your tongue," replied the young man, making at the same time a movement of his head, very slight, but full of indescribable pride.

Henry's gaze showed an increase of interest. He had heard that name, White Lightning. Before he went south to New Orleans it was beginning to have ominous significance on the border. White Lightning had fought in the great battle when the emigrant train was saved at the crossing of the river, but it was only since then that he had become a head chief, with the opportunity to display his terrible talents. An intensity of purpose and action like the fire that burns white had caused men to give to him the name, White Lightning, in English, but in his own Wyandot tongue he was Timmendiquas, which means The Lightning.

Henry had risen to his feet, and as they stood eye to eye each felt that the other was a worthy opponent. The chief marked the great proportions and lofty bearing of the captive youth, and a glint of approval appeared in his eyes.

"The Wyandots are happy to have taken such a prisoner," he said, "and now we will go."

He made a gesture, and instantly the group fell into single file, as he led the way through the forest. Henry was the fourth man in the file. All his strength had come back, but he was far too wise to attempt escape. His hands were bound behind him, and he would have no chance with such woodsmen. He must bide his time, and he marched without protest.

When they had gone about a mile all stopped at a signal from White Lightning. The chief dropped back to a subordinate place in the line, although his was still the air and actual manner of command, and his place at the head of the file was taken by a heavy, middle-aged warrior who carried at his belt one of the hideous trophies at which Henry would not look. But he understood Indian custom well enough to know the cause of this change. The middle-aged warrior had taken the first scalp in battle, and therefore it was his honor to lead the party back in triumph to their village or camp.

13

White Lightning remained but a moment or two in his place. Then he stepped forth, while the others stood rigid, and drew a medicine bag from beneath the folds of his blanket. He held the bag for a moment poised in his hand, as if it were a sacred object, which, in fact, it was to the Wyandots, while the warriors regarded it with reverential eyes.

Then every warrior took his totem from some secure place next to his body where it had been tied. The totems were small objects various in kind, such as the skin of a snake, a piece of the tail of a buffalo, a part of the horn of a buck, or a little packet of feathers. But every totem was sacred, and it was handled with worshipful care. The chief put them one by one into the medicine bag, which he handed to the temporary leader, the first scalp-taker, who would bear it in triumph home.

Henry watched the proceeding with interested eyes. He knew the Indian way. In his early captivity he had seen the entire rite, which was practically sacred. He knew that before these Wyandots had started on the war-path every man had put his totem in the bag, and then White Lightning had carried it bound securely to his body. Whenever they halted the bag was laid down in front, and no one might pass it. The warriors, now on the war-path, were not allowed to talk of home, wife, or sweetheart, lest it weaken their hearts and turn them to water. When they camped at night the heart of whatever animal they had killed in the course of the day was cut into small pieces and burned. During the burning no man was allowed to step across the fire, but must walk around it in the direction of the sun. When they laid the ambush, and the enemy came into sight, the chief gave back his totem to every man, and he wore it on his body in the conflict as a protection given by Manitou.

Henry noticed the rapt, worshipful air with which every man regarded his totem before it was replaced in the medicine bag. He was a child of the forest and the wilderness himself, and, while he knew that this was superstition, he could not find it in his heart to criticize it. It was their simple belief, the best that they knew, and here was the proof of its power. They had suffered no loss in the ambush, while they had slain two and taken one.

The elderly warrior who now bore the medicine bag and who was to lead them back home preserved a stoical face while the brief ceremonies were going on, but Henry knew that his heart was swollen with pride. He had achieved one of the greatest triumphs of an Indian's life, and the memory of it would remain with his tribe as long as he lived.

"You are now our leader, O Anue (Bear)," said the young chief in Wyandot to the successful warrior.

"I take the trust, O Timmendiquas (Lightning)," replied Anue as he stepped back to the head of the line.

But the spirit and authority of Timmendiquas were still omnipotent, despite the formal leadership of Anue, and he turned to the prisoner, regarding him a moment or two with his piercing glance.

14

"You have come with the great white force up Yandawezue?" he said interrogatively.

"Yandawezue?" repeated Henry, who was not familiar with the Wyandot tongue.

"The great river," repeated Timmendiquas, waving his hand toward the southwest.

"Ah, I understand," said Henry. "You mean the Mississippi. Yes, we have come up it all the way from New Orleans, and we have a strong force, many men with many rifles and with cannon. We had a great battle far down the river, and we defeated all the Indians and white men, their renegade allies."

Timmendiquas, the White Lightning of the whites, the great young chief of the Wyandots, drew himself up in all the majesty of a perfectly proportioned six feet three, and the fierce, Roman-like features contracted into a scornful smile.

"No Wyandots were there," he said. "But they are here, and with them their allies, the Miamis, the Shawnees, the Ottawas, the Delawares, and the Illinois. You may be many, you may have cannon, and you may be brave, and you have come up Yandawezue, but you will find Ohezuhyeandawa" (the Ohio—in the Wyandot tongue, "something great") "closed to you."

"Ohezu—do you mean the Ohio?" asked Henry.

"In your language, the Ohio," replied the young chief with dignity, "but the Wyandots had given it its right name, Ohezuhyeandawa, long before the white people came."

"I suppose you're right in that," said Henry reflectively, "but your name for it is too long. Ohio is better. As for our fleet, I think, in spite of what you say, that it will make its way up the Ohio to Pittsburgh, although I do admit that the dangers are great."

White Lightning merely shook his head. His dignity would not permit him to argue further with a prisoner. Henry regarded him with secret admiration. He did not believe that the chief could be over twenty-five or twenty-six years of age, but his great qualities were so obvious that it seemed natural for him to lead and command.

The chief stepped back into the line, Anue gave the signal, and the band resumed its rapid march toward the northeast. So swift, indeed, was the pace of the warriors that none but the forest-bred could have maintained it. They never stopped for a moment, striding on over the ground with a long, easy step that was like the trot of a horse, and almost as fast. Nor did they make any sound. It was like the passing of so many ghostly forms, phantoms flitting through the wilderness.

Henry noticed bye and bye that the pace increased. The legs of the warrior in front of him worked with the speed and regularity of machinery. But no perspiration appeared upon the bare brown neck, there was no evidence of fatigue, and Henry was sure that all the others were moving with the same ease and vigor. He wondered at first at this new speed, and then he divined the cause. It was to test him, and he was sure that some sort of signal had passed between Timmendiquas and Anue.

This was a picked band of warriors, there was not a man in it under six feet in height, and all were lean, but muscled powerfully and with great shoulders and chests. They had an intense pride in physical strength and prowess, such necessary qualities to them, and they would show the white prisoner, large as he was and strong as he looked, how much inferior he was to the chosen warriors of the Wyandots.

Henry accepted the challenge. They did not know his natural powers and the perfection of his training. He answered them, stride for stride. He filled his lungs with the fresh air of the woods, but he kept his breathing steady and regular. No gasp, no quick breath should ever show that he was not a match for them, one and all. His own pace increased. He almost trod upon the man in front of him, a warrior whom he had heard Timmendiquas address as Hainteroh (The Raccoon).

Hainteroh said nothing and did not look back, but he felt the strong step that narrowly missed his heels, the step of a white youth, a prisoner, and he moved faster—a great Wyandot warrior could not suffer such an indignity as to be crowded by a captive, one whom he had regarded as a physical inferior. Those in front moved faster, also, and now the second increase in speed had been caused by the prisoner himself.

Henry had become for the time as primitive, as much a child of the wilderness as they. An ironical spirit laid hold of him. They would test him! Well, he would test them! The inside of his chest bubbled with malicious laughter. Once more Hainteroh, great warrior of the Wyandots, mighty hunter, taker of scalps, fearless among men, felt the planting of that vigorous step at his very heels, almost upon him. It would not be pleasant to have so much weight come down upon them, and it would be a disgrace in the tribe to have been trodden upon by a white prisoner.

A third time the line increased its speed, and a second time it was the captive youth who caused it. They fairly fled through the forest now, but the breathing of every man was yet steady and regular.

They came to a wide brook, almost a creek. Anue never paused for an instant, but took it with a light leap, nor pausing an instant on the other side, sped on. The second man took it in the same way, then Hainteroh, and Henry, so close behind that the moccasins of the Wyandot were scarcely twinkling in the air before the feet of Henry were resting where his had been.

Henry heard the light sound of the others behind him as one by one they leaped into his place, but he never looked back. He was still pushing the Raccoon hard, and a terrible fear was slowly eating its way to the heart of the redoubtable Hainteroh, chosen warrior of the Wyandots, the bravest of all races. Sooner or later this demon white youth would tread upon his heels. He could feel already the scrape of his moccasins, the ineffable disgrace. He shuddered from head to

16

foot. Such a thing could not be endured. He fairly leaped through the air, and once more a new impulse was communicated to the line.

The way now became rougher, leading over stony hills, but there was no slackening of speed, the line remaining as even and regular as the links of a chain, Timmendiquas from his position in seventh place looking now and then with admiration over the heads of the men in front of him at the captive.

They crossed the hills, entered the deep and tangled woods again, and sped on as few war parties had ever traveled. The miles fell swiftly behind them, no one spoke, they heard nothing but the regular breathing of one another, and Henry did not yet see the drops of perspiration on the bare brown back in front of him. The sun passed far down the western arch. Shadowy twilight was already creeping up, the distant waves of the forest were clothed in darkening mists, but they did not stop. Anue gave no word, and Timmendiquas, for the time, would wait upon the formal leader.

Henry, always keenly sensitive to everything about him, noticed that the air was changing. It was growing heavier, and it had in it a touch of damp, but so slight that an ordinary person would not have observed it. There was, too, a faint circle of mist about the sun, and he believed that the beautiful weather was passing.

His mind returned to the broad bare back in front of him. The figure of Hainteroh was still working like a perfect machine, but the keen eyes of the youth saw the sight for which he had long been looking. Squarely in the middle of that brown surface a silver bead was forming. The yellow light of the low sun struck upon it, revealing clearly its nature and growth. Nor did it remain long alone. Brothers and sisters and cousins, near and then distant, gathered around it, and the great brown back of Hainteroh was wide enough for them all.

Henry enjoyed the sight. It appealed to the powerful, primitive instincts in his nature, and again the inside of his chest bubbled with silent laughter. His wicked delight increased when a slight wheezing sound came to his ears. Hainteroh's breath was growing short. Now the wheeze at intervals became something dangerously resembling a gasp, and there could be no doubt that Hainteroh, mass of muscle and mighty warrior of the Wyandots, was growing tired, while the prisoner, the white youth just behind him, seemed still fresh and strong, and would step in Hainteroh's tracks before the latter was fairly clear of them.

Henry heard the same slight wheezing sound behind him, and took one quick glance over his shoulder. The face of the warrior next to him was bedewed, but that of Timmendiquas was as cool and calm as his own. It seemed to him that just the touch of a smile appeared in the eyes of the chief, as if he understood and appreciated, and the fleeting look of Henry was not too brief to give back the smile. A singular bond of mutual respect was established in quick time between White Lightning and himself.

On sped the dusky line. The sun sank in a cloud of mist and vapors. Thick night crept up, broken only when heat lightning flared on the far horizon, but Anue, bearer of the medicine bag, taker of the first scalp, honored among warriors, still led.

CHAPTER III

THE SONG OF THE LEAVES

The night had come a full hour when Anue stopped in a little glade hemmed in by mighty oaks and beeches. The heat lightning flared again at that moment, and Henry saw that every one besides Timmendiquas and himself was panting. Enduring as were all Wyandots, they were glad that Anue had stopped, and they were generous enough to cast looks of approval at the captive who stood among them still calm and still breathing regularly. Timmendiquas did more. He stepped into the circle, put one hand on Henry's shoulder, and looked him directly in the eyes.

"You are strong," he said gravely, "stronger even than most Wyandots, and your soul is that of the eagle. If the boy is what he is, what will the man be?"

Henry knew that the words were meant, and he felt pride, but his modesty would not let him show it.

"I thank you, White Lightning," he replied with a similar gravity. "Your Manitou was kind enough to give me a strong body, and I, like you, have lived in the woods."

"As I see," said the chief sententiously. "Now I tell you this. We will take the bonds from your arms if you promise us not to seek to escape to-night. Else you must lie among us bound, hand and foot, to a warrior on either side. See, we are willing to take your word."

Henry felt pride again. These Wyandots, mortal enemies, who had never seen him before, would believe what he said, putting absolute faith in their reading of his character. He looked up at the dusky sky, in which not a single star twinkled, and then at the black forest that circled about them. Bound, and with a lightly sleeping Wyandot at either elbow, he would have a slender chance, indeed, of escape, and he could well bide his time.

"I give the promise and with it my thanks, White Lightning," he said.

White Lightning cut the thongs with one sweep of his knife, and Henry's arms fell free. Sharp pains shot through them as the circulation began to flow with its old freedom, but he refused to wince. He had chosen a policy, the one that he thought best fitted to his present condition, and he would abide by it through all things. He merely stepped a little to one side and watched while they made the camp.

The task was quickly done. Three or four warriors gathered fallen brushwood and set it on fire with flint and steel. Then they cooked over it strips of venison from their pouches, giving several strips to Henry, which he ate with no appearance of haste or eagerness, although he was quite hungry.

It was growing very dark, and the lightning on the horizon became vivid and intense. The air was heavy and oppressive. The fire burned with a languid drooping flame, and the forest was absolutely still, except when the thunder grumbled like the low, ominous mutter of a distant cannonade.

"A storm comes," said Timmendiquas, glancing at the lowering skies.

"It will be here soon," said Henry, who knew that the words were spoken to him.

Every warrior carried a blanket, which he now wrapped closely about his body, but Henry asked for nothing. He would not depart from his policy.

He stood in the center of the glade listening, although there was yet nothing to hear. But it was this extraordinary breathless silence that impressed him most. He felt as he breathed the heavy air that it was the sign of impending danger. The warning of the wind among the leaves had not been more distinct.

A long, rolling crash came from their right. "Heno (Thunder)!" said White Lightning. He did not mean to say the obvious, but his emphasis indicated that it was very loud thunder.

The thunder sank away in a low, distant note that echoed grimly, and then the breathless silence came again. A minute later the whole forest swam in a glare of light so dazzling that Henry was compelled to close his eyes. It passed in an instant, and the wilderness was all black, but out of the southwest came a low, moaning sound.

"Iruquas (The wind)!" said the chief in the same sententious tone.

The groan became a rumble, and then, as the vanguard of the wind, came great drops of rain that pattered like hail stones.

"Inaunduse (It rains)," said the chief.

But it was merely a brief shower like a volley from withdrawing skirmishers, and then the rumble of the wind gave way to a crash which rose in a moment to a terrible roar.

"A hurricane!" exclaimed Henry. As he spoke a huge compressed ball of air which can be likened only to a thunderbolt struck them.

Strong as he was, Henry was thrown to the ground, and he saw the chief go down beside him. Then everything was blotted out in pitchy blackness, but his ears were filled with many sounds, all terrible, the fierce screaming of the wind as if in wrath and pain, the whistling of boughs and brushwood, swept over his head, and the crash of great oaks and beeches as they fell, snapped through at the trunk by the immense force of the hurricane.

Henry seized some of the bushes and held on for his life. How thankful he was now that he had given his promise to the chief, and that his hands were free! A shiver swept over him from head to foot. Any moment one of the trees might fall

19

upon him, but he was near the center of the glade, the safest place, and he did not seek to move.

He was conscious, as he clung to the bushes, of two kinds of movement. He was being pulled forward and he was being whirled about. The ball of air as it shot from southwest to northeast revolved, also, with incredible rapidity. The double motion was so violent that it required all of Henry's great strength to keep from being wrenched loose from his bushes.

The hurricane, in its full intensity, lasted scarcely a minute. Then with a tremendous rush and scream it swept off to the northeast, tearing a track through the forest like a tongue of flame in dry grass. Then the rain, pouring from heavy black clouds, came in its wake, and the lightning, which had ceased while the thunderbolt was passing, began to flash fitfully.

Henry had seen hurricanes in the great Ohio Valley before, but never one so fierce and violent as this, nor so tremendous in its manifestations. Awe and weirdness followed in the trail of that cannon ball of wind. The rumble of thunder, far and echoing, was almost perpetual. Blackest darkness alternated with broad sheets of lightning so intense in tint that the forest would swim for a moment in a reddish glare before the blackness came. Meanwhile the rain poured as if the bottom had dropped out of every cloud.

Henry struggled to his feet and stood erect. He could have easily darted away in the confusion and darkness among the woods, but such a thought did not occur to him. He had given his promise, and he would keep it despite the unexpected opportunity that was offered. He remained at the edge of the circle, while Timmendiquas, the real leader, hastily gathered his men and took count of them as best he could.

The chief, by the flare of the lightning, saw Henry, upright, motionless, and facing him. A singular flash of understanding quicker than the lightning itself passed between the two. Then Timmendiquas spoke in the darkness:

"You could have gone, but you did not go."

"I gave my promise to stay, and I stayed," replied Henry in the same tone.

The lightning flared again, and once more Henry saw the eyes of the chief. They seemed to him to express approval and satisfaction. Then Timmendiquas resumed his task with his men. Hainteroh of the broad back had been dashed against a sapling, and his left arm was broken. Another man had been knocked senseless by a piece of brushwood, but was sitting up now. Three or four more were suffering from severe bruises, but not one uttered a complaint. They merely stood at attention while the chief made his rapid inspection. Every man had wrapped his rifle in his blanket to protect it from the rain, but their bodies were drenched, and they made no effort now to protect themselves.

Hainteroh pointed to his broken arm. The chief examined it critically, running his hand lightly over the fracture. Then he signaled to Anue, and the two, seizing the arm, set the broken bone in place. Hainteroh never winced or uttered a word.

Splints, which White Lightning cut from a sapling, and strips of deerskin were bound tightly around the arm, a sling was made of more deerskin from their own scanty garb, and nature would soon do the rest for such a strong, healthy man as Hainteroh.

They stood about an hour in the glade until the lightning and thunder ceased, and the rain was falling only in moderation. Then they took up the march again, going by the side of the hurricane's path. It was impossible for them to sleep on the earth, which was fairly running water, and Henry was glad that they had started. It was turning much colder, as it usually does in the great valley after such storms, and the raw, wet chill was striking into his marrow.

The line was re-formed just as it had been before, with Anue leading, and they went swiftly despite the darkness, which, however, was not so dense as that immediately preceding and following the hurricane. The trained eyes of the Wyandot and of the prisoner could now easily see the way.

The coldness increased, and the diminishing rain now felt almost like hail stones, but the clouds were floating away toward the northeast, and the skies steadily lightened. Henry felt the warming and strengthening influence of the vigorous exercise. His clothing was a wet roll about him, but the blood began to flow in a vigorous stream through his veins, and his muscles became elastic.

They followed by the side of the hurricane's track for several miles, and Henry was astonished at the damage that it had done. Its path was not more than two hundred yards wide, but within that narrow space little had been able to resist it. Trees were piled in tangled masses. Sometimes the revolving ball had thrown them forward and sometimes it had thrown them, caught in the other whirl, backward.

They turned at last from this windrow of trees, and presently entered a little prairie, where there was nothing to obstruct them. The rain was now entirely gone, and the clouds were retreating far down in the southwest. Timmendiquas looked up.

"Washuntyaandeshra (The Moon)," he said.

Henry guessed that this very long name in Wyandot meant the moon, because there it was, coming out from the vapors, and throwing a fleecy light over the soaked and dripping forest. It was a pleasing sight, a friendly one to him, and he now felt unawed and unafraid. The wilderness itself had no terrors for him, and he felt that somehow he would slip through the hands of the Wyandots. He had escaped so many times from great dangers that it seemed to him a matter of course that he should do so once more.

They made greater speed on the prairie, which was covered only with long grass and an occasional clump of bushes. But near its center something rose up from one of the clumps, and disappeared in a streak of brown.

"Oughscanoto (Deer)," said the chief.

But Henry had known already. His eyes were as quick as those of Timmendiquas.

21

They crossed the prairie and entering the woods again went on without speaking. The moonlight faded, midnight passed, when Anue suddenly stopped at the entrance to a rocky hollow, almost a cave, the inner extension of which had escaped the sweep of the storm.

"We rest here," said White Lightning to Henry. "Do you still give your promise?"

"Until I awake," replied the youth with a little laugh.

He entered the hollow, noticed that the dry leaves lay in abundance by the rocky rear wall, threw himself down among them, and in a few moments was asleep, while his clothes dried upon him. All the warriors quickly followed his example except Timmendiquas and Anue, who sat down at the entrance of the hollow, with their rifles across their knees, and watched. Neither spoke and neither moved. They were like bronze statues, set there long ago.

Henry awoke at the mystical hour when the night is going and the dawn has not yet come. He did not move, he merely opened his eyes, and he remembered everything at once, his capture, the flight through the forest, and the hurricane. He was conscious of peace and rest. His clothes had dried upon him, and he had taken no harm. He felt neither the weight of the present nor fear for the future. He saw the dusky figures of the Wyandots lying in the leaves about him sound asleep, and the two bronze statues at the front of the stony alcove.

Clear as was Henry's recollection, a vague, dreamy feeling was mingled with it. The wilderness always awoke all the primitive springs within him. When he was alone in the woods—and he was alone now—he was in touch with the nymphs and the fauns and the satyrs of whom he had scarcely ever heard. Like the old Greeks, he peopled the forest with the creatures of his imagination, and he personified nearly everything.

Now a clear sweet note came to his half-dreaming ear and soothed him with its melody. He closed his eyes and let its sweetness pierce his brain. It was the same song among the leaves that he had heard when he was out with the shiftless one, the mysterious wind with its invisible hand playing the persistent and haunting measure on the leaves and twigs.

It was definite and clear to Henry. It was there, the rhythmic note ran through it all the time, and for him it contained all the expression of a human voice, the rise, the fall, the cadence, and the shade.

But its note was different now. It was not solemn, ominous, full of warning. It was filled with hope and promise, and he took its meaning to himself. He would escape, he would rejoin his comrades, and the great expedition would end in complete success.

Stronger and fuller swelled the song, the mysterious haunting note that was played upon the leaves, and Henry's heart bounded in response. He was still in that vague, dreamy state in which things unseen look large and certain, and this was a call intended for him. He glanced at the brown statues. If they, too, heard, they made no sign. He glanced at the leaves, and he saw them moving gently as they were played by the unseen hand.

Henry closed his eyes again and listened to the note of hope, sweeter and more penetrating than ever. A great satisfaction suffused him, and he did not open his eyes again. The dreamy state grew, and presently he floated off again into a deep, restful slumber.

When Henry awoke the glade was flooded with brilliant sunlight. A warm west wind was blowing and trees and grass were drying. Several of the Wyandots were, like himself, just rising from sleep, but it was evident that others had been up far before, because at the edge of the glade lay a part of the body of a deer, recently killed and dressed. Other Wyandots were broiling strips of the flesh on sharpened twigs over a fire built in the center of the glade. The pleasant savor came to Henry's nostrils, and he sat up. Just at that moment a Wyandot, who had evidently been hunting, returned to the glade, carrying on his arm a large bird with beautiful bronze feathers.

"Daightontah," said Timmendiquas.

"I suppose that word means turkey," said Henry, who, of course, recognized the bird at once.

The chief nodded.

"Turkey is fine," said Henry, "but, as it won't be ready for some time, would you mind giving me a few strips of Oughscanoto, which I think is what you called it last night."

The young chief smiled.

"You learn fast," he said. "You make good Wyandot."

Henry seemed to see a significance in the tone and words, and he looked sharply at White Lightning. A Spaniard, Francisco Alvarez, had tried to tempt him once from his people, but the attempt was open and abrupt. The approach of the chief was far different, gentle and delicate. Moreover, he liked White Lightning, and, as Henry believed, the chief was much the better man of the two. But here as before there was only one answer.

The chief nodded at one of the men, who handed the broiled strips, and the boy ate, not with haste and greediness, but slowly and with dignity. He saw that his conduct in the night and the storm had made an impression upon his captors, and he meant to deepen it. He knew the Indian and his modes of thought. All the ways of his life in the northwestern tribe readily came back to him, and he did the things that were of highest esteem in the Indian code.

Henry showed no anxiety of any kind. He looked about him contentedly, as if place and situation alike pleased him more than any other in the world. But this was merely an approving, not an inquiring look. He did not seem to be interested in anything beyond the glade. He was not searching for any way of escape. He was content with the present, ignoring the future. When the time came for them to go he approached White Lightning and held out his hands.

23

"I am ready to be bound," he said.

A low murmur of approval came from two or three of the Wyandots who stood near.

"Let the promise go another day?" said White Lightning with a rising inflection.

"If you wish," said Henry. He saw no reason why he should not give such a promise. He knew that the Wyandots would watch him far too well to allow a chance of escape, and another such opportunity as the storm was not to be expected.

The chief said not another word, but merely motioned to Henry, who took his old place as fourth in the line with Anue at the head. Then the march was resumed, and they went steadily toward the northeast, moving in swiftness and silence. Henry made no further effort to embarrass Hainteroh, who again was just before him. His reasons were two—the Wyandot now had a broken arm, and the boy had already proved his quality.

The day was beautiful after the storm. The sky had been washed clean by wind and rain, and now it was a clear, silky blue. The country, an alternation of forest and little prairies, was of surpassing fertility. The pure air, scented with a thousand miles of unsullied wilderness, was heaven to the nostrils, and Henry took deep and long breaths of it. He had suffered no harm from the night before. His vigorous young frame threw off cold and stiffness, and he felt only the pleasure of abounding physical life. Although the wind was blowing, he did not hear that human note among the leaves again. It was only when his mind was thoroughly attuned and clothed about in a mystical atmosphere that it made a response. But his absolute belief that he would escape remained.

Henry was troubled somewhat by the thought of his comrades. He was afraid, despite his warning to them, that they would leave the fleet and search for him when he did not return, and he knew that Adam Colfax needed them sorely. This was the country that they knew best, the country Adam Colfax and his men knew least. It was best for another reason that they did not seek him. So wary a foe as the Wyandot could keep away help from the outside, and, if he escaped, he must escape alone.

They traveled swiftly and almost without a word until noon, when they stopped for a half hour and ate. They did not light any fire, but took cold food from their pouches, of which they had a variety, and once more Timmendiquas was most hospitable.

"Oghtaeh (Squirrel)," he said, holding up a piece.

"Yes, thank you," replied the boy, who thought he recognized the flesh.

"Yuingeh (Duck)?" said the chief, holding up another piece.

"I'll take that, too," replied Henry.

"Sootae (Beaver)?" said the chief, producing a third.

"I'll risk that, too," replied Henry. "It looks good."

"Yungenah (Dog)?" said the hospitable Timmendiquas, offering a fourth fragment of meat.

Henry looked at it suspiciously.

"Yungenah?" he said. "Now, Chief, would you tell me what Yungenah means?"

"Dog," replied the Wyandot sententiously.

"No, no!" exclaimed Henry. "Take it away."

Timmendiquas smiled benevolently.

"Dog good," he said, "but not make you eat it. Wyandot glad enough to get it."

They continued the journey throughout the afternoon, and did not stop until after sunset. Henry's promise was renewed for the second time, and he slept quietly within the circle of the Wyandots. He awakened once far in the night, and he saw that the watch was most vigilant. White Lightning was awake and sitting up, as also were three warriors. The night was clear and bright save for a few small harmless clouds. Henry saw that he had made no mistake in renewing his promise. The chance of escape had not yet come.

White Lightning noticed that his captive's eyes were open and he walked over to him. This youth, so strong and so skillful, so brave and so frank, appealed to the young chief. He would regret the necessity of putting him to death. A way of escaping it would be welcome.

"It is not like last night," he said pleasantly.

"No," said Henry. "There is no chance of another storm."

"Oghtserah," said the chief, pointing to the small, harmless clouds.

"But they are too little to mean anything," said Henry, guessing from the chief's gesture that "Oghtserah" meant clouds.

"You learn Wyandot," said the chief in the same pleasant tone. "You learn fast. See Tegshe."

He glanced up.

"Stars?" guessed Henry.

The chief smiled again.

"It is right," he said. "You stay long with us, you learn to talk to Wyandot. Look!"

He held up one finger.

"Scat," he said.

He held up two.

"Tindee," he said.

He held up three.

25

"Shaight," he said.

He held up four. "Andaught."

Five—"Weeish."

Six—"Washaw."

Seven—"Sootare."

Eight—"Acetarai."

Nine—"Aintru."

Ten—"Aughsah."

"Now you count ten," he said somewhat in the tone of a schoolmaster to Henry.

"All right," said Henry tractably. "Here goes: Scat, Tindee, Shaight, Andaught, Weeish, Washaw, Sootare, Acetarai, Aintru, Aughsah."

The chief's smile deepened.

"You good memory," he said. "You learn very fast." Then he added after a moment's hesitation: "You make good Wyandot. Wyandots small nation, but bravest, most cunning and most enduring of all. Wyandot being burned at the stake calls for his pipe and smokes it peacefully while he dies in the fire."

"I don't doubt it," said Henry, who had heard of such cases.

The chief glanced at him and concluded that he said enough on that point. Once more he looked up.

"Washuntyaandeshra."

"The moon," said Henry. "Yes, it's bright."

"You learn. You remember," said the chief. "Now you sleep again."

He walked away, and Henry closed his eyes, but did not go to sleep just yet. He had understood Timmendiquas perfectly, and it troubled him. He liked the young chief, but white he was and white he would remain. He resolutely forced the question out of his mind, and soon he was fast asleep again.

CHAPTER IV

THE FOREST VILLAGE

They traveled another day and another, always rapidly. Henry continued his policy and asked no questions. He divined, however, that the Wyandots were on the way to a village of theirs, either permanent or temporary, probably the latter, as they were far west of the country conceded by the other Indians to be Wyandot.

He surmised, also, that the red alliance against the white vanguard had been enlarged until it included all the tribes of the Ohio Valley north of the river. He knew very well how all these tribes were situated, their great villages at Chillicothe, Piqua, and other places, whence it was easy for them to make raids upon the settlements south of the Ohio and then retreat into the vast wilderness north of it, where it was exceedingly dangerous to follow them. Should he escape, he would not be sorry to have been a prisoner, since he might learn all their plans, knowledge as precious as diamonds.

On the fourth day they checked their speed, and a lithe young Indian whom Henry heard called Thraintonto, which means in Wyandot The Fox, stripped himself of his breech clout, gave his long and defiant scalp lock a somewhat fiercer curl, and darted ahead of the band.

He was the swiftest runner in the war party, chosen specially by Timmendiquas for an important duty, and Henry knew very well the nature of his errand. The Wyandot village now lay not far away, and Thraintonto sped ahead, a messenger, to tell that the war party had achieved victory, and was approaching with the proof of it.

He watched the figure of Thraintonto dart away and then disappear, a flash of brown in the green wilderness. He knew that The Fox was filled with the importance of his mission. None could be more welcome to an Indian.

The band resumed its march after the brief stop, now proceeding in leisurely fashion through a beautiful country, magnificently wooded and abounding in game. Little brooks of clear fresh water, the characteristic of the Ohio Valley, abounded everywhere. They were never a half mile from one, and now and then they came to a large creek. Henry was quite sure that they would soon reach the river that received all these creeks.

They stopped two or three hours later, and went through a solemn rite. Brushes and paint were produced—everything had been arranged for in advance—and all the members of the band were painted grotesquely. Red, blue, and yellow figures were depicted upon their faces, shoulders, and chests. Not a square inch of exposed skin was left without its pictorial treatment. Then every man put on a beautiful headdress of white feathers taken from different birds, and, when all was done, they formed in single file again, with Timmendiquas, in place of Anue, now at their head. The chief himself would lead the victorious band to the village, which was certainly near at hand.

The advance was resumed. It was not merely a return. It partook in its nature of a triumphal progress, like some old festival of the Greeks or Ph[oe]nicians. They came presently to a cedar tree, and from this White Lightning broke a branch, upon which he hung the two scalps that they had taken. Then, bearing the branch conspicuously in his right hand, he advanced and began a slow monotonous chant. All the warriors took up the chant, which had little change save the rising and falling of the note, and which, like most songs of savages, was plaintive and melancholy.

27

Henry, who, as usual, followed the broad brown back of Hainteroh, observed everything with the keenest attention. He was all eyes and ears, knowing that any detail learned now might be of value to him later.

They crossed the crest of a low hill, and he caught sight of lodges, a hundred perhaps in number, set in a warm valley, by the side of the small clear river that he had surmised was near. The lodges of buffalo or deerskin stood in a cluster, and, as it was a full quarter mile on every side to the woods, there was no chance for a lurking foe to lie in ambush. Henry noticed at once that there were no fields for maize or beans, and he was confirmed in his opinion that the village was temporary. He noticed, too, that the site of the place was chosen with great judgment. It lay in the angle of the river, which formed an elbow here, flowing between high banks, and on the other two sides rows of fallen logs formed an admirable defense in forest warfare.

The band paused a few moments at the crest of the hill, and began to chant more loudly. In front of the village was a concourse of warriors, women, and children, who joined in the song, and who opened out to receive the victors as they came marching on.

The chant swelled in volume, and its joyous note was now marked. But not one of the marching warriors relaxed a particle from his dignity. White Lightning strode majestically, a magnificent figure of savage man, and led the way to a war pole in the center of the village, in front of a council house built of poles. Near the foot of this pole a fire was burning.

Henry stepped from the line when they came to the war pole, and the warriors, secretly admiring their splendid trophy, closed in about him, cutting off all chance of escape, should he try it. But he had no thought of making such an attempt. His attention was centered now on the ceremonies.

The war band formed in a group, the war pole in the center. Then two warriors fastened two blocks of wood on a kind of rude ark that lay near the war pole. This wooden ark, carved like a totem, was the most sacred of all objects to the Wyandots.

All the returned warriors sat down upon the ground, and the great young chief, Timmendiquas, inquired gravely whether his lodge was ready for him. An old man replied that it had been swept clean and prepared by the women, and Timmendiquas and his warriors, rising from the ground, uttered a tremendous whoop. Then they marched gravely in a circle about the pole, after which they took up the ark and carried it solemnly to the council house. When they entered the council house, bearing the ark with them, they closed the door behind them.

The whole population of the village was packed densely in front of the council house, and when the door was shut upon the victorious war band all the female kin of the warriors within, except those too young or too old to take part, advanced, while the crowd swung back to give them room, and arranged themselves in two parallel lines, facing each other on either side of the door of the council house.

28

These women were dressed in all their barbaric finery. They wore beautiful headdresses of feathers, red and white and blue and yellow. Their faces were painted, but not so glaringly as those of the warriors. Even here in the wilderness woman's taste, to a certain extent, prevailed. They wore tunics of finely dressed deerskins, or, in some cases, bright red and blue shawls, bought at British posts, deerskin leggings, and moccasins. Much work had been lavished upon the moccasins, which were of the finest skin, delicately tanned and ornamented with hundreds of little beads, red, yellow, blue, green and every other color.

Many of the younger women, not yet wrinkled or bent by hard work, were quite pretty. They were slim and graceful, and they had the lightness and freedom of wild things. Henry was impressed by the open and bold bearing of them all, women as well as men. He had heard much of the Wyandots, the flower of all the western tribes, and now at close range he saw that all he had heard was true, and more.

As soon as the two lines were formed, and they were arranged with the greatest exactitude and evenness, the women, as they faced one another, began a slow monotonous chant, which, however, lasted only a minute. At the end of this minute there was profound silence for ten minutes. The women, trained for these ceremonies, stood so perfectly still that Henry could not see a body quiver. At the end of the ten minutes there was another minute of chanting, and then ten more minutes of silence, and thus, in this proportion of ten minutes of silence to one minute of song, the alternation would be kept up all day and all night.

Once every three hours Timmendiquas would come forth at the head of his warriors, raise the war whoop, pass around the war pole, bearing aloft a branch of cedar, and then return to the council house, closing the door firmly as before.

Meanwhile Henry's attention was taken from the ceremonies by a most significant thing. He had been conscious for a while that some one in the closely packed ring of Wyandot spectators was watching him. He had a sort of feeling as of cold upon the back of his neck, and he shivered a little. He knew, therefore, that the look directed upon him was evil, but pride kept him from showing undue curiosity before the Wyandots, who were trained to repress every emotion. He too, had, in these respects, instincts kindred with those of the Wyandots.

Presently he turned slowly and carelessly, and found that he was looking into the savage, sneering eyes of Braxton Wyatt, the young renegade, who more than once had sought the destruction of Henry and his comrades. Although they could not find his body, he had hoped that Wyatt had perished in the great battle on the Lower Mississippi, because it might save the border much, but, now that he was alive and here, Henry refused to show surprise, alarm, or any other emotion. He merely shrugged his shoulders ever so slightly, and his glance passed on. But he knew that Braxton Wyatt was swelling with malignant triumph. Fortune had changed her face, and it was his day to smile. Henry Ware was there, a prisoner among the Wyandots—and a prisoner of the Wyandots seldom escaped—while he, Braxton Wyatt, could exult over him and see him die. Truly, it was an amazing turn of the wheel, and Henry felt all the bitterness of it, although his expression did not alter a particle.

The boy's eyes roamed back again, and he saw that Braxton Wyatt's was not the only white face in the crowd. Five men stood near him, and, tanned and browned as they were, it was obvious that they belonged to the white race. He surmised readily by their air of perfect confidence and freedom that they were renegades, also, and he was not wrong. As he was soon to learn, they were Simon Girty, name of incredible infamy on the border, Moses Blackstaffe, but little his inferior in cunning and cruelty, and McKee, Eliot and Quarles. So Braxton Wyatt, white youth among the Indians, was not alone. He had found men of his race as bad as himself, and Henry knew that he would thrive in such company.

Henry guessed that the renegade who stood a little in front of the others, who seemed by his manner and bearing to consider himself their leader, was the terrible Girty, a man who left behind him an almost unbelievable record for cruelty and treachery to his own race. He was partly in Indian, partly in white dress, and when his glance fell upon Henry it was full of most inhuman mockery. The boy's wrath flamed up. He did not seek now to practice the Indian stoicism and repress his feelings. His eyes, blazing with indignation, looked straight into those of Girty, with a gaze so stern and accusing and so full of contempt that the renegade, unable to withstand it, lowered his own eyes.

Braxton Wyatt had seen this little passage, and Henry's triumph of the moment increased his hatred. He longed to say something, to taunt him with his position, something that his ignoble soul was not above, but he did not dare to do it just then. He and his fellow renegades wished to sway the Wyandots to a purpose of theirs, and any interruption now of the ceremonies, which, in fact, were a sacred rite, would bring fierce anger down upon his head.

Henry remained about four hours in the crowd, and then, an old man, whose dignity and bearing showed that he held a chief's rank, tapped him on the shoulder.

"Come," he said in fair English, "I am Heno, and you are our prisoner."

Henry had learned already that Heno in Wyandot meant Thunder, and he answered cheerfully.

"Very well, my good Thunder, lead on, and I'll follow."

The old chief gravely led the way, and the throng opened out to let them pass. Henry glanced back at the two swaying lines of women, now engaged in one of their minute-long chants, and he wondered at the illimitable patience of the red race, to whom time seemed nothing.

Unless some great movement, like a sudden attack by an enemy or the necessity of a forced march, interfered, the warriors would go in and out of the council house for three days, when all except the leader and one attendant warrior would go forth to their lodges, which would be swept clean for them, and which would be decorated with twigs of cedar or pieces of scalps to satisfy the ghosts of departed friends. But Timmendiquas and his attendant would remain three more days and nights in the council house to complete their purification. When they emerged the medicine bag would be hung before the lodge door of Timmendiquas. Unless the village was removed, it would hang there a month, and the people would sing and dance before it at intervals.

As Henry passed through the throng, following close behind old Heno, many admiring glances were bent upon him by the great little red nation of the Wyandots. These children of the wilderness knew the value of a tall, straight figure, powerful shoulders, a splendid chest and limbs that seemed to be made of woven wire. Here was one, already mighty among his kind, although but a boy.

Heno led the way to a bark lodge in the center of the village, and motioned to Henry to enter.

"I must bind you," he said, "because if I did not you are so strong and so swift that you might escape from us. If you will not suffer me to tie the cords I shall call the help of other warriors."

"There is no need of a fight about it, Thunder," said Henry genially. "I know you can bring in enough warriors to overpower anybody, so go ahead."

He held out his hands, and the old chief looked somewhat embarrassed at the willingness and cheerfulness of the captive. Nevertheless, he produced deerskin cords and bound the boy's wrists, not so tightly that the cords hurt, but with ingenious lacings that Henry knew he could neither slip nor break. Then, as the captive sat down on a rush mat and leaned against the bark wall of the lodge, old Heno regarded him attentively.

Thunder, old but brave warrior of the Wyandots, was a judge of promising youth, and he thought that in his sixty years of life he had never seen another so satisfactory as this prisoner, save perhaps the mighty young chief, known to his own people as Timmendiquas and to the settlers as White Lightning. He looked at the length of limb and the grand development of shoulders and chest, and he sighed ever so gently. He sighed because in his opinion Manitou should have bestowed such great gifts upon a Wyandot, and not upon a member of the white race. Yet Heno did not actually hate the prisoner. Coiled at the bottom of his heart, like a tiny spring in a watch, was a little hope, and this little hope, like the tiny spring, set all the machinery of his mind in motion.

"You no like being captive, held in lodge, with arms tied?" he said gently.

Henry smiled.

"No, I don't enjoy it," he replied. "It's not the situation that I should choose for myself."

"You like to be free," continued old Heno with the same gentle gravity. "You like to be out in the forest with Whoraminta?"

"Yes," replied Henry, "I'd like to be free, and I'd like to be out in the forest, but I don't know about Whoraminta. I'm not acquainted with him, and he might not be a pleasant comrade."

"Whoraminta! Whoraminta!" repeated Heno. "Cannot think of your word for it. It is this!"

He threw himself into a firm attitude, held out one hand far, extended the other about half so far, shut his left eye, and looked with the right intently along the level of his two hands. Henry understood the pantomime perfectly.

"I know," he said. "Whoraminta is a rifle. You're right, Thunder, I'd like mighty well to be out in the forest with my Whoraminta, one of the trustiest and best comrades I ever had."

Heno's smile answered that of the captive.

"And with plenty of Teghsto?" he said.

"Teghsto?" said Henry. "That's new to me. Can't you think of the English word for it?"

Heno shook his head, but closed his right hand until it formed approximately the shape of a horn, then elevated it and held it as if he were pouring something into the open palm of his left hand.

"Use in Whoraminta," he said.

"That's not hard," said Henry. "Powder you mean."

"That right," said Heno, smiling again. "Teghsto go in Whoraminta, and Yeatara go in Whoraminta, too. You want plenty of Yeatara."

"Lead! bullets!" said Henry at a guess.

"Yes. That it. Yeatara is lead, and you snap with Taweghskera; fire spark jump out flash! bang! You want Taweghskera, too."

"Taweghskera must be flint," said Henry, and old Heno nodded. "Yes, Thunder, I'd want the flint, too, or I couldn't do anything at all with Whoraminta, Teghsto and Yeatara. I'll remember those words, my friend. Thanks for your free teaching."

"You learn fast. You make good Wyandot," said Heno in the most friendly manner. "You have your arms, your feet free, Whoraminta with you, you go with the warriors on great hunt, you gone many moons, you kill the deer, buffalo, bear, panther, you have no care, no sorrow, you live. I, too, was a young hunter and warrior once."

Old Heno slowly drew his figure up at the glorious picture that he had painted. His nostrils were distended, and the fire of his youth came back into his eyes. He saw the buffaloes trampling down the grass, and heard the shout of his enemies in the forest combat.

"I'm thinking, Heno," said Henry sincerely, "that you're yet a good deal of a young hunter and warrior."

"You not only make good warrior, but you make good chief, too. You know how to talk," said Heno.

32

Nevertheless, he was pleased, and he was still smiling when he left a few moments later. Nobody else came for a day and night, old Heno bringing him his food and water. He did not suffer any actual physical pain, as his bonds permitted him to move a little and the circulation was not impeded, but he chafed terribly. The picture that Heno had drawn of the great forest and the great hunt was most alluring. He longed for freedom and his "Whoraminta."

A visitor came on the second morning. The lodge door was opened and a thick figure filled it a moment as a man entered. Henry was sitting on a mat at the farthest part of the lodge, and he could see the man very clearly. The stranger was young, twenty-seven or twenty-eight perhaps, thick set and powerful, tanned to the brownness of an Indian by sun, wind and rain, but the features obviously were those of the white race. It was an evil face, but a strong one. Henry felt a shiver of repulsion. He felt that something demoniac had entered the lodge, because he knew that this was Simon Girty, the terrible renegade, now fully launched upon the career that made his name infamous throughout the Ohio Valley to this day.

But after the little shiver, Henry was without motion of expression. Show apprehension in the presence of such a man! He would rather die. Girty laughed and sat down on the mat on the other side of the lodge. But it was a small lodge, and their faces were not more than four feet apart. Henry read in the eyes of Girty a satisfaction that he did not seek to conceal.

"It isn't so pleasant to be trussed up in that fashion, is it?" he asked.

Henry refused to answer.

Girty laughed again.

"You needn't speak unless you feel like it," he said. "I can do the talking for both of us. You're tied up, it's true, but you're treated better than most prisoners. I've been hearing a good deal about you. A particular friend of yours, one Braxton Wyatt, a most promising lad, has told me a lot of stories in which you have a part."

"I know Braxton Wyatt very well," said Henry, "and I'm glad to say that I've helped to defeat some of his designs. He has a great ambition."

"What is that?" asked Girty.

"To become as bad a man as you are."

But Girty was not taken aback at all. His lips twisted into a peculiar grin of cruel satisfaction.

"They do fear me," he said, "and they'll fear me more before long. I've joined the Indians, I like them and their ways, and I'm going to make myself a great man among them."

"At the expense of your own kind?"

"Of course. What is that to me. I'm going to get all the tribes together, and sweep the whites out of the Ohio Valley forever."

"I've heard that these same Indians with whom you're so thick burned your step-father at the stake?" said Henry.

"That's true," replied the renegade without the slightest feeling. "That was when I was a little child, and they captured our family. But they didn't burn me. So what have I to complain of?"

Henry could not repress a shudder, but Girty remained as cool as ice.

"Why shouldn't I be a great man among the Indians?" he said. "I know the tricks of both white and red now. The Continentals, as they call themselves—rebels I call them—held McKee, Eliot and myself prisoners at Fort Pitt, the place they call Pittsburgh, but we escaped and here we are. We've been joined by Blackstaffe, Quarles, and the boy, Braxton Wyatt. The Indians trust us and listen to us; we're going to draw all the valley Indians together—Shawnees, Miamis, Wyandots, Ottawas, Delawares and Illinois—and we'll light such a flame on both sides of the river that no white man will ever be able to put it out."

"You've got to reckon with some brave men first," said Henry.

"Yes, I know that the settlers have good woodsmen, Boone and Kenton—Simon Kenton was my comrade once—but they are too few, and as for this expedition to which you belonged, that is coming up the river, we're going to cut that off, too, not only because we'll be glad to wipe out those people, but because we want the rifles, the ammunition, the stores, and, above all, the cannon that your fleet carries. What will the wooden walls in Kentucky be to us when we get those big guns?"

"When you get them!" said Henry defiantly. This man inspired increasing horror and repulsion. The exulting way in which he talked of destroying his own people would have been incredible, had Henry merely heard of it from others. But the man was here before his face, glorying in the deeds that he expected to commit.

"Oh, we'll get them," said Girty confidently. "You think you can help to keep us from it, but you won't be there when it's done. Two things are going to be offered to you, and you'll have to choose between them."

"What are they?" asked Henry, who had resumed his calm, at least, so far as looks went.

"It's what I mainly came here to talk to you about. Timmendiquas is young, but he's a mighty man among the Wyandots. All the older chiefs are willing to step aside in his favor, and when men do that without being made to do it, there's something great in the one that's favored, something that everybody is bound to see. He's first among the Wyandots, and you know what that means when I tell you that the last of the Wyandots are as good as the first of most people."

"Why do you talk to me about Timmendiquas?" asked Henry. "I've seen him, I've been with him for days, I know what he is."

"I'm coming to it. Timmendiquas likes you. He thinks you're fitted for the forest and a life like the one he leads. Other Wyandots who have observed you agree with him, and to tell you the truth I think so, too, myself."

"Well!" said Henry. He now divined what Girty was going to reveal, but he wished the renegade to tell it himself.

"Timmendiquas will be in the council house several days longer, purifying himself, but when he does come out, they'll say to you: 'Be a Wyandot or die.' They'll put it to you plain, just as it has been put to white men before you."

Henry stirred a little. Certainly he did not wish to die, nor did he expect to die, but he would risk the alternative.

"Girty," he said, slowly, "an offer something like this was made to me once before. It was made by a Spaniard far down in the south. You never knew him—he's dead now—but your friend, Braxton Wyatt did—but the other thing wasn't death, nor did he ask me, if I took his offer, to make war upon the settlements in Kentucky. Before I'd turn Indian like you and Braxton Wyatt and the others, and murder my own people, you infamous renegade, I'd be torn to pieces or burned at the stake a dozen times over!"

The words were hurled out by passion and feeling as the flash of powder sends forth the bullet. The renegade shrank back, and rose to his feet, his eyes aflame, but in a moment or two he sank down again, laughing a little.

"That's what I knew you'd say," he said, "and I came here to hear you say it. I wanted to force the hand of Timmendiquas, and I've done it. I don't want you to join us, and I'll tell you why. I intend to be first here, first among the white leaders of the Indians, but if you were to come with us you'd be first yourself in three or four years, and I'd be only second. See how much I think of your powers."

"I don't thank you for your compliment," said Henry boldly, "but I'll thank you if you'll get out of this lodge. I think you're the worst man I've ever seen."

Simon Girty frowned again, and raised his hand as if to strike the bound youth, but refrained.

"We don't see things alike," he said, and abruptly left the lodge.

Henry felt his evil presence long after he had gone, as if some foul animal had entered the lodge, and presently, when old Heno came, he asked him as a great favor to leave the door open for a while. When the cool, fresh air rushed in he breathed it in great draughts and felt relieved. He admired Timmendiquas. He respected the Wyandots. He could not blame the Indian who fought for his hunting grounds, but, with all the strength of his strong nature, he despised and hated every renegade.

That evening, after old Heno had gone, he sought for the first time to slip or break his bonds. He wanted to get away. He wanted to rejoin his comrades and the fleet. He wanted to help them prepare for the new dangers. But strain as he might with all his great strength, and twist as he would with all his ingenuity, he

35

could not get free. He gave it up after a while and lay on his rush mat in a state of deep depression. It seemed that the Wyandots, cunning and agile, flower of the red men, would give him no chance.

He had asked Heno to leave the door of the lodge partly open a while longer that he might have plenty of fresh air, and the old warrior had done so. He heard faint noises from the village, but bye and bye they ceased, and Henry at last fell asleep.

Deep in the night he heard a musical sound, a small note but clear and sweet. It reached him easily, although it seemed to come from the forest four or five hundred yards away, and it spoke in almost audible tones, telling him to be of good faith, that what he wished would come to pass. It was the wind among the leaves again, something mystical but almost human to him. It was the third time that it had sung to him, once in warning, twice in hope, and the depression that he had felt when he laid down vanished utterly. A deep sense of peace and content pervaded his whole being. It was a peace of the senses and mind alike, driving away all trouble either for the present or the future.

He was called to deeper rest. The voice of the forest still sang to him, becoming softer and softer and fainter and fainter, and the feeling of absolute content was overwhelming. He did not seek to move, but permitted himself, as if under an opiate, to drift away into a far slumberland, while the note from the forest sank to nothing.

When he awoke the next morning he did not know whether he had really heard or had merely dreamed.

CHAPTER V

PLAY AND COUNCIL

Henry was still a prisoner in the lodge when the purification of Timmendiquas was finished. He had been permitted to go forth now and then under a strong guard, but, no matter how closely he watched, not the slightest chance of escape presented itself. He saw the renegades about, Braxton Wyatt among them, but none of these men spoke to him. It was evident to him, however, from the respectful manner in which the Wyandots treated Girty that he had great influence among them.

The warriors seemed to be in no hurry about anything. The hunters were bringing in plenty of game, and the village life went forward merrily. But Henry judged that they were merely waiting. It was inconceivable that the Wyandots should remain there long in peace while the Indian world of all that great valley was seething with movement.

Timmendiquas came to see him at the end of the sixth day of purification, and treated him with the courtesy due from a great chief to a distinguished prisoner.

"Have our warriors been kind to you?" he asked.

"They have done everything except let me slip away," replied Henry.

Timmendiquas smiled.

"That is the one thing that we do not wish," he said. "They think as I do that you are fit to be a Wyandot. Come, I will loose your hands, and together we will see our young men and young women play ball."

Henry was not at all averse. Both his nature and his long but friendly captivity in a far northwestern tribe made him have a keen sympathy with many traits in the Indian character. He could understand and like their sports.

"I'll go gladly, White Lightning," he said. "I don't think you need ask me to give any promise not to escape. I won't find any such chance."

The chief smiled with pleasure at the compliment, undid the bonds, and the two walked out into the brilliant sunshine. Henry felt at once that the village was tingling with excitement. All were hurrying toward a wide grassy meadow just at the outskirts of the village, and the majority of them, especially the young of either sex, laughed and chattered volubly. There was no restraint. Here among themselves the Indian repression was thrown aside.

Henry, with the shadow of great suffering and death over him, felt their thrill and excitement. The day was uncommonly fine, and the setting of the forest scene was perfect. There was the village, trim and neat in its barbaric way, which in the sunshine was not an unpleasant way, with the rich meadows about it, and beyond the great wilderness of heavy, circling dark green.

All were now gathered at the edge of the meadow, still laughing, chattering, and full of delight. Even the great Timmendiquas, red knight, champion and far-famed hero at twenty-five, unbent and speculated with keen interest on the result of the ball game, now about to be played. Henry felt his own interest increasing, and he rubbed shoulders with his old friends, Heno the Thunder, Anue the Bear, and Hainteroh the Raccoon. The gallant Raccoon still carried his arm in a sling, but he was such a healthy man that it would be well in an incredibly brief period, and meantime it did not interfere at all with his enjoyment of a ball game.

The meadow was about a hundred yards wide and a hundred and fifty yards long. The grass upon it was thick, but nowhere more than three or four inches in height. All along the edges of the longer sides, facing each other, stakes had been driven at intervals of six feet, and amid great cheering the players formed up on either side next to the line of the stakes.

But all the players on one side were women, mostly young, strong, and lithe, and all the players on the other side were men, also mostly young, strong and lithe. They wore no superfluous garments, although enough was left to save modesty, and young braves and young squaws alike were alert and eager, their eyes

37

flushing with excitement. There were at least one hundred players on each side, and it seemed a most unequal match, but an important proviso was to come.

Timmendiquas advanced to the edge of the meadow and held up his hand. Instantly all shouting, cheering, and talking ceased, and there was perfect silence. Then old Heno, holding in his hand a ball much larger than the modern baseball, but much smaller than the modern football, advanced gravely and solemnly into the meadow. The eyes of two hundred players, young warriors and young girls were intent upon him.

Old Thunder, despite his years, was a good sport and felt the importance of his duty. While all were watching him, and the multitude did no more than breathe, he walked gingerly over the grass, and with a keen old eye picked out a point that was equally distant from the long and short sides of the parallelogram. Here he stood gravely for a few moments, as if to confirm himself in the opinion that this was the proper place, and extended his right arm with the big ball lying in the open palm.

There was a long breath of excitement from players and spectators alike, but Big Thunder was a man of experience and deliberation who was not to be hurried. He still held his right arm extended with the big ball lying in the open palm, and then sent a warning look to each hundred, first to the men and then to the women. These two sides were already bent far over, waiting to jump.

The stakes, the field, the positions of the players were remarkably like the modern game of football, although this was wholly original with the Indians.

The eyes of old Heno came back from the players to the ball lying in the palm of his right hand and regarded it contemplatively a moment or two. Then the fingers suddenly contracted like lightning upon the ball, and he threw it high, perfectly straight up in the air, at the same time uttering a piercing shout.

Henry saw that the ball would fall almost where Heno stood, but the old warrior ran swiftly away, and the opposing sides, men and women, made a dash for it before it fell. The multitude, thrilled with the excitement, uttered a great shout, and bent forward in eagerness. But no one—not a player—encroached upon the meadow. Warriors as guards stalked up and down, but they were not needed. The discipline was perfect. Henry by the side of Timmendiquas shared in the general interest, and he, too, bent forward. The chief bent with him.

Young warriors and young girls who made a dash for the ball were about equal in speed. Wyandot women were not hampered by skirts, and forest life made them lithe and sinewy. Both were near the ball, but Henry yet saw nothing to tell which would reach it first. Suddenly a slim brown figure shot out from the ranks of the women, and, with a leap, reached the ball, when the nearest warrior was yet a yard away.

There was a great cry of applause, as the girl, straightening up, attempted to run with the ball through the ranks of the men, and throw it between the stakes at their side of the field. Two warriors promptly intercepted her, and now Henry saw why the match between girls and warriors was not so unequal as it had appeared at first. When the warriors intercepted the girl she threw the ball over their heads and as far as she could toward the coveted goal posts. Three warriors ran for it, but the one who reached it kicked it with all his might back toward the goal posts of the girls. It fell into a dense throng there, and a girl promptly threw it back, where it was met by the returning kick of a warrior. The men were allowed to use only their feet, the girls could use both hands and feet. If any warrior touched the ball with his hands he was promptly put off the field by the umpires, and the ball was restored to its original position.

The match, well balanced, hotly contested, swayed back and forth. Now the ball was carried toward the women's goal, and then toward the men. Now all the two hundred players would be in a dense throng in the center, and then they would open out as some swift hand or foot sent the ball flying. Often the agile young squaws were knocked down in the hurly burly, but always they sprang up laughing.

All around the field the people cheered and laughed, and many began to bet, the wagers being mostly of skins, lead, powder or bright trinkets bought at the British posts.

For over a half hour the ball flew back and forth, and so far as Henry could see, neither had gained any advantage. Presently they were all packed once more in a dense throng in the center of the field, and the ball was invisible somewhere in the middle of the group. While the crowd watched for its reappearance all the shouting and cheering ceased.

The ball suddenly flew from the group and shot toward the goal posts on the side of the women and a stalwart warrior, giving it another kick, sent it within ten yards of victory for the men.

"Ah, the warriors are too strong for them," said White Lightning.

But he spoke too soon. There was a brown streak across the grass, and the same girl who had first seized the ball darted ahead of the warrior. She picked up the ball while it was yet rolling and ran swiftly back with it. A warrior planted himself in her way, but, agile as a deer, she darted around him, escaped a second and a third in the same way, and continued her flight toward the winning posts.

The crowd gave a single great shout, subsiding after it into a breathless silence.

"The Dove runs well," murmured Timmendiquas in English.

Henry's sympathies were with her, but could the Dove evade all the warriors? They could not touch the ball, but they might seize the girl herself and shake her until the ball fell from her hands. This, in fact, was what happened when an agile young warrior succeeded in grasping her by the shoulder. The ball fell to the ground, but as he loosed her and prepared to kick it she made a quick dive and seized it. The warrior's foot swung in the empty air, and then he set out after the flying Dove.

Only one other guard was left, and it was seen that he would intercept her, but she stopped short, her arm swung out in a curve, and she threw the ball with all her might toward the goal posts. The warrior leaped high to catch it, but it passed six inches above his outstretched fingers, sailed on through the air, cleared the goal posts, and fell ten feet on the other side. The Dove had won the game for her side.

The crowd swarmed over the field and congratulated the victorious girls, particularly the fleet-footed Dove, while the beaten warriors drew off in a crestfallen group. Timmendiquas, with Henry at his side, was among the first to give approval, but the renegades remained in their little group at the edge of the field. Girty was not at all pleased at the time consumed by the Wyandots in this game. He had other plans that he wished to urge.

"But it's no use for me to argue with them," he said to Braxton Wyatt. "They're as set in their ways as any white people that ever lived."

"That's so," said Wyatt, "you're always right, Mr. Girty, I've noticed, too, since I've been among the Indians that you can't interfere with any of their rites and ceremonies."

He spoke in a deferential tone, as if he acknowledged his master in treachery and villainy, and Girty received it as his due. He was certainly first in this group of six, and the older ones, Blackstaffe, McKee, Eliot, and Quarles, recognized the fact as willingly as did Braxton Wyatt.

The crowd, the game finished, was dissolving, and Girty at the head of his comrades strolled toward Timmendiquas, who still had Henry at his side.

"Timmendiquas," he said in Wyandot, "beware of this prisoner. Although but a boy in years, he has strength, courage and skill that few men, white or red, can equal."

The eyes of the young chief, full of somber fire, were turned upon the renegade.

"Since when, Girty," he asked, "have the Wyandots become old women? Since when have they become both weak and ignorant?"

Girty, bold as he was, shrank a little at the stern tone and obvious wrath of the chief.

"I meant nothing wrong, Timmendiquas," he said. "The world knows that the Wyandots are both brave and wise."

White Lightning shrugged his shoulders, and turned away with his prisoner. Henry could understand only a word or two of what they said, but he guessed its import. Already skilled in forest diplomacy, he knew that it was wisdom for him to say nothing, and he walked on with White Lightning. He watched the chief with sharp side glances and saw that he was troubled. Two or three times he seemed on the point of saying something, but always remained silent. Yet his bearing towards Henry was most friendly, and it gave the captive boy a pang. He knew the hope that was in the mind of White Lightning, but he knew that hope could never come true.

"We do not wish to make you suffer, Ware," he said, when they came to the door of Henry's prison lodge, "until we decide what we are to do with you, and before then much water must flow down Ohezuhyeandawa (The Ohio)."

"I do not ask you to do anything that is outside your customs," said Henry quietly.

"We must bind you as before," said Timmendiquas, "but we bind you in a way that does not hurt, and Heno will bring you food and water. But this is a day of rejoicing with us, and this afternoon our young men and young maids dance. You shall come forth and see it."

Henry was re-bound, and a half hour later old Heno appeared with food, meat of the deer and wild turkey, bread of maize, and a large gourd filled with pure cold water. After he had loosened Henry's wrists that he might eat and drink he sat by and talked. Thunder, with further acquaintance, was disclosing signs of volubility.

"How you like ball game?" he asked.

"Good! very good!" said Henry sincerely, "and I don't see, Thunder, how you could throw that ball so straight up in the air that it would come down where you stood."

"Much practice, long practice," said the old man modestly. "Heno been throwing up balls longer by twice than you have lived."

When the boy had finished eating, old Heno told him to come with him as the dance was now about to begin, and Henry was glad enough to escape again from the close prison lodge.

The dancers were already forming on the meadow where the ball game had been played, and there was the same interest and excitement, although now it was less noisy. Henry guessed from their manner that the dance would not only be an amusement, but would also have something of the nature of a rite.

All the dancers were young, young warriors and girls, and they faced each other in two lines, warriors in one and girls in the other. As in the ball game, each line numbered about a hundred, but now they were in their brightest and most elaborate raiment. The two lines were perfectly even, as straight as an arrow, the toe of no moccasin out of line, and they were about a rod apart.

At the far end of the men's line a warrior raised in his right hand a dry gourd which contained beads and pebbles, and began to rattle it in a not unmusical way. To the sound of the rattle he started a grave and solemn chant, in which all joined. Then the two lines, still keeping their straightness and evenness, danced toward each other slowly and rhythmically. All the time the song went on, the usual monotonous Indian beat, merely a rising and falling of the note with scarcely any variation.

The two lines, still dancing, came close together, and then both bent forward until the head of every warrior touched the head of the girl opposite him. They remained in this position a full half minute, and a young warrior often whispered sweet words in the ear of the girl whose head touched him. This, as Henry learned later, was the wooing or courting dance of the Wyandots.

41

Both sides suddenly straightened up, uttered a series of loud shouts, and began to dance back toward their original position, at the same time resuming the rising and falling chant. When the full distance was reached they danced up, bowed, and touched heads again, and this approaching or retreating was kept up for four hours, or until the sun set. It became to Henry extremely monotonous, but the Indians seemed never to tire of it, and when they stopped at darkness the eyes of all the dancers were glowing with pleasure and excitement.

It was quite dark when Henry returned to the lodge for the second time that day, but this time old Heno instead of Timmendiquas was his escort back to prison.

"Play over now," said Heno. "Great work begin to-morrow."

The old man seemed to be full of the importance of what he knew, and Henry, anxious to know, too, played adroitly upon his vanity.

"If any big thing is to be done, I'm sure that you would know of it, Heno," he said. "So they are to begin to-morrow, are they?"

"Yes," replied Heno, supposing from Henry's words that he had already received a hint from Timmendiquas. "Great chiefs reach here to-night. Hold council to-morrow."

"Ah, they come from all the tribes, do they not?" said Henry, guessing shrewdly.

"From all between Ohezuhyeandawa (The Ohio) and the Great Lakes and from the mountains to Yandawezue (The Mississippi)."

"Illinois, Ottawas, Miamis, Shawnees, and Delawares?" said Henry.

"Yes," said Heno, "Illinois, Ottawas, Miamis, Shawnees, and Delawares. All come to smoke pipes with the Wyandots and hear what we have to say. We small nation, but mighty warriors. No Wyandot ever coward."

"That is true," said Henry sincerely. "I've never heard of a Wyandot who flinched in battle. My people think that where one Wyandot warrior walks it takes two warriors of any other tribe to fill his footprints."

Old Heno smiled broadly.

"Maybe you be at council to-morrow," he said. "You make good Wyandot."

"Maybe I could," said Henry to himself, "but it's certain that I never will."

Old Heno withdrew, still smiling, and Henry was left alone in the darkness of the prison lodge, full of interest over what was to occur on the morrow, and anxious that he might be present to see. He knew that the conference of the chiefs would be concerning the new war on Kentucky, and now he was not so anxious to escape at once. A week later would be better, and then if the chance came—he never faltered in his belief that it would come—he could carry with him news worth the while. The young chief, Timmendiquas, was a man whom he admired, but, nevertheless, he would prove a formidable leader of such a coalition, the most dangerous to the white people that could be found.

Henry listened again for the song among the leaves that had the power to fill him with hope, but he did not hear it. Nevertheless, his courage did not depart, and he felt that the longer the Wyandots waited to dispose of him the better were his chances.

Heno came the next morning with his breakfast and announced that all the chiefs of the Ohio Valley had arrived and were now in conference in the council house.

"They talk later outside," he said, "and maybe Timmendiquas let you come and hear wise words that great chiefs say."

"I'd like to hear," said Henry. "I know that the Indians are great orators."

Heno did not reply, but Henry had divined that he was susceptible to flattery. He understood, too, that it was the policy of White Lightning to impress him with the skill and power of the tribes. So he waited patiently.

Meanwhile fifty famous chiefs representing all the great nations of the Ohio Valley sat in the temporary council house of the Wyandots, the smallest but the wisest and bravest tribe of them all. They were mostly men of middle age or older, although two or three were nearly, but not quite, as young as Timmendiquas himself. This chief was at once the youngest, the tallest, and the handsomest man present. They sat in rows, but where he sat was the head of the council. All looked toward him.

Every chief was in his finest dress, moccasins, leggings, and hunting coat of beautifully tanned deerskin, with blanket of bright color looped gracefully over the shoulder. In one of the rows in a group sat the six renegades, Girty, Blackstaffe, McKee, Eliot, Quarles, and Braxton Wyatt. Every man was bent forward in the stooped formal attitude of one who listens, and every one had the stem of a pipe in his mouth.

In one group sat the chiefs of the Ottawas, the most distant of the tribes, dwellers on the far shores of Lake Huron, sometimes fish-eaters, and fugitives at an earlier day from the valley of the Ottawa River in Canada, whence they took their name. The word "Ottawa" in their language meant "trader," and they had received it in their ancient home because they had ideas of barter and had been the "go betweens" for other tribes. They worshiped the sun first and the stars second. Often they held festivals to the sun, and asked his aid in fishing and hunting. They occupied a secondary position in the Ohio Valley because they were newer and were not as fierce and tenacious in war as the older tribes. Ottawa chiefs did not thrust themselves forward, and when they spoke it was in a deprecatory way.

Next to the Wyandots were the Illinois, who lived in the valley of the Illinois and who were not numerous. They had been beaten often in tribal wars, until their spirit lacked that fine exaltation which means victory. Like the Ottawas, they felt that they should not say much, but should listen intently to the words of the chiefs who sat with them, and who represented great warrior nations.

Next to the Illinois were the Delawares, or, in their own language, the Lenni Lenape, who also were an immigrant race. Once they had dwelt much farther east, even beyond the mountains, but many warlike tribes, including the great league of the Iroquois, the Six Nations, had made war upon them, had reduced their numbers, and had steadily pushed them westward and further westward, until they reached the region now called Ohio. Here their great uncles, the Wyandots, received them with kindness, told them to rest in peace and gave them extensive lands, fine for hunting, along the Muskingum River.

The Lenni Lenape throve in the new land and became powerful again. But never in their darkest days, when the world seemed to be slipping beneath their feet, had they lost the keen edge of their spirit. The warrior of the Lenni Lenape had always been willing to laugh in the face of flames and the stake, and now, as their chiefs sat in the council, they spoke often and they spoke boldly. They feared to look no one in the face, not even the far-famed Timmendiquas himself. They were of three clans: Unamis, which is the Turtle; Unaluchtgo, which is the Turkey; and Minsi, the Wolf. Minsi was the most warlike and always led the Lenni Lenape in battle. Chiefs of all three clans were present.

Next to the Lenni Lenape were the valiant Shawnees, who held all the valley of the Scioto as far west as the Little Miami or Mud River. They had a record for skill and courage that went far back into the mists of the past, and of all the tribes, it was the Shawnees who hated the whites most. Their hostility was undying. No Shawnee would ever listen to any talk of peace with them. It must be war until the white vanguard was destroyed or driven back over the mountains. So fearless were the Shawnees that once a great band of them, detaching from the main tribe, had crossed the Ohio and had wandered all the way through the southern country, fighting Chickasaws, Creeks, and Choctaws, until they reached the sea, more than a thousand miles from their old home. A cunning chief, Black Hoof, who could boast that he had bathed his feet in the salt water, had led them safely back more than twenty years before, and now this same Black Hoof sat here in the council house of the Wyandots, old and wrinkled, but keen of eye, eagle-beaked, and as shrewd and daring as ever, the man who had led in an almost unknown border exploit, as dangerous and romantic as the Retreat of the Ten Thousand.

The Shawnees claimed—and the legend was one that would never die among them—that they originated in a far, very far, land, and that they were divided into 12 tribes or sub-tribes. For some cause which they had forgotten the whole nation marched away in search of a new home. They came to a wide water that was bitter and salt to the taste. They had no canoes, but the sea parted before them, and then the twelve tribes, each with its leader at its head, marched on the ocean bottom with the wall of waters on either side of them until they reached a great land which was America. It is this persistent legend, so remarkable in its similarity to the flight of the children of Israel from Egypt, even to the number of the tribes, that has caused one or two earlier western writers to claim that the Shawnees were in reality the Ten Lost Tribes of Israel.

Next to the Shawnees were the Miamis, more numerous perhaps, but not more warlike. They lived along the rivers Miami and Maumee and were subdivided

44

into three clans, the Twigtees, the Weas, and the Piankeshaws. Chiefs of all three clans were present, and they could control many hundreds of warriors.

The Wyandots, who lived to the eastward in Ohio, held themselves back modestly. They were a small tribe, but the others often called them "The Nation-That-Never-Knew-a-Coward," and there was no reason for them to push themselves forward. When the time came for a Wyandot chief to speak the time would come for the others to listen. They did speak, and throughout that morning the great question was argued back and forth. Girty and Blackstaffe, the second of the renegades in influence, sometimes participated, and they were listened to with varying degrees of respect, according to the character of the advice they gave. These white men, with their cunning and knowledge of their own people, were of value, but once or twice when they spoke the lips of some of the younger chiefs, always including Timmendiquas, curled with scorn.

At noon they came forth from the council house, and Timmendiquas, accompanied by Heno, went to the lodge in which Henry was confined. Heno carried particularly tempting food to Henry. Besides venison and turkey, he brought maple sugar and hominy with a dressing of bear's oil and sugar.

Henry had become used to Indian food long since, and he ate with relish. Timmendiquas stood by, regarding him attentively.

"You are a strong and valiant foe, Ware," he said at length. "I fight against the white people, but I do not dislike you. I wish, then, that you would come forth and see the great council of the allied tribes in the meadow. The council of the chiefs was held this morning. This afternoon we lay the matter before all the warriors."

"I'll come gladly," said Henry.

CHAPTER VI

THE GANTLET

Timmendiquas and Heno left the lodge, but in about ten minutes Heno returned, bringing with him Hainteroh.

"Well, how's your arm, Raccoon?" said Henry, wishing to be friendly.

Raccoon did not know his English words, but he understood Henry's glance, and he smiled and touched his arm. Then he said something in Wyandot.

"He say arm soon be well," said old Heno. "Now you come out and see council, great talk, me on one side of you, Hainteroh on the other."

"Yes, I know you've got to guard me," said Henry, "but I won't try to run."

They loosed his bonds, and he stepped out with them, once more to see all the people pouring toward the meadow as they had done at the time of the ball game. The crowd was greatly increased in numbers, and Henry surmised at once that many warriors had come with the chiefs from the other tribes. But he noticed, also, that the utmost concord seemed to exist among them.

When they reached the meadow they stopped at the edge, and Heno and Hainteroh stood on either side of him. The people were gathered all about, four square, and the chiefs stood on the meadow enclosed by the square.

"Now they speak to the Wyandot nation and the visiting warriors," said Heno.

A chief of ripe years but of tall and erect figure arose and stood gravely regarding the multitude.

"That Kogieschquanohel of the clan of the Minsi of the tribe of the Lenni Lenape," said Heno, the herald. "His name long time ago Hopocan, but he change it to Kogieschquanohel, which mean in language of the Yengees Maker of Daylight. He man you call Captain Pipe."

"So that is Captain Pipe, is it?" said Henry.

Captain Pipe, as the whites called him, because his later Indian name was too long to be pronounced, was a Delaware chief, greatly celebrated in his day, and Henry regarded him with interest.

"Who is that by the side of Captain Pipe?" he asked, indicating another chief of about the same height and age.

"That Koquethagaaehlon, what you call Captain White Eyes," replied Heno. "He great Delaware chief, too, and great friend of Captain Pipe."

Henry's eyes roamed on and he saw two other chiefs whom he knew well. They were Yellow Panther, head chief of the Miamis, and Red Eagle, head chief of the Shawnees. He had no doubt that Braxton Wyatt would tell them who he was, and he knew that he could expect no mercy of any kind from them. Timmendiquas stood not far away, and in a group, as usual, were the renegades.

Captain Pipe stretched forth a long arm, and the multitude became silent. Then he spoke with much strong simile drawn from the phenomena of nature, and Henry, although he knew little of what he said, knew that he was speaking with eloquence. He learned later that Captain Pipe was urging with zeal and fire the immediate marching of all the tribes against the white people. They must cut off this fleet on the river, and then go in far greater force than ever against the white settlements in Kain-tuck-ee.

He spoke for half an hour with great vigor, and when he sat down he was applauded just as a white speaker would be, who had said what the listeners wished to hear.

His friend, Captain White Eyes, followed, and the gist of his speech, also, Henry learned somewhat later from Heno. He was sorry to differ from his friend, Captain Pipe. He thought they ought to wait a little, to be more cautious, they had already suffered greatly from two expeditions into Kain-tuck-ee, the white

46

men fought well, and the allied tribes, besides losing many good warriors, might fail, also, unless they chose their time when all the conditions were favorable.

The speech of Captain White Eyes was not received with favor. The Wyandots and nearly all the visiting warriors wanted war. They were confident, despite their previous failures, that they could succeed and preserve their hunting grounds to themselves forever. Other speeches, all in the vein of Captain Pipe, followed, and then Girty, the renegade, spoke. He proclaimed his fealty to the Indians. He said that he was one of them; their ways were his ways; he had shown it in the council and on the battle field; the whites would surely hang him if they caught him, and hence no red man could doubt his faith. The tribes should strike now before the enemy grew too strong.

Great applause greeted Girty. Henry saw that he stood high in the esteem of the warriors. He told them what they wished to hear, and he was of value to them. The boy's teeth pressed down hard on his lips. How could a white man fight thus against his own people, even to using the torch and the stake upon them?

When Girty sat down, Timmendiquas himself stood up. His was the noblest figure by far that had faced the crowd. Young, tall, splendid, and obviously a born leader, he drew many looks and murmurs of approval and admiration. He made a speech of great grace and eloquence, full of fire and conviction. He, too, favored an immediate renewal of the war, and he showed by physical demonstration how the tribes ought to strike.

He spread a great roll of elm bark upon the ground, extending it by means of four large stones, one of which he laid upon each corner. Then with his scalping knife he drew upon it a complete map of the white settlements in Kain-tuck-ee and of the rivers, creeks, hills, and trails. He did this with great knowledge and skill, and when he held it up it was so complete that Henry, who could see it as well as the others, was compelled to admire. He recognized Wareville and its river perfectly, and Marlowe, too.

"We know where they are and we know how to reach them," said Timmendiquas in the Wyandot tongue, "and we must fall upon them in the night and slay. We must send at once to Tahtarara (Chillicothe, the greatest of the Indian towns in the Ohio Valley) for more warriors, and then we must wait for this fleet. Tuentahahewaghta (the site of Cincinnati, meaning the landing place, where the road leads to the river) would suit well, or if you do not choose to wait that late we might strike them where Ohezuhyeandawa (the Ohio) foams into white and runs down the slope (the site of Louisville). This fleet must be destroyed first and then the settlements, or the buffalo, the deer and the forest will go. And when the buffalo, the deer, and the forest go, we go, too."

Great applause greeted the speech of Timmendiquas, and the question was decided. Captain White Eyes, who had a melancholy gift of foresight, was in a minority consisting of himself only, and swift runners were dispatched at once to the other tribes, telling the decision. Meanwhile, a great feast was prepared for the visiting chiefs that they might receive all honor from the Wyandots.

Escorted by Heno and Hainteroh, Henry went back to his prison lodge, sad and apprehensive. This was, in truth, a formidable league, and it could have no more formidable leader than Timmendiquas. He had seen, too, the boastful faces of the renegades, and he was not willing that Braxton Wyatt or any of them should have a chance to exult over their own people.

Timmendiquas came to him the next morning and addressed him with gravity, Henry seeing at once that he had words of great importance to utter.

"I was willing for you to see the council yesterday, Ware," said White Lightning, "because I wished you to know how strong we are, and with what spirit we will go forth against your people. I have seen, too, that many of our ways are your ways. You love the forest and the hunt, and you would make a great Wyandot."

He paused a moment, as if he would wait for Henry to speak, but the boy remained silent.

"You are also a great warrior for one so young," resumed Timmendiquas. "The white youth, Wyatt, says that it is so, and the great chiefs, Yellow Panther of the Miamis, and Red Eagle of the Shawnees, tell of your deeds. They are eager to see you die, but the Wyandots admire a brave young warrior, and they would make you an offer."

"What is your offer, Chief?" asked Henry, knowing well that, whatever the offer might be, Timmendiquas was the head and front of it—and despite his question he could surmise its nature.

"It is this. You are our prisoner. You are one of our enemies, and we took you in battle. Your life belongs to us, and by our laws you would surely die in torture. But you are at the beginning of life. Manitou has been good to you. He has given you the eye of the eagle, the courage of the Wyandot, and the strength of the panther. You could be a hunter and a warrior more moons than I can count, until you are older than Black Hoof, who led the Shawnees before you were born, to the salt water and back again.

"Is death sweet to you, just when you are becoming a great warrior? There is one way, and one only to escape it. If a prisoner, strong and brave like you, wishes to join us, shave his head and be a Wyandot, sometimes we take him. That question was laid before the chiefs last night. The white men, Girty, Blackstaffe, Wyatt, and the others, were against it, but I, wishing to save your life and see you my brother in arms, favored it, and there were others who helped me. We have had our wish, and so I say to you: 'Be a Wyandot and live, refuse and die.'"

It was put plainly, tersely, but Henry had expected it, and his answer was ready. His resolution had been taken and could not be altered.

"I choose death," he said, adopting the Wyandot's epigrammatic manner.

A shade of sadness appeared for a moment on the face of Timmendiquas.

"You cannot change?" he asked.

"No," replied Henry. "I belong to my own people. I cannot desert them and go against them even to escape death. Such a temptation was placed in my way once before, Timmendiquas, but I had to refuse it."

"I would save your life," said the chief.

"I know it, and I thank you. I tell you, too, that I have no fancy for fire and the stake, but the price that you ask is too much."

"I cannot ask any other."

"I know it, but I have made my choice and I hope, Timmendiquas, that if I must go to the happy hunting grounds I shall meet you there some day, and that we shall hunt together."

The eyes of the chief gleamed for a moment, and, turning abruptly, he left the lodge.

There was joy among the renegades when the decision of Henry was made known, and now he was guarded more closely than ever. Meanwhile, all the boys about to become warriors were being initiated, and the customs of the Ohio Valley Indians in this particular were very different from the ways of those who inhabited the Great Plains.

Every boy, when he attained the age of eight, was left alone in the forest for half a day with his face blackened. He was compelled to fast throughout the time, and he must behave like a brave man, showing no fear of the loneliness and silence. As he grew older these periods of solitary fasting were increased in length, and now, at eighteen, several boys in the Wyandot village had reached the last blackening and fasting. The black paint was spread over the neophyte's face, and he was led by his father far from the village to a solitary cabin or tent, where he was left without weapons or food. It was known from his previous fasting about how long he could stand it, and now the utmost test would be applied.

The father, in some cases, would not return for three days, and then the exhausted boy was taken back to the village, where his face was washed, his head shaved, excepting the scalp lock, and plentiful food was put before him. A small looking-glass, a bag of paint, and the rifle, tomahawk, and knife of a warrior were given to him.

While these ceremonies were going on Henry lay in the prison lodge, and he could not see the remotest chance of escape. He listened at night for the friendly voice among the leaves, but he did not hear it. Timmendiquas did not come again, and two old squaws, in place of Heno, brought him his food and drink. He had no hope that the Wyandots would spare him after his refusal to leave his own people and become an Indian. He knew that their chivalry made no such demand upon them. The hardest part of it all was to lie there and wait. He was like a man condemned, but with no date set for the execution. He did not know when they would come for him. But he believed that it would be soon, because the Wyandots must leave presently to march on the great foray.

The fourth morning after the visit of Timmendiquas the young chief returned. He was accompanied by Heno and Hainteroh, and the three regarded the youth with great gravity. Henry, keen of intuition and a reader of faces, knew that his time had come. What they had prepared for him he did not know, but it must be something terrible. A shiver that was of the spirit, but not of the muscles, ran through him. Torture and death were no pleasant prospect to him who was so young and so strong, and who felt so keenly every hour of his life the delight of living, but he would face them with all the pride of race and wilderness training.

"Well, Timmendiquas," he said, "I suppose that you have come for me!"

"It is true," replied Timmendiquas steadily, "but we would first prepare you. It shall not be said of the Wyandots that they brought to the ordeal a broken prisoner, one whose blood did not flow freely in his veins."

Henry's bonds were loosened, and he stood up. Although he had been bound securely, his thongs had always allowed him a little movement, and he had sought in the days of his captivity to keep his physical condition perfect. He would stretch his limbs and tense his muscles for an hour at a time. It was not much, it was not like the freedom of the forest, but pursued by one as tenacious and forethoughtful as he, it kept his muscles hard, his lungs strong, and his blood sparkling. Now, as he stood up, he had all his strength, and his body was flexible and alert.

But Heno and Hainteroh seized him by each hand and pulled strongly. He understood. They were acting in a wholly friendly manner for the time being, and would give him exercise. He tried to guess from it the nature of the first ordeal that awaited him, but he could not. He pulled back and felt his muscles harden and tighten. So strong was he that both warriors were dragged to his side of the wigwam.

"Good!" said Timmendiquas. "Prison has not made you soft. You shall prove to all who see you that you are already a great warrior."

Then they rubbed his ankles and wrists with bear's oil that any possible stiffness from the bonds might be removed, and directed him to walk briskly on the inside circuit of the lodge for about fifteen minutes. He did readily as they suggested. He knew that whatever their motives—and after all they were Indians with all the traits of Indians—they wished him to be as strong as possible for the fate that awaited him outside. The hardier and braver the victim, the better the Indians always liked it. Over a half hour was passed in these preparations, and then White Lightning said tersely and without emotion:

"Come!"

He led the way, and Henry, following him, stepped from the lodge into the sunlight with Hainteroh and Heno close behind. The boy coming from the half darkness was dazzled at first by the brilliant rays, but in a few moments his eyes strengthened to meet them, and he saw everything. A great crowd was gathered for a third time at the meadow, and a heavy murmur of anticipation and excitement came to his ears.

Henry felt that everybody in the Wyandot village was looking at him. It gave him a singular feeling to be thus the center of a thousand eyes, and the little mental shiver came again, because the eyes were now wholly those of savages. He felt a cool breath on his face. The wind was blowing, and from the forest came the faint rustle of the leaves. He listened a moment that he might hear that hopeful note, the almost human voice that had spoken to him, but it was not there. It was just an ordinary wind blowing in the wilderness, and he ceased to listen because now his crisis was at hand.

Timmendiquas led toward the meadow, and Heno and Hainteroh came close behind. Now Henry saw what they had prepared for him as the first stage of his ordeal. He was to run the gantlet.

Two parallel lines had already been formed, running the longest way of the meadow and far down into an opening of the forest, and all were armed with switches or sticks, some of the latter so heavy, that, wielded by a strong hand, they would knock a man senseless. No sympathy, no kindliness showed in the faces of any of these people. The spirit of the ball and the dance was gone. The white youth was their enemy, he had chosen to remain so, and they knew no law but an eye for an eye and a tooth for a tooth. Children and women were as eager as men for the sport. It was a part of their teaching and belief.

Henry looked again down the line, and there he saw the renegades, three on one side and three on the other. It seemed to him that theirs were the most cruel faces of all. He saw Braxton Wyatt swinging a heavy stick, and he resolved that it should never touch him. He could bear a blow from an Indian, but not from Braxton Wyatt.

Then he looked from the cruel face of the renegade to the forest, so green, so fresh, and so beautiful. What a glorious place it was and how he longed to be there. The deep masses of green leaves, solid in the distance, waved gently in the wind. Over this great green wilderness bent the brilliant blue sky, golden at the dome from the high sun. It was but a fleeting glance, and his eyes came back to earth, to the Wyandots, and to his fate.

"I was able to make it the gantlet first," Timmendiquas was saying in his ear. "Others wished to begin at once with the fire."

"Thank you, White Lightning," said Henry.

He looked for the third time at the line, and he saw that no human being, no matter how great his strength and dexterity, could reach the end of it. It was at least a quarter of a mile in length, and long before he was half way he would be beaten to the earth, limbs broken. They had not intended that he should have the remotest chance of escape. Nor, look as he would, could he see any.

Hark! What was that? It was a sound from the forest, a low, sweet note, but clear and penetrating, the wind among the leaves, the voice, almost human, that told him to be of good faith, that even yet in the face of imminent death he would escape. It was no longer an ordinary wind blowing through the wilderness; it was some voice out of space, speaking to him. White Lightning saw the face of his prisoner suddenly illumined, and he wondered.

Henry looked down the line for the fourth time, and then the way came to him. He knew what to do, and he drew himself together, a compact mass of muscles, and tense like steel wire. Then, while the clear song from the forest still sang in his ear, he glanced up once more at the beneficent heavens, and uttered his wordless prayer:

"O Lord, Thou who art the God of the white man and the Manitou of the red man, give me this day a strength such as I have never known before! Give me an eye quick to see and a hand ready to do! I would live. I love life, but it is not for myself alone that I ask the gift! There are others who need me, and I would go to them! Now, O Lord, abide with me!"

They were his thoughts, not his words, but he was the child of religious parents, who had given him a religious training, and in the crisis he remembered.

It was the duty of Timmendiquas to give the word, but he waited, fascinated by the singular look on the face of the prisoner. He saw confidence, exaltation there, and he still wondered. But the crowd was growing impatient for its sport. They were bedecked in their gayest for this holiday scene, and the size and obvious strength of the captive indicated that it would be continued longer than common.

Timmendiquas glanced at the prisoner again, and for an instant the eyes of the two met. The chief saw purpose written deep in the mind of the other, and Henry caught the fleeting glimpse of sympathy that he had noticed more than once before.

"Are you ready?" asked Timmendiquas in tones so low that no one else could hear.

"Ready!" replied Henry as low.

"Go!" called Timmendiquas. His voice was so sharp that it cracked like a pistol.

Henry made a mighty leap forward, and shot down between the lines so swiftly that the first blows aimed at him fell after he had passed. Then a switch cut him across the shoulders, a stick grazed his head, another glanced off his back as he fled, but he was so quick that the sticks and switches invariably fell too late. This was what he had hoped for; if he could keep ahead of the shower of blows for forty or fifty yards all might go well. It would go well! It must go well! Hope flamed high in him, and he seemed to grow stronger at every leap. The Indians were shouting with delight at the sport, but so intent was he upon his purpose that he did not hear them.

Henry looked up for a moment, and he saw near him the face of Timmendiquas, who had followed him down the line, seeking, it seemed, to give a blow on his account. Beside him, a warrior held a heavy club poised to strike. Henry saw that he could not escape it, and his heart sank, like a plummet in a pool. But the great chief, so sure of foot, stumbled and fell against the warrior with the poised club. The blow went wide, and Henry was untouched. He ran on, but he understood.

He had marked a spot in the line, fifty yards on, perhaps, where it seemed weakest. With the exception of the leader of the renegades, Girty, it was mostly women and children who stood there. Now he was nearing them. He saw Girty's cruel, grinning face, and the heavy stick in his hand poised for a blow.

He could not run in a perfectly straight line, because he was compelled to dodge right or left to escape the clubs, and he was not always successful. One, a glancing blow, made his head ring, but in a moment his will threw off the effect, and the sting of it merely incited him to greater effort. Now the face of Girty was just before him, and the shouting of the Indians was so loud that he could not but hear.

He saw Girty raise his club, and, quick as lightning, Henry, turning off at a right angle, hurled himself directly at Girty, passed within the circle of the falling club, seized the renegade's arm, and wrenched his weapon from his grasp.

It was done in a second, but the Indian warriors near instantly sprang for the pair. The impact of Henry's body knocked Girty to his knees and, as he fell, the youth made a sweeping blow at him with the captured club. Had Henry been left time to balance himself for the stroke, the evil deeds of Simon Girty would have stopped there, and terrible suffering would have been spared to the border. But he struck as he ran, and, although Girty was knocked senseless, his skull was not fractured.

Henry darted away at a right angle from the line toward the forest. He had done what was achieved a few times by prisoners of uncommon strength and agility. Instead of continuing between the rows he had broken out at one side, and now was straining every effort to reach the forest, with the whole Wyandot village yelling at his heels.

Timmendiquas had seen the deed in every detail. He had marked the sudden turn of the fugitive and the extraordinary quickness and strength with which he had overthrown Girty, at the same time taking from him his weapon, and his eyes flashed approval. But he was a Wyandot chief, and he could not let such a captive escape. After a few moments of hesitation he joined in the pursuit, and directed it with voice and gesture.

Henry's soul sang a song of triumph to him. He would escape! There was nobody between him and the forest, and they would not fire just yet for fear of hurting their own people. His strength redoubled. The forest came nearer. It seemed to reach out great green branches and invite him to its shelter.

An old woman suddenly sprang up from the grass and seized him by the knees. He made a mighty effort, threw her off, and leaped clear of her clawing hands. But he had lost time, and the warriors had gained. One was very near, and if he should lay hands upon him Henry knew that he could not escape. Even if the warrior were able to hold him only a half minute the others then would be at hand. But he was still keyed up to the great tension with which he had started down the line. His effort, instead of reaching the zenith, was still increasing, and, turning sideways as he ran, he hurled the stick back into the face of the warrior who was so near. The Wyandot endeavored to dodge it, but he was not quick enough. It struck him on the side of the head and he fell, knocked senseless as

Girty, the renegade, had been.

Then the fleeing youth made another supreme effort, and he drew clear of his pursuers by some yards. The forest was very much nearer now. How cool, how green, and how friendly it looked! One could surely find shade and protection among all those endless rows of mighty trunks! He heard a report behind him and a bullet sang in his ear. The Wyandots, now that he had become a clear target in front of them, began to fire.

Henry, remembering an old trick in such cases, curved a little from side to side as he ran. He lost distance by it, but it was necessary in order to confuse the marksmen. More shots were fired, and the Wyandots, shouting their war cries, began to spread out like a fan in order that they might profit by any divergence of the fugitive from a straight line. Henry felt a pain in his shoulder much like the sting of a bee, but he knew that the bullet had merely nipped him as it passed. Another grazed his arm, but the God of the white man and the Manitou of the red to whom he had prayed held him in His keeping. The Wyandots crowded one another, and as they ran at full speed they were compelled to fire hastily at a zig-zagging fugitive.

He made one more leap, longer and stronger than all the rest, and gained the edge of the forest. At that moment he felt a tap on his side as if he had been struck by a pebble, but he knew it to be a bullet that had gone deeper than the others. It might weaken him later, but not now; it merely gave a new impulse to his speed, and he darted among the trees, spurning the ground like a racing deer.

The bullets continued to fly, but luck made the forest dense, the great trees growing close to one another, and now the advantage was his. Only at times was his body exposed to their aim, and then he ran so fast that mere chance directed the shots. None touched him now, and with a deep exulting thrill, so mighty that it made him quiver from head to foot, he felt that he would make good his flight. Only ten minutes of safety from the bullets, and he could leave them all behind.

Henry's joy was intense, penetrating all his being, and it remained. Yes, life here in this green wilderness was beautiful! He had felt the truth of it with all its force when they brought him forth to die, passing from one torture to another worse, and he felt it with equal poignancy now that he had turned the impossible into the possible, now that the coming gift to him was life, not death. His spirit swelled and communicated itself to his body. Fire ran through his veins.

He took a single fleeting look backward, and saw many brown figures speeding through the forest. He knew their tactics. The fan would develop into a half curve, and pursue with all the fleetness and tenacity with which the Indian— above all the Wyandot—was capable. If he varied but a single yard from the direct line of his flight some one in the half curve would gain by it. He must not lose the single yard! He glanced up through the green veil of foliage at the sun, and noticed that he was running toward the southeast, the way that he wanted to go. Other such glances from time to time would serve to keep him straight, and again he felt the mighty and exultant swell that was in the nature of spiritual exaltation.

The war cries ceased. The Wyandots now pursued in silence, and it would be a pursuit long and tenacious. It was their nature not to give up, and they were filled with chagrin that so notable a prisoner had slipped from them, breaking through their lines and gaining the forest in the face of the impossible. Henry knew all these things, too, and he had no intention of relaxing his speed until he was beyond the range of their rifles. It was well for him that his muscles and sinews were like woven wire, and that he had striven so hard to keep himself in physical trim while he lay a prisoner in the lodge. His breathing was still long and free, and his stride did not decline in either length or quickness.

The ground rolled slightly, and was free from undergrowth for the first half mile. Then he came to clumps of bushes, but they did not decrease his speed, and when he looked back again he saw no Wyandot. The fleetest among them had not been able to equal him, and before long he heard them calling signal cries to one another. The chiefs were giving directions, seeking to place the fugitive, who was now lost to sight, but Henry only ran the faster. He did not delude himself with any such foolish belief that they would quit the pursuit because they could no longer see him.

CHAPTER VII

ALONE IN THE WILDERNESS

When Henry looked back a third time and saw that no Wyandot had yet come into view, he made another spurt, one in which he taxed his power of muscle and lung to the utmost. He maintained his speed for a half mile and then slowed down. He had no doubt that he had increased his lead over them, and now he would use cunning in place of strength and speed. It was a country of springs and brooks, and he looked for one in order that he might use this common device of the border—wading in the water to hide his tracks. But he saw none. Here fortune was not kind, and he ran on in the long, easy stride like the gallop of a horse.

He still sought to keep a perfectly straight course toward the southeast. It would not permit that deadly half circle to close in, and it would carry him toward his friends and the fleet. He reached rougher ground, low hills with many outcroppings of stone, and he leaped lightly from rock to rock. His moccasined feet, for a space, left no traces, and when he came to the softer earth again he paused. They would certainly lose the trail at the hills, and it would take them five, perhaps ten, minutes to find it once more.

He leaned against a tree, drawing great breaths and relaxing his muscles. He permitted everything to give way for a minute or two, knowing that in such manner he would procure the most rest and resiliency. Meanwhile he listened with all the powers of those wonderful, forest-bred ears of his, but heard nothing save a far, faint call or two.

After about five minutes he resumed his flight, going at the long, easy frontier lope, and a little later he came to a great mass of tangled and fallen forest where a hurricane had passed. Fortune that had failed him with the brook served him with the trees, and he ran lightly along in the path of the hurricane, leaping from trunk to trunk. He had turned for the first time from his direct course, but now he could afford to do so. It would take the shrewdest of the Wyandot warriors some time to pick up a trail that was lost for a full quarter of a mile, and he did not leave the windrow until fully that distance was covered.

He passed some low hills again, and just beyond them he came to a large creek flowing between fairly high banks. This was better luck than he had hoped. The waters felt cool and fresh, and, hot from his long run, he drank eagerly. But the creek would serve another and better purpose, the hiding of his trail. It flowed in the very direction in which he was going, and he waded down stream for forty or fifty yards. Then he went over his head. The creek had suddenly deepened, but he came up promptly and swam easily with the current.

Swimming rested him in a way. A new set of muscles came into play, and he swam placidly for two or three hundred yards. Then he turned over on his back and floated as far again. Now, as he floated, he found time to take thought. He saw that the sun was still shining brilliantly overhead, and the forest grew in a dense green wall to the water's edge on either side.

He had come so far. It seemed that he had made good his escape, but he was able for the first time to take a survey of his situation. He was alone in the wilderness and without arms. What a ship is to the sailor, so the rifle was to the borderer. It was his meat and drink, his defense, his armor, his truest and trustiest comrade; without it he must surely perish, unless some rare chance aided him, as once in a thousand times the shipwrecked sailor reaches the lone island.

Henry knew that he was a long distance from the Ohio, and it would be difficult to locate the fleet. It would have to move slowly, and it may have tied up several times for weather.

He floated two or three hundred yards further, and then at a dip in the bank he emerged, the water running in streams from his clothing. He stood there a minute or two, watching and listening, but nothing alarming came to his eye or ear. Perhaps he had shaken off the Wyandots, but he was far too well versed in forest cunning and patience to take it for granted. He was about to start again when he felt a little pain in his side. He remembered now the light impact as if a pebble had struck him, and he knew that the wound had been caused by a bullet. But no blood was there. It had all been washed away by the waters of the creek. The cold stream, moreover, had been good for the wound.

He lifted his wet clothing and examined his hurt critically. It might be serious. It would certainly weaken him after a few hours, although the bullet had passed through the flesh, and a few hours now were more precious to him than weeks later. But his pride and joy in life were not yet diminished. He was free and he would not be re-taken. The country around him was as beautiful as any that he had ever seen. The banks of the creek were high and rocky, and its waters were very clear. Splendid forests swept away from either side, and on one far horizon showed the faint line of blue hills. The sun was still shining bright and warm.

He re-entered the forest, continuing his flight toward the southeast, and swung along at a good pace. Exercise restored the warmth to his body and also brought with it now and then the little stitch in his side. His clothing gradually dried upon him, and he did not cease his long, easy trot until he noticed that the sun was far down in the west. It had already taken on the fiery red tint that marks it when it goes, and in the east gray shadows were coming.

Henry believed that he had shaken off the pursuit for good now, and he sat down upon a log to rest. Then a sudden great weakness came over him. The forest grew dim, the earth seemed to tip up, and there was a ringing sound in his ears. He looked at his hand and saw that it was shaking. It required a great effort of the will to clear his vision and steady the world about him. But he achieved it, and then he took thought of himself.

He knew very well what was the matter. His wound had begun to assert itself, and he knew that he could no longer refuse to listen to its will.

The sun sank in a sea of red and yellow fire, and the veil of darkness was drawn over the vast primeval wilderness. Henry welcomed the coming of the dusk. Night is kindly to those who flee. He left the log and walked slowly toward the horizon, on which he had seen the dim, blue line of the hills. He would be more likely to find there rude shelter of some sort.

The reflex from long and strenuous action both physical and mental—no one fights for anything else as he does for his life—had come, and his body relaxed. The dizziness returned at times, and he knew that he must have rest.

He was aware, too, that he needed food, but it was no time to hunt for it. That must be done on the morrow, and intense longing for his rifle assailed him again. It would be more precious to him now than gold or diamonds.

A melancholy note came lonesomely through the forest and the twilight. It was the cry of the whippoorwill, inexpressibly mournful, and Henry listened to it a minute or two. He thought at first that it might be a signal cry of the Wyandots, but when it was twice repeated he knew that it was real. He banished it from his mind and went on.

A gobble came from a tree near by. He caught the bronze gleam of the wild turkeys sitting high on the branches. They may have seen him or heard him, but they did not stir. Something sprang up in the bushes, ran a little way and stopped, regarding him with great lustrous eyes. It was a deer, but it was unafraid. The behavior of deer and turkey was so unusual that a curious idea gripped Henry. They knew that he was unarmed, and therefore they did not feel the need to run.

He always felt a close kinship with the wild things, and he could not put aside this idea that they knew him as he now was, a helpless wanderer. It humiliated him. He had been a lord of creation, and now he was the weakest of them all. They could find their food and shelter with ease, but only luck would bring him either. He felt discouragement because he had suddenly sunk to the lowest place among living things, and that stitch in his side began to grow stronger. It did not come now at intervals but stayed, and soon he must lie down and rest if he had nothing more than the shelter of a tree's outspread boughs.

But he came to the hills and, after some hunting, found a rocky alcove, which he half filled with the dead leaves of last year. There he lay down and drew some of the leaves over him. It was wonderfully soothing and peaceful, and the stitch in his side became much easier. As his nerves resumed their normal state, he grew very hungry. But he would have to endure it, and he tried to think of other things.

It was quite dark now, but he heard noises about him. He knew that it was the night prowlers, and some of them came very near. It was true that they knew him to be unarmed. In some mysterious way the word had been passed among them that their greatest enemy, man, could do them no harm, and Henry saw bright little eyes looking at him curiously through the darkness.

The boy felt deeply his sense of helplessness. Small shadowy forms hopped about through the thickets. He fancied that they were rabbits, and they came very near in the most reckless and abandoned fashion. He was overwhelmed with shame. That a little rabbit eight inches long and weighing only two or three pounds should defy him who had slain bears and buffaloes, and who had fought victoriously with the most powerful and cunning of Indian warriors, was not to be endured. He raised himself up a little and threw a stone at them. They disappeared with a faint noise of light, leaping feet, but in a few moments they came back again. If he frightened them it was only for an instant, and it took an effort of his will to prevent an unreasoning anger toward the most timid and innocent of forest creatures.

The night now was well advanced, but full of dusky beauty. The stars were coming out, bright and confident, and their silvery twinkle lighted up the heavens. Henry looked up at them. They would have been to most people mere meaningless points in the vast, cold void, but they made him neither lonely nor afraid. The feeling of weakness was what troubled him. He knew that he ought to sleep, but his nerves were not yet in the perfect accord that produces rest.

He resolutely shut his eyes and kept them shut for five minutes. Then he opened them again because he felt a larger presence than that of the rabbits. He saw another half circle of bright eyes, but these were much higher above the ground, and presently he made out the lean forms, the sharp noses, and the cruel white teeth of wolves. Still he was not afraid. They did not seem to be above four or five in number, and he knew that they would not attack him unless they were a large pack, but he felt the insult of their presence. He hated wolves. He respected a bear and he admired a buffalo, but a wolf, although in his way cunning and skillful beyond compare, did not seem to him to be a noble animal.

Such contempt for him, a hunter and a warrior, who could slay at two hundred yards, given his rifle, must be avenged, and he felt around at the edge of the hollow until his hand closed upon a stone nearly as large as his fist. Then he closed his eyes all but a tiny corner of the right one and lay so still that even a wolf, with all his wolfish knowledge and caution, might think him asleep. By the faint beam of light that entered the tiny corner of his right eye he saw the wolves drawing nearer, and he marked their leader, an inquiring old fellow who stood three or four inches taller than the others, and who was a foot in advance.

The wolves approached slowly and with many a little pause or withdrawal, but the youth was fully as patient. He had learned his lessons from the forest and its creatures, and on this night nothing was cheaper to him than time. It was another proof of natural power and of the effect of long training that he did not move at all for a quarter of an hour. The old wolf, the leader, who stood high in the wolf tribe, who had won his position by genuine wolfish wisdom and prowess, could not tell whether this specimen of man was alive or dead. He inclined to the opinion that he was dead. Certainly he did not move, he could not see a quiver of the eyelash, and he noticed no rising and falling of the chest under the buckskin hunting shirt. A doubled up hand—the one that enclosed the stone—lay pallid and limp upon the leaves, and it encouraged the wise old leader to come closer. He had seen a dead warrior in his time, and that warrior's hand had lain upon the grass in just such a way.

The old leader took a longer and bolder step forward. The dead hand flashed up from the leaves, flew back, and then shot forward. Something very hard, that hurt terribly, struck the leader on the head, and, emitting a sharp yelp of pain and anger, he fled away, followed by the others. The warrior, whom he in all his wisdom had been sure was dead, had played a cruel joke upon him.

Henry Ware laughed joyously, and turned into a more comfortable position upon the leaves. He was not in his normal frame of mind, or so small an incident would not have caused him so much mirth. But it brought back the divine spark of courage which so seldom died within him. Unarmed as he was, he was not without resources, and he had driven off the wolves. He would find a way for other things.

The wind began to blow gently and beneficently, and the murmur of it among the leaves came to him. He interpreted it instantly as the wilderness voice that, calling to him more than once in his most desperate straits, had told him to have faith and hope. He fell asleep to its music and slept soundly all through the night.

He awoke the next morning after the coming of the daylight, and sprang to his feet. The sudden movement caused a slight pain in his side, but he knew now that the wound was not serious. Had it been so it would have stiffened in the night, and he would now be feverish, but he felt strong, and his head was clear and cool. Another proof of his healthy condition was the fierce hunger that soon assailed him. A powerful body was demanding food, the furnace needed coal, and there was no way just yet to supply it. This was the vital question to him, but he took wilderness precautions before undertaking to solve it.

He made a little circle, searching the forest with eye and ear, but he found no sign that the Wyandots were near. He did not believe that they had given up the pursuit, but he was quite sure that they had not been able to find his last trail in the night. When he had satisfied himself upon this point, he washed his wound carefully in the waters of a brook, and bound upon it a poultice of leaves, the use of which he had learned among the Indians. Then he thought little more about it. He was so thoroughly inured to hardship that it would heal quickly.

Now for food, food which he must take with his bare hands. It was not late enough in the year for the ripening of wild fruits and for nuts, but he had his mind upon blackberries. Therefore he sought openings, knowing that they would not grow in the shade of the great trees, and after more than an hour's hunting he found a clump of the blackberry briars, loaded with berries, magnificent, large, black, and fairly crammed with sweetness.

Henry was fastidious. He had not tasted food for nearly a day, and he ached with hunger, but he broke off a number of briars containing the largest stores of berries, and ate slowly and deliberately. The memory of that breakfast, its savor and its welcome, lingered with him long. Blackberries are no mean food, as many an American boy has known, but Henry was well aware that he must have something stronger, if he were to remain fit for his great task. But that divine spark of courage which was his most precious possession was kindled into a blaze. Food brought back all his strength, and his veins pulsated with life. Somehow he would find a way for everything.

He fixed his course once more toward the southeast. The country here was entirely new to him, much rougher, the hills increasing in height and steepness, and he inferred that he was approaching a river, some tributary of the Ohio.

When he reached the crest of a hill steeper than the rest, he dropped down among the bushes as if he had been shot. He had happened to look back, and he caught a passing glimpse of brown among the green. It was quick come, quick gone, but he had seen enough to know that it was an Indian following him, undoubtedly one of the pursuing Wyandots, who, by chance, had hit upon his trail.

Had Henry been armed he would have felt no fear. He considered himself, with justice, more than a match for a single warrior, but now he must rely wholly upon craft, and the odds against him were more than ten to one. He was at the very verge of a steep descent, and he knew that he could not slip down the crest of the hill and get away without being seen by the Wyandot, who, he was sure, was aware of his presence.

He lay perfectly still for at least five minutes, watching for the warrior and at the same time trying to form a plan. He saw only the waving green bushes, but he knew that he would hear the warrior if he approached. His trained ear would detect the slightest movement among grass or bushes, and he had no doubt that the Wyandot was as still as he.

Luck had been against Henry because the crest of the hill was bare, so if he undertook to slip away in that direction he would become exposed, but it favored him when it made the thicket dense and tall where he lay. As long as he remained in his present position the Wyandot could not see him unless he came very close, and he resolved that his enemy should make the first movement.

The infinite test of patience went on. A quarter of an hour, a half hour, and an hour passed, and still Henry did not stir. If a blade of grass or a twig beside him moved it was because the force of the wind did it. While he lay there, he examined the thicket incessantly with his eyes, but he depended most upon his ears. He listened so intently that he could hear a lizard scuttling through the grass, or the low drone of insects, but he did not hear the warrior.

He looked up once or twice. The heavens were a solid, shimmering blue. Now and then birds, fleet of wing, flashed across its expanse, and a blue jay chattered at intervals in a near tree. The peace that passeth understanding seemed to brood over the wilderness. There was nothing to tell of the tragedy that had just begun its first act in the little thicket.

After the first hour, Henry moved a little, ever so little, but without noise. He did not intend to get stiff, lying so long in one position, and, as he had done when a prisoner in the lodge, he cautiously flexed his muscles and took many deep breaths, expanding his chest to the utmost. He must rely now upon bodily strength and dexterity alone, and he thanked God that Nature had been so kind to him.

He flexed his muscles once more, felt that they were elastic and powerful, and then he put his ear to the earth. He heard a sound which was not the scuttling of a lizard nor the low drone of insects, but one that he ascribed to the slow creeping of a Wyandot warrior, bent upon taking a life. Henry was glad that it was so. He had won the first victory, and that, too, in the quality in which the Indian usually excelled, patience. But this was not enough. He must win also in the second test, skill.

The stake was his life, and in such a supreme moment the boy had no chance to think of mercy and kindliness. Nearly all the wilderness creatures fought for their lives, and he was compelled to do so, too. He now sought the Wyandot as eagerly as the Wyandot sought him.

He resumed the pursuit, and he was guided by logic as well as by sight and hearing. The Wyandot knew where he had first lain, and he would certainly approach that place. Henry would follow in that direction.

Another dozen feet and he felt that the crisis was at hand. The little waving of grass and bushes that marked the passage of the Wyandot suddenly stopped, and the slight rustling ceased to come. Nerving everything for a mighty effort, Henry sprang to his feet and rushed forward. The Wyandot, who was just beginning to suspect, uttered a cry, and he, too, sprang up. His rifle leaped to his shoulder and he fired as the terrible figure sprang toward him. But it was too late to take any sort of aim. The bullet flew wide among the trees, and the next instant Henry was upon him.

The Wyandot dropped his empty rifle and met his foe, shoulder to shoulder and chest to chest. He was a tall warrior with lean flanks and powerful muscles, and he did not yet expect anything but victory. He was one of the many Wyandots who had followed him from the village, but he alone had found the fugitive, and he alone would take back the scalp. He clasped Henry close and then sought to free one hand that he might draw his knife. Henry seized the wrist in his left hand, and almost crushed it in his grasp. Then he sought to bend the Indian back to the earth.

The Wyandot gave forth a single low, gasping sound. Then the two fought wholly in silence, save for the panting of their chests and the shuffling sound of their feet. The warrior realized that he had caught a foe more powerful than he had dreamed of and also that the foe had caught him, but he was still sure of his triumphant return to the village with the fugitive scalp. But as they strove, shoulder to shoulder and chest to chest, for full five minutes, he was not so sure, although he yet had visions.

The two writhed over the ground in their great struggle. The warrior endeavored to twist his hand loose, but in the unsuccessful attempt to do so, he dropped the knife to the ground, where it lay glittering in the grass whenever the sunbeams struck upon its blade. Presently, as they twisted and strove, it lay seven or eight feet away, entirely out of the reach of either, and then Henry, suddenly releasing the warrior's wrist, clasped him about the shoulders and chest with both arms, making a supreme effort to throw him to the ground. He almost succeeded, but this was a warrior of uncommon strength and dexterity, and he recovered himself in time. Yet he was so hard pushed that he could make no effort to reach the tomahawk that still hung in his belt, and he put forth his greatest effort in order that he might drag his foe from his feet, and thus gain a precious advantage.

The last lizard scuttled away, and the drone of the insects ceased. Henry, as he whirled about, caught one dim glimpse of a blue jay, the same that had chattered so much in his idle joy, sitting on a bough and staring at the struggling two.

It was a titanic contest to the blue jay, two monstrous giants fighting to the death. All the other forest people had fled away in terror, but the empty-headed blue jay, held by the terrible fascination, remained on his bough, watching with dilated eyes. He saw the great beads of sweat stand out on the face of each, he could hear the muscles strain and creak, he saw the two fall to the ground, locked fast in each other's arms, and then turn over and over, first the white face and then the red uppermost, and then the white again.

The blue jay's eyes grew bigger and bigger as he watched a struggle such as he had never beheld before. They were all one to him. It did not matter to him whether white or red conquered, but he saw one thing that they did not see. As they rolled over and over they had come to the very brink of the hill, and the far

62

side went down almost straight, a matter of forty or fifty feet. But this made no impression upon him, because he was only a blue jay with only a blue jay's tiny brain.

The two monstrous giants were now hanging over the edge of the precipice, and still, in their furious struggles, they did not know it. The blue jay, perceiving in a dim way that something tremendous was about to happen in his world, longed to chatter abroad the advance news of it, but his tongue was paralyzed in his throat, and his eyes were red with increasing dilation.

The two, still locked fast in each other's arms, went further. Then they realized where they were, and there was a simultaneous writhe to get back again. It was too late. The blue jay saw them hang for a moment on the brink and then go crashing into the void. His paralyzed voice came back to him, and, chattering wildly with terror, he flew away from the terrible scene.

CHAPTER VIII

THE SHADOW IN THE WATER

Henry Ware and the Wyandot warrior were clasped so tightly in each other's arms that their hold was not broken as they fell. They whirled over and over, rolling among the short bushes on the steep slope, and then they dropped a clear fifteen feet or more, striking the hard earth below with a sickening impact.

Both lay still a half minute, and then Henry rose unsteadily to his feet. Fortune had turned her face toward him and away from the Wyandot. The warrior had been beneath when they struck, and in losing his life had saved that of his enemy. Henry had suffered no broken bones, nothing more than bruises, and he was recovering rapidly from the dizziness caused by his fall. But the warrior's neck was broken, and he was stone dead.

Henry, as his eyes cleared and his strength returned, looked down at the Indian, a single glance being sufficient to tell what had happened. The warrior could trouble him no more. He shook himself and felt carefully of his limbs. He had been saved miraculously, and he breathed a little prayer of thankfulness to the God of the white man, the Manitou of the red man.

He did not like to look at the fallen warrior. He did not blame the Wyandot for pursuing him. It was what his religion and training both had taught him to do, and Henry was really his enemy. Moreover, he had made a good fight, and the victor respected the vanquished.

It was his first impulse to plunge at once into the forest and hasten away, but it got no further than an impulse, His was the greatest victory that one could win. He had not only disposed of his foe; he had gained much beside.

He climbed back up the hill and took the gun from the bushes where it had fallen. He had expected a musket, or, at best, a short army rifle bought at some far Northern British post, and his joy was great when he found, instead, a beautiful Kentucky rifle with a long, slender barrel, a silver-mounted piece of the finest make. He handled it with delight, observing its fine points, and he was sure that it had been taken from some slain countryman of his.

He recovered the knife, too, and then descended the hill again. He did not like to touch the dead warrior, but it was no time for squeamishness, and he took from him a horn, nearly full of powder, and a pouch containing at least two hundred bullets to fit the rifle. He looked for something else which he knew the Indian invariably carried—flint and steel—and he found it in a pocket of his hunting shirt. He transferred the flint and steel to his own pocket, put the tomahawk in his belt beside the knife, and turned away, rifle on shoulder.

He stood a few moments at the edge of the forest, listening. It seemed to him that he heard a far, faint signal cry and then another in answer, but the sound was so low, not above a whisper of the wind, that he was not sure.

Whether a signal cry or not, he cared little. The last half hour had put him through a wonderful transformation. Life once more flowed high in every vein never higher. He, an unarmed fugitive whom even the timid rabbits did not fear, he, who had been for a little while the most helpless of the forest creatures, had suddenly become the king of them all. He stood up, strong, powerful, the reloaded rifle in his hands, and looked and listened attentively for the foe, who could come if he chose. His little wound was forgotten. He was a truly formidable figure now, whom the bravest of Indian warriors, even a Wyandot, might shun.

Still hearing and seeing nothing that told of pursuit, he entered the forest and sped on light foot on the journey that always led to the southeast. The low rolling hills came again, and they were covered densely with forest, not an opening anywhere. The foliage, not yet touched with brown, was dark green and thick, forming a cool canopy overhead. Tiny brooks of clear water wandered through the mass and among the tree trunks. Many birds of brilliant plumage flew among the boughs and sang inspiringly to the youth as he passed.

It was the great, cool woods of the north, the woods that Long Jim Hart had once lamented so honestly to his comrades when they were in the far south. Henry smiled at the memory. Long Jim had said that in these woods a man knew his enemies; the Indians did not pretend to be anything else. Jim was right, as he had just proved. The Wyandots had never claimed to be anything but his enemies, and, although they had treated him well for a time, they had acted thus when the time again came.

Henry smiled once more. He had an overwhelming and just sense of triumph. He had defeated the Wyandots, the bravest and most skillful of all the Western tribes. He had slipped through the hundred hands that sought to hold him, and he was going back to his own, strong and armed. The rifle was certainly a splendid trophy. Long, slender, and silver mounted, he had never seen a finer, and his critical eye assured him that its quality would be equal to its appearance.

64

He did not stop running while he examined the rifle, and when he put it back on his shoulder the wind began to blow. Hark! There was the song among the leaves again, and now it told not merely of hope, but of victory achieved and danger passed. Henry was sure that he heard it. He had an imaginative mind like all forest-dwellers, like the Indians themselves, and he personified everything. The wind was a living, breathing thing.

He stopped at the end of two or three hours. The sun was sailing high in the heavens, and he had come at last to a little prairie. Game, it was likely, would be here, and he meant now to have food, not blackberries, but the nutritious flesh that his strong body craved. He could easily secure it now, and he stroked the beautiful rifle joyously.

Except for the great villages at Chillicothe, Piqua, and a few other places, the Indians shifted their homes often, leaving one region that the game might increase in it again, until such time as they wished to come back, and Henry judged that the country in which he now was had been abandoned for a while. If so, the game should be plentiful and not shy.

The prairie was perhaps a mile in length, and at its far edge two deer were grazing. It was not difficult to stalk them, and Henry, choosing the doe, brought her down with an easy shot. He carried the body into the woods, skinned it, cut off the tenderer portions, and prepared for a solid dinner. With his food now before him, he realized how very hungry he was. Yet he was fastidious, and, as usual, he insisted upon doing all things in season, and properly.

He brought forth the Indian's flint and steel—he was very glad now that he had had the forethought to take them—and after much effort set about kindling a fire. Flint and steel are not such easy things to use, and it took Henry five minutes to light the blaze, but five minutes later he was broiling tender, juicy slices of deer meat on the end of a twig, and then eating them one by one. He ate deliberately, but he ate a great many, and when he was satisfied he put out the fire. He crushed the coals into the earth with his heels and covered them with leaves, instinctive caution making him do it. Then he went deep into the forest, and, lying down in a thicket, rested a long time.

He knew that the Indian tribes intended to gather at Tuentahahewaghta (the site of Cincinnati), the place where the waters of the Licking, coming out of the wild Kentucky woods, joined the Ohio, and he believed that the best thing for him to do was to go to that point. He calculated that, despite his long delay at the Wyandot village, he could yet arrive there ahead of the fleet, and after seeing the Indian mobilization, he could go back to warn it. Only one thing worried him much now. Had his four faithful comrades taken his advice and stayed with the fleet, or were they now in the forest seeking him? He well knew their temper, and he feared that they had not remained with the boats after his absence became long.

But these comrades of his were resourceful, and he was presently able to dismiss the question from his mind. He had acquired with the patience of the Indian

65

another of his virtues, an ability to dismiss all worries, sit perfectly still, and be completely happy. This quality may have had its basis originally in physical content, the satisfaction that came to the savage when he had eaten all he wished, when no enemy was present, and he could lie at ease on a soft couch. But in Henry it was higher, and was founded chiefly on the knowledge of a deed well done and absolute confidence in the future, although the physical quality was not lacking.

He felt an immense peace. Nothing was wrong. The day was just right, neither too hot nor too cool. The blaze of the brilliant skies and of the great golden sun was pleasantly shaded from his eyes by the green veil of the leaves. Those surely were the finest deer steaks that he had ever eaten! There could not be such another wilderness as this on the face of the earth! And he, Henry Ware, was one of the luckiest of human beings!

He lay a full two hours wrapped in content. He did not move arm or leg. Nothing but his long, deep breathing and his bright blue eyes, shaded by half-fallen lashes, told that he lived. Every muscle was relaxed. There was absolutely no effort, either physical or mental.

Yet the word passed by the forest creatures to one another was entirely different from the word that had been passed the night before. The slackened human figure that never moved was dangerous, it was once more the king of the wilderness, and the four-footed kind, after looking once and fearfully upon it, must steal in terror away.

The wolf felt it. Slinking through the thicket, he measured the great length of the recumbent shape, observed the half-opened eye, and departed in speed and silence; a yellow puma smelt the human odor, thought at first that the youth was dead, but, after a single look, followed the wolf, his heart quaking within him. A foolish bear, also, shambled into the thicket, but he was not too foolish, after he saw Henry, to shamble quickly away.

When Henry rose he was as thoroughly refreshed and restored as if he had never run a gantlet, made a flight of a night and a day, and fought with a Wyandot for his life. The very completeness of it had made him rest as much in two hours as another would have rested in six. He resumed his flight, taking with him venison steaks that he had cooked before he put out his fire, and he did not stop until the night was well advanced and the stars had sprung out in a dusky sky. Then he chose another dense thicket and, lying down in it, was quickly asleep.

He awoke about midnight and saw a faint light shining through the woods. He judged that it was a long distance away, but he resolved to see what made it, being sure in advance that it was the glow of an Indian camp fire.

He approached cautiously, looked from the crest of a low hill into a snug little valley, and saw that his surmise was true.

About fifty warriors sat or lay around a smouldering fire, and he inferred from their dress and paint that they were Shawnees. Four who sat together were talking earnestly, and he knew them to be chiefs. It was impossible to hear what they said, but he believed this to be a party on the way to the great meeting at the mouth of Licking. It was evident that he had not escaped too soon, and he withdrew as cautiously as he had approached.

An excitable youth would have hastened on in the night at full speed, but Henry knew better and could do better. He returned to his nest in the thicket and fell asleep again, as if he had seen nothing alarming. But he rose very early in the morning, and after a breakfast on the cold deer meat, made a circle around the Indian camp, and continued his southeastern journey at great speed.

He traveled all that day, and he saw that he was well into the enemy's country. Indian signs multiplied about him. Here in the soft earth was the trace of their moccasins. There they had built a camp fire and the ashes were not yet cold. Further on they had killed and dressed a deer. There was little effort at concealment, perhaps, none. This was their own country, where only the roving white hunter came, and it was his business, not theirs, to hide. Henry felt the truth of it as he advanced toward the Ohio. He was compelled to redouble his caution, lest at any moment he plunge into the very middle of a war band.

He passed more than a half dozen trails of large parties, and he felt sure that, according to arrangement, they were converging on the Ohio, at the point where the Licking emptied the waters and silt of the Kentucky woods into the larger stream. Timmendiquas, no doubt, would be there, and Henry's heart throbbed a little faster at the thought that he would meet such a splendid foe.

He lay in a thicket about noonday, and saw over a hundred warriors of the Ottawas, worshipers of the sun and stars, go by. They were all in full war paint, and he had no doubt that they had come from the far western shore of Lake Huron to join the great gathering of the tribes at Tuentahahewaghta and to help destroy the fleet and all river posts if they could.

That evening, taking the chances that the Indians would or would not hear him, he shot a wild turkey in a tree, traveled two or three miles further, built a small fire in the lee of a hill, where he cooked it, then ran in a curve three or four miles further, until he came to a thicket of pawpaw bushes, where he ate heartily by a faint moonlight. He watched and listened two hours, and then, satisfied that no one had heard the shot, he went to sleep with the ease and confidence of one who reposes at home, safe in his bed.

The night was warm. Sleeping in the open was a pleasure to such as Henry Ware, and he was not disturbed. He had willed that he should wake before daylight, and his senses obeyed the warning. He came back from slumber while it was yet dark. But he could feel the coming dawn, and, eating what was left of the turkey, he sped away.

He saw the sun shoot up in a shower of gold, and the blue spread over the heavens. He saw the green forest come into the light with the turning of the world, and he felt the glory of the great wilderness, but he did not stop for many hours. The day was warmer than the one before, and when the sun was poised just overhead he began to feel its heat. He was thirsty, too, and when he heard a gentle trickling among the bushes he stopped, knowing that a brook or spring was near.

He pressed his way through the dense tangle of undergrowth and entered the open, where he stood for a few minutes, cooling his eyes with the silver sparkle of flowing water and the delicate green tints of the grass, which grew thickly on the banks of the little stream. He was motionless, yet even in repose he seemed to be the highest type of physical life and energy, taller than the average man, despite the fact that he was yet but a boy in years, and with a frame all bone and sinew. Blue eyes flashed out of a face turned to the brown of leather by a life that knew no roof-tree, and the uncut locks of yellow hair fell down from the fur cap that sat lightly upon his head.

Around him the wilderness was blazing with all the hues of spring and summer, yet untouched by autumn brown. The dense foliage of the forest formed a vast green veil between him and the sun. Some wild peach trees in early bloom shone in cones of pink against the green wall. Shy little flowers of delicate purple nestled in the grass, and at his feet the waters of the brook gleamed in the sunshine in alternate ripples of silver and gold, while the pebbles shone white on the shallow bottom.

He stood there, straight and strong like a young oak, a figure in harmony with the wilderness and its lonely grandeur. He seemed to fit into the scene, to share its colors, and to become its own. The look of content in his eyes, like that of a forest creature that has found a lair to suit him, made him part of it. His dress, too, matched the flush of color around him. The fur cap upon his head had been dyed the green of the grass. The darker green of the oak leaves was the tint of his hunting shirt of tanned buckskin, with the long fringe hanging almost to his knees. It was the tint, too, of the buckskin leggings which rose above his moccasins of buffalo hide.

But the moccasins and the seams of the leggings were adorned with countless little Indian beads of red and blue and yellow, giving dashes of new color to the green of his dress, just as the wild flowers and peach blossoms and the silver and gold of the brook varied the dominant green note of the forest. A careless eye would have passed over him, his figure making no outline against the wall of forest behind him. It was the effect that he sought, to pass through wood and thicket and across the green open, making slight mark for the eye.

Henry was not only a lover of the wilderness and its beauty, but he was also a conscious one. He would often stop a moment to drink in the glory of a specially fine phase of it, and this was such a moment. Far off a range of hills showed a faint blue tracery against the sky of deeper blue. At their foot was a band of silver, the river to which the brook that splashed before him was hurrying. Everywhere the grass grew rich and rank, showing the depth and quality of the soil beneath. A hundred yards away a buffalo grazed as peacefully as if man had never come, and farther on a herd of deer raised their heads to sniff the southern wind.

68

It was pleasant to Henry to gaze upon the stretch of meadow before him. So he stood for a minute or two, looking luxuriously, his rifle resting across his shoulder, the sun glinting along its long, slender, blue barrel. Then he knelt down to drink, choosing a place where a current of the swift little brook had cut into the bank with a circular sweep, and had formed a pool of water as clear as the day, a forest mirror.

Henry did not feel the presence of any danger, but he retained all his caution as he knelt down to drink, a caution become nature through all the formative years of practice and necessity. His knees made no noise as they touched the earth. Not a leaf moved. Not a blade of grass rustled. The rifle remained upon his shoulder, his right hand grasping it around the stock, just below the hammer, the barrel projecting into the air. Even as he rested his weight upon one elbow and bent his mouth to the water, he was ready for instant action.

The water touched his lips, and was cool and pleasant. He had come far, and was thirsty. He blew the bubbles back and drank, not eagerly nor in a hurry, but sipping it gently, as one who knows tastes rare old wine. Then he raised his head a little and looked at his shadow in the water, as perfect as if a mirror gave back his face. Eyes, mouth, nose, every feature was shown. He bent his head, sipping the water a little more, and feeling all its grateful coolness. Then he raised it again and saw a shadow that had appeared beside his own. The mirror of the water gave back both perfectly.

An extraordinary thrill ran through him but he made no movement. The blood was leaping wildly in his veins, but his nerves never quivered. In the water he could yet see his own shadow as still as the shadow that had come beside it.

Henry Ware, in that supreme moment, did not know his own thoughts, save that they were full of bitterness. It hurt him to be trapped so. He had escaped so much, he had come so far, to be taken thus with ease; although life was full and glorious to him, he could have yielded it with a better will in fair battle. There, at least, one did not lose his forest pride. He had gloried in the skill with which he had practiced all the arts of the wilderness, and now he was caught like any beginner!

But while these thoughts were running through his mind he retained complete command of himself, and by no motion, no exclamation, showed his knowledge that he was not alone. He suppressed his rebellious nerves, and refused to let them quiver.

The shadow in the water beside his own was distinct. He could see the features, the hair drawn up at the top of the head into a defiant scalp-lock, and the outstretched hand holding the tomahawk. He gazed at the shadow intently. He believed that he could divine his foe's triumphant thoughts.

The south wind freshened a little, and came to Henry Ware poignant with the odors of blossom and flower. The brook murmured a quiet song in his ears. The brilliant sunshine flashed alike over grass and water. It was a beautiful world, and never had he been more loth to leave it. He wondered how long it would be until the blow fell. He knew that the warrior, according to the custom of his race, would prolong his triumph and exult a little before he struck.

Given a chance with his rifle, Henry would have asked no other favor. Just that one little gift from fortune! The clutch of his fingers on the stock tightened, and the involuntary motion sent a new thought through him. The rifle lay unmoved across his shoulder, its muzzle pointing upward. Before him in the water the shadow still lay, unchanged, beside his own. He kept his eyes upon it, marking a spot in the center of the forehead, while the hand that grasped the rifle crept up imperceptibly toward the hammer and the trigger. A half minute passed. The warrior still lingered over his coming triumph. The boy's brown fingers rested against the hammer of the rifle.

Hope had come suddenly, but Henry Ware made no sign. He blew a bubble or two in the water, and while he seemed to watch them break, the muzzle of the rifle shifted gently, until he was sure that it bore directly upon the spot in the forehead that he had marked on the shadow in the water.

The last bubble broke, and then Henry seemed to himself to put all his strength into the hand and wrist that held the rifle. His forefinger grasped the hammer. It flew back with a sharp click. The next instant, so quickly that time scarcely divided the two movements, he pulled the trigger and fired.

CHAPTER IX

THE GATHERING OF THE FIVE

As the report of his shot sped in echoes through the forest, Henry Ware sprang to his feet and stood there for a little space, his knees weak under him, and drops of perspiration thick on his face. The rifle was clenched in his hands, and a light smoke came from the muzzle.

Thus he stood, not yet willing to turn around and see, but when the last echo of the shot was gone there was no sound. The wind had ceased to blow. Not a leaf, not a blade of grass stirred. He was affected as he had never been in battle, because he knew that a man whose shadow alone he had seen lay dead behind him.

He shifted the rifle to one hand only, and wiped his face with the other. Then, as his knees grew stronger and he was able to control the extraordinary quivering of the nerves, he turned. The warrior, the red spot upon his forehead, lay stretched upon his back. He had died without a sound, as if he had been struck by a bolt of lightning. The handle of the tomahawk was still clutched in his fingers, but his rifle had fallen beside him. The single minute that he had paused to exult over the foe who seemed so completely in his power had been fatal.

Henry took the powder and bullets from the fallen warrior and added them to his own store—the bullets he found would fit his rifle—but he did not wish to burden himself with the extra rifle, knife, and tomahawk. Nor did he wish to abandon them. Their value was too great in the wilderness. He chose a middle course. He thrust all three in a hollow tree that he found about a mile further on. They were so well hidden in the trunk that there was not one chance in a million of anybody but himself ever finding them.

"I may need you again some day," he murmured to the inanimate weapons, "and if so you'll be here waiting for me."

He noted well the locality, the trees, and the lay of the land. Everything was photographed on his memory and would remain there until such time as he needed the use of the picture. Then he continued his advance, at the long easy walk that he had learned from the frontiersmen, and soon his shaken nerves were restored.

He began to calculate now how far he might be from the Ohio, and, as he was traveling more east than south, he reckoned that it would be several days before he reached the mouth of the Licking. But he felt assured that he would reach it, despite the dangers that were still thick about him. In the afternoon he saw smoke on the horizon, and, going at once to ascertain its cause, he found a small Shawnee village in a cozy valley. He saw signs of preparation among the warriors in it, and he divined that they, too, were destined for the "landing place" on the Ohio, opposite the mouth of the Licking.

He left the village after the cursory look and plunged again into the unbroken wilderness. Two or three hours later he decided that he was being followed. He had not seen or heard anything, but it was a sort of divination. He sought to throw it aside, telling himself that it was mere foolishness, but he could not do it. The thought stayed with him, and then he knew that it must be true.

He cared little for a single warrior, but he did not wish to be delayed. He increased his speed, but the sense of being followed did not depart. He was not alarmed, but he was annoyed intensely. He had already encountered two warriors, triumphing each time, and it seemed to him that he ought now to be let alone.

He made a complete circle, coming back on his own tracks in order to convince himself absolutely that he was or was not followed, and he found a few traces in the soft earth to show him that his sixth sense had not warned him in vain. There moccasins had passed, and the owner of them was undoubtedly pursuing Henry. For what else but his life?

It was hard necessity, but he resolved to have it out with this warrior who trailed him so relentlessly. Night was coming on, and he must sleep and rest, but he could not do so with an enemy so near. Hence he now dropped the role of the pursued, and became the pursuer.

It was a difficult task, but an occasional trace in the earth helped him, and he followed unerringly. So intent was he upon his object that he did not notice for some time that he was still traveling in a circle, and that his mysterious foe was doing the same. They were going around and around. Both were pursuers and both pursued.

Henry's annoyance increased. He had never been irritated so much before in his life. He could not continue forever with this business and let his mission go. Moreover, night was now much nearer. The western world was already sinking into darkness, and the twilight would soon reach him. He wished to deal with his enemy, while it was yet light enough to see.

He turned directly about on his own trail and, after advancing a little, lay hidden in the bushes. The warrior, unless uncommonly wary, would soon come in sight. But he did not come. Henry was not able either to see or hear a sign of him. The bushes were tinged with the reddish light of the setting sun, but they moved only in the way in which the wind blew them. His foe had not come into the trap, and Henry knew now that he would not come.

He remained a full half hour in his hiding place, and then, turning again, he tried the other way around the circle. A slight motion in the thicket behind him told that his foe was still there, and he stopped. His annoyance gave way to admiration. This was undoubtedly a great warrior who trailed him, a man of courage, the possessor of all forest skill. It must surely be the best of the whole Wyandot tribe. Henry was willing to give full credit.

But he must deal with such a foe. His safety and perhaps the safety of many others depended upon it. He could not shake him off; therefore, he must fight him, and he summoned all his energy and faculties for the task.

Now began the forest combat between invisible and noiseless forces, but none the less deadly because neither could see nor hear his foe. Yet each knew that the other was always there. It was the slight waving of a bush or the flutter of a leaf, stirred by a moccasin, that told the tale.

As the hunt, the deadliest of all hunts, proceeded, each became more engrossed in it, neglecting no precaution, seeking incessantly some minute advantage. Henry was by nature generous and merciful, but at this time he did not think of those things. Wilderness necessity did not permit it.

The reddish tint on trees and bushes faded quite away, the sun was gone, and the night came, riding down on the world like a black horseman, but the eyes of the two grew used to the dark as it came, and they continued their invisible battle, circling back and forth in the forest.

Henry's admiration for his foe increased. He had never encountered another such warrior. Surpassing skill was his. He knew every trick, every device of the forest. Every move that Henry tried he met on equal terms, and, strive as Henry would to see him, he was still unseen.

This singular duel would have exhausted the patience of most men. One or the other, finding it unbearable, would have exposed himself, but not so these two. An hour, two hours, passed, and they were still seeking the advantage. The moon had come out and touched trees and bushes with silver, but they were still creeping to and fro, seeking a chance for a shot.

It was Henry who secured the first glimpse. He saw for an instant a face in a bush fifty yards away, and at the same moment he fired. But he knew almost before his finger ceased to pull the trigger that he would miss, and he threw down his head to escape the return shot. He was barely in time. He heard the bullet pass over him, and it seemed to him that it sung a taunting little song as it went by. But he was busy reloading his rifle as fast as he could, and he knew that his foe was doing the same.

The rifle reloaded, a sudden extraordinary idea leaped up in his brain. It seemed impossible, but the impossible sometimes comes true. It was the merest of fleeting glimpses that he had caught of that face, but his eye was uncommonly quick, and his mind equally retentive.

His mind would not let go of the idea; an impression at first, it quickly became a belief and then a conviction. He was lying on his chest, and, raising his head a little, he emitted the call of the night-owl, soft, long, and weird. He uttered the cry twice and waited. From the woods fifty yards away came the answering hoot of an owl, once, twice, thrice. Henry gave the cry twice again, and the second reply came from the same place, once, twice, thrice.

Henry, without hesitation, sprang up to his full length, and walked boldly forward. A second tall figure had risen and was coming to meet him. The moonlight streamed down in a silver shower upon the man who had stalked him so long, and revealed Shif'less Sol.

"Sol!" exclaimed Henry. "And I shot at you, thinking that you were a Wyandot."

"You did not shoot any harder at me than I did at you," said Shif'less Sol, "an' me all the time thinkin' that you wuz one o' them renegades!"

"Thank God we both missed!" said Henry, fervently.

"An' thank God that you're here, an' not tied down back thar in the Wyandot village," said Shif'less Sol.

Their hands met in the strong firm clasp of those who have been friends through the utmost dangers.

"It's fine to see you again, Sol," said Henry. "Are the others well?"

"When I last saw 'em," replied the shiftless one.

"Tell me how you ran across my trail and what went before," said Henry, as they sat down on a fallen log together.

"You'll ricolleck," said Shif'less Sol, "that you told us not to hunt you ef you didn't come back, but to go on with the fleet. I reckon it wuz easier fur you to give that advice than for us to keep it. We knowed from what the others said that you wuz captured, but we hoped that you'd escape. When you didn't come, we agreed right quick among ourselves that we had more business huntin' you than we had with that fleet.

73

"We didn't have much to go by. We guessed thar was a Wyandot village somewhar in these parts, an' we hunted fur it. Last night me an' Tom Ross saw some Injuns who wuz in camp an' who wuz rather keerless fur them. Some white men wuz with 'em, an' we learned from scraps o' talk that we could pick up that you had escaped, fur which news we wuz pow'ful glad. We heard, too, that they wuz goin' to the Ohio at the mouth o' the Lickin,' whar thar wuz to be a great getherin' o' 'em. One or two o' the white men wuz to go on ahead this mornin'. So we let 'em alone an' we spread out so we could find you.

"When I run across your trail afore sundown, I wuz shore it belonged to one o' them renegades I heard called Blackstaffe, and I made up my mind to git him."

"You come mighty near getting the fellow who stood in his place," said Henry. "I thought I had against me about the best warrior that was ever in these woods."

The moonlight disclosed the broad grin and shining teeth of the shiftless one.

"I reckon I ain't been sleepin' on no downy couch myself fur the last two hours," he said. "Henry, what's all this about the getherin' at the mouth o' the Lickin'?"

"All the tribes will be there—Wyandots, Shawnees, Miamis, Delawares, Ottawas, and Illinois. I've heard them in council. They mean to begin a new and greater war to drive the whites from their hunting ground. The fleet will be attacked in great force again, and all the settlements will have to fight."

"Then," said Shif'less Sol, "we'd better pick up the other fellers, Tom an' Saplin' an' Paul, ez soon ez we kin, an' git ahead o' the Indians."

"Where are the others?" asked Henry.

"Off that way lookin' fur you," replied Sol, waving his hand toward the southeast. "We scattered so ez to cover ez much ground as we could."

"We must hunt them and use our signal," said Henry, "two hoots of the owl from the first, three from the others, and then the same over again from both. It's a mighty good thing we arranged that long ago, or you and I, Sol, might be shooting at each other yet."

"That's so, an' we're likely to need them bullets fur a better use," rejoined the shiftless one. "Pow'ful good gun you've got thar, Henry. Did the Injuns make you a present o' that before you ran away?"

"It was luck," replied Henry, and he told his story of the fight with the Wyandot, the fall over the cliff, and his taking of the rifle and the ammunition.

"That fall wuz luck, maybe," said Shif'less Sol sagely, "but the rest o' it wuz muscles, a sharp eye, quickness, an' good sense. I've noticed that the people who learn a heap o' things, who are strong and healthy, an' who always listen and look, are them that live the longest in these woods."

"You're surely right, Sol," said Henry with great emphasis.

But Henry was in the best of humors. The shiftless one was a power in himself, as he had proved over and over again, and the two together could achieve the impossible. Moreover, the rest of his comrades were near. He felt that the God of the white man, the Manitou of the red man, had been kind to him, and he was grateful.

"Do you think we ought to try the signal for the others now, Sol?" he asked.

"Not now. I'm shore that they're too fur off to hear. Ef the Injuns heard us signalin' so much they'd come down on us hot-foot."

"Just what I was thinking," said Henry. "Suppose we push on a few miles, wait a while and then send out the cry."

"Good enough," said the shiftless one.

They advanced three or four miles and then stopped in a dense cluster of hickory saplings, where they waited. Within the thicket they could see to some distance on either side, while they themselves lay hidden. Here they talked now and then in low voices, and Shif'less Sol, although he did not speak of his feelings, was very happy. He had believed all the time that Henry would escape, but believing is not as good as knowing.

"You shorely had a pow'ful interestin' time in the Wyandot village, Henry," he said, "an' that chief, White Lightning—I've heard o' him afore—'pears to hev been good to you. What did you say his Injun name wuz?"

"Timmendiquas. That means Lightning in Wyandot, and our people have tacked on the word 'white.' He's a great man, Sol, and I think we're going to meet him again."

"Looks likely. I don't blame him for puttin' up sech a pow'ful good fight fur the huntin' grounds, 'though they look to me big enough for all creation. Do you know, Henry, I hev sometimes a kind o' feelin' fur the Injuns. They hev got lots o' good qualities. Besides, ef they're ever wiped out, things will lose a heap o' variety. Life won't be what it is now. People will know that thar scalps will be whar they belong, right on top o' thar heads, but things will be tame all the time. O' course, it's bad to git into danger, but thar ain't nothin' so joyous ez the feelin' you hev when you git out o' it."

The night advanced, very clear and pleasantly cool. They had heard occasional rustlings in the thicket, which they knew were made by the smaller wild animals, taking a look, perhaps, at those curious guests of theirs and then scuttling away in fright. Now absolute stillness had come. There was no wind. Not a twig moved. It seemed that in this silence one could hear a leaf if it fell.

Then Henry sent forth the cry, the long, whining hoot of the owl, perfectly imitated, a sound that carries very far in the quiet night. After waiting a moment or two he repeated it, the second cry being exactly the same in tone and length as the first.

"Now you listen," said Shif'less Sol.

There was another half minute of the absolute silence, and then, from a point far down under the southeastern horizon came an answering cry. It was remote and

75

low, but they heard it distinctly, and they waited eagerly to see if it would be repeated. It came a second time, and then a third. Henry answered twice, and then the other came thrice. Call and answer were complete, and no doubt remained.

"I judge that it's Saplin' who answered," ruminated Shif'less Sol. "He always did hev a hoot that's ez long ez he is, an' them wuz shorely long."

"I think, too, that it was Long Jim," said Henry, "and he'll come straight for us. In five minutes I'll send out the cry again, and maybe another will answer."

When Henry gave the second call the answer came from a point almost due east.

"That's Tom," said the shiftless one decisively. "Couldn't mistake it. Didn't that owl hoot sharp and short fur an owl? Jest like Tom Ross. Don't waste any words that he kin help, an' makes them that he has to use ez short ez he kin."

Another five minutes, and Henry gave the third call. The answer came from the southwest, and the shiftless one announced instantly that it was Paul.

"O' course we know it's Paul," he said, "'cause we know that his owl is the poorest owl among the whole lot o' us, an' I've spent a lot o' time, too, trainin' his hoot. No Injun would ever take Paul's owl to be a real one."

Henry laughed.

"Paul isn't as good in the woods as we are," he said, "but he knows a lot of other things that we don't."

"O' course," said Shif'less Sol, who was very fond of Paul. "It's shorely a treat to set by the camp fire an' hear him tell about A-Killus, an' Homer, an' Virgil, an' Charley-mane, and all the other fierce old Roman warriors that had sech funny names."

"They'll be here in less than half an hour," said Henry. "So we'd better leave the thicket, and sit out there under the big trees where they can see us."

They took comfortable seats on a fallen log under some giant maples, and presently three figures, emerging from various points, became palpable in the dusk. "Tom," murmured Henry under his breath, "and Jim—and Paul."

The three uttered low cries of joy when they saw the second figure sitting on the log beside that of Shif'less Sol. Then they ran forward, grasped his hands, and wrung them.

"How did you escape, Henry?" exclaimed Paul, his face glowing.

"Shucks! he didn't escape," said Shif'less Sol, calmly. "Henry owes everything that he is now, includin' o' his life, to me. I wuz scoutin' up by the Wyandot village, an' I captured in the thickets that thar chief they call White Lightnin'— Timmendiquas he told me wuz his high-toned Injun name. I took him with my hands, not wishin' to hurt him 'cause I had somethin' in mind. Then I said to him: 'Look at me,' an' when he looked he began to tremble so bad that the beads on his moccasins played ez fine a tune ez I ever heard. 'Is your name Hyde?' said he.

'It is,' said I. 'Solomon Hyde?' said he. 'Yes,' said I. 'The one they call Shif'less Sol?' said he. 'Yes,' said I. 'Then,' said he, 'O great white warrior, I surrender the whole Wyandot village to you at once.'

"I told him I didn't want the whole Wyandot village ez I wouldn't know what to do with it ef I had it. But I said to him, puttin' on my skeriest manner: 'You've got in your village a prisoner, a white boy named Henry Ware, a feller that I kinder like. Now you go in that an' send him out to me, an' be mighty quick about it, 'cause ef you don't I might git mad, an' then I can't tell myself what's goin' to happen.'

"An' do you know, Saplin'," he continued, turning a solemn face upon Jim Hart, "that they turned Henry over to me out thar in the woods inside o' three minutes. An' ef I do say it myself, they got off pow'ful cheap at the price, an' I'm not runnin' down Henry, either."

Long Jim Hart, a most matter-of-fact man, stared at the shiftless one.

"Do you know, Sol Hyde," he said indignantly, "that I believe more'n half the things you're tellin' are lies!"

Shif'less Sol burst into a laugh.

"I never tell lies, Saplin'," he said. "It's only my gorgeeyus fancy playin' aroun' the facts an' touchin' 'em up with gold an' silver lights. A hoe cake is nothin' but a hoe cake to Saplin' thar, but to me it's somethin' splendid to look at an' to eat, the support o' life, the creater o' muscle an' strength an' spirit, a beautiful thing that builds up gran' specimens o' men like me, somethin' that's wrapped up in poetry."

"Ef you could just live up to the way you talk, Sol Hyde," said Long Jim, "you'd shorely be a pow'ful big man."

"Maybe Indians have heard our calls," said Henry, "and if so, they'll come to look into the cause of them. Suppose we go on four or five miles and then sleep, all except one, who will watch."

"The right thing to do," said Tom Ross briefly, and they proceeded at once, Tom leading the way, while Henry and Paul, who followed close behind, talked in low voices.

A long, lonesome sound came from the north, and then was repeated three or four times. Henry laughed.

"That's real," he said. "I'd wager anything that if we followed that sound we'd find a big owl, sitting on a limb, and calling to some friend of his."

"You ain't mistook," said Tom Ross sententiously.

As they walked very fast, it did not take them long to cover the four or five miles that they wished, and they found a comfortable, well-hidden place in a ravine. The darkness also had increased considerably, which was good for their purpose, as they were hunting for nobody, and wished nobody to find them.

All save Tom Ross lay down among the bushes and quickly fell asleep. Tom found an easy seat and watched.

CHAPTER X

THE GREAT BORDERER

Tom Ross watched until about an hour after midnight, when he awoke Henry, who would keep guard until day.

"Heard anything?" asked the boy.

"Nuthin'" replied Tom with his usual brevity, as he stretched his long figure upon the ground. In a minute he was fast asleep. Henry looked down at the recumbent forms of his comrades, darker shadows in the dusk, and once more he felt that thrill of deep and intense satisfaction. The five were reunited, and, having triumphed so often, he believed them to be equal to any new issue.

Henry sat in a comfortable position on the dead leaves of last year, with his back against the stump of a tree blown down by some hurricane, his rifle across his knees. He did not move for a long time, exercising that faculty of keeping himself relaxed and perfectly still, but he never ceased to watch and listen.

About half way between midnight and morning, he heard the hoot of the owl and also the long, whining cry of the wolf. He did not stir, but he knew that hoot of owl and whine of wolf alike came from Indian throats. At this hour of the night the red men were signaling to each other. It might be the Wyandots still in pursuit of the escaped prisoner, or, more likely, it was the vanguard of the hosts converging on Tuentahahewaghta (the landing place opposite the mouth of the Licking, the site of Cincinnati).

But Henry felt no apprehension. The night was dark. No one could follow a trail at such a time. All the five were accomplished borderers. They could slip through any ring that might be made, whether by accident or purpose, around them. So he remained perfectly still, his muscles relaxed, his mind the abode of peace. Cry of owl and wolf came much nearer, but he was not disturbed. Once he rose, crept a hundred yards through the thicket, and saw a band of fifty Miamis in the most vivid of war paint pass by, but he was yet calm and sure, and when the last Miami had disappeared in the darkness, he returned to his comrades, who had neither moved nor wakened.

Dawn came in one great blazing shaft of sunlight, and the four awoke. Henry told all that he had seen and heard.

"I'm thinkin' that the tribes are all about us," said Shif'less Sol.

"Shorely," said Tom Ross.

"An' we don't want to fight so many," said Long Jim.

"An' that bein' the case," said Shif'less Sol, "I'm hopin' that the rest o' you will agree to our layin' quiet here in the thicket all day. Besides, sech a long rest would be a kindness to me, a pow'ful lazy man."

"It's the wisest thing to do," said Henry. "Even by daylight nothing but chance would cause so faint a trail as ours to be found."

It was settled. They lay there all day, and nobody grew restless except Paul. He found it hard to pass so much time in inaction, and now and then he suggested to the others that they move on, taking all risks, but they merely rallied him on his impatience.

"Paul," said Long Jim, "thar is one thing that you kin learn from Sol Hyde, an' that is how to be lazy. Uv course, Sol is lazy all the time, but it's a good thing to be lazy once in a while, ef you pick the right day."

"You don't often tell the truth, Saplin'," said Shif'less Sol, "but you're tellin' it now. Paul, thar bein' nuthin' to do, I'm goin' to lay down ag'in an' go to sleep."

He stretched himself upon a bed of leaves that he had scraped up for himself. His manner expressed the greatest sense of luxury, but suddenly he sat up, his face showing anger.

"What's the matter, Sol?" asked Paul in surprise.

The shiftless one put his hand in his improvised bed and held up an oak leaf. The leaf had been doubled under him.

"Look at that," he said, "an' then you won't have the face to ask me why I wuz oncomf'table. Remember the tale you told us, Paul, about some old Greeks who got so fas-tee-ge-ous one o' 'em couldn't sleep 'cause a rose leaf was doubled under him. That's me, Sol Hyde, all over ag'in. I'm a pow'ful partickler person, with a delicate rearin' an' the instincts o' luxury. How do you expect me to sleep with a thing like that pushed up in the small o' my back. Git out!"

As he said 'Git out,' he threw the leaf from him, lay down again on his woodland couch, and in two minutes was really and peacefully asleep.

"He is shorely won'erful," said Long Jim admiringly. "Think I'll try that myself."

He was somewhat longer than the shiftless one in achieving the task, but in ten minutes he, too, slept. Paul was at last able to do so in the afternoon, when the sun grew warm, and at the coming of the night they prepared to depart.

They traveled a full eight hours, by the stars and the moon, through a country covered with dense forest. Twice they saw distant lights, once to the south and once to the east, and they knew that they were the camp fires of Indians, who feared no enemy here. But when dawn came there was no sign of hostile fire or smoke, and they believed that they were now well in advance of the Indian parties. They shot two wild turkeys from a flock that was "gobbling" in the tall trees, announcing the coming of the day, and cooked them at a fire that they built by the side of a brook. After breakfast Henry and Tom Ross went forward a little to spy out the land, and a half mile further on by the side of the brook they saw two or three faint prints made by the human foot. They examined them long and carefully.

"Made by white men," said Henry at last.

"Shorely," said Tom Ross.

"Now, I wonder who they can be," said Henry. "It's not the renegades, because they would not leave the Indians."

"S'pose we go see," said Tom Ross.

The trail was faint and difficult to follow, but they managed to make it out, and after another half mile they saw two men sitting by a small camp fire under some trees. The fire was so situated that no one could come within rifle shot of it without being discovered by those who built it, and Henry knew that the two men sitting there had noticed him and Ross.

But the strangers did not move. They went on, calmly eating pieces of buffalo steak that they were broiling over the coals. Although nearly as brown as Indians, they were undoubtedly white men. The features in both cases were clearly Caucasian, and, also, in each case they were marked and distinctive.

Henry and Ross approached fearlessly, and when they were near the fire the two men rose in the manner of those who would receive visitors. When they stood erect the distinction of their appearance, a distinction which was not of dress or cultivation but which was a subtle something belonging to the woods and the wilderness, was heightened. They differed greatly in age. One was in middle years, and the other quite young, not more than twenty-two or three. Each was of medium height and spare. The face of the elder, although cut clean and sharp, had a singularly soft and benevolent expression. Henry observed it as the man turned his calm blue eyes upon the two who came to his fire. Both were clad in the typical border costume, raccoon skin cap, belted deerskin hunting shirt, leggings and moccasins of the same material, and each carried the long-barreled Kentucky rifle, hatchet, and knife. Their dress was careful and clean, and their bearing erect and dignified. Their appearance inspired respect.

Henry looked at them with the greatest curiosity. He believed that he knew the name of the elder man, but he was not yet sure.

"My name is Henry Ware," said Henry, "and my friend is Tom Ross. Our home is at Wareville in Kentucky, whenever we happen to be there, which hasn't been often lately."

"I think I've heard of both of you," said the elder man in mild tones that accorded well with his expression. "Mine is Boone, Dan'l Boone, and this young fellow here with me is Simon Kenton. Simon's a good boy, an' he's learnin' a lot."

Henry instinctively took off his cap. Already the name of Boone was celebrated along the whole border, and it was destined to become famous throughout the English-speaking world. The reputation of Simon Kenton, daring scout, explorer, and Indian fighter, was also large already.

"We're proud to see you, Mr. Boone and Mr. Kenton," said Henry, "and to shake your hands. When we saw this fire we did not dream what men we were to find sitting beside it."

Daniel Boone laughed in his kindly, gentle way, and his fine large eyes beamed benevolence. Nor was this any assumption or trick of manner, as Henry soon learned. The man's nature was one of absolute simplicity and generosity. With a vast knowledge of the woods and a remarkable experience, he was as honest as a child.

"I'm nothin' but plain Dan'l Boone," he said, "an' there ain't any reason why you should be proud to see me. But white folks ought to be glad when they meet one another in these woods. Simon, fry some more o' them buffalo steaks for our friends."

Kenton, who had said nothing but who had listened attentively, went about his task, working with skill and diligence.

"Set down," said Boone.

Henry and Tom obeyed the hospitable invitation and took the crisp steaks that Kenton handed to them. They were not hungry, but it was the custom of the border for white men when they met to take meat together, as the Arabs taste salt. But the steaks were uncommonly tender and juicy, and they were not compelled to force their appetites.

Both Boone and Kenton looked admiringly at Henry as he ate. But a boy in years, he had filled out in an extraordinary manner. He was not only a youthful giant, but every pound of him was bone and muscle and lean flesh.

"I've heard of you more than once, Henry Ware," Boone said. "You've been a captive 'way out among the Indians o' the northwest, but you came back, an' you've fought in the battles in Kentucky. I was a prisoner, too, for a long time among the Indians."

"I've heard all about it, Mr. Boone," said Henry eagerly. "I've heard, too, how you saved Boonesborough and all the other wonderful things that you've done."

Boone, the simple and childlike, blushed under his tan, and Simon Kenton spoke for the first time.

"Now don't you be teasin' Dan'l," he said. "He's done all them things that people talk about, an' more, too, that he's hid, but he's plum' bashful. When anybody speaks of 'em he gets to squirmin'. I'm not that way. When I do a big thing, I'm goin' to tell about it."

Boone laughed and gave his comrade a look of mild reproof.

"Don't you believe what he tells you about either him or me," he said. "Simon's a good boy, but his tongue runs loose sometimes."

Henry knew that an explanation of his and Tom's appearance there was expected, and now he gave it.

"I've just escaped from the Indians, a Wyandot band, Mr. Boone," he said, "and I was lucky enough to meet in the forest four old comrades of mine. The other three are back about a mile. We came on ahead to scout. Indians of different tribes are in great numbers behind us."

"We reckoned that they were," said Boone. "Me an' Simon have been takin' a look through the woods ourselves, and we know that mighty big things are stirrin'."

"The biggest yet," said Henry. "We've been to New Orleans, and we've come back up the Mississippi into the Ohio with a big fleet of boats and canoes loaded with arms, ammunition, and all kinds of supplies. It is commanded by a brave man, Adam Colfax, and they mean to take all these things up the river to Pittsburgh, where they will be carried over the mountains to our people in the east who are fighting Great Britain."

"I've heard of that fleet, too," said Boone, "an' it's got to get to Pittsburgh, but it won't have any summer trip. Now, what did you hear among the Wyandots?"

"I saw chiefs from all the valley tribes, Wyandots, Shawnees, Miamis, Lenni-Lenape, Ottawas, and Illinois," replied Henry, "and they've bound themselves together for a great war. Their bands are on the march now to the meeting place on the Ohio, opposite the mouth of the Licking. The renegades, too, are with the Wyandots, Mr. Boone. I saw with my own eyes Girty, Blackstaffe, McKee, Eliot, Quarles, and Braxton Wyatt."

Boone's mild eyes suddenly became threatening.

"They'll all be punished some day," he said, "for making cruel war on their own kind. But I can tell you somethin' else that we've just found out. While you were down the Mississippi, some new people have built a settlement an' fort on the south bank of the Ohio some distance before you get to the mouth of the Licking. I think it was a plum' foolish thing to do to settle so far north, but they've got a strong fort and the river is narrow there. They say that they can stop the Indian canoes from passing and help our own people. They call their place Fort Prescott."

"But won't it help, Mr. Boone?" asked Henry.

"It would if they could hold it, but that man Girty has gone on ahead with five hundred picked warriors to take it. It's only a little fort, an' there ain't more than seventy or eighty men in it. I'm afraid he'll take it."

"They must have help," said Henry impulsively. "My friends and I travel light and fast, and we can at least warn them of what is coming. There's a lot in being ready."

"That's so," said Boone, "an' I reckoned that you'd go when you heard what I had to say. Me an' Simon would have gone if we didn't have to warn another place back of the river. But we'll come with help, if they can hold out a while."

"Then it's all settled," said Henry.

"It's settled," said Daniel Boone.

82

Tom Ross at once went back for the others, and they quickly came. They, too, were delighted to meet the famous Boone and Kenton, but they wasted little time in talk. Boone, with his hunting knife, drew a map on deerskin, and he added verbal details so explicit that skilled forest runners like the five could not fail to go straight to Fort Prescott.

In a quarter of an hour they started. When they reached the forest they glanced back and saw Boone and Kenton leaning on their long rifles, looking at them. Paul impulsively waved his hand.

"These are two men to trust!" he exclaimed.

"Shorely!" said Tom Ross.

They did not speak again for a long time. Dropping into Indian file, Henry in the lead, they traveled fast. They knew that the need of them at Fort Prescott was great. Evidently the men who had built the fort were inexperienced and too confident, and Henry, moreover, had a great fear that Girty and his army would get there first. The renegade was uncommonly shrewd. He would strike as quickly as he could at this exposed place, and if successful—which in all likelihood he would be—would turn the captured cannon against the fleet of Adam Colfax. If superhuman exertions could prevent such a disaster, then they must be made.

It was a warm day, and Paul was the first to grow weary. The way led wholly through woods, and it seemed to him that the heat lay particularly heavy under the boughs of the great trees which served to enclose it and which shut out wandering breezes. But he would not complain. He strove manfully to keep up with the others, step for step, although his breath was growing shorter.

Henry about noon looked back, noticed that Paul was laboring, and stopped for a rest of a half hour. Two or three hours later they struck a great trail, one so large that all knew at least five hundred warriors must have passed. It was obvious that it had been made by Girty and his army, and they saw with a sinking of the heart that it was hours cold. The Indian force was much ahead of them, and its trail led straight away to Fort Prescott.

"I'm afraid they'll beat us to the fort," said Henry. "They've got such a big start. Oh, that Girty is a cunning man! If we could only warn the garrison! Surprise is what they have most to dread."

"It means that we must get there somehow or other and tell them," said Paul. "We've got to do the impossible."

"Shorely," said Tom Ross.

"That is so," said Henry quietly. "We must try for Fort Prescott. If all of us cannot get there in time, then as many as can must. If only one can do it, then he must reach it alone."

"It is agreed," said the others together, and the file of five resumed its swift flight toward the Ohio.

CHAPTER XI

THE RACE OF THE FIVE

They followed for a while in the trail of Girty and his band, and they inferred from all the signs that the Indian force was still moving very fast. The element of surprise would certainly be a great aid to those who attacked, and Henry judged that this was not alone the plan of Girty. The master mind of Timmendiquas was somewhere back of it.

The day marched on. The skies were without a cloud, and the sun became a hot blue dome. No air stirred in the deep forest, and every face became wet with perspiration, but the pace was not decreased until midway between noon and twilight, when they stopped for another half hour of complete rest.

They had left Girty's trail, but they had crossed several other trails, evidently of bands varying in numbers from twenty to fifty. But all converged on the point which their map showed to be Fort Prescott, and the dangers had thickened greatly. They were now near the Ohio, and the savages swarmed in all the woods before them. They must not merely reach Fort Prescott, but to do it they must pass through a cloud of their foes.

"I'm thinkin' that we'll have to fight before we reach the river," said Shif'less Sol to Henry.

"More than likely," replied the boy. "But remember our agreement. Some one of us must get into Fort Prescott."

"O' course," said Shif'less Sol.

When they started again they kept carefully into the deepest of the woods, taking the thickets by preference. Their speed was decreased, but they had reached the point now where it was of vital importance not to be detected.

They passed the remains of two camp fires. At both the bones of buffalo and deer, eaten clean, had been thrown about carelessly, and at the second the ashes were not yet cold. Moreover, they began to hear the Indian calls in the forest, cry of bird or beast, and Henry watched anxiously for the setting sun. Warriors might strike their trail at any moment, and darkness would be their greatest protection.

The sun had never before been so slow to sink, but at last it went down under the horizon, and the dusky veil was drawn over the earth. But the moon soon came out, an uncommonly brilliant moon, that flooded the forest with a pure white light, so intense that they could mark every ridge in the bark of the big trees. The stars, too, sprang out in myriads, and contributed to the phenomenal brightness.

"This is bad," said Henry. "This is so much like daylight that I believe they could follow our tracks."

The long plaintive howl of a wolf came from a point directly behind them, not a quarter of a mile away.

"They hev it now," said Long Jim, "an' they're follerin' us fast."

"Then there is nothing to do but run," said Henry. "We must not stop to fight if we can help it."

They broke into the long frontier trot, still heading south, slightly by east, and they did not hear the plaintive cry again for a half hour, but when it came it was nearer to them than before, and they increased their gait. A mile further on, Henry, who was in the lead, stopped abruptly. They had come to the steep banks of a wide and deep creek, a stream that would be called a river in almost any other region.

"We can't wade it," said Tom Ross.

"Then we must swim it," said Shif'less Sol.

"Yes. But listen," said Henry Ware.

From a point up the stream came a low, measured beat, like a long sigh.

"Paddles," said Henry, speaking low, "and those paddles belong to Indian canoes, at least a dozen of them. They are coming down the creek, which must empty into the Ohio not a great many miles from here."

"If we run along the bank uv the creek we give them behind us a chance to gain," said Tom Ross.

"And then be enclosed between the war party and the canoes," said Henry. "No, we must swim for it at once. Every fellow tie his ammunition around his neck, and hold his rifle above his head. If we have to fight we must have weapons for the fighting."

His counsel was quickly taken, and then there was a plunk as he sprang into the creek. Four more plunks followed almost instantly, as every one leaped into the water in his turn. Four heads appeared above the surface of the stream and, also, four outstretched arms holding rifles. It was not such an easy task to swim with a single arm, but all five had learned to do it, and across the creek they went, still in single file, Henry leading the way. Here, with no boughs and leaves to intercept it, the moonlight fell with uncommon brilliancy upon the water. The entire surface of the creek, a deep and placid stream, was turned to molten silver, shimmering slightly under the night wind. The heads, necks, and outstretched arms of the swimmers were outlined perfectly against it. Every feature of the five was disclosed, and behind them, shown clearly, was the crumbling wake of every one.

They were compelled to swim somewhat with the stream, because the opposite bank was so steep that to climb it would take time that could not be spared. Henry, as he swam, with the strong, circular sweep of a single arm, listened, and he heard the rhythmical sweep of the paddles growing louder. The creek curved before him, and the steep bank, too deep to climb at such a moment, was still there. He saw, too, that it ran on for at least a hundred yards more, and meanwhile the canoes, with nothing in their way, were coming swiftly. He could almost count the strokes of the paddles.

He glanced back and looked into the eyes of Shif'less Sol directly behind him. He knew by his comrade's look that he, too, had heard. The faces of the others showed the same knowledge.

"Swim as fast as you can, boys," he whispered, "but be careful not to splash the water!"

They scarcely needed this advice, because they were already making supreme efforts. Meanwhile, the unconscious pursuit was coming nearer. Only the curve that they had just turned kept them hidden from the occupants of the canoes.

It was a terribly long hundred yards, and it seemed to all of the five that they scarcely moved, although they were swimming fast.

"I've been chased by the Injuns through the woods an' over the hills an' across the prairies," groaned Shif'less Sol, "an' now they've took to chasin' me through the water. They'd run me through the sky if they could."

"Look out, Sol," said Henry. "The Indians are so near now that I think I can hear them talking."

The sound of low voices came, in fact, from a point beyond the curve, and now they could hear not only the beat of the paddles, but the trickle of the water when one was lifted occasionally from the stream. In another minute the canoes would turn the curve, and their occupants could not keep from seeing the fugitives.

Henry swam desperately, not for himself alone, but to lead the way for his comrades. At last he saw the shelving bank, twenty yards away, then ten, then five. His feet touched bottom, he ran forward and sprang ashore, the water running from him as if from some young river god. But rifle and ammunition had been kept above the flood, and were dry.

Just as he reached the bank a shout of triumph, having in it an indescribably ferocious note, filled all the forest and was returned in dying echoes. The Indians in their canoes had turned the curve and had instantly seen the fugitives, four of whom were still in the creek. Exultant over this sudden find and what they regarded as a sure capture, they plied their paddles with such a spasm of energy that the canoes fairly leaped over the water.

Henry, on the bank, knew that only instant and deadly action could save his comrades. He threw up his rifle, took a single glance along the polished barrel, which glittered in the moonlight, and fired. An Indian in the foremost canoe, uttering a cry which was all the more terrible because it was checked half way, dropped his paddle into the water, fell over the side of the canoe, hung there a moment, and then sank into the creek.

86

The boat itself stopped, and the one just behind it, unable to check its impetus, ran into it, and both capsized. Despite Indian stoicism, cries arose, and six or seven warriors were struggling in the water. Meanwhile, Shif'less Sol and Ross also gained the land and fired. Another warrior was slain, and another wounded.

All the canoes, menaced by such a deadly aim, stopped, and several of the occupants fired at the five on the bank. But firing from such an unsteady platform, their bullets went wild, and only cut the leaves of the forest. Henry had now reloaded, but he did not pull the trigger a second time. He had noticed a movement in the woods on the opposite bank of the creek, the one that they had just left. Bushes were waving, and in a moment their original pursuers came into view. Henry sent his bullet toward them, and Shif'less Sol did the same. Then the five turned to flee.

A great medley of shouts and yells arose behind them, yells of anger, shouts of encouragement as the two Indian parties, the one from the canoes and the other from the woods, joined, and Henry heard splash after splash, as pursuing warriors sprang into the water. He knew now that, in this instance, at least, the race would be to the swift, and the battle to the strong.

They did not run in Indian file, but kept well abreast, although Henry, at the right end of the line, made the course. No one spoke. The only sounds were the light, swift tread of moccasins and of rapid breathing. Their pursuers, too, had ceased to shout. Not a single war cry was uttered, but every one of the five knew that the warriors would hang on hour after hour, throughout the night, and then throughout all the next day, if need be.

For an hour they sped through the woods, and once or twice in the more open places, as Henry looked back, he saw dim brown figures, but they were never near enough for a shot. Then he would increase his pace, and his four comrades would do the same.

Fortune, which had favored them so many times, did not do so now. It persisted in remaining an uncommonly brilliant night. It seemed to Henry's troubled mind that it was like the full blaze of noonday. The moon that rode so high was phenomenal, a prodigy in size, and burnished to an exasperating degree. Every star was out and twinkling as if this were its last chance.

They reached the crest of a little hill, and now they saw the dusky figures behind them more plainly. The Indians fired several shots, and Henry and Tom Ross replied, reloading as they ran.

"Faster! A little faster!" cried Henry, and their breath grew shorter and harder as they dashed on. The muscles of their legs ached. Little pains smote them now and then in the chest, but they could not stop. It was just such a border fight and pursuit as the woods, both north and south of the Ohio, often witnessed, and of most of which there was never any historian to tell.

Their speed was now decreasing, but they knew that the speed of the Indians must be decreasing, too. All were trained runners alike, pursuers and pursued, but they could not go on at such a high pace forever.

Fortunately the far side of the hill and much of the ground beyond was covered thickly with hazel-nut bushes. Into these they dashed, and now they were hidden again from view. The closeness of the bushes caused them to drop once more into Indian file, and now Henry, with those keen backward glances of his, examined his comrades with an eye that would not be deceived.

Paul showed signs of great weariness. He swayed a little from side to side as he ran, and the red of exertion in his face gave place to the white of exhaustion. Henry reckoned that he could not last much longer and he prayed for darkness and deep thickets without end.

He looked up again. Surely the dazzling splendor of that exasperating moon had been dimmed a little! And among the myriads of stars some were twinkling with less fervor, if he could believe what he saw. Would bad fortune turn to good? He looked again in five minutes, and now he was sure. A cloud, light and fleecy, but a cloud, nevertheless, was drawing itself closely across the face of the moon. Many of the stars, actually grown bashful, were not twinkling now at all, and others had become quite pale and dim. The thickets, too, were holding out, and their pursuers were not now in sight. They continued thus for a half hour more, and the blessed clouds, not clouds of rain, but clouds of mists and vapors, were increasing. The moon had become but a dim circle and the last reluctant star was going. The forest was full of shadows. Henry turned once more to Paul, whose breath he could hear coming in gasps.

"Turn north, Paul," he said. "They will follow us and they will miss you in the darkness and these thickets. Hide in some good place and we'll come back for you."

He held out his hand, Paul gave it one clasp, and turned away at a sharp angle. He ran northward while the pursuit rushed past him, and then he fell down in a thicket, where he lay panting.

The four, who had been a few minutes before the five, kept on, saying nothing, but all thinking of Paul. They had not deserted him. It was in the compact that even one should continue as long as he could. They would return for him. But would any one live to come back?

The way grew rougher. Once, as they crossed a hill, they were outlined for a moment on its crest, and a half dozen shots were fired by the pursuers. Long Jim checked an exclamation, but Shif'less Sol heard the slight sound.

"What is it, Jim?" he asked.

"Nuthin'," replied Long Jim, "'cept I stumbled a little. Them must be Wyandots an' Shawnees follerin' us, Sol, from the way they hang on."

"It don't make much difference what they are so long ez they don't quit."

The four went on now with measured tread under the dusky heavens, over hillocks, down little valleys, and across brooks, which they leaped with flying feet. It seemed that they would never tire, but the trained warriors behind them were no less enduring. Once, twice, thrice they caught sight of them, and when a longer period of invisibility passed they knew, nevertheless, that they were still there. Now Long Jim suddenly wavered, but gathered himself together in an instant and continued his long leaps. Henry glanced at him and saw a patch of red on the sleeve of his buckskin hunting shirt.

"You've been hit, Jim," he said.

"It's nuthin'," said Long Jim doggedly, but he staggered again as he spoke.

"Turn to the north, Jim," said Henry sharply. "We'll come for you, too!"

Long Jim lifted a face of agony to the heavens. It was not agony of the body, but agony of the spirit, because he could not go on with the others.

"Go, Jim, while they can't see you," repeated Henry.

Long Jim waved his hand in a gesture of farewell, and, turning abruptly, disappeared in the bushes as quickly as if great waters had closed over him.

The three, who had been a minute before the four, did not look back. There were still life and strength in them, and the power to run. The Ohio could not be far away now, and they ought to strike it before morning.

"I'd like to stop an' fight," breathed Shif'less Sol. "I don't partickerly mind bein' chased sometimes, but I do mind bein' chased all the way back to New Or-lee-yuns."

Henry, despite their desperate situation, could not withhold a smile, which, however, was hidden from the shiftless one by the darkness.

"No choice seems to be left to us," he said. "It's run, Sol, run and keep on running."

A groan of weariness from the shiftless one was his only reply. But he kept by the side of Henry. Tom Ross was on the other side, and the three flitted through the bushes with a long swinging stride that still covered ground at a remarkable rate. Once they came to low, marshy soil, a swamp almost, where back water from the Ohio or the creek evidently stood in flood time, and they were forced to curve about, thus giving their pursuers a chance to come diagonally and to make a great gain upon them.

As they turned due south, skirting the side of the marsh, Tom Ross was in the woods furthest away from the soft ground. A rifle shot from some point deeper in the forest was fired at him, but the bullet only whistled by his ear and passed on to be lost in the marsh. Henry saw a dusky figure spring from the darkness and hurl itself upon Tom. He and the shiftless one instantly whirled about to help their comrade, but Tom and the warrior were now rolling over and over in the struggle of life and death.

Neither combatant in such a close grip could use his rifle, but each had drawn a knife, and the blades glittered as the men sought for a blow. Henry and the shiftless one looked for an opening, but they could not strike without as much danger to their comrade as to themselves, and they stood by, lost for the moment in doubt, knowing that all the time the pursuing band was coming nearer.

It was a furious struggle of bodily strength and passion, exerted to the utmost, and while the time seemed very long to those who would help, but could not find the chance, it was in reality not more than a minute. Then both knives flashed. One figure suddenly relaxed and lay still, but the other sprang to its feet.

It was Tom Ross who arose, and a cry of relief, low, but very deep, broke from each of the spectators. But Tom had not gone unscathed. The blade of the warrior had ripped open all the clothing on his left shoulder and had also cut deep into the flesh. Already the black blood was dripping upon the leaves.

"Bound to weaken me, an' I must stop somewhar to tie it up," said Tom tersely. "You two go on."

"We'll come back for you, too, Tom," said Henry, deeply moved, knowing how much it cost Silent Tom Ross to fall by the way.

"I turn to the east," said Tom. "I'll be restin' somewhar in the woods."

He slid away through the bushes and in an instant was gone. Henry, in order to keep the pursuit in the main channel and let the departure of Tom Ross pass unnoticed, sent back a fierce and challenging cry, the first that the fugitives had given forth that night. It was answered instantly from a point very near, the triumphant shout issuing from the throats of men who believed their victory sure and at hand.

"We must reach the Ohio, Sol," said Henry, "you and I, or you or I."

"Both or one," said Shif'less Sol. "Come on."

His face was upturned a little and, although there was no moonlight now, Henry saw it clearly. There was nothing of listlessness or despair in the face of the shiftless one. The look of exaltation that sometimes came upon him shone from his eyes. Dauntless and true, he would remain to the last.

"Thar's a gleam among the trees," he said ten minutes later, "an' it looks like water."

"It must be the Ohio! It surely is the Ohio!" said Henry. "We must swim for it, Sol."

The shiftless one only nodded in reply, but both as they ran tied their ammunition again around their necks, seeing at the same time that their powder horns were stopped up tightly. The trees thinned fast, open muddy ground appeared, and before them stretched a broad yellow current, the Ohio. They called up the last reserve of their strength and ran as swiftly as they could over the moist, sinking earth. But they were now visible to their pursuers, who had not yet emerged from the forest, and more bullets were fired.

"Are you hit, Sol?" asked Henry, anxiously of his comrade.

"No," replied the shiftless one. "Too dark fur 'em to take good aim."

The river seemed to widen as they approached it. It might be narrow enough somewhere near here for cannon to command it, but it was a giant stream, nevertheless, and a swimming head upon its surface would be exposed for a long way to rifle shots. Shif'less Sol wheeled and fired at the group that was now emerging from the woods, causing it to hesitate and then stop for a few minutes, although several shots were fired in return. The shiftless one felt a sharp, stinging pain in his side as a bullet glanced off his ribs, but he did not wince.

"Jump, Henry," he cried, "jump ez fur out into the river ez you kin!"

The bank at the very edge of the water was about a dozen feet high, and Henry leaped as far as he could. He heard a splash behind him as Sol, too, sprang into the water of the Ohio, but the shiftless one remained in the shadow of the bank.

"What is it, Sol?" cried Henry in alarm.

"I've been touched a leetle by a mite o' lead. It don't amount to much, but to-night I don't believe I kin swim the Ohio. I'll drift down river under the bank an' they'll never see me."

Sol was already floating away with the stream in the deepest shadow, and Henry, swimming as before with only one arm, struck out strongly for the Kentucky shore.

CHAPTER XII

THE ONE WHO ARRIVED

Henry Ware, when his last comrade, hurt and spent, drifted away in the darkness, felt that he was alone in every sense of the word. But the feeling of failure was only momentary. He was unhurt, and the good God had not given him great strength for nothing. He still held the rifle in his left hand above his head and swam with the wide circular sweep of his right arm. The yellow waves of the Ohio surged about him and soon he heard the nasty little spit, spit of bullets upon the water near his head and shoulders. The warriors were firing at him as he swam, but the kindly dusk was still his friend, protecting him from their aim.

He would have dived, swimming under water as long as his lungs would hold air. But he did not dare to wet his precious rifle and ammunition, which he might need the very moment he reached the other shore—if he reached it.

He heard the warriors shooting, and then came the faint sound of splashes as a half dozen leaped into the water to pursue him. Henry changed the rifle alternately from hand to hand in order to rest himself, and continued in a slanting course across the river, drifting a little with the current. He did not greatly fear the swimmers behind him. One could not attack well in the water, and they were likely, moreover, to lose him in the darkness, which was now heavy, veiling either shore from him. Had it not been for the rifle it would have been an easy matter to evade pursuit. Swimming with one arm was a difficult thing to do, no matter how strong and skillful one might be. But the pursuing warriors, who would certainly carry weapons, suffered from the same disadvantage. He heard another faint report, seeming to come from some point miles away, and a bullet struck the water near him, dashing foam in his eyes. It was fired from the bank, but it was the last from that point. He was so far out in the river now that his head became invisible from the shore, and he was helped, also, by the wind, which caused one wave to chase another over the surface of the river.

Henry was now about the middle of the stream, here perhaps half a mile in width, and he paused, except for the drifting of the current, and rested upon arm and shoulder. He looked up. The sky was still darkening, and only a faint silvery mist showed where the moon was poised. Then he looked toward either shore. Both were merely darker walls in the general darkness. He did not see any of the heads of the swimming warriors on the surface of the river, and he believed that they had lost him in the obscurity.

Refreshed by his floating rest of a minute or two, he turned once more toward the Kentucky shore. It was an illusion, perhaps, but it seemed to him that he had been lying at the bottom of a watery trough, and that he was now ascending a sloping surface, broken by little, crumbling waves.

He swam slowly and as quietly as possible, taking care to make no splash that might be heard, and he was beginning to believe that he was safe, when he saw a dark blot on the yellow stream. Far down was another such blot, but fainter, and far up was its like.

They were Indian canoes, and the one before him contained but a single occupant. Henry surmised at once that they were sentinels sent there in advance of the main force, and that the trained eyes of the warriors in the canoes would pierce far in the darkness. It seemed that the way was shut before him, and that he would surely be taken. He felt for an instant or two a sensation of despair. If only the firm ground were beneath his feet he could fight and win! But the watching warrior before him was seated safely in a canoe and could pick him off at ease. Undoubtedly the sentinels had been warned by the shots that a fugitive was coming, and were ready.

But he was not yet beaten. He called once more upon that last reserve of strength and courage, and, as he floated upon his back, holding the rifle just over him, he formed his plan. He must now be quick and strong in the water, and he could not be either if one hand was always devoted to the task of keeping the rifle dry. He must make the sacrifice, and he tied it to his back with a deerskin strap used for that purpose. Then, submerged to his mouth, he swam slowly toward the waiting canoe.

It was a tremendous relief to use both hands and arms for swimming, and fresh energy and hope flowed into every vein. It was a thing terrible in its delicacy and danger that he was trying to do, but he approached it with a bold heart. He was absolutely noiseless. He made not a single splash that would attract attention, and he knew that he was not yet seen. But he could see the warrior, who was high enough above the water to stand forth from it.

The man was a Wyandot, and to the swimming eyes, so close to the surface of the river, he seemed very formidable, a heavily-built man, naked to the waist, with a thick scalp lock standing up almost straight, an alert face, and the strong curved nose so often a prominent feature of the Indian. One brown, powerful hand grasped a paddle, with an occasional gentle movement of which he held the canoe stationary in the stream against the slow current. A rifle lay across his knees, and Henry knew that tomahawk and knife were at his belt. He not only seemed to be, but was a formidable foe.

Henry paused and sank a little deeper in the water, over his mouth, in fact, breathing only through his nose. He saw that the warrior was wary. Some stray beams of moonlight fell upon the face and lighted up the features more distinctly. It was distinctly the face of the savage, the hunter, a hunter of men. Henry marked the hooked nose, the cruel mouth, and the questing eyes seeking a victim.

He resumed his slow approach, coming nearer and yet nearer. He could not be ten yards from the canoe now, and it was strange that the Indian did not yet see him. His whole body grew cold, but whether from the waters of the river he did not know. Yet another yard, and he was still unseen. Still another yard, and then the questing eyes of the Wyandot rested on the dark object that floated on the surface of the stream. He looked a second time and knew that the head belonged to some fugitive whom his brethren pursued. Triumph, savage, unrelenting triumph filled the soul of the Wyandot. It had been his fortune to make the find, and the trophy of victory should be his. It never entered into his head that he should spare, and, putting the paddle in the boat, he raised the rifle from his knees.

The Wyandot was amazed that the head, which rose only a little more than half above the water, should continue to approach him and his rifle. It came on so silently and with so little sign of propelling power that he felt a momentary thrill of superstition. Was it alive? Was it really a human head with human eyes looking into his own? Or was it some phantasy that Manitou had sent to bewilder him? He shook with cold, which was not the cold of the water, but, quieting his nerves, raised his rifle and fired.

Henry had been calculating upon this effect. He believed that the nerves of the Wyandot were unsteady and, as he saw his finger press the trigger, he shot forward and downward with all the impulse that strong arms and legs could give, the bullet striking spitefully upon the water where he had been.

It was a great crisis, the kind that seems to tune the faculties of some to the highest pitch, and Henry's mind was never quicker. He calculated the length of his dive and came up with his lungs still half full of air. But he came up, as he had intended, by the side of the canoe.

The Wyandot, angry at the dexterity of the trick played upon him, and knowing now that it was no phantasy of Manitou, but a dangerous human being with whom he had to deal, was looking over the side of the canoe, tomahawk in hand, when the head came up on the other side. He whirled instantly at the sound of splashing water and drew back to strike. But a strong arm shot up, clutched his, another seized him by the waist, and in a flash he was dragged into the river.

Henry and the warrior, struggling in the arms of each other, sank deep in the stream, but as they came up they broke loose as if by mutual consent and floated apart. Henry's head struck lightly against something, and the fierce cry of joy that comes to one who fights for his life and who finds fortune kind, burst from him.

It was the canoe, still rocking violently, but not overturned. He reached out his hand and grasped it. Then, with a quick, light movement, he drew himself on board.

The Wyandot was fifteen feet away, and once more their eyes met. But the positions were reversed, and the soul of the Wyandot was full of shame and anger. He dived as his foe had done, but he came up several feet away from the canoe, and he saw the terrible youth with his own rifle held by the barrel, ready to crush him with a single, deadly blow. The Wyandot perhaps was a fatalist and he resigned himself to the end. He looked up while he awaited the blow that was to send him to another world.

But Henry could not strike. The Indian was wholly helpless now and, his first impulse gone, he dropped the rifle in the canoe, seized the paddle, and with a mighty sweep sent the canoe shooting toward the Kentucky shore. He had turned none too soon. Other canoes drawn by the shot were now coming from both north and south. The Wyandot turned and swam toward one of them, while Henry continued his flight.

Henry was so exultant that he laughed aloud. A few minutes before he had been swimming for his life. Now he was in a canoe, and nothing but the most untoward accident could keep him from reaching the Kentucky shore. One or two shots were fired at long range from the pursuing canoes, but the bullets did not come anywhere near him, and he replied with an ironic shout.

The Wyandot's bullet pouch and powder horn, torn from him in the struggle, were lying in the boat. Henry promptly seized them, and reloaded the Wyandot's rifle. Just as he finished the task his canoe struck against the shore, and, as he leaped out, he gave it a push with his foot that sent it into the current. Then carrying the Indian's rifle in addition to his own, strapped on his back, he darted into the woods.

Once more Henry Ware trod the soil of Kain-tuck-ee, and for an instant or two he did not think of his wounded or exhausted companions behind. Nature had been so kind to him in giving him great physical power, which formed the basis of a sanguine character, that he always and quickly forgot hardships and dangers passed and was ready to meet a new emergency. The muddy Ohio was flowing from him in plentiful rills, but one rifle was loaded, and he had of dry ammunition enough to serve. Moreover, his trifling wound was forgotten. His mind responded to his triumph, and, laughing a little, he shook his captured rifle gleefully.

He stopped three or four hundred yards from the river in a dense clump of oak and elm and listened. He could hear no sound that betokened the approach of the Indians, nor did he consider further pursuit likely. They would be too busy with their intended attack on Fort Prescott to be searching the woods in the night for a lone fugitive, who, moreover, had shown a great capacity for escaping.

The night was dark and a cool wind was blowing. A less hardy body would have been chilled by the immersion in the Ohio, but Henry did not feel it. He was now studying the country, half by observation and half by instinct. It was hilly, as was natural along the course of the river, but the hills seemed to increase in height toward the north and east, that is, up the stream. It was reasonable to infer that Fort Prescott lay in that direction, as its builders would choose a high point for a site.

Henry began his advance, sure that the fort was not far away. The wind rose, drying his yellow hair and blowing it about his face. His clothing, too, began to dry, but he was unconscious of it. The dusky sky served him well. There were but few stars, and the moon was only half-hearted. Nevertheless, he kept well in the thickets, although he veered back toward the Ohio, and now and then he saw its broad surface turned from yellow to silver in the faint moonlight. He saw, also, two or three dark spots near the shore, moving slowly, and he knew that they were Indian canoes. Girty and his force were almost ready for the attack on the fort. A portion of the band was already crossing to the southern shore, and it was likely that the attack would be made from several sides.

Henry increased his pace and came into a little clearing partly filled with low stumps, while others that had either been partially burned or dragged out by the roots lay piled on one side. It looked like a poor little effort of man to struggle with the wilderness, and Henry smiled in the darkness. If this tiny spot were left alone, and it surely would be if Fort Prescott fell, the forest would soon claim it again. But he was glad to see it, because it was a sign that he was approaching the fort.

A little further on he came to a small field of Indian corn, the fresh green blades shimmering in the moonlight and giving forth a pleasant, crooning sound as the wind blew gently upon them. Beyond, on the crest of the hill, he saw a dark line that was a palisade, and beyond that a blur that was roofs. This obviously was Fort Prescott, and Henry examined it with the eye of a general.

The place was located well for defense, on the top of a bare hill, with the forest nowhere nearer than two hundred yards and the underbrush cut cleanly away in order that it might afford no ambush. Henry judged that a spring, rising somewhere inside the palisade, flowed down to the Ohio. He had no fault to find with the place except that it was advanced too far into the Indian country, but that single fault was most serious and might prove fatal.

The fort seemed strong and well built and it was likely that one or two sentinels were on the watch, although he could not see from the outside. One of his hardest problems was now before him, how to enter the fort and give the warning without first being fired upon as an enemy. He had no time to waste, and he decided upon the boldest course of all.

He drew all the air that he could into his lungs, and then, uttering a piercing shout, magnified both in loudness and effect by the quiet night, he rushed directly for the lowest point in the palisade. "Up! up!" he cried. "You are about to be attacked by the tribes! Up! Up! if you would save yourselves!"

Before he was half way to the palisade two heads looked over it, and the muzzles of two long rifles were thrust toward him.

"Don't shoot!" he cried. "I'm a friend and I bring warning! Don't you see I'm white?"

It was hard in the darkness of night to see that one so brown as he was white, but the bearers of the rifles were impressed by his forcible words and withdrew their weapons. Henry ran on, and, despite the burden of his two rifles, seized the top of the parapet with his hands and in a moment was over. As he disappeared on the inside, a rifle shot was fired from some point behind, and a bullet whistled where he had been. Henry alighted upon his feet and found facing him two men in buckskin, rifle in hand and ready for instant action. His single glance showed that they were men of resolution, not awed either by his dramatic appearance or the rifle shot fired with such evident hostile intent.

"Who are you?" asked one.

"My name is Henry Ware," replied Henry rapidly, "and I bring you word that you are about to be attacked by a great force of the allied tribes led by the famous chiefs, Timmendiquas, Yellow Panther, and Red Eagle and the renegades, Girty, Blackstaffe, Eliot, McKee, Quarles, and Wyatt."

It was a terrible message that he delivered, but his tone was full of truth, and both men paled under their tan. While Henry was speaking, lights were appearing in the log houses within the palisades, and other men, drawn by the shot, were approaching. One, tall, well built, and of middle age, was of military appearance, and Henry knew by the deference paid to him that he must be the chief man of the place.

"What is it?" he asked in a voice of much anxiety.

"The stranger brings news of an attack," replied one of the sentinels.

"Of an attack by whom?"

"By Indian warriors in great force," said Henry. "I've just escaped from them myself, and I know their plans. They are in the woods now beyond the clearing."

"To the palisade, some of you," said the man sharply, "and see that you watch well. I believe that this boy is telling the truth."

"I would not risk my life merely to tell you a falsehood," said Henry quietly.

"You do not look like one who would tell a falsehood for any purpose," said the man.

He looked at Henry with admiration, and the boy's gaze met his squarely. Nor was it lacking in appreciation. Henry knew that the leader—for such he must be —was a man of fine type.

"My name is Braithwaite, Major Braithwaite," said the man, "and I believe that I am, in some sort, the commander of the fort which I now fear is planted too deep in the wilderness. I had experience with the savages in the French war and I know how cunning and bold they are."

Henry learned later that he was from Delaware, that he had earned the rank of major in the great French and Indian war, and that he was brave and efficient. He had opposed the planting of the colony on the river, but, being out-voted, he had accepted the will of the majority.

Major Braithwaite acted with promptness. All the men and larger boys were now coming forth from the houses, bringing their rifles, and as he assigned them to places the Indian war cry rose in the forest on three sides of the fort, and bullets pattered on the wooden palisade.

CHAPTER XIII

AT THE FORT

The cry of the warriors in the woods was answered by a single cry from the log houses. It was that of the women and children, but it was not repeated. They had learned the frontier patience and courage and they settled themselves down to helping—the women and all the children that were large enough—and to waiting. The men at the palisade replied to the Indian volley, some shooting from the crest, while others sent their bullets through loopholes.

Major Braithwaite was standing erect near Henry. After the volley and reply, followed by silence, he took one look about to see that the palisade was well-manned. Then it seemed to Henry that his figure stiffened and grew taller. His nostrils distended and a spark appeared in his eyes. The old soldier smelt the fire and smoke of battle once more, and the odor was not wholly ungrateful to him.

"Young sir," he said, turning to Henry, "we owe you a great debt. You got here just in time to save us from surprise."

"I'm glad," replied Henry, "that one of us was lucky enough to get through."

"One of you? What did you mean? Did others start?"

Henry flushed. He had not meant to say anything about the circumstances of his coming. It was a slip, but he could not take it back.

"There were five of us when we started," he said. "We were sure that at least one of us would get here."

"Good God! You do not mean to tell me that the others have all been killed?"

"No," replied Henry confidently. "They were wounded or broke down. I'll find 'em or they'll find me. We've been ahead of a fleet that is carrying arms, ammunition, and other things for our people in the east. That fleet ought to reach here in a few days."

The Major's face showed a little relief.

"Pray God it will come in time," he said earnestly. "We need it here, and so do our brethren in the east. What do you think is likely to happen here? My experience with the Indians on the Canada frontier tells me that I can never know what to expect of them. But you've probably had more experience in that way."

The boy, before answering, looked up at the sky. It had grown darker. It was a very timid moon, and nearly every star had withdrawn.

"They'll try to rush us soon," he replied. "The night helps them. How many men have you got?"

"About eighty, but counting the half-grown boys and several women who can shoot we are able to put a hundred rifles into the defense."

"Then we can hold 'em back for a long time," said Henry. "Tell the men to watch well at the palisade, and I'll take a look around."

He glided naturally into his position of wilderness leader, and Major Braithwaite, a cultivated man with a commission, a man who was old enough to be his father, yielded to him without pique or the thought of it. The wild youth of great stature and confident bearing inspired him with a deep sense of relief at such a crisis.

Henry went swiftly among the log houses, which were arranged in rows much after the fashion of Wareville, with a central blockhouse, from the upper story of which riflemen could fire upon enemies who sought to rush across the clearing against the palisade. In a little hollow just beyond the group of houses a cool, clear spring bubbled up, trickled away, passed under the palisade, and flowed into the Ohio. It was an invaluable spring inside the walls and Henry thought its presence, together with the beauty and healthfulness of the site, had determined the location of Fort Prescott.

On the side of the river, the bank dropped down rather steeply to the Ohio, which was not more than a hundred yards away, and which was contracted here to less than half its usual width. Cannon planted on this height could easily sweep the river from shore to shore, and Henry drew a sudden sharp breath. He believed that he had half defined the plan of Timmendiquas, Girty, and their confederates —to seize Fort Prescott, command the river, and shut off the fleet. But how? He could not yet see where they would obtain the means.

The river was dusky, but Henry's eyes, used to the darkness, could search its surface. He saw a number of moving black dots, three near the center of the stream and others at the farther shore. He could not discern the outlines because of the distance, but he was sure that they were Indian canoes, always watching.

He went back to Major Braithwaite and he was conscious, on the way, that many eyes were gazing at him with curiosity from the open doors of the log houses. It was quickly known to all that a stranger, a most unusual stranger, had come with a warning so quickly justified, and when they saw him they found that the report was true. But Henry took no apparent notice. He found Major Braithwaite standing near the southern side of the palisade.

"Well, what do you think of us?" asked the Major, smiling rather wanly.

"It's a good fort," replied Henry, "and that spring will be a great thing for you. We came near being taken once in our own fort of Wareville because the wells failed and we had no spring. Have you put any men in the top of the blockhouse?"

"Eight of our best riflemen are there."

"Tell them never to stop watching for a second and tell the men at the palisades to do the same. In their fights with us the warriors always rely on their belief that they have more patience than we have, and usually they have."

The Major breathed hard.

"I would that this thing were well over," he said. "I have a wife and two little children in one of those houses. Speaking for myself and all the rest of us, too, I cannot thank you too much, young sir, for coming to the fort with this warning."

"It is what we always owe to one another in the woods," said Henry. "I think it likely that they will attack about three or four o'clock in the morning. If I were you, sir, I'd have coffee served to the riflemen, that is, if you have coffee."

"We have it," said the Major, and soon the women were preparing the coffee. Everybody drank, and then the riflemen resumed their watch upon the forest. Some were men of experience and some were not. Those who were not believed, as the weary hours passed, that it was a false alarm and wished to go to sleep, leaving perhaps a half dozen sentinels to keep guard. But Major Braithwaite would not allow it. Not an expert in the forest himself, he believed that he knew an expert when he saw one, and he already had implicit faith in Henry Ware. The two were together most of the time, passing continually around the enclosure. Henry looked up at the sky, where no ray of moonlight now appeared, and where rolling clouds increased in the darkness. The forest was merely a black shadow, and the clearing between it and the palisade lay in heavy gloom. The wise forethought of Major Braithwaite had caused a narrow platform, or rather ledge, to be run around the inside of the palisade at such a height that a man could stand upon it and fire over the top of the stakes.

Henry and the Major stepped upon the ledge and looked at the clearing. The Major saw nothing—merely the black background of earth, forest and sky. Nor did Henry see anything, but he believed that he heard something, a faint, sliding sound, perhaps like that of a great serpent when it trails its long length over the grass and leaves. It was such a noise as this that he was expecting, and he sought with attentive ear and eye to locate it.

Ear guided eye, and he became sure that the sound came from a point fifteen or twenty yards in front of them, but approaching. Then eye discerned a darker blot against the dark face of the earth, and presently turned this blot into the shape of a creeping warrior. There were other creeping forms to right and left, but Henry, raising his rifle, fired at the first that he had seen.

All the warriors, dozens of them, sprang to their feet, uttering their cry, and rushed upon the wall, firing their rifles as they came. The defenders replied from the top of the palisade through the loopholes and from the upper story of the blockhouse. The Indians kept up their war cries, terrifying in their nature and intended for that purpose, while the white men shouted encouragement to one another. The sharp, crackling fire of the rifles was incessant, and mingled with it was the sighing sound of bullets as they struck deep into the wood of the palisade.

It was a confused struggle, all the more grim because of the darkness. Many of the Indians reached the palisade. Some were shot down as they attempted to climb over. Others knelt under the wall and fired through the very loopholes. One warrior leaped over the palisade, escaping all the bullets aimed at him, and, tomahawk in hand, ran toward a woman who stood by one of the houses with the intention of striking her down. He was wild with the rage of battle, but a lucky shot from the window of the blockhouse slew him. He fell almost at the feet of the horrified woman, and it was seen the next morning that he belonged to the fearless Wyandot nation.

Henry stood for a time on the ledge, firing whenever he saw a chance, wasting no bullets, but after a while he sprang down and ran along the line, believing that he could be of more service by watching as well as fighting. He knew that the brunt of the Indian attack would be likely to veer at any moment, and presently it shifted to the eastern side. Luckily he was there, and at his call the Major came with more men. The warriors were repelled at this point, also. At the end of a half hour the attack sank, and then ceased on all sides. The defenders were victorious for the time, and there was great rejoicing among those who did not know all the ways of the forest.

"It is merely a withdrawal for another and better opportunity, is it not?" said Major Braithwaite to Henry.

"Of course," replied the boy. "They do not give up as easy as that. It was so dark that I don't think much damage was done to either side. Besides, a lot of them are there yet, hiding against the palisade, and if they get a chance they will pick off some of your men."

As Henry spoke, a bullet whizzed through a loophole, and a defender was struck in the shoulder. The others quickly moved out of range. Major Braithwaite was very grave.

"Those savages are a great danger," he said. "How are we to get at them."

"If we lean over the wall to shoot down at 'em," said Henry, "they can shoot up at us, and they can see us better. It's a big question. Ah, I know what to do. Those stakes are green wood, are they not?"

"Yes. Why?"

"They won't burn unless the fire is nursed?"

"I shouldn't think so."

"Then we'll have our red friends out without much danger to ourselves."

Henry quickly told his plan, and the Major was all approval. Pots and kettles were filled with coals from the smouldering fires in the houses—in every Kentucky pioneer cabin the fire was kept over night in this manner ready for fresh wood in the morning—and then they were carried to the wooden barrier, the bearers taking care to keep out of range of the loopholes. A line of men stood along the ledge, and at a whispered word from Henry twenty heaps of red hot coals were dropped over the palisade, falling down at its foot. A series of howls, wild with pain, arose, and a dozen figures, leaping up, darted toward the forest. Two were shot by the riflemen in the blockhouse, but the rest made good the wood. More coals and boiling water, also, were emptied along the whole line of the stockade, but only three more warriors were roused up, and these escaped in the darkness. All were gone now.

Henry laughed quietly, and Major Braithwaite joined in the laugh.

"It was a good plan," he said, "and it worked well. Now, I think, young sir, you ought to get a little sleep. I don't think they can surprise us, and it will not be long before day."

Henry lay down on a bed of furs in one of the houses, with the first rifle that he had taken by his side—the other he had already given to the defenders—and soon he slept soundly. He was troubled somewhat by dreams, however; in these dreams he saw the faces of his four lost comrades. He awoke once while it was yet dark, and his mind was heavy. "I must go back for them at the very first chance," he said to himself, and then he was asleep again.

He awoke of his own accord two hours after sunrise, and after he had eaten a breakfast that one of the women brought him, he went forth.

A splendid sun was ascending the heavens, lending to the green wilderness a faint but fine touch of gold. The forest, save for the space about the fort and a tiny cutting here and there, was an enclosing wall of limitless depth. It seemed very peaceful now. There was no sign of a foe in its depths, and Henry could hear distantly the song of birds.

But the boy, although sure that the warriors were yet in the forest, looked with the most interest and attention toward the river. The morning sunshine turned its yellow to pure gold, and the far hills rising abruptly were a green border for the gold. But Henry was not seeking either beauty or grandeur. He was looking for the black dots that he had seen the night before. They were not on the surface of the river, but he believed that he could detect them against the bank, hidden partly in the foliage. Yet he was not sure.

"Good morning, my young friend, I trust that you slept well and are refreshed," said a cheery voice behind him.

It was Major Braithwaite, dressed now in the buff and blue of a colonial officer, who saluted him, his fine, tall figure upright and military, and his face expressing confidence. He noticed Henry's eyes on his buff and blue and he said:

"I brought with me the new uniform of our army and I put it on. It is the first time that I have ever worn in battle the uniform of what I trust will prove to be a new nation. I serve in the deep wilderness, but still I serve."

Henry might have smiled at such precision of speech and a certain formality of manner, but he knew it to be the result of a military training, and it did not decrease his liking for the Major.

"I've slept well and I'm rested," he replied. "What damage did they do to us last night?"

"Two of our men were slain—brave fellows—and we have already buried them. Five more were wounded, but none severely. Do you think, Mr. Ware, that having had a taste of our mettle, they have withdrawn?"

"No," replied Henry emphatically. "They wouldn't think of leaving. They, too, must have suffered little loss. You see, sir, the darkness protected both sides, and they are in the woods there now, trying to think of the easiest way to take Fort Prescott."

But Henry, as he spoke, turned his eyes from the woods toward the river, and Major Braithwaite, impressed even more in the daylight than in the night by his manner and appearance, noticed it. The Major, although not a skilled forest fighter, despite his experience in the great French and Indian war, was a shrewd observer and judge of mankind.

"Why do you look so often and with so much anxiety toward the Ohio?" he asked. "What do you expect there?"

"I believe it's our greatest source of danger."

"In what way?"

"I don't know, I may be mistaken," replied Henry, not wishing to cause an alarm that might prove groundless. "We must pay attention to the forest just now. Something is moving there."

He was looking again toward the green wall, upon which a white spot suddenly appeared.

"It's a white cloth of some kind," said Major Braithwaite. "That means a flag of truce. Now what in the name of Neptune can they want?"

"We'll soon see," said Henry, as he and the Major advanced to the palisade and stepped upon the ledge. Many others did the same, and not a few among them were women and children. The Major did not send them away, as a bullet from the forest could not reach them there.

A man came from among the trees, waving a white rag on a stick, but stopped out of rifle shot. The man was tanned almost as brown as an Indian, and he was dressed in Indian style, but his features were undoubtedly Caucasian.

"Do you know who he is?" asked the Major.

"Yes," replied Henry, "it is the worst scoundrel in all the west, the leader of the men who fight against their own people, the king of the renegades, Simon Girty."

"Girty coming to us under a white flag!" exclaimed the Major. "What can he want?"

"We'll soon see," said Henry. "Look, there are the chiefs."

A dozen stately figures issued from the green gloom and stood beside Girty, silent and impressive, their hands folded upon the muzzles of their rifles, which rested upon the ground, their figures upright, figure and face alike motionless, an eagle feather waving defiantly in every scalp lock. There was something grand and formidable in their appearance, and all those who looked from the palisade felt it.

"Do you know any of them?" asked Major Braithwaite.

"Yes," replied Henry. "I see Yellow Panther, head chief of the Miamis; Red Eagle, head chief of the Shawnees, and Captain Pipe and Captain White Eyes, Delaware chiefs, but I do not see Timmendiquas, the White Lightning of the Wyandots, the bravest and greatest of them all. There are two more renegades behind the chiefs. They are Blackstaffe and Braxton Wyatt."

"Girty is coming forward. He is going to speak," said the Major.

The renegade advanced another dozen feet, still holding the white flag above him, and hailed them in a loud voice.

"Ho, you within the fort!" he cried. "I wish to speak with your leader, if you have one."

Major Braithwaite stepped upon the highest point of the ledge. He showed above the palisade from the waist up, and the morning sunshine touched his cocked hat and buff and blue with an added glory. It was a strange figure in the forest, but the face under the cocked hat was brave and true.

"I am the commander here," said Major Braithwaite in a clear and penetrating voice. "What does Simon Girty want with us?"

"I see you know me," said the renegade laughing. "Then you ought to know, too, that it's worth while to listen to what I have to say."

Henry stood on a lower part of the ledge. Only his head appeared above the palisade, and Girty and Wyatt had not yet noticed him. But Major Braithwaite, almost unconsciously, looked down to him for advice.

"Draw him out as much as you can," said Henry.

"I am listening," said the Major. "Proceed."

"I want to tell you," called Girty, "that this place is surrounded by hundreds of warriors. We've got the biggest force that was ever gathered in the west, and it ain't possible for you to escape us."

A groan came from the palisade. It was some of the women who uttered it. But the Major waved his hand in reproof, and no one cried out again.

"You have yet to prove what you say," he replied. "We beat you off last night."

"That was only a little skirmish," said Girty. "We were just feeling of you. See, here are a dozen great chiefs beside me, Shawnee, Miami, Delaware, and others, which shows that we can send against you a thousand warriors, two thousand, if we wish. But we mean to be merciful. I'm a white man and the chiefs will listen to me. But if you don't do as I say, nothing will be left of this place two days from now but ashes and coals. All the men will be dead, and the women and children will be carried away, the women to be squaws of our warriors, the children to grow up as Indians, and never to know that they were white."

Faces along the barrier blanched. Major Braithwaite himself shuddered, but he replied in a strong voice:

"And what is the alternative that you offer us?"

"We admit that we would lose lives in taking your fort, lives that we wish to save. So we promise you that if you surrender, your women and young children shall go safely up the Ohio on boats to Pittsburgh, the men to be held for ransom."

"Don't think of accepting, Major!" exclaimed Henry. "Don't think of it, even if they had ten thousand warriors! If you put your people in his power, Girty would never dream of keeping his promise, and I doubt if the chiefs understand what he is saying while he is speaking English!"

"Never fear that I shall do such a thing, my boy," said Major Braithwaite. "Meekly surrender a place like this to a scoundrel like Girty!"

Then he called out loudly:

"It may be that you can take us in two days as you say, but that you will have to prove, and we are waiting for you to prove it."

"You mean, then," said Girty, "that we're to have your scalps?"

"Major," said Henry earnestly, "let me speak to them. I've lived among the Indians, as I told you before, and I know their ways and customs. What I say may do us a little good!"

"I believe in you, my boy," said Major Braithwaite with confidence. "Speak as you please, and as long as you please."

He stepped from the high point of the ledge, and Henry promptly took his place. Braxton Wyatt uttered a cry of surprise and anger as the figure of the great youth rose above the palisade, and it was repeated by Simon Girty. The two knew instinctively who had put Fort Prescott on guard, and their hearts were filled with black rage.

"Simon Girty," called Henry in the language of the Shawnees, which he spoke well, "do you know me?"

He had deliberately chosen the Shawnee tongue because he was sure that all the chiefs understood it, and he wished them to hear what he would have to say.

"Yes, I know you," said Girty angrily, "and I know why you are here."

Henry suddenly put on the manner of an Indian orator. He had learned well from them when he was a captive in the Northwestern tribe, and for the moment the half-taunting, half-boastful spirit which he wished to show really entered into his being.

"Simon Girty," he called loudly, "I came here to save these people and to defeat you, and I have succeeded. You cannot take this fort and you cannot frighten its men to surrender it. Renegade, murderer of your kind, wretch, liar, I know and these people know that if they were to surrender you would not keep your word if you could. How can any one believe a traitor? How can your Indian allies believe that the man who murders his own people would not murder them when the time came?"

Girty's face flamed with furious red, but Henry went on rapidly:

"If Manitou told me that I should fall in fair fight with a Wyandot or a Shawnee or a Miami I should not feel disgraced, but if I were to be killed by the dirty hand of you, Girty, or the equally dirty hand of Braxton Wyatt, who stands behind you, I should feel myself dishonored as long as the world lasts."

Girty, choking with rage, drew his tomahawk from his belt and shook it at Henry, who was more than a hundred yards away. The chiefs remained motionless, silent and majestic as before.

"And you great chiefs," continued Henry, "listen to me. You will fail here as you have failed before. Help, great help, is coming for these people. I brought them the warning. I aroused them from sleep, and I know that many men are coming. Pay heed to me, Yellow Panther, head chief of the Miamis, and Red Eagle, head chief of the Shawnees, that you may know who I am, and that my words are worth hearing. I am that bearer of belts, Big Fox, who came with Brown Bear and The Bat into the council lodge of the Miamis and sent the warriors of the Shawnees and the Miamis astray. I was white and my comrades were white, but you did not know me, cunning as you are."

Now Yellow Panther and Red Eagle stirred. These were true things that he told, and curiosity and anger stirred in them.

"Who is this that taunts us?" they asked of Girty.

"It's a young fiend," replied the renegade. "Wyatt has told me all about him. Boy as he is, he's worth a whole band of warriors to the people behind those walls."

"There is more that you should remember, Red Eagle and Yellow Panther," continued Henry, wishing to impress them. "It was I and my comrades who carried the message to the wagon train that you fought at the ford, where you were beaten, where you lost many warriors. I see that you remember. Tell your warriors that Manitou favors my friends and me, that we have never yet failed. We were present when the Indians of the south and many renegades like Girty and Wyatt here, men with black hearts who told lies to their red friends, were beaten in a great battle. As they failed in the south, so will you fail here. A mighty fleet is coming, and it will scatter you as the winter wind scatters the dead leaves."

Henry paused. He had calculated his effects carefully. He wished to create feeling between red man and renegade, and he wished to plant in the red mind the belief that he was really protected by Manitou. The tribes, at least, might hesitate and delay, and meanwhile the fleet was coming.

"I'll see that you're burned at the stake when we take this place," shouted Girty, "and I'll see that it's the slowest fire a man ever died over."

"I've said what I had to say," called back the youth.

He stepped down from the wall. The renegades and the chiefs retired to the woods.

"What were you saying to them?" asked Major Braithwaite.

"I was telling them of their former failures," replied Henry. "I was trying to discourage them and to make them hate the renegades."

CHAPTER XIV

SIX FIGURES IN THE DUSK

The hours moved slowly, and Henry began to believe that his grandiloquent speech—purposely so—had met with some success. No attack was made, and delay was what he wanted. The woods seemed to remain the home of peace and quiet. Major Braithwaite had a pair of strong military glasses, and, as an additional precaution, he and Henry searched the woods with them from the upper windows of the blockhouse. Still there was no evidence of Indian attack, and Henry turned the glasses upon the river. He could now make out definitely the canoes, half hidden under the foliage on the far bank, but no stir was there. All things seemed to be waiting.

Henry turned the glasses down the river. He had a long view, but he saw only the

Ohio and its yellow ripples. He lowered the glasses with an impatient little movement and handed them back to their owner.

"Why are you disappointed?" asked Major Braithwaite.

"I was hoping that the fleet might be coming, which would be a vast help to you here, but I see no sign of its approach. Of course it's slow work for rowers and oarsmen to come week after week against a strong current, and they have been delayed, too, by storms."

The news, confined hitherto to a few, spread through the fort, that a fleet might come soon to their help, and there was a wonderful revival of spirits. People were continually climbing to the cupola of the blockhouse, and the Major's glasses were in unbroken use. Always they were pointed down the stream, and women's eyes as well as men's looked anxiously for a boat, a boat bearing white men, the vanguard of the force that would come to save them. The sight of these women so eagerly studying the Ohio moved Henry. He knew, perhaps better than they, that they had the most to fear, and he resolved never to desert them.

In this interval of quiet Henry went down to the little spring which was just east of the last row of houses, but a full twenty yards from the palisade. The ground sank away abruptly there, leaving a little bluff of stone three or four feet high. The stream, two inches deep and six inches broad, beautifully clear and almost as cold as ice, flowed from an opening at the base of the bluff. A round pool, five or six feet across and two feet deep, had been cut in the stone at the outlet of the spring, and a gourd lay beside it for the use of all who wished to drink.

Henry drank from the pool and sat down beside it with his back against a rock. He watched the water, as it overflowed the pool, trickle away toward the river, and then, closing his eyes, he thought of his comrades, the faithful four. Where were they now? He felt a powerful temptation, now that he had warned Fort Prescott, to slip away in the darkness of the night that was to come and seek them. Three of them were wounded and Paul, who alone was unhurt, did not have the skill of the others in the forest. But powerful as the temptation was, it was a temptation only and he put it away. They must wait, as he himself would have been glad to wait, had it been Shif'less Sol or any other who had arrived instead of himself.

He kept his eyes shut a long while. It seemed to him at this time that he could think more strongly and clearly with all external objects shut out. He saw now without any flattery to self that his presence in the fort was invaluable. Major Braithwaite did not understand forest strategy, but nature and circumstance combined had compelled the boy to learn them. He knew, too, of the fleet of Adam Colfax and its elements, and the plans of the allied tribes and their elements. He seemed to hold the very threads of fate in his hands, whether for good or ill.

Henry Ware opened his eyes, and chance directed that he should open them when his gaze would rest up the stream. There was a black beam in the very center of the circle of vision, and he stared at it. It was moving, and he rose to his feet. He knew that the object was a boat, but it was much larger than an Indian canoe, much larger even than the great war canoes that they sometimes built, capable of carrying thirty or forty men. It was not long, slim, and graceful, but broad of beam, and came slowly and heavily like one of the large square flatboats in which the pioneers sometimes came down the Ohio.

Henry believed this boat an object to be dreaded, and he walked swiftly toward the blockhouse, where Major Braithwaite was standing. The Major noticed his manner and asked:

"Is it anything alarming?"

"I am afraid so. It's the big boat that you see out there in the river. Suppose we go to the top of the blockhouse and look at it through your glasses."

The Major went without a word. He was unconsciously relying more and more upon the boy whom he variously addressed as "Young sir" and "My young friend." Nor did he take the first look. He handed the glasses to Henry, who made a long examination of the boat and then, sighing, passed them back to the Major.

Major Braithwaite's survey was not so long and he looked puzzled when he took the glasses down.

"Now, what in the name of Neptune do you make of it, young sir?" he asked.

"It's a flatboat that once belonged to an emigrant party," said Henry. "Such boats, built for long voyages and much freight, are of heavy timbers and this is no exception. They have mounted upon it two cannon, twelve pounds at least. I can see their muzzles and the places that have been cut away in the boat's side to admit them."

Major Braithwaite's face whitened.

"Cannon here in the wilderness!" he exclaimed.

"One of our stations in Kentucky has been attacked with cannon."

"Where do they get them?"

"They are brought all the way from Canada and they are worked by the renegades and white men from Canada."

"This is a great danger to us."

"It is certainly a very great danger, Major."

Henry took another look through the glasses. The boat, driven by great sweeps, came on in a diagonal course across the river, bearing down upon the fort. Nobody on board it could yet be seen, so well protected were they by the high sides. It was near enough now to be observed by everybody in the fort, and many curious eyes were turned upon it, although the people did not yet know, as Henry and the Major did, the deadly nature of its burden.

The two descended from the blockhouse. The boat was now much nearer, still coming on, black and silent, but behind it at some distance, hovered a swarm of canoes filled with warriors.

The big boat stopped and swayed a little in the current. There was a flash of flame from her side, a puff of smoke, and a crash that traveled far up and down the river. A cannon ball struck inside the palisade, but buried itself harmlessly in the ground, merely sending up a shower of dirt. There was a second flash, a second puff and crash, and another cannon ball struck near its predecessor, like the first doing no harm.

But consternation spread inside the fort. They could reply to rifles with rifles, but how were they to defend themselves from cannon which from a safe range could batter them to pieces?

While the terrible problem was yet fresh in their minds, the attack on land was resumed. Hundreds of the warriors issued from the woods and began to fire upon the palisade, while the cannon shot were sent at intervals from the floating fortress.

Major Braithwaite retained his courage and presence of mind. All the women and children were told to remain within the heavy log houses, which were thick enough to turn cannon balls, and the best shots of the garrison manned the palisade, replying to the Indian fire.

Henry did not yet take much part in the combat. He believed that the attack upon the palisade was largely in the nature of a feint, intended to keep the defenders busy while the cannon did the real work. Not even Wyandots would storm in broad daylight walls held by good riflemen. He soon knew that he was right, as the rifle fire remained at long range with little damage to either side, while the flatboat was steadily drawing nearer, and the cannon were beginning to do damage. One man was killed and another wounded. Several houses were struck, and here and there stakes in the palisade were knocked away.

Major Braithwaite, despite his courage, showed alarm.

"How can we fight those cannons?" he said.

"Who is the best marksman you have?" asked Henry.

"Seth Cole?" replied the Major promptly.

"Will you call Seth Cole?"

Seth Cole came promptly. He was a tall, thin man, cool of eye and slow of speech.

"Are you ready to go with me anywhere, Mr. Cole?" asked Henry.

"I'm thinkin' that what another feller kin stand I kin, too," replied Seth.

"Then you're ready," said Henry, and he quickly told his plan.

Major Braithwaite was astonished.

"How in the name of Neptune do you ever expect to get back again, my young friend?" he exclaimed.

"We'll get back," replied the boy confidently. "Let us slip out as quietly as we can,

109

Major, but if you see any movement of the Indians to gain that side you might open a covering fire."

"I'll do it," said the Major, "and God bless you both."

He wrung their hands and they slipped away.

The palisade fronting the river ran along the very edge of the cliff, which rose at a sharp angle and was covered with bushes clustering thickly. It was impossible for a formidable Indian force to approach from that side, climbing up the steep cliff, and but little attention was paid to it.

Henry and Seth Cole waited until one of the cannon was fired, hiding the flatboat in its smoke, and then they leaped lightly over the palisade, landing among the bushes, where they lay hidden.

"You're sure that no one saw us?" said Henry.

"I'm thinkin' that I'm shore," replied Seth.

"Then we'll go on down the cliff."

Nimble and light-footed, they began the descent, clinging to rocks and bushes and sedulously keeping under cover. Luckily the bushes remained thick, and three-fourths of the way to the bottom they stopped, Henry resting in the hollow of a rock and Seth lying easily in a clump of bushes. They were now much nearer the flatboat, and while hidden themselves they could see easily.

Henry had uncommonly keen sight, and the eyes of the sharpshooter Seth Cole were but little inferior to his. He now saw clearly the muzzles of the two cannon, elevated that they might pitch their balls into the fort, and he marked those who served them, renegades and men from Canada, gunners, spongers, and rammers. He could even discern the expression upon their faces, a mingling of eagerness and savage elation. Behind the flatboat, at a distance of fifty or sixty yards, still hovered the swarm of canoes filled with Wyandots, Shawnees, Miamis, Illinois, Ottawas, and Delawares, raising a fierce yell of joy every time a shot struck within the palisade.

"Do you think you can reach them with a bullet, Seth Cole?" asked Henry Ware.

"I'm thinkin' I kin."

"I'm sure *I* can. See them reloading the cannon. You take the fellow with the sponge and I'll attend to the gunner himself."

"I'm thinkin' I'll do it," said Seth Cole. "Jest you give the word when to pull the trigger."

The two remained silent, each settling himself a little firmer in his position in the thick shrubbery. The sponger ran his sponge into the muzzle of the cannon, cleaned out the barrel, and an Indian next to him, evidently trained for the purpose, handed him a fresh charge. The gunner took aim, but he did not fire. A bullet struck him in the heart, and he fell beside the gun. The sponger, hit in the head, fell beside him. Both died quietly. The Indian, staring for a few moments, snatched up the sponge, but Henry had reloaded swiftly, and a third shot struck him down.

There was consternation on the flatboat. The light wisps of white smoke made by the rifles of the sharpshooters were lost in the dusky cloud raised by the cannon fire, and they did not know whence these deadly bullets came.

The second cannon was ready a couple of minutes later, but, like the first, its load was not discharged at the fort. The gunner was struck down at his gun and the rammer, hit in the shoulder, fell into the stream. Two Indians standing near were wounded, and panic seized the warriors at the sweep. The Ohio had seldom witnessed such sharpshooting, and Manitou was certainly turning his face away from them. They began to use the sweeps frantically, and the boat with its cannon sheered away to escape the deadly bullets.

Henry and Seth were reloading with quickness and dispatch.

"These are good rifles of ours that carry far, and they're still within range," said Henry.

"I'm thinkin' that we kin reach 'em," said Seth.

"I'll take the warrior near the head of the boat."

"I'll take the one a leetle further down."

"Ready, Seth?"

"I'm thinkin' I am."

The two pulled trigger at the same time, and both warriors fell. The boat, rocking heavily under the efforts of many hands at the sweeps, was driven furiously out of range, and Henry and Seth laughed low, but with pleased content. This was war, and they were fighting for the lives of women and children.

"I'm thinkin' that we've put 'em to guessin' for a while," said Seth.

"We surely have," said Henry, "and as those cannon won't come into action again for some time we'd better get back into the fort."

"Yes, we had," said Seth, "but I'm thinkin' I'm mighty glad you brought me along. Don't know when I've enjoyed myself so much. Curious, though, they didn't spot us there."

"Too much of their own cannon smoke floating about. Anyway, we've beat cannon balls with rifle bullets—that is, for the present. See, all the canoes, too, are going back to the other side of the river."

"Yes, an' the firin' on the fur side o' the fort's dyin' down. They must have seen what's happened, and are changin' tactics."

The ascent of the cliff was more difficult, but they managed to make it, still keeping under cover, and scaled the palisade. Major Braithwaite greeted them with joy and gratitude.

"I was afraid that neither of you would ever come back," he said, "but here you

111

are and you've driven off the cannon with rifles. It was great work, in the name of Neptune, it was!"

"No work at all," said Seth Cole, "jest play. Enjoyed myself tremenjeously."

The attack from the woods now ceased, as Henry reckoned it would when the cannon were driven off. He believed that there was concerted action on land and water, and that Timmendiquas had arrived. All the movements of the besieging force showed the mind of a general.

When the last shot was fired the Major and Henry made a tour about the fort. Three more lives had been lost and there were wounds, some serious, but they were upborne by a second success and the courage of the garrison grew. Several of the houses had been struck by cannon balls, but they were not damaged, and three or four small boys were already playing with a ball that they had dug from the earth.

"I wish we had cannon with which to reply to them," said Major Braithwaite. "Every fort in this wilderness should have at least one. You have driven away the boat with its guns, but it will come back, and when it returns it will be on guard against your sharpshooting."

"It will certainly come back if it has a chance," said Henry.

There was significance in his tone, and the Major looked at him.

"If it has a chance? What do you mean by those words?" he asked.

"We've got to put that boat out of action."

"Sink it?"

"No, if we sank it they might raise it again and have the cannon ready for action again in a few hours. We've got to burn the boat and then the cannon will be warped and twisted so they can't fix it short of a foundry."

"But we can't get at the boat."

"It must be done or this fort will surely be taken to-morrow. You know what that means."

Major Braithwaite groaned. He had a vision of his own wife and children, but he thought of the others, too.

"How?" he asked.

Henry talked to him earnestly, but the Major shook his head.

"Too dangerous!" he said. "You would all be lost. I cannot sanction such an enterprise. The fort cannot spare good men, nor could I let you go in this way to your death."

Henry talked more earnestly. He urged the necessity, the cruel necessity, of such an attempt, and the Major yielded at last, although with great reluctance.

"You want volunteers, I suppose?" he said.

112

"Yes. I know that Seth Cole will go, and I'm sure that others, too, will be willing to do so."

The remainder of the day passed without any demonstration from the besiegers, and Henry noticed with pleasure that the coming night promised to be dark. Already he had selected his assistants, Seth Cole and four others, all powerful swimmers, but the enterprise was kept a secret among the six and Major Braithwaite.

He ate a hearty supper, lay down and slept a while. When he awoke, he found that the promise of the night was fulfilled. It was quite dark, with clouds and light flurries of rain. There was no moon.

It was past midnight, and the Indian encampment, both on land and water, showed no sign of movement. The woods were without camp fires, but at the far bank of the river several lights could be seen. The river itself was in shadow. Most of the people at the fort, exhausted by their long labors and watches, were asleep, but Henry and his five comrades gathered near the spring, carrying with them three little iron pots, carefully covered with tin tops.

"It's a pity we haven't two or three hand grenades," said Major Braithwaite. "These are rather cumbrous things."

"I've heard Paul say that they used pots like these in ancient times," said Henry, "and I guess that if they did so, we can, too. What do you say, Seth?"

"I'm thinkin' that we kin," said Seth confidently. "Leastways, I'm thinkin' that we're ready to try."

"That is surely the right spirit," said Major Braithwaite, with a little tremor in his voice. "You lads are about to embark upon a desperate undertaking. I would not say that the chances are against you, if you did not know it already, but there is nothing truer than the fact that fortune favors those who dare much. I pray that all of you may come back."

He shook hands with them all, and stood by the palisade as, one by one, they climbed over it and dropped into the dark.

Henry and his five comrades on the outside of the palisade remained for a little space crouched against the wooden wall. All six searched the thickets on the slope with eye and ear, but they could neither see nor hear anything that betokened the presence of an enemy. It was not likely that Indian scouts would be lying in such a place, practically hanging to the side of the cliff between the palisade and the river, but Henry was not willing to neglect any precaution. The slightest mischance would ruin all. He gave silent but devout thanks that this night of all nights should prove to be so dark.

It was a singular file that made its way down the cliff through the thick brush, six dusky figures carrying rifles, and three of them, in addition, gingerly bearing small iron pots. When nearly to the bottom of the cliff their singularity increased. They stopped in a little alcove of the rocks, hid their rifles and ammunition among the bushes, took off every particle of clothing, all of which they hid, also, except their belts.

They buckled the belts tightly around their bare waists, but every belt carried in it a tomahawk and hunting knife. They still bore the three little iron pots which they handled so gingerly.

Six white figures slipped through the remaining bushes, six white figures reached the edge of the river, and then all six slid silently into the water, which received them and enveloped them to the chin. Henry, Seth Cole, and a man named Tom Wilmore bore the three iron pots above their heads, swimming with a single hand.

CHAPTER XV

THE DEED IN THE DARK

Henry was the leading swimmer, but he paused ten yards from the shore and the others paused with him. Six black dots hung in a row on the dark surface of the river. But so well did they blend with the shadow of the stream that an Indian eye on the bank, no matter how sharp, might have passed them over.

"The thing to do," said Henry, "is to make no noise. We must swim without splashing and we've got to find that flatboat with the cannon on it. You understand?"

Not a word was said in reply, but five heads nodded, and the silent six resumed their swim across the Ohio. They had entered the stream as far up as possible in order that they might go diagonally toward the south, thus taking advantage of the current.

Henry turned over on his back, floating easily with the help of one hand and holding the little pot above his face. Once he opened it a little to feel that it was still warm from within, and, satisfied that it was so, he floated silently on. His position made it easiest for him to look upward, but not much was to be seen there. The promise of the night still held good in performance. Rolling clouds hid the moon and stars, and again Henry gave thanks for so favorable a night.

His comrades swam so silently that he turned a little on his side to see that they were there. Five black dots on the water followed him in a close row, and, proud of their skill, he turned back again and still floated with his face to the skies.

They soon passed the middle of the river, and now the extremely delicate part of their task was come. The lights on the northern bank had increased to a half dozen and were much larger. They seemed to be camp fires. Dim outlines of canoes appeared against the bank.

Henry paused, and the five black heads behind him paused with him. He raised his head a little from the water and studied the shore. A shape, bigger and

114

darker than the others, told him where the flatboat lay. Owing to its greater draught, it was anchored in deeper water than the canoes, which was a fortunate thing for the daring adventurers. Henry saw the muzzles of the cannon, and a dark figure by each, evidently the warriors on guard. He could see them, but they could not see him and his comrades, whose heads were blurred with the darkness of the river. He turned on his side and whispered to Seth, who was next to him:

"I think we'd better swim above the flatboat, keeping at a good distance, and then drop down between it and the bank. They will not be expecting an enemy from that side. What do you think of it, Seth?"

Seth Cole nodded, and they swam silently up stream. If any one splashed the water it passed for the splash of a leaping fish, and there was no alarm in the Indian camp. Henry, studying the shore minutely as he swam with slow stroke, could not see motion anywhere. The fires burned low, and now that they were dropping down near the shore he saw the dim outlines of figures beside them. Some of the warriors slept in a sitting posture with their heads upon their knees, which were clasped in their arms, while others lay in their blankets. The canoes, in which Indians also slept, were tied to saplings on the bank.

They swam now with the greatest slowness, barely making a stroke, drifting rather. Henry knew that not all the warriors on the bank were asleep. Sentinels stood somewhere among the trees, and it was hard to escape the vigilance of an Indian on watch. Only a night of unusual darkness made an approach such as theirs possible.

A broad shape rose out of the obscurity. It was the flatboat, now not twenty feet away, and Henry paused a moment, the five heads pausing with him.

"Nobody is watching on this side of the boat," whispered the youthful leader, "and it will not be hard to climb over the side. We must all do so at once and make a rush."

"I'm thinkin' you're right," Seth Cole whispered back.

They headed straight for the flatboat and each put a hand upon its side. A Miami sentinel on the bank heard a splash a little louder than usual, and he saw a gleam of white in the water beside the flatboat.

The Miami sprang forward for a better look, but he was not in time. Six white figures rose from the water. Six white figures gave a mighty heave, and the next moment they were upon the deck. The sentinels, looking toward the middle of the river, heard the sound of light, pattering footsteps behind them, and wheeled about. Despite their courage, they uttered a cry of superstitious horror. Surely these white, unclad figures were ghosts, or gods come down from the skies! One in his fright sprang overboard, but the other, recovering himself somewhat, fired at the foremost of the invaders. His bullet missed, and Henry, not noticing him, rushed toward the little cabin. Here he saw some bedding, evidently taken with the boat from its former owners, and he emptied the coals from the iron pot among it. A blaze instantly sprang up and spread with great rapidity. Despite the

115

heat, Henry scattered the burning cloth everywhere with a canoe paddle that lay on the floor. Seth Cole and Tom Wilmore were also setting the boat on fire in a half dozen places.

The flames roared around them, and then they rushed upon the deck, where the sounds of conflict had begun. There were renegades as well as Indians upon the boat, and both soon realized that the invaders were human beings, not spirits or ghosts. Several shots were fired. A man from Fort Prescott was slightly wounded in the shoulder, and the red blood was streaking his white skin. But one of the invaders had used his tomahawk to terrible purpose—the figure of a warrior lay motionless upon the deck.

As Henry sprang to the relief of his comrades he ran directly into some one. The two recoiled, but their faces were then not more than a foot apart, and Henry recognized Braxton Wyatt. Wyatt knew him, too, and exclaimed: "Henry Ware!" He had been sleeping upon the boat and instantly he raised a pistol to make an end of the one whom he hated. Henry had no time to draw tomahawk or knife, but before the trigger could be pulled he seized the renegade in the powerful clasp of his bare arms.

The excitement of the moment, the imminence of the crisis, gave a superhuman strength to the great youth. He lifted Braxton Wyatt from his feet, whirled him into the air, and then sent him like a stone from a sling into the deep water of the Ohio. The renegade uttered a cry as he sank, but when he came up again he struggled for the shore, not for the boat. The renegade McKee had already been driven overboard, and the Indians, who alone were left on the boat, felt their superstition returning when they saw Braxton Wyatt tossed into the river as if by the hand of omnipotence. The flames, too, had gained great headway, and were now roaring high above the deck and the heat was increasing fast. If these were devils—and devils they certainly must be!—they had brought with them fire which could not be fought.

The Indians hesitated no longer, and the last of them, leaping overboard, swam for the land.

"It's time for us to go, too," said Henry to his panting comrades. "They'll get over their fright in a minute or two and be after us."

"I'm thinkin' you're right," said Seth Cole, "but nothin' kin save this boat now. She must be an old one. She burns so fast."

Henry sprang into the river and the five followed him, swimming with their utmost power toward the southern shore. They heard behind them the crackling of the flames, and a crimson light was cast upon the water.

Henry looked back over his shoulder. The boat was blazing, but the light from it reached his comrades and himself. The Indians on the bank saw them. Hasty bullets began to flick the water near them. Canoes were already starting in chase.

"If that light keeps up, they're bound to git us," said Seth Cole.

"But it won't keep up," said Henry. "Swim, boys! Swim with all your might! It's not Indians alone that we've got to dodge!"

Tired as they were, they increased their speed by a supreme effort for a minute or so, and then as if by the same impulse all looked back. The boat was a mass of flame, a huge core of light, casting a brilliant reflection far out over the river and upon the bank, where trees, bushes, and warriors alike stood out in the red flare.

The boat seemed to quiver, and suddenly it leaped into the air. Then came a tremendous explosion and a gush of overpowering flame. Henry and his comrades dived instantly and swam as far as they could under water toward the eastern shore. When they came up again the flatboat and its terrible cannon were gone, heavy darkness again hung over land and water, and pieces of burning wood were falling with a hissing splash into the river. But they heard the voices of warriors calling to each other, organizing already for pursuit. Their expedition was a brilliant success, but Henry knew that it would be a hard task to regain Fort Prescott. Led by the renegades and driven on by their bitter chagrin, the Indians would swarm upon the river in their canoes, seeking for them everywhere with eyes used to darkness.

"Are you all here, boys?" he asked. He had been scorched on the shoulder by a burning fragment, but in the excitement he did not notice it. Two of the men were slightly wounded, but at that time they thought nothing of their hurts. All six were there, and at Henry's suggestion they dived again, floating down stream as long as they could hold their breath. When they came up again the six heads were somewhat scattered, but Henry called to them softly, and they swam close together again. Then they floated upon their backs and held a council of war.

"It seems likely to me," said Henry, "that the Indian canoes will go straight across the stream after us, naturally thinking that we'll make at once for Fort Prescott."

"I'm thinkin' that you're tellin' the truth," said Seth Cole.

"Then we must drop down the stream, strike the bank, and come back up in the brush to the place where our rifles and clothes are hid."

"Looks like the right thing to me," said Tom Wilmore. "I'll want my rifle back, but 'pears to me I'll want my clothes wuss. I'm a bashful man, I am. Look thar! they've got torches!"

Indians standing up in the canoes were sweeping the water with pine torches in the search for the fugitives, and Henry saw that they must hasten.

"We must make another dash for the bank," he said. "Keep your heads as low down on the water as you can."

They swam fast, but the Indian canoes were spreading out, and one tall warrior who held a burning pine torch in his hand uttered a shout. He had seen the six dots on the stream.

"Dive for it again," cried Henry, "and turn your heads toward the land!"

He knew that the Indians would fire, and as he and his comrades went under he heard the spatter of bullets on the water. When they rose to the surface again they were where they could wade, and they ran toward the bank. They reached dry land, but even in the obscurity of the night their figures were outlined against the dark green bush, and the warriors from their canoes fired again. Henry heard near him a low cry, almost suppressed at the lips, and if it had not been for the red stain on Tom Wilmore's shoulder he would not have known who had been hit.

"Is it bad, Tom?" he exclaimed.

"Not very," replied Wilmore, shutting his teeth hard. "Go on. I can keep up."

A boat suddenly shot out of the dusk very near. It contained four Indian warriors, two with paddles and two with upraised rifles. One of the rifles was aimed at Henry and the other at Seth Cole, and neither of them had a weapon with which to reply. Henry looked straight at the muzzle which bore upon him. It seemed to exercise a kind of terrible fascination for him, and he was quite confident that his time was at hand.

He saw the warrior who knelt in the canoe with the rifle aimed at him suddenly turn to an ashy paleness. A red spot appeared in his forehead. The rifle dropped from his hands into the water, and the Indian himself, collapsing, slipped gently over the side and into the Ohio. The second Indian had fallen upon his back in the canoe, and only the paddlers remained.

Henry was conscious afterward that he had heard two shots, but at the time he did not notice them. The deliverance was so sudden, so opportune, that it was miraculous, and while the frightened paddlers sent their canoe flying away from the bank, Henry and his comrades darted into the thick bush that lined the cliff and were hidden from the sight of all who were on the river.

"Our clothes and our rifles," whispered Henry. "We must get them at once."

"They fired from the fort just in time," said Tom Wilmore.

Henry glanced upward. The palisade was at least three hundred yards away.

"Those bullets did not come from Fort Prescott," he said. "It's too far from us, and they were fired by better marksmen than any who are up there now."

"I think so, too," said Seth Cole, "an' I'm wonderin' who pulled them triggers."

Shif'less Sol and Tom Ross were first in Henry's mind, but he knew that both had suffered wounds sufficient to keep them quiet for several days, and he believed that the timely shots were the work of other hands. Whoever the strangers might be they had certainly proved themselves the best and most timely of friends.

They reached the thicket in which they had hidden their clothes and rifles, and found them untouched.

"Queer how much confidence clothes give to a feller!" exclaimed Seth Cole, as he slipped on his buckskins.

"It's so," said Henry, "and it's so, too, that you're not a whole man until you get

118

back your rifle."

When he grasped the beautiful weapon which had been his prize he felt strength flowing in a full tide in every vein. Before he was halt, a cripple, but now he was a match for anybody. He heard a quick, gasping breath, and the sound of a soft fall.

Tom Wilmore had sunk forward, prone in the bushes. His wound in the shoulder was deeper than he had admitted. Through the thicket came the sounds of pursuit. The warriors had left the canoes and were seeking them on land.

But the borderers had no thought of deserting their senseless comrade. Two of the men raised him up between them, and Henry, Seth Cole, and the sixth, armed with weapons of range and precision, protected the rear. Up the slope they went toward the fort. Henry presently heard light footsteps among the bushes and he fired toward the sound. He did not believe that he could hit anything in the darkness and uncertainty, but he wished to attract the attention of the watchers of the palisade. The diversion was effective, as shots were fired over their heads when they came near the wooden walls, and the pursuers drew back.

Tom Wilmore revived and demanded to be put down. It hurt his pride that he should have to be carried. He insisted that he was not hurt seriously, and was on his feet again when they reached the palisade. The anxious voice of Major Braithwaite hailed from the dark.

"Is it you, Ware; is it you, young sir?"

"We are here, all of us," replied Henry, and the next instant they were at the foot of the palisade, where Major Braithwaite and at least twenty men were ready to receive them.

When they were helped over the wall the Major counted quickly:

"One! two! three! four! five! six! all here, and only two wounded! It was a wonderful exploit! In the name of Neptune, how did you do it?"

"We took the flatboat just as we planned," replied Henry with pardonable pride. "We set it on fire, and it blew up, also just as we planned. Those cannon are now twisted old iron lying at the bottom of the Ohio River."

"We saw the fire and we heard the explosion," said the Major. "We knew that your daring expedition had succeeded, but we feared that your party would never be able to reach the fort again."

"We are here, however, thanks to the assistance of somebody," said Henry, "and nobody is hurt badly except Tom Wilmore there."

"An' I ain't hurt so bad, neither," said Tom shame-facedly. "Things did git kinder dark down thar, but I'm all right now, ready for what may happen to be needed."

A few scattering shots were fired by the Indians in the woods at the foot of the bluff, and a few more from canoes on the river, but the garrison did not take the trouble to reply. Henry was quite sure that the Indians would not remain in the brush on the cliff, as the morning would find them, if there, in an extremely dangerous position, and, deeply content with the night's work, one of the best that he had ever done, he sought sleep in the log house which had been assigned to him.

It was a little one-roomed cabin with a bed of buffalo robes and bearskins, upon which the boy sank exhausted. He had made sure, before withdrawing, that Tom Wilmore was receiving the proper attention, and hence he had little upon his mind now. He could enjoy their triumph in its full measure, and he ran back rapidly over incidents of their daring trip. Everything was almost as vivid as if it were occurring again, and he could account for detail after detail in its logical sequence until he came to the two gunshots that had saved them. Who had fired the bullets? In any event, it was evident that they had effective friends outside the walls, and while he was still wondering about them he fell asleep.

The siege the next day was desultory. There were occasional shots from the forest and the river, but the far-reaching cannon were gone, and the garrison paid little attention to rifle bullets that fell short. Moreover, they were all—men, women and children—full of courage. The exploit of the six in blowing up the flatboat and sending the cannon to the bottom of the river seemed to them a proof that they could do anything and defeat any attempt upon Fort Prescott.

But Henry and Major Braithwaite in the cupola of the blockhouse once more looked southward over the surface of the Ohio and wondered why the fleet did not come. Henry, with the coming of the day, felt new misgivings. The Indians, with the whole forest to feed them and freedom to go and come as they pleased—vast advantages—would persist in the siege. Timmendiquas would keep them to it, and he might also be holding back the fleet. White Lightning was a general and he would use his forces to the best advantage. After a last vain look through the glasses down the river, he took another resolve.

"I'm going out again to-night, Major," he said. "I'm going to hasten the fleet."

"We can ill spare you, my lad," said the Major, putting an affectionate hand upon his shoulder, "but perhaps it is best that you should go. You saved us once, and it may be that you will save us twice. I'll not say anything about your going to the people in general. They think you bring good fortune, and it might discourage them to know that you are gone."

It was night, and only Major Braithwaite and Seth Cole saw Henry leave Fort Prescott.

"I'll be back in a few days, Major," said the boy, "and I'll bring help."

"You've given us great help already, young sir," said Major Braithwaite. "How, in the name of Neptune, we can ever thank you sufficiently, I don't know."

"I'm thinkin' we do owe you a lot," said Seth Cole tersely.

The boy smiled in the dark as he shook their hands. He was not foolish to conceal from himself that he liked their praise, but he tried to disclaim credit.

"I was merely a little luckier than my comrades," he said, "but don't you let them surprise you, Major. Keep a good watch. Since those cannon were blown up and sunk, you can hold them."

"We'll do it or, in the name of Neptune, we'll die trying," said Major Braithwaite.

"I'm thinkin' we kin do it," said Seth Cole.

Then Henry was over the palisade and gone, slipping away so quietly that Major Braithwaite was startled. The boy was there, and then he wasn't.

Henry dropped over the wall on the side next to the river, which he knew to be the safest way of departure because the least guarded. Twenty or thirty yards from the fort he lay among the bushes and listened. He was full of confidence and eager for his task. Rest and sleep had restored all his strength. He had his fine rifle, a renewed supply of ammunition, and had no fear of either the wilderness or the darkness.

He crept down through the bushes much nearer to the bank, and he saw a half dozen Indian canoes moving slowly up and down the river not far from the shore. They were patrols. The warriors did not intend to be surprised by another dash from the fort. Henry indulged himself in silent laughter. His comrades and he had certainly put a spoke in the savage wheel.

He watched the boats a few moments and in one of them he saw two white faces that he recognized. They belonged to Braxton Wyatt and Blackstaffe. Again Henry laughed silently. He remembered the look on Braxton Wyatt's face when he threw him into the Ohio. But Wyatt deserved much more than to be hurled into muddy water, and the villain, Blackstaffe, was worse because he was older, knew more, and had done more crime. Henry raised his rifle a little. From the point where he lay he might reach Blackstaffe with a bullet, but he could not do it. He could not shoot a man from ambush.

He moved carefully along the side of the cliff down the river. It was steep footing, but it would be perhaps impossible to pass anywhere else, and he proceeded with slowness, lest he set a pebble rolling or make the bushes rattle. He reached the place where they had scrambled ashore after burning the flatboat and he paused there a moment. His mind returned to the two mysterious shots that had saved them. Could he have been mistaken in his surmise, and could it have been Shif'less Sol and Tom Ross or perhaps Long Jim who had fired the timely bullets?

He was not one to spend his time in guesses that could not be answered, and he resumed his advance, increasing his speed as the cliff became less precipitous. It was an average night, not a black protecting one, and he knew that he must practice great caution. He intended when further down to swim the river, but it was not yet safe to expose himself there, and he clung to the southern bank.

He soon had proof that all his caution was needed. He heard a soft footstep and quietly sank down in the bushes. A Miami sentinel passed within twenty feet of him, and the boy did not rise again until he was out of sight. Twenty yards further he saw another, and then the glow of lights came through the trees. He knew it to be an Indian camp fire, although the warriors themselves were hidden from him by a swell of the earth. But he felt an intense desire to see this fire, or rather those about it. It was a legitimate wish, as any information that he might obtain would be valuable for the return—and he intended to return.

He crept to a point near the crest of the swell, and then he lay very close, glad that the bushes there were so thick and that they hid him so well. Six men were coming and he recognized them. Two were white, Girty and Blackstaffe, and there were Yellow Panther, Red Eagle, Captain Pipe, the Delaware, and White Lightning, the great Timmendiquas of the Wyandots. They were talking in the Shawnee tongue, which he understood well, and despite all his experience and self-control, a tremor shook him.

They stopped near him and continued their conversation. Every word that they said reached the listener in the bush.

"The place was warned, as Ware said. There's no doubt of it," said Girty viciously, nodding toward the hill on which stood Fort Prescott. "His boast was true. Braxton Wyatt knows him. He was tossed by him into twenty feet of the Ohio. It must have been worth seeing."

Girty laughed. He could take a malignant pleasure in the misfortune of an ally. Henry also saw the white teeth of Timmendiquas gleam as his lips curved into a smile. But in him the appeal was to a sense of humor, not to venom. He seemed to have little malice in his nature.

"It is so," said Timmendiquas in Shawnee. "It was certainly the one called Ware, a bold youth, and powerful. It was wonderful the way in which he broke through our lines at the running of the gantlet and escaped. He must be a favorite of Manitou."

"Favorite of Manitou! It was his arms and legs that got him away," snarled Girty.

His tone was insolent, domineering, and the dark eyes of Timmendiquas were turned upon him.

"I said he was a favorite of Manitou," he said, and his words were edged with steel. "Our friend, Girty, thinks so, too."

His hand slipped down toward the handle of his tomahawk, but it was the eye more than the hand that made the soul of Girty quail.

"It must be as you say, Timmendiquas," he replied, smoothly. "He surely seemed to have been helped by some great power, but it's been a bad thing for us. If he hadn't come, we could have taken Fort Prescott with our first rush. Then with our cannon on the hill we could have stopped this fleet which is coming."

"I have heard that in the far South this fleet beat another fleet which had cannon," said Timmendiquas.

"Yes," said Girty. "Braxton Wyatt was there and saw it done. Red men and white were allied, and they had a ship of their own, but it was blown up in the battle.

But here our cannon would have been on a hill. It is a long way to Canada and we cannot send there for more."

"We can win without cannon," said White Lightning with dignity. "Do you think that all the nations and all the chiefs of the great valley are assembling here merely for failure? Have we not already held back the white man's fleet?"

"We've certainly held it for a few days," replied Girty, "but we've not taken Fort Prescott."

"We will take it," said Timmendiquas.

Henry listened with the greatest eagerness. He did not wish to miss a word. Now he understood why the fleet had not come. It had been delayed in some manner, probably by rifle fire at narrow portions of the river, and it would be the tactics of Timmendiquas to beat it and the fort separately. It would be his task to bring them together and defeat Timmendiquas instead. Yet he felt all his old admiration and liking for the great young chief of the Wyandots. The other chiefs were no mean figures, but he towered above them all, and he had the look of a king, a king by nature, not by birth.

Henry hoped that they would stay and talk longer, that he might hear more of their plans, but they walked away toward the camp fire, where he could not follow, and, rising from the bushes, he passed swiftly between the fire and the river, pursuing his journey down stream. He saw two more Indian sentinels, but they did not see him, and when he looked back the flare of the camp fire was gone.

Two miles below the fort the river curved. No watching canoe would be likely to be there, and Henry thought it would be a good place to swim the river. He was about to prepare himself for his task, when by the moonlight, which was now clear, he saw the print of footsteps in the soft earth near the shore. There was a trail evidently made by two men. It ran over the soft earth twenty feet, perhaps, and was then lost among the bushes.

He examined the footsteps carefully and he was sure that they were made by white men and within the hour. He crouched among the bushes and uttered a faint, whining cry like the suppressed howl of a wolf. It was a cry literally sent into the dark, but he took the chance. A similar cry came back from a point not very far away, and he moved toward it. He heard a light rustle among the bushes and leaves and he stopped, lying down in order that he might be hidden and, at the same time, watch.

Henry was quite convinced that those who made the footprints had also made the noise, and he was still sure that they were white men. They might be renegades, but he did not think so. Renegades were few in number, and they were likely at such a time to stay closely in the Indian camp. He was puzzled for a little while how to act. He might stalk these strangers and they might stalk him in the darkness for hours without either side ascertaining a single fact concerning the identity of the other. He decided upon a bold policy and called loudly: "Who is there?"

123

His was unmistakably a white voice, the voice of a white Anglo-Saxon, and back came the reply in the same good English of the white man: "Who are you?"

"A friend from the Kentucky settlements," replied Henry, and stood up. Two figures, also, rose from the brush, and after a few moments' inspection advanced.

Henry could scarcely restrain a cry of pleasure as he recognized the men. They were Daniel Boone and Simon Kenton. Boone laughed in his quiet, low way as they came forward.

"About to take another night swim in the Ohio, Indians or no Indians?" he said.

Henry understood at once. It was these two who had saved them; the timely bullets had come from the rifles of these famous borderers.

"We owe our lives to you and Mr. Kenton, Mr. Boone," he said, grasping the hand that Daniel Boone held out to him.

Boone laughed again in his quiet fashion. No sound came from his lips, but his face quivered with mirth.

"You certainly were a good swimmer," he said. "I never saw a fellow walk through the water faster in my life."

"We had every reason to swim fast," said Henry with a smile.

"Don't say anything more about our savin' you," said Daniel Boone. "It's what anybody else in our place ought to have done an' would have done. We've been hangin' around the fort havin' worned another place first, waitin' for a chance to help. Some hunters are comin' up from the South and we expect to join them to-morrow, but we won't be strong enough to do much."

"All the tribes are here, are they not?" asked Henry.

"Bands from 'em all are here. They must have two or three thousand warriors scattered around Fort Prescott. I reckon I can tell you where most of the big bands are placed."

The three sat down on the ground and talked low. Henry felt greatly encouraged by the presence of these two men, so skillful and so renowned. Watchful sentinels, but little could evade them, and they would be a source of valuable strength to fort and fleet alike.

"You saw Timmendiquas?" said Boone.

"Yes, he is here," said Henry, "and he is leading the attack."

"Then our people have got to look out," said Boone emphatically. "We'll watch around here the best way we can while you go on with what you're tryin' to do."

He held out his hand again as Henry rose to depart. For a man who lived a life of constant danger and who had passed through so many great adventures, he had a singularly gentle and winning manner. Henry's admiration and respect were mingled with a deep liking. He would have referred again to the saving of his life, but he knew that the great borderer would not like it.

"Good-by, Mr. Boone," he said, and their hands met in a hearty clasp. He and Kenton also bade farewell in the same friendly manner, and then Henry went down to the river.

"We'll watch again," said Boone, laughing in his dry way; "you can't tell when you'll need us."

CHAPTER XVI

THE RETURN TRAIL

Henry, with the aid of Boone and Kenton, rolled the trunk of a small fallen tree to the river. Then he took off his clothes, made them and his arms and ammunition into a bundle, which he put on the log, said good-by to the two men, and launched himself and his fortunes once more upon the Ohio. He pushed the log before him, taking care to keep it steady, and swam easily with one hand.

Fifty yards back he looked out and saw the two hunters standing on the bank, leaning on the muzzles of their long rifles. They were watching him and he waved his free hand in salute. Boone and Kenton took off their raccoon skin caps in reply. He did not look back again until he was nearly to the northern shore, and then they were gone.

He reached the bank without obstruction, moored his log among some bushes, and, when he was dry, dressed again. Then he went down stream along the shore for several miles, keeping a watch for landmarks that he had seen before. It was a difficult task in the night, and after an hour he abandoned it. Finding a snug place among the bushes, he lay down there and slept until dawn. Then he renewed his search.

Henry, at present, was not thinking much of the fleet. His mind was turning to his faithful comrades who had dropped one by one on the way. Both fleet and fort could wait a while. So far as he was concerned, they must wait. He roved now through the bushes and along the water's edge, looking always for something. It was a familiar place that he sought, one that might have been seen briefly, but, nevertheless, vividly, one that he could not forget. He came at last to the spot where he and Shif'less Sol had sprung into the water. Just there under the bank the shiftless one had drifted away, while he swam on, drawing the pursuit after him. It had been only a glimpse in the dusk of the night, but he was absolutely sure of the place, and as he continued along the bank he examined every foot of it minutely.

Henry did not expect to find any traces of footsteps after so many days, but the bank for some distance was high and steep. It would not be easy to emerge from the river there, but he felt sure that Shif'less Sol had left it—if he survived—at the first convenient point.

In about three hundred yards he came to a dip in the high bank, a gentle slope upon which a man could wade ashore. Shif'less Sol, wounded and drifting with the current, would certainly reach this place and use it. Henry, without hesitation, turned aside into the woods and began to look for a trail or a sign of any kind that would point a way. Twenty yards from the landing he found a dark stain on an oak tree, a little higher than a man's waist.

"Shif'less Sol," he murmured. "He was wounded and he leaned here against this tree to rest after he came from the river. Now, which way did he go?"

He tried to make a reckoning of the point at which Tom Ross had been compelled to turn aside, and he reckoned that it lay northwest. It seemed likely to him that Shif'less Sol, if he could travel at all, would go in the direction or supposed direction of Tom Ross, and Henry went northwestward for about a mile before stopping, following a narrow little valley, leading back from the river and not well wooded. The traveling was easy here, and easy traveling was what a wounded man would certainly seek. His stop was made because he had come to a brook, a clear little stream that flowed somewhere into the Ohio.

Henry again used his reasoning faculties first, and his powers of observation afterward. Wounds made men hot and thirsty, and hot and thirsty men would drink cool water at the first chance. He got down on his knees and examined the grass minutely up and down the brook on both banks. He was not looking for footprints. He knew that time would have effaced them here as it had done back by the river. He was searching instead for a dim spot, yellowish red, somber and ugly.

He came presently to the place, larger and more somber than he had anticipated. "Here is where Sol knelt down to drink," he murmured, "and his blood flowed upon the grass while he drank. Poor old Sol!" He was afraid that Sol had been steadily growing weaker and weaker, and he dreaded lest he should soon find a dark, still object among the bushes.

A hundred yards further he found something else that his eyes easily read. The ground had been soft when a man passed and, hardening later, had preserved the footsteps. The trail lay before him, clear and distinct for a distance of about a rod, but it was that of a staggering man. A novice even could have seen it. The line zigzagged, and the footprints themselves were at irregular distances. "Poor old Sol," Henry murmured again. Just beyond the soft ground he found another of the somber splotches, and his heart sank. No one could stand a perpetual loss of blood, and for a dark moment or two Henry was sure that Shif'less Sol had succumbed. Then his natural hopefulness reasserted itself. Shif'less Sol was tough, enduring, the bravest of the brave. It seemed to Henry's youthful mind that his lion-hearted comrade could not be killed.

He continued his advance, examining the ground carefully everywhere, and following that which offered the least obstacle to a wounded and weak man. He saw before him a mass of grass, high and inviting, and when he looked in the center of it he found what he hoped, but not what he dreaded. Some one had lain

126

down there and had rested a long time or slept, perhaps both, and then had been able to rise again and go on.

The crushed grass showed plainly the imprint of the man's body, and the somber stains were on either side of the impression. But the grass had not been threshed about. The man, when he lay there, had scarcely moved. Henry was in doubt what inference to draw. It was certain that Shif'less Sol had not been feverish, or he might have lain in utter exhaustion.

As long as the grass lasted, its condition, broken or swept aside, showed the trail, but when he came into the woods again it was lost. There was no grass here and the ground was too hard. Nor did the lie of the land itself offer any hint of Shif'less Sol's progress. It was all level and one direction was no more inviting than another. Henry paused, at a loss, but as he looked around his eyes caught a gleam of white. It came from a spot on a hickory tree where the bark had been deftly chipped away with a hatchet or a tomahawk, leaving the white body of the tree, exposed for two or three square inches. Henry read it as clearly as if it had been print. In fact, it was print to him, and he knew that it had been so intended. Shif'less Sol had felt sure that Henry would come back after his friend, and this was his sign of the road. Shif'less Sol knew, too, that the attention of the tribes would be concentrated upon the fort and the fleet, and the warriors would not be hunting at such a time for a single atom like himself.

Henry found a second chipped tree, a third, and then a fourth. The four made a line pointing northwestward, but more west than north. He was quite sure now of the general direction that he must pursue, and he advanced, the chipped trail leading deeper and deeper into a great forest. At the crossing of another brook he looked for the somber sign, but it was not there. Instead, a short distance farther on, he found some tiny fragments of buckskin, evidently cut into such shape with a sharp knife. Near them were several of the reddish stains, but much smaller than any he had seen before.

It was again a book of open print to Henry, and now he felt a surge of joyous feeling. Shif'less Sol had washed his wound at the brook back there and he had stopped here to bind it up with portions of his buckskin clothing, cutting the bandage with his sharp knife. The act showed, so Henry believed, that he was gaining in strength, and when he next saw a chipped tree he observed the mark carefully. It was about the same in width and length, but it was much deeper than usual. A piece of the living wood had gone with the bark.

Henry smiled. His strong imagination reproduced the scene. There was Shif'less Sol standing erect and comparatively strong for the first time since the last night of the flight. He had raised his tomahawk, and then, in the pride of his strength, had sunk it four times into the tree, cutting out the thick chip. Henry murmured something again. It was not now "Poor old Sol," it was "Good old Sol."

He lost the trail at the end of another mile, but after some searching found it again in another chipped tree, and then another close by. It still pointed in a northwesterly direction, more west than north, and Henry hence was sure that he could never lose it long. Soon he came upon a little heap of ashes and dead coals with feathers and bones lying about. The feathers were those of the wild turkey, and this chapter of the book was so plain that none could mistake it. Sol had shot a wild turkey, and here he had cooked it and eaten of it. His fever had gone down or he would have had no appetite. Undoubtedly he was growing much stronger.

He traveled several miles further without seeing anything unusual, and then he came abruptly out of the deep forest upon a tiny lake, a genuine jewel of a little lake. It was not more than a half of a mile long, perhaps a hundred and fifty yards across, and its deep waters were very clear and beautiful.

The chipped trail—the last tree was not more than twenty feet back—pointed straight to the middle of this lake and Henry was puzzled. His own shore was low, but the far one was high and rocky.

Henry was puzzled. He could not divine what had been in Shif'less Sol's mind, and, a tall erect figure, rifle on shoulder, he stared at the lake. Across the water came a mellow, cheerful hail: "Henry! Oh-h-h, Henry!"

Henry looked up—he had recognized instantly the voice of Shif'less Sol, and there he was, standing on the bluff of the far shore. "Swim over!" he called, "and visit me in my house!" Henry looked down toward the end of the lake. It would be a half mile walk around it, and he decided in favor of swimming. Again he made his clothes and arms into a bundle, and in three or four minutes was at the other side of the lake.

As he came to the cliff Shif'less Sol extended a helping hand, but Henry, noticing that he was pale and thin, did not take it until he had sprung lightly upon the rocks. Then he took it in a mighty clasp that the shiftless one returned as far as his strength would permit.

"I'm pow'ful glad to see you, Henry," said Shif'less Sol, "but I don't think you look respeckable without some clothes aroun' you. So put 'em on, an' I'll invite you into my house."

"It's fine to see you again, Sol! Alive and well!" exclaimed Henry joyfully.

"Wa'al, I'm alive," said Shif'less Sol, "but I ain't what you would sca'cely call well. A bullet went clean through my side, and that's a thing you can't overlook just at the time. I ain't fit yet for runnin' races with Injuns, or wrastlin' with b'ars, but I've got a good appetite an' I'm right fond o' sleep. I reckon I'm what you'd call a mighty interestin' invalid."

"Invalid or not, you're the same old Sol," said Henry, who had finished dressing. "Now show me to this house of yours."

"I can't say rightly that it's the mansion o' a king," said Shif'less Sol solemnly. "A lot o' the furniture hasn't come, an' all the servants happen to be away at this minute. Guess I'll have to show you 'roun' the place myself."

"Go ahead; you're the best of guides," said Henry, delighted to be with his old comrade again.

The shiftless one, still going rather weakly, led the way a few steps up the almost precipitous face of the rock toward some bushes growing in the crevices. Then he disappeared. Henry gazed in amazement, but Shif'less Sol's mellow laugh came back.

"Walk right in," he said. "This is my house."

Henry parted the bushes with his hand and stepped into a deep alcove of the rock running back four or five feet, with a height of about five feet. The entrance was completely hidden by bushes.

"Now, ain't this snug?" exclaimed Shif'less Sol, turning a glowing face upon Henry, "an' think o' my luck in findin' it jest when I needed it most. Thar ain't a better nateral house in all the west."

It was certainly a snug niche. The floor was dry and covered with leaves, some pieces of wood lay in a corner, on a natural shelf was the dressed body of a wild turkey, and near the entrance was a heap of ashes and dead coals showing where a fire had been.

"It is a good place," said Henry emphatically, "and you certainly had wonderful luck in finding it when you did. How did it come about, Sol?"

"I call it Fisherman's Home," returned the shiftless one, "because me that used to be a hunter, scout, explorer an' Injun-fighter, has to fish fur a while fur a livin'. When I wuz runnin' away from the warriors, with my side an' my feelin's hurtin' me, I come to this lake. I knowed that jest ez soon ez you got the chance, providin' you wuz still livin', you'd foller to find me, an' so I blazed the trail. But when I got here it set me to thinkin'. I saw the high bank on this side, all rocks an' bushes. I reckoned I could come over here an' hide among 'em an' still see anybody who followed my trail down to the other side. I wuz strong enough by that time to swim across, an' I done it. Then when I wuz lookin' among the rocks an' bushes fur a restin' place, I jest stumbled upon this bee-yu-ti-ful mansion. It ain't furnished much yet, ez I told you, but I've sent an order to Philadelphy, an' I'm expectin' a lot o' gor-gee-yus things in a couple o' years."

"And you live by fishing, you say?"

"Mainly. You remember we all agreed a long time ago always to carry fishin' lines an' hooks, ez we might need 'em, an' need 'em pow'ful bad any time. It looked purty dang'rous to shoot off a gun with warriors so near, although I did bring down wild turkeys twice in the night. But mostly I've set here on the ledge with my bee-yu-ti-ful figger hid by the bushes, but with my line an' hook in the water."

"Is the fishing good?"

"Too good. I don't s'pose the fish in Hyde Lake—that's what I've named it—ever saw a hook before, an' they've been so full o' curiosity they jest make my arm ache. It's purty hard on a lazy man like me to hev to pull in a six or seven pound bass when you ain't rested more'n half a minute from pullin' in another o' the

129

same kind. I tell you, they kep' me busy, Henry, when what I wuz needin' wuz rest."

Henry smiled.

"Were you fishin' when you saw me?" he asked.

"I shorely wuz. I'm mostly fishin', an' when I'm fishin' I mostly keep my eyes turned that way. I've been sayin' to myself right along for the last two or three days: 'Henry will be along purty soon now. He shorely will. When he comes, he'll follow that chipped trail o' mine right down to the edge o' the water. Then he'll stan' thar wondering an' while he's standin' and wondering I'll give him an invite to come over to my bee-yu-ti-ful mansion,' and, shore enough, that's jest what happened."

Henry sat down on a heap of leaves and leaned luxuriously against the wall.

"You cook at night?" he said.

"O' course, and I always pick a mighty dark hour. Hyde Lake, desarvin' its name, is full o' eight or ten kinds o' fine fish, an' here are some layin' under the leaves that I cooked last night. I eat pow'ful often myself. Livin' such a lazy life here, I've growed to be what Paul calls a eppycure. Remember them tales he used to tell about the old Romans an' Rooshians an' Arabiyuns and Babylonians that got so fine they et hummin' birds' tongues an' sech like, an' then the flood wuz sent to drown 'em all out 'cause they wuzn't fitten to live. I don't think hummin' birds' tongues a sustainin' kind o' diet, anyway."

"I remember the tales, but not just that way, Sol. However, it doesn't matter."

"Hev a fish, Henry. You've traveled fur, an' I made up my mind from the fust that I'd offer refreshment an' the fat o' the water to anybody comin' to my house. We kin cook the turkey to-night, an' then eat him, too."

He handed to Henry a fine specimen of lake trout, admirably broiled, and the boy ate hungrily. Shif'less Sol took another of the same kind and ate, also. Henry, from his reclining position, could see through the screen of leaves. The surface of the little lake was silver, rippling lightly under the gentle wind, and beyond was the green wall of the forest. He felt a great peace. He was rested and soothed, both body and mind. The shiftless one, too, felt a deep content, although he had always been sure that Henry would come.

For nearly a quarter of an hour neither spoke again, and Henry could hear the faint lapping of the water on the rocks below. It was the shiftless one who at last broke the silence.

"You reached Fort Prescott, o' course?" he asked.

"Yes," replied Henry. "I got in, and I warned them in time. We beat off a land attack, and then they advanced on us by the river."

"What could canoes do against a fort on a hill?"

"They had cannon brought from Canada."

"Cannon! Then I s'pose they battered the fort down with 'em, an' you're all that's left."

"No, they didn't. They might have done it, but they lost their cannon."

"Lost 'em! How could that happen?"

"The boat carrying them was blown up, and the cannon with it."

The shiftless one looked at Henry, and the boy grew uncomfortable, blushing through his tan. Shif'less Sol laughed.

"Ef them cannon wuz blowed up—an' they shorely wuz ef you say so," he said, "it's mighty likely that you, Henry Ware, had a lot to do with it. Now, don't be bashful. Jest up an' tell me the hull tale, or I'll drag it out o' you."

Henry, reluctantly and minimizing his part as much as he could, told the story of the blowing up of the flatboat and the cannon. Shif'less Sol was hugely delighted.

"Them shore wuz lively doin's," he said. "Wish I'd been thar. I'll always be sorry I missed it. An' at the last you wuz saved by Dan'l Boone an' Simon Kenton. Them are shorely great men, Henry. I ain't ever heard o' any that could beat 'em, not even in Paul's tales. I reckin Dan'l Boone and Simon Kenton kin do things that them Carthaginians, Alexander an' Hannibal an' Cæsar an' Charley-mane, couldn't even get started on."

"They certainly know some things that those men didn't."

"More'n some. They know a pow'ful lot more. I reckon, Henry, that Dan'l Boone is the greatest man the world has yet seed."

Henry said nothing. The shiftless one's simple admiration and faith appealed to him. They rested a while longer, and then Henry asked:

"Sol, do you think that we can find Tom Ross?"

"Ef he's alive, we kin. We jest got to."

"I knew that would be your answer. Do you think you will be strong enough to start in the morning?"

"I've been weak, Henry, but I'm gainin' now mighty fast. I didn't suffer much 'cept loss o' blood, an' me bein' so healthy, I'm making gallons o' new first-class blood every day. Yes, Henry, I think I kin start after Tom to-morrow mornin'."

"Then we'll find him if he's alive, but we'll spend the time until then in quiet here."

"'Ceptin' that I'm boun' to cook my turkey to-night."

Henry presently climbed to the top of the bank, a distance of eight or ten feet above the hollow, but precipitous. It was probably this steepness that had prevented any large wild animal from using the place as a lair. It would also make attack by Indians, should any come, extremely difficult, but Henry did not anticipate any danger from them now, as their attention was centered on the fort and the fleet.

Shif'less Sol followed him up the cliff, and when they stood on the hill Henry noticed again the thinness of his comrade. But the color was returning to his cheeks, and his eye had regained the alert, jaunty look of old. Henry calculated that in a week Shif'less Sol would be nearly as strong as ever. The shiftless one saw his measuring look, and understood it.

"My time ez a fisherman is over," he said. "I'll be a hunter, an' explorer, an' fighter of warriors ag'in. But I think, Henry, we ought to remember the hollow, an' keep it ez one o' them places Paul calls inns. Ef we wuz ever 'roun' here ag'in, we might want to drop in an' rest a while."

Henry agreed with him, and examined the country for a distance of about a half mile. He did not see any evidence of warriors, but he knew they could not be far away and he returned to the hollow, where he and Shif'less Sol spent the rest of the day, each lying upon a bed of leaves and gazing through the screen of bushes toward the shimmering surface of the lake. Nor did they say much, only a word or two now and then.

Henry felt a great sense of luxury. He did not realize fully until now all that he had been through recently, the mighty strain that had been put upon his nervous organization, and the absolute freedom from any sort of effort, whether mental or physical, was precious to him.

It was almost the twilight hour when they heard the faint whirring of wings. Henry looked up through half-closed eyes. A cloud of wild ducks, hundreds of them, settled down upon the lake.

"I'd like to take a shot at them," he said. "There's nothing better than a wild duck cooked as Jim Hart can cook it."

"But I wouldn't shoot jest now if I were you," said the shiftless one, "'cause somebody else is ahead of you."

Henry came at once from his dreamy state and rose to a sitting position. Two Indians were walking down to the edge of the lake. He saw them clearly through the curtain of bushes and leaves. They held guns in their hands, and their eyes were on the ducks, which fairly blackened a portion of the lake's surface.

"They're lookin' fur food, not scalps," whispered the shiftless one. "Tain't likely they'll see my blazed tree, specially since dark is comin' on."

The two Indians fired into the cloud of ducks, then waded in and took at least a dozen dead ones. The foolish ducks flew further up the lake and settled down again, where a further slaughter was committed. Then the Indians, loaded with the spoil, went away.

"Them warriors had shotguns," said Shif'less Sol, "an' they were out huntin' fur some big war party, most likely, one o' them that's watchin' the fort. But they ain't dreamin' that fellers like you and me are aroun' here, Henry."

The night dropped down like a great black mask over the face of the world, and Shif'less Sol announced that he was going to cook his turkey.

"I'm tired o' fish," he said, "fish fur breakfast, fish fur dinner, an' fish fur supper. Ef it keeps on this way, I'll soon be covered with scales, my blood will be cold, an' I'll die ef I'm left five minutes on dry land. Don't say a word, Henry, I'm goin' to cook that turkey ef I lose my scalp."

Henry did not say anything. He thought there was little danger, the night was so dark, and Sol broiled his bird to a turn over smothered coals. When it was done he took it up by the leg and held it out admiringly.

"I don't believe Jim Hart hisself could beat that," he said, "an' Jim is shorely a pow'ful good cook, I guess about the best the world has ever seed. Don't you think, Henry, that ef Jim Hart had been thar to cook wild turkey an' venison an' buffler meat for all them old Romans an' Egyptians, an' sech like, with the cur'ous appetites, always lookin' fur new dishes, they'd have rested satisfied, an' wouldn't hev decayed down to nothin'? 'Pears strange to me why they'd keep on lookin' roun' fur hummin' bird tongues an' them other queer things when they could have had nice cow buffler steak every day o' thar lives."

The two ate the turkey between them, and Shif'less Sol, thumping his chest, said:

"Now, let us set forth. It is Solomon Hyde hisself ag'in, an' he feels fit fur any task."

They started about ten o'clock, curved around the lake, and traveled in a general northwesterly course. Henry went slowly at first, but when he noticed that Shif'less Sol was breathing easily and regularly, he increased the pace somewhat.

"What's your opinion about the place where we'll find Tom, if we find him at all?" he asked.

"Ef we find Tom Ross, it'll be mighty close to the place whar we left him. Tom never wastes any words, an' he ain't goin' to waste any steps, either. Are you shore we come along this way, Henry? I wuz runnin' so pow'ful fast I only hit the tops o' the hills ez I passed."

"Yes, this is the place," said Henry, looking carefully at hills, gullies, rocks, and trees, "and it was certainly somewhere near here that Tom was forced to turn aside."

"Then we'll find him close by, livin' or dead," said Shif'less Sol succinctly.

"But how to do it?" said Henry.

"Yes, how?" said Sol.

They began a careful search, radiating continually in a wider circle, but the night that hid them from the warriors also hid all signs of Tom Ross.

"Tom's the kind o' feller who wouldn't make the least bit o' noise," said Shif'less Sol, "an' I'm thinkin' we've got to make a noise ourselves, an' let him hear it."

"What kind of a noise?"

"We might try our old signal, the call that we've so often made to one another."

133

"Yes," said Henry, "that is what we must do."

CHAPTER XVII

PICKING UP THE STRANDS

Henry sat down in the underbrush, and Shif'less Sol sat down close to him. Their figures were hidden by the darkness and the bushes.

"Do your best, Henry," said the shiftless one.

Henry opened his mouth and emitted a long, mournful cry, so like that of the owl that Shif'less Sol, at a little distance, could not have told the difference. After a silence of a few seconds he repeated the cry, to show that they were two.

"Don't see why you can't let a tired and sick man sleep, 'specially when he needs it so bad," said a voice so near them that both started up in astonishment.

It was the voice of Tom Ross, as they knew when the very first words were uttered, and they saw him standing erect in a little clump of trees and looking reproachfully at them. It was night, and Tom was fifty yards away, but they would have known his figure and attitude anywhere. They rushed to him, each seized a hand and shook it.

"Don't shake too hard," said Tom. "Jest gittin' well uv a pow'ful bad headache."

They saw that a rude bandage encircled his head, and was tied tightly.

"Injun bullet hit my skull," said Tom briefly. "Couldn't git in, so it went 'round an' come out on the other side. Made my head ache most a week. Been campin' here till you'd come."

"Where have you been camping?" asked Henry.

"Over thar in the bushes," replied Tom, and he led the way to a very thick clump at the side of a huge, up-thrust root of an oak. Sheltered partly by the bushes and partly by the big root had been the lair of some wild animal that Tom had dispossessed. But he had relined it first with dry leaves and little boughs, turning it into a man's nest.

"Found it the night I dropped out," said Tom. "Couldn't be partickler then. Had to lay down somewhar. Remember, after I'd been here an hour or two, some big yeller animal with yellerish-green eyes come starin' in at me through the bushes, angry and reproachful-like. Said to me plain as day: 'You've took my house. Git out.' Felt like a robber, I did, slippin' into another man's bed while he wuz away, an' takin' up all the room. But I jest had to hold on, me feelin' pow'ful bad. I p'inted my rifle at him, looked down the sights and said: 'Git.' He must have knowed what a rifle meant, 'cause git he did, an' he ain't ever come back to claim his mansion. Then, jest havin' strength enough left to bind up my head, I fell over

134

into a sleep, an' I reckon I slep' 'bout three days an' three nights, 'cause I ain't got any idea how much time hez passed sence I left you that night, Henry.

"But I felt better after my long sleep, though still weak an' wobbly. I'd hev made myself some herb tea, but I wuz beginnin' to git tre-men-jeous-ly hungry. Managed to watch at a spring not far from here until a deer came down to drink one night, an' I shot him. Been livin' on deer meat since then, an' waitin' fur my headache to go away. Expected you an' Sol or one uv you would come fur me."

Tom stopped abruptly and took a mighty breath. He did not make so long a speech more than once a year, and he felt mentally exhausted.

"Well, we've found you, Tom," said Henry joyfully.

"Ef you hadn't come, I'd have started myself in a day or two to find *you*," said Ross.

"I don't wonder that Injun bullet turned aside, when it run ag'in Tom Ross' skull," said the shiftless one. "That shorely wuz a smart bullet. It knowed it wuzn't worth while to beat its head ag'in a rock."

"Don't be impydent, Sol," said Tom with a quiet chuckle. "Now that we three are together ag'in, I s'pose the next thing fur us to do is to track Jim Hart to his hidin' place."

"That comes next," said Henry.

It did not occur to any of the three that Long Jim might have been slain. Their belief in their own skill, endurance, and good fortune, was so great that they did not reckon on anything more than a wound, fever, and exhaustion.

"I believe we'd better stop here to-night," said Shif'less Sol. "Tom can widen his den, and all three of us kin sleep in it."

Henry and Tom agreed. Silent Tom, although he said little, was greatly rejoiced over the coming of his comrades, and he brought from the fork of a tree his store of deer meat, of which they ate. Then, in accord with the shiftless one's suggestion, they widened the den, and the three slept there, turns being taken at the watch.

Henry had the last turn, and it was about two o'clock in the morning when he was awakened for it. Shif'less Sol, who had awakened him, instantly fell asleep, and Henry sat at the edge of the lair, his rifle across his knees, and his eyes turned up to the great stars, which were twinkling in a magnificent blue sky.

Henry had imbibed much of the Indian lore and belief. It was inevitable where human beings were so few, and the skies and the forest were so immense, that he should feel the greatness of nature and draw his symbols from it. He wondered in a vague sort of way on which of the bright stars Manitou dwelt, and if on all of them there were hunting grounds like those in which he and his comrades roved.

He watched with his ears, that is, he listened for the sound of anything that

135

might be moving in the forest, but he kept his eyes on the high heavens. His thoughts were solemn, but not at all sad. He could see much in the Indian belief of the happy hunting grounds in which strong, brave warriors would roam forever. It appealed to him as a very wise and wholesome belief, and he asked no better hereafter than to roam such forests himself through eternity with those who were dear to him.

Some clouds gathered in the southwest, and a faint, far rumble came to his ears. "Baimwana (thunder)," he murmured, speaking almost unconsciously in Iroquois, a little of which he had learned long ago. He was sorry. Rain would not be pleasant, particularly for the two who were not yet fully recovered from their wounds. But the thunder did not come again, the clouds passed, and he knew there would be no rain.

A wind, gentle and musical, began to blow. "Wabun (the East Wind)," he murmured. He personified the winds, because it was in his nature to do so, and because the Indians with whom he had dwelt did it. It was this gift of his, based on a powerful imagination, that now made him hear the human voice once more in the wind. It was a low voice, but penetrating, thrilling him in every nerve, and its note was hope. He had heard it before at crises of his life, and its prophecy had not failed to come true. Nor did he believe that it would do so now.

The wind shifted. "Kabibanokka (the North Wind)," he murmured. But the note was unchanged. It was still a voice that brought courage. They would find Jim and Paul, and the fleet and the fort alike would triumph.

He heard, soon, light sounds in the bush, but they were not the footsteps of enemies. He knew it because he had heard them all before. A tawny beast came down through the grass, but halted at a respectful distance. Henry caught a glimpse of one yellow eye, and he felt a sort of amused sorrow for the panther. The rightful owner of this house had been driven out, as Tom Ross confessed, and he was there not far away looking reproachfully at the robbers. Well, he should have his house back on the next night, and perhaps he could then keep it all the rest of his life.

The yellow eye disappeared. The sorrowful and reproachful panther had gone away. The wind shifted, and its odor was fresh with the dawn, which would soon be whitening the east. A troop of deer, led by a splendid stag, passed so close that Henry could see their forms in the dusk. The wind was taking the odor of himself and his comrades away from them, and he watched the dusky file as it passed. Even had the country been clear of Indians, he would not have taken a shot at them, because he had no desire to slay merely for the sake of slaying.

The deer passed. Light sprang up in the east. The white turned to red, the red to gold, and the gold at last became blue. An eagle, in an early search for food, sailed far above Henry's head, outlined—wing, beak and talon—against the blue. The whole world, grass and leaves wet with dew, basked in the morning light, wonderfully fresh and beautiful.

Henry awoke his comrades, who instantly sat up, every trained faculty thoroughly alive.

"All been quiet, Henry?" asked Shif'less Sol.

"Nothing happened," replied the boy, "except that the owner of this house looked in once, called Tom Ross here an infamous robber, and then went away, saying he would have revenge if he had to live a hundred years to get it."

"Ef he's ez dang'rous ez that," said Shif'less Sol, lightly, "I say let's move on right now, an' give him back his gor-gee-yous mansion."

The sense of humor and joy of life had fully returned to the shiftless one. Another night's rest had added wonderfully to his strength, and the coming of Henry and the finding of Tom contributed so much to the uplift of his spirits that he considered himself as good, physically, as ever.

"I'm ready for anything now, from a fight to a foot-race," he said, "but ef choosin' is to be mine, I'd rather hev breakfast. Tom, bring out that deer meat o' yourn."

They quickly disposed of their food and resumed the reverse journey in the path of their former flight. They passed through woods and tiny prairies, crossed little brooks, and kept a sharp watch for landmarks. Henry said at last that they had come to the place where Jim Hart had been forced to turn aside.

"Do you reckon that Jim wuz hit hard?" asked Shif'less Sol.

"I hope not," replied Henry earnestly, "and the chances are all in his favor. Stray bullets in the dark don't often kill."

"I figger," said Tom Ross, "that he waded up this little creek that comes down here, and turns off to the south. It would be the thing that any man would naterally do to hide his trail."

"We'll jest go along it," said Shif'less Sol, "rememberin' that Jim is pow'ful long legged an' ef he took a notion would step out o' the water an' up a cliff ten feet high."

They followed the creek nearly a mile, but did not see any place at which a man would be likely to emerge. It was a swift stream coming down from a mass of high hills, the blue outline of which they saw three or four miles ahead of them.

"It's my belief," said Henry, pointing to the blue hills, "that Jim's in there."

"It's pow'ful likely," said Shif'less Sol. "Injuns tryin' to take a fort an' a fleet ain't likely to bother about a pile o' hills layin' out o' their path. They go fur what they want."

"Best place fur him," said Tom Ross.

They now left the bed of the stream and advanced swiftly toward the hills, which turned from blue to green as they came nearer. They were high and stony, but clothed densely in dark forest. The shiftless one had truly said that Indians on the war path, seeking the greatest prizes that had ever come within their reach, would not bother about a patch of such isolated and difficult country.

137

It was a long walk through the forest, but the day was come, and the air made for briskness and elasticity. They searched occasionally by the side of the brook for a footstep preserved in mud, or any other sign that Long Jim had passed, but they found nothing. Nevertheless, they still felt sure of their original opinion. Jim would have lain in the bush through the night, and to make for the hills when he saw them in the morning was the most natural thing to do.

When they came finally to the hills, they found them exceedingly steep, jagged masses, thrown together in the wildest fashion.

"Ef we don't find Long Jim in here," said Shif'less Sol, "then I'm a mighty bad guesser."

They sought everywhere for a trail but found none, and at last, crossing a sharp crest of rock, they saw before them a little valley completely hidden by cliff and forest from any but the closest observer. They began the descent of the slope, passing among trees and thick bushes, and Henry, who was in the lead, suddenly stopped and, smiling broadly, pointed straight ahead.

"If that isn't the stamp and seal of Long Jim, then I'm blind," he said.

They saw a small snare for rabbits, made by bending over a stout bush, to which was attached a cord of strong deerskin, cut perhaps from Long Jim's clothing. This cord was fastened around a little circle of sticks set in the ground. A little wooden trigger in the center of the circle was baited with the leaves which rabbits love. When Mr. Foolish Rabbit reached over for his favorite food, he sprang the trigger, the noose slipped, caught him around the neck, the released bush flew back with a jerk, and he was quickly choked to death.

"That's Long Jim all over," said Shif'less Sol admiringly. "I kin see him in that buckskin cord, them sticks, an' that noose. Too weak to go huntin', he sets a trap. Oh, he's smart, he is! An' he's been ketchin' somethin', too. See this bit o' rabbit fur."

"Trust Long Jim to get something to eat," said Henry, "and to cook it the best way that ever could be found. We must be coming pretty close to him now."

"Yes, here are signs of his trail," said Tom Ross. "I'd bet my scalp that he's got a dozen uv these snares scattered around through the valley, an' that he's livin' on the fat uv the land without ever firin' a shot. Stop, do you smell that?"

They stopped and sniffed the air inquiringly. A faint, delicate aroma tickled the nostrils of all three. It was soothing and pleasant, and they sniffed again.

"Now, that is Long Jim an' no mistake," whispered Shif'less Sol. "It's shorely his sign."

"Seems to me you're right," Henry whispered back, "but we mustn't make any mistake."

They crept down the slope, among the bushes, with such care that neither could hear either of the other two moving. All the while that enchanting aroma grew stronger. Shif'less Sol, despite his caution, was obliged to raise his nose and take another sniff.

"It's Long Jim! It must be Long Jim! It can't be anything else but Long Jim at work!" he murmured.

After ten minutes of creeping and crawling down the slope, Henry softly pulled aside a thick bush and pointed with a long forefinger.

In a little dip, almost a pit, a long-legged, long-bodied man sat before a rude oven built of stones evidently gathered from the surrounding slopes. Within the oven smoldered coals which gave out so little smoke that it was not discernible above the bushes. On the flat top of the oven strips of rabbit steak were broiling, and from them came the aroma which had been so potent a charm in the nostrils of the three.

The long-legged man sat in Turkish fashion, and his eyes were intent upon his oven and steaks. One hand rested in a rude sling, but the other held a stick with which he now and then poked up the coals. It was obvious that he was interested and absorbed as no other task in the world could interest and absorb him. The soul of an artist was poured into his work. He lingered over every detail, and saw that it was right.

"Now, ain't that old Long Jim through an' through?" whispered Shif'less Sol to Henry. "Did you ever see a feller love cookin' ez he does? It's his gift. He's done clean furgot all about Injuns, the fort, the fleet, us, an' everything except them thar rabbit steaks. Lemme call him back to the world, that good, old, ornery, long-legged, contrary Jim Hart, the best cook on this here roun' rollin' earth o' ours."

"Go ahead," said Henry.

Shif'less Sol raised his rifle and took a long, deliberate aim at Long Jim. Then he called out in a sharp voice:

"Give 'em up!"

Long Jim sprang to his feet in astonishment, and uttered the involuntary question:

"Give up what?"

"Them rabbit steaks," replied the shiftless one, emerging from the bushes, but still covering Long Jim with his rifle. "An' don't you be slow about it, either. What right hev you, Jim Hart, to tickle my nose with sech smells, an' then refuse to give to me the cause o' it? That would be cruelty to animals, it would."

"Sol Hyde! and Henry Ware! and Tom Ross!" exclaimed Long Jim joyfully. "So you hev come at last! But you're late."

They grasped his hand, one by one, and shook his good arm heartily.

"Was that where you caught the bullet?" asked Henry, looking at the bad arm.

Long Jim nodded.

139

"Broke?"

Long Jim shook his head.

"Thought so at first," he replied, "but it ain't. Bruised more'n anything else, but it's been terrible sore. Gittin' better now, though. I'll hev the use uv it back all right in a week."

"It seems that you haven't been faring so badly," said Henry.

Long Jim looked around the little valley and grinned in appreciation.

"I knowed I couldn't do anything about the fort with this bad arm," he said. "Weakened ez I wuz, I wuzn't shore I could swim the river with one arm, an' even ef I ever reached the fort I'd be more likely to be a hindrance than a help. So I found this place, an' here I've stayed, restin' an' recuperatin' an' waitin' fur you fellers to come back. I didn't want to shoot, 'cause them that I didn't want to hear might hear it, an' 'cause, too, I knowed how to set traps an' snares."

"We saw one of them as we came along," said Henry.

"They've worked bee-yu-tiful," said Long Jim, an ecstatic look coming over his face. "I've caught rabbits an' a 'possum. Then I set to work and built this oven, an' I've learned a new way to broil rabbit steaks on the hot stones. It's shorely somethin' wonderful. It keeps all the juice in 'em, an' they're so tender they jest melt in your mouth, an' they're so light you could eat a hundred without ever knowin' that you had 'em."

"That's what I'm thinkin'," said Shif'less Sol, reaching for his rifle. "Gimme about twenty o' them steaks quicker'n you kin wink an eye, Jim Hart, or I'll let you hev it."

Long Jim, the soul of an artist still aflame within him, willingly produced the steaks, and all ate, finding that they were what he had claimed them to be. But he waited eagerly for the verdict, his head bent forward and his eyes expectant.

"Best I ever tasted," said Henry.

Long Jim's eyes flashed.

"Finer than silk," said Shif'less Sol.

Sparks leaped from Long Jim's eyes.

"Could eat 'em forever without stoppin'," said Tom Ross.

Long Jim's eyes blazed.

"I couldn't 'a' stood it ef you fellers hadn't liked my finest 'chievement," he said. "Shows you've got more sense than I thought you had."

"Jim feels like Columbus did that time he discovered Ameriky," said Shif'less Sol. "Knowed it wuz thar all the time, but wanted other people to know that he knowed it wuz thar."

"It's a snug place, Jim, this little valley, or rather pit, of yours," said Henry, "but we must leave it at once and find Paul."

"That's shorely so," said Long Jim, casting a regretful look at his oven, "but I wish we could come back here an' stay a while after we found him. That thar oven don't look much, but it works pow'ful. I b'lieve I could make some more uv them Columbus dis-kiv-er-ies with it."

"I don't think we will be back this way for a long time," said Henry, "but your oven will keep. Sol is compelled to bear a similar sorrow. He has the snuggest nest in the side of a cliff that ever you did see, but he has left it just as it is, and he hopes to see it again some day."

"That bein' the case," said Long Jim, "I think I kin stand it, since Sol here is my brother in sorrow."

They left the deep little valley, although Jim Hart cast more than one longing glance behind, and began the search for Paul, who had been the first to fall by the way. The four were a unit in believing that this would be the most difficult task of all. Paul, although he had learned much, was not a natural woodsman in the sense that the others were. Henry had reckoned all the time upon certain laws of the forest which Sol, Tom, and Jim would obey. He was with them like the skilled boxer meeting the skilled opponent, but Paul might at any time strike a blow contrary to science, and therefore unexpected. Although Paul had not been wounded, Henry felt more apprehension about him than he had ever felt about any one of the others, because of this very uncertainty.

They returned upon the back trail, and with four minds and four pairs of eyes working, they had no great difficulty in locating the point at which Paul had left them. Like most of the country it was heavily wooded, and one could easily find a hiding place so long as the dark lasted.

They located their own line of flight, not because any visible signs of it were left, but because they remembered the region through which they had run.

"Here is whar Paul turned away an' jumped into the bushes," said Shif'less Sol, "an' he shorely didn't go fur, 'cause he wuz pow'ful tired. I reckon Paul wuz tired enough to last him fur a month."

They turned to the eastward, and about a half mile further on, after long search, they found a place in the densest bushes that showed signs of crushing. Some twigs were broken, and several of the smaller bushes, bent to one side by a heavy body, had not returned to their normal position.

"Here is where Paul laid down to rest," said Henry.

"An' he wuz so tired he fell asleep an' slep' all night," said Shif'less Sol.

"He shorely did," said Tom Ross, "'cause these bushes wuz bent so long they ain't had time to straighten out ag'in."

"An' him with nothin' to eat the next mornin', poor feller," said Long Jim sympathetically.

141

They were able to follow Paul's trail a rod or so by the bent bushes, but then they lost it, and they stood conferring. Henry's eye fell upon a mass of wild flowers on a distant hill slope, red, blue, and delicate pink. He admired them at first, and then his eyes brightened with sudden comprehension.

"Paul has always loved beautiful things," he said to his comrades. "He does not forget to see them even in moments of danger, and he would naturally go toward that slope over there covered with wild flowers."

Shif'less Sol slapped his knee in approval.

"You do reason fine, Henry," he said. "Paul would shorely make fur them flowers, jest 'cause he couldn't help it."

They invaded the flower field, and, as all of them confidently expected, they saw signs that Paul had been there. Some of the flowers were broken down, but not many—Paul would take care not to injure them in such a way. But Henry's shrewd eye noticed where several had been cut from the stem. Paul had done this with his hunting knife, and probably he had thrust one or more of the flowers into his buckskin hunting coat.

When they crossed the flower field the trail was lost again.

"Now," said Long Jim, "how are you goin' to tell what Paul wuz thinkin' when he wuz comin' 'long here?"

Henry and Shif'less Sol wrinkled their brows in thought.

"Paul was not wounded," he replied. "After his night's sleep—and probably he did not wake up until long after daylight had come—he was thoroughly rested and as strong as ever. After making sure of his direction from the hill top here, he would go toward the river, thinking it his duty yet to reach the fort if he could."

"An' naterally," said Shif'less Sol, "he'd go whar the walkin' wuz easiest, but whar thar wuz kiver so he couldn't be seen by warriors. So he'd choose the easy slope under them big trees thar, an' go south toward that valley."

"Reckon you're right," said Long Jim in a convinced tone. "That's just about what Paul would do."

They descended the slope, an easy one, for a quarter of a mile, and came to a valley thickset with bushes and blackberry vines containing sharp briars.

"Paul wouldn't go crashin' into a briar patch," said Long Jim.

"He wouldn't, an' fur that reason he'd take this path," said Tom Ross, pointing to a narrow opening in the bushes and briars.

It was evidently a trail made by animals, trodden in the course of time in order to avoid a long circuit about the thicket, but they followed it, believing that Paul had gone that way. When nearly through, Henry saw something lying in the path. He stooped and held up the stem of a rose with one or two faded petals left upon it.

"It fell out o' his coat, an' he never noticed it," said Shif'less Sol.

142

"Right, uv course," said Tom Ross.

Not far beyond the thicket was a brook of uncommon beauty, a clear little stream bordered by wild flowers.

"Paul would stop here to drink an' look at all these here bee-yu-ti-ful scenes," said Shif'less Sol.

"He would," said Henry, "and, being terribly hungry, he would then climb that wild plum tree there beyond the oaks."

"Might throw up a stick an' knock 'em down," said Long Jim.

"There is no fallen wood here," said Henry, "and, being so ragingly hungry, Paul would not hunt for a stick. He'd shin up that tree at once."

"Tree itself will show," said Tom Ross.

"And it certainly does show," said Henry as they looked.

Little pieces of the bark on the trunk were broken off, evidently by a heavy body as it had struggled upward. Shif'less Sol also found two plum skins on the ground not far from the tree. The shiftless one held them up for the others to see.

"Now, ain't that Paul all over?" Tom Ross said. "Knows all about how the Carthygenians fit the French, an' how the English licked the Persians, but here he goes droppin' plum skins on the groun' fur any wanderin' warrior to see."

"Don't you go to attackin' Paul," said Shif'less Sol, "'cause Paul is a scholar like me. I ain't had the opportunities fur learnin', but I take naterally to it, 'specially history. So I kin understand why Paul, thinkin' all the time about Hannibal an' Belisarry an' all them great battles a long time ago, should throw his plum skins 'roun' loose, knowin' thar ain't no Carthygenians an' Persians about these days to see 'em."

"Paul is shorely a good boy," said Tom Ross, "an' ef he wants to throw plum skins, he kin. Now, we've got to figger on what he'll do next."

"Let's go to the top of that hill over there," said Henry, "and take a look at the country."

The survey showed a tangled mass of forest and low hills, which seemed to be monotonously alike in every direction. They could not see the Ohio from their summit.

"I think it likely," said Henry, "that Paul has got lost. Maybe he has been wandering about in a circle. I heard my Indians say that one lost on the Great Plains often did that."

"Might be a good guess," said Shif'less Sol. "Let's go back to the plum tree and try to take up his trail."

Paul's trail from the plum tree led in a northeasterly direction, and they were sure now that he was lost, as the river lay to the south. But the trail could not be followed more than twenty yards, and then they held another council.

143

"Bein' lost," said Tom Ross, "it ain't likely that he's ever got more'n two or three miles from here. Been spendin' his time goin' up an' down an' back an' forth. Ef we'd fire a rifle he might hear it."

Henry shook his head.

"I wouldn't," he said. "We would be just as likely to draw the Indians upon us, and we can find him, anyhow."

"Guess you're right," said Tom. "S'pose we spread out in a long line an' go huntin' through the thickets, follerin' the general direction that his little piece of trail showed."

The suggestion was approved, and in ten minutes a whistle from Tom Ross drew them to a central point.

"Paul killed a wild turkey here," said Tom. "These woods seem to be full uv 'em, an' he lighted a fire with his flint and steel. Had a hard time doin' it, too. Knelt down here so long tryin' to knock out a blaze that the prints uv his knees haven't gone away yet."

"But he did get it to goin' at last," said Shif'less Sol, "an' he cooked his turkey an' et it, too. Here's the wishbone, all white an' shinin', jest ez he throwed it down."

"And down here is the spring where he picked the turkey after he heated it on the fire, and where he washed it," said Henry. "Paul was so hungry he never thought about hiding the feathers, and a lot of 'em are left, caught in the grass and bushes."

"I don't blame Paul," said Long Jim, his gastronomic soul afire. "Ef I wuz hungry ez he must have been, I'd hev et it ef all the warriors uv all the tribes on this continent wuz standin' lookin' on."

"Paul felt a pow'ful sight better after eatin'," said Shif'less Sol, "an' he took the rest uv the turkey with him. Seems likely to me that Paul would follow the brook, thinkin' it would flow into the Ohio."

"That's almost a certainty," said Henry.

They went with the stream, but it was one of those brooks common throughout the West—it came out of the ground, and into the ground it went again, not more than half a mile from the point at which they took up its course. The stream disappeared under a natural stone arch in the side of the hill.

"Paul was greatly disappointed," said Henry, "and of course he went to the top of the hill to see if he could get a reckoning."

But the new hill merely revealed the same character of country.

"Seein' that he wuzn't gittin' anywhar, Paul, o' course, changed his direction," said Shif'less Sol.

"Naturally," said Henry.

"Now which way do you figger that he would go?" said Tom Ross.

"Down through that big grove there," replied Henry. "Having killed one turkey, he'd be on the look-out for another, and he knows that they roost in tall trees."

"Looks to me like a kind o' mind readin'," said Shif'less Sol, "but I think it's right. Lead on, Henry. Whar A-killus Ware will go, the dauntless soul o' Hector Hyde ain't afeard to foller."

They searched for some time among the trees, and then Henry pointed to a great elm. A section of bark nearly a foot square had been cut from it. The bark was lying on the ground, but the inner lining had been clipped from it and was gone.

"I jedge that this wuz done about a day ago," said Shif'less Sol. "Now, what in thunder did Paul do it fur?"

"Suppose you ask him," said Henry, who had gone on ahead, but who had now turned back and rejoined his comrades.

Astonished, they looked at him.

"He's sitting in a little valley over there, hard at work," said Henry. "Come and see, but don't make any noise. It would be a pity to disturb him."

Henry endeavored to speak lightly, but he felt an immense relief. They followed him silently and looked cautiously into a pleasant little glade. There they beheld Paul, alive, and to all appearances strong and well.

But Paul was absorbed in some great task. He sat upon the ground. His rifle lay on the grass beside him. A sheet of white was supported upon his knees, and his face was bent over it, while he drew lines there with the point of his hunting knife. So intensely interested was he, and so deeply concentrated was his mind, that he did not look up at all.

"It's the inner bark of the elm tree, and he's drawing something on it," said Henry.

Jim Hart stirred. His knee struck a little stick that broke with a snap. Paul heard it, and instantly he threw down the bark, snatched up his rifle, and began to investigate.

"He'll come up here spyin'," whispered Shif'less Sol. "While he's lookin', let's steal his bark away from him an' see what's on it."

"We'll do it," said Henry, and while Paul, rifle in hand, ascended the slope to see what had caused the noise, they deftly slipped away, descending to the other side of the glade.

When Paul entered the bushes, Shif'less Sol ran out, picked up the roll of bark, and returned silently with it to his comrades, who lay in a dense thicket. Filled with curiosity, all looked at it promptly.

"It's a map," whispered Henry, "and he's trying to locate himself in that way. See, this long line is the Ohio, here is the route of our own flight, this place is where he thinks he left us, and this line, I suppose, shows his own course after he dropped out. This deep mark here indicates where he now is. It's pretty good, but he's got everything turned around. South is where east ought to be, and north has taken the place of west."

"But what good is a map ef it don't take you anywhar?" asked Jim Hart.

"That's a plum' foolish question fur you to ask, Jim Hart," said Shif'less Sol disdainfully. "Great scholars like me an' Paul always draw maps. What does it matter ef you don't git anywhar? Thar's your map, anyhow."

"Sh!" whispered Tom Ross. "He's comin' back, havin' diskivered that thar's nothin' in the bushes. Now what'll he do?"

Paul, his mind relieved, returned to the glade, put back his rifle on the grass, and looked for the precious map that was costing him so much time and thought. It was not there, and great was the boy's amazement. He had certainly laid it down at that very spot, and he had not been gone a minute. He looked all around, and even up into the air, and the four in the brush were forced to smile at his puzzled face.

Paul stood staring at the place where his precious map had lain, but where it lay no more, and his amazement deepened. They admired Paul and had a deep affection for him, but they thought that their little joke might keep him nearer to the earth when he was in a dangerous Indian country.

"Mebbe he thinks Alfred the Great an' his Mogul Tartars hev come an' took it away," whispered Shif'less Sol.

Then Paul held up his hand.

"Feelin' o' the wind," said Shif'less Sol. "He hez now come to the conclusion that the wind took his map away, and so he thinks ef he kin find out which way it's blowin' he kin find out which way the map hez blowed, too."

Paul concluded that the light wind was blowing toward the east, and going in that direction he began to search for his map among the bushes that enclosed the glade. The moment his figure was hidden Henry whispered to the others:

"Come on!"

They came silently from the thicket, ran to the center of the glade, where Henry, kneeling down, spread out the map on the ground and began to examine it with the greatest attention. The others knelt beside him, and they also became absorbed in a study of the map. The four heads almost touched over the sheet of bark.

Paul, failing to find his map in the bushes, turned back to the glade. Then he stood transfixed with astonishment. He saw four figures, the backs of two, and the heads and shoulders of two more. Heads, backs, and shoulders were familiar. Could it really be they? He winked his eyes rapidly to clear away any motes. Yes, it was they, the four faithful comrades with whom he had roved and hunted and fought so long. He uttered a shout of joy and rushed toward them.

Paul's hands were shaken so often and so hard that his fingers were numbed. A

146

little moisture gathered on the eyelids of the sensitive boy when he saw how glad they were to see him.

"You've found me," he said, "and it's so good to see you again that I enjoy with you the little trick you've played on me."

"Pow'ful fine map, this o' yours, Paul," said Shif'less Sol, holding up the sheet of bark. "'Pears to me you kin find everything on it, 'cept whar you are."

"That was just the trouble with it, Sol," said Paul frankly. "It looked fine to me, but I couldn't make it work."

"Well," said Henry, "here we are, together again, all five of us, ready for anything. Isn't that so, boys, and isn't it fine?"

"Shorely," said Shif'less Sol, speaking for them all.

"Now, Paul," said Henry, "what were you trying to do?"

"I had an idea that I could reach the river," said Paul. "If I did so, then I might be able to swim across it in the night, and take a warning to Fort Prescott, if it wasn't too late."

"Got anything to eat left?" asked Tom Ross.

"I've had wild fruit," replied Paul, "and I shot a turkey, the last of which went this morning, but I was hoping for more luck of that kind."

"Well," said Tom, "we, too, hev about et up all that we had. So we'll hev to take a little hunt together. 'Twon't take long. Country's full uv game."

They shot a deer within an hour, feasted abundantly and retained enough more to last them several days.

"Wish we had Jim Hart's oven here," said Shif'less Sol as they ate. "While Jim wuz waitin', Paul, he made more improvements in the art o' cookin'."

Long Jim grinned with appreciation. It was a compliment that he liked.

"Now," said Henry, "the next thing for us to do is to find the fleet. Mr. Boone told me that it was being held up in a narrow part of the river by the Indian sharpshooters. I suppose that Adam Colfax doesn't want to lose any more men for fear that he will grow short-handed before he reaches Pittsburgh."

"But he's got to get through, an' he's got to help the fort, too," said Shif'less Sol.

"That's so," said Henry, "and we must find him just as soon as we can."

Rising, they sped toward the southwest.

CHAPTER XVIII

THE HALTING OF THE FLEET

Adam Colfax had been making slow progress up the Ohio, far slower than he had hoped, and his brave soul was worn by hardships and troubled by apprehensions. A great hurricane had caused him serious alarm for his smaller boats. They had been saved from sinking with the greatest difficulty, and the precious stores had to be kept well and guarded well.

He was grieved and troubled, too, over the disappearance of the five, the valiant five who had continually been doing him such great service from the very moment of the start at New Orleans. He liked them all, and he mourned them for their own sakes as well. He also realized quickly that he had lost more than the five themselves. His fleet seemed to have come into a very nest of dangers. Men who went ashore to hunt never returned. At narrow points in the river they were fired upon from the dense forest on the bank, and if they sent a strong force ashore, they found nothing. If they camped at night, bullets drew blood or scattered the coals at their feet.

Invisible but none the less terrible foes hung upon them continually, and weakened their spirits. The men in the fleet were willing and eager to fight a foe whom they could see, but to be stung to death by invisible hornets was the worst of fates.

Adam Colfax missed the "eyes of the fleet" more and more every day. If Henry Ware and Shif'less Sol and their comrades had been there, they could have discovered these unseen foes, and they could have told him what to do. At night he often saw signal fires, blazing on either side of the Ohio and, although he did not know what they meant, he felt sure that they were lighted by his enemies, who were talking to one another.

Two or three of his men who had been originally woodsmen of the great valley told him that the allied tribes had come to destroy him. They had seen certain signs in the forest that could not be mistaken. The woods were full of warriors. They had heard, too, that further on was a fort on the river bank which the Indians had probably taken by this time, and which they would certainly use against the fleet. Adam Colfax wished once more for the five, who were more familiar than anybody else with the country, and who were such magnificent scouts. Never had he felt their absence more.

He came at last to the narrowest place in the river that he had yet seen, enclosed on either bank by jutting hills. As the fleet approached this watery pass a tremendous fire was opened upon it from either shore. The bullets not only came from the level of the water, but from the tops of the hills, and the sides of the boat offered no protection against the latter. The men of the fleet returned the fire, but their lead was sent into the forest and the undergrowth, and they did not know whether it hit anything except inoffensive wood and earth.

148

Adam Colfax drew back. He felt that he might have forced the pass, but the loss in men and stores would be too great. It was not his chief object to fight battles even if every battle should prove a victory.

When he withdrew, the forest relapsed into silence, but when he attempted the passage again the next day he was attacked by a similar, though greater, fire. He was now in a terrible quandary. He did not wish another such desperate battle as that which he had been forced to fight on the Lower Mississippi. He might win it, but there would be a great expenditure of men and ammunition, and at this vast distance from New Orleans neither could be replaced.

He drew back to a wider part of the river and decided to wait a day or two, that is, to take counsel of delay.

Adam Colfax was proud of his fleet and the great amount of precious stores that it carried. The reinforcements after the Battle of the Bayou had raised it to more than its original strength and value. All the men had recovered from their wounds, and everybody was in splendid health. He had made up his mind that fleet and cargo should be delivered intact at Pittsburgh, otherwise he could never consider his voyage wholly a success.

The night after he fell back from the watery pass he held a council of his captains and guides on his own flat boat, which had been named the *Independence*. He had with him Adolphe Drouillard, a brave and devoted French Creole from New Orleans; James Tilden, a Virginian; Henry Eckford, a south Carolinian; Charles Turner, a New Yorker, and William Truesdale, and Eben Barber, New Englanders, and besides these, Nat Thrale and Ned Lyon, the best of the scouts and guides since the disappearance of the five, were present.

The fleet was anchored in the middle of the river, out of rifle shot for the present, but Adam Colfax knew very well that the enemy was in the dense wood lining either bank. He had sent skirmishers ashore in the afternoon, and they did not go many yards from the stream before they were compelled to exchange shots with the foe. Thrale and Lyon, who were on the southern bank, reported that the Indians were still thick in the forest.

"They see us here on the river," said Thrale, "an' ef we don't keep well in the middle uv it they kin reach us with thar bullets. But we won't be able to see the least speck or sign uv them."

Adam Colfax had sighed when he heard these words, and now, as his little council gathered, it seemed that all predictions of evil were about to be fulfilled. A smoky red sun had set behind the hills, and the night, true to the promise of the sun, had come on dark and cloudy. It was not exactly the cloudiness of rain; it was rather that of heat and oppressiveness, and it had in it a certain boding quality that weighed heavily upon the spirits of Adam Colfax.

The boats were anchored in a double row in the exact center of the stream, swaying just a little with the gentle current. All those carrying sails had taken them down. Adam Colfax's boat was outside the two lines, slightly nearer to the southern shore, but still beyond rifle shot.

149

While the leader sat in the stern of his boat waiting for the two scouts who were last to come, he surveyed the fleet with the anxious eyes of one who carries a great responsibility. In the darkness the boats were not much more than dark lines on the darker river. Now and then they were lighted up by flares of heat lightning, but the eyes of Adam Colfax turned away from them to the banks, those high banks thick with forest and undergrowth, which contained so many dangers, real dangers, not those of the imaginary kind, as he had ample proof. Now and then a shot, apparently as a taunt, was fired from either shore, and two or three times he heard the long, whining yell which is the most ominous of human cries. This, too, he knew, was a taunt, but in every case, cunning, ferocity and power lay behind the taunt, which was another truth that he knew.

They were all soon gathered on the deck of the little *Independence*, and the faces of the two scouts who came last were very grave.

"What do you think of it, Lyon?" said Adam Colfax.

Lyon gave his head one brief shake.

"We're right in the middle of the biggest hornet's nest the country ever saw," he replied. "Looks ez ef we couldn't git past without another terrible fight."

"And you, Drouillard?" Adam Colfax asked of the Creole.

"Eet ees hard to go on," replied Drouillard in his broken English, "but we cannot go back at all. So eet ees true that we must go on. Eet ees is the only thing we can do."

"But how?" said Adam Colfax. "We cannot use up all the ammunition that we have in these battles. If we were to reach Pittsburgh in that condition we'd be a burden instead of a help."

"But as Mr. Drouillard says, we can't go back," said Truesdale.

They sat dumbly a minute or two, no one knowing what to propose, and all looking toward the southern bank, where they believed the chief danger to lie. The dark green forest made a high black line there in the night, a solid black until it was broken by a pink dot, which they knew to be the flash of a rifle.

"They are jeering at us again," said Adam Colfax.

"'Tain't no jeer, either," said Thrale, as five or six pink dots appeared where the one had been, and faint sounds came to their ears.

Lyon confirmed the opinion of his brother scout.

"So many wouldn't let off their guns at once jest fur fun," he said. "I wonder what in tarnation it means!"

The spray of pink dots did not reappear, and they turned their minds once more to their great problem, which seemed as insoluble as ever. The flowing of the current, gentle but deep and strong, swung the *Independence* a little further from the two lines of boats, but those on board, in their absorption, did not notice it. Three or four minutes passed, and there was the report of a rifle shot from the southern bank, followed an instant later by another. Two bullets splashed in the water near the *Independence*.

"We'd better pull back a leetle," said Drouillard. "We are drifting within range of ze warriors."

"So we are," said Lyon, laying his hand on a sweep. "Now, what under the moon is that?"

He pointed to a dark object, a mere black dot on the dusky surface of the river. But it was not a stationary dot, and in its movement it came toward the *Independence*.

"Shorely they don't mean to come swimmin' to attack us," said the other guide, Thrale. "That's a human head on top uv the water an' thar's a body belongin' to it under the water. An' see, thar's another head behind it, an' behind that another, an' likely thar's more."

"Eet ees certainlee the warriors trying to reach us on the water," said Adolphe Drouillard, and, raising his rifle, he took aim at the first swimming head.

"Hold a little," said Adam Colfax, pushing down the barrel of the weapon. "Look, as they come closer now, you can see a fourth and a fifth head and then no more. Five swimming heads on the water must mean something, I hope; yet I'm afraid I hope too much."

The foremost of the swimming figures raised a hand out of the water, and held it high in token of amity. Instantly the four behind did the same thing.

"Most amazing," said Adolphe Drouillard. "Ees eet possible that they are friends?"

"I think it not only possible, but probable," said Adam Colfax with a rising tone of joy in his voice. "They are near now, and that first head looks familiar to me. I devoutly hope that I'm not mistaken."

The leader's head, propelled by the powerful strokes of the arms below, came within a yard or two of the *Independence*, and some stray rays of the moon, falling upon it, brought it from dusk into light. It was the face of a young river god, strong features cut cleanly, a massive projecting chin, and long yellow hair from which the water flowed in streams.

The head was raised from the water, the hands grasped the edge of the boat, and the figure sprang lightly on board, standing perfectly erect for a moment, while the water ran from his fringed hunting shirt, his moccasins, the knife and tomahawk at his belt, and flowed away over the boards.

"Henry Ware alive!" exclaimed Adam Colfax, springing forward and seizing the hand which dripped water from the tip of every finger.

"An' don't furgit me," said Shif'less Sol, as he leaped aboard and stood beside Henry, a tiny cataract pouring from every seam of his clothing.

"Nor me," said Tom Ross briefly, taking his place with his comrades.

151

"An' I'm here, too," said Jim Hart, uprearing his thin six feet four.

"So am I," said Paul, as he drew himself over the rail of the *Independence*.

"All of you alive and well!" exclaimed Adam Colfax, departing for once from his New Hampshire calm. "All returned from the dead together! I feel as if an army had come to our relief!"

"We ain't been dead," said Shif'less Sol. "An' we ain't been havin' sech a hard time, either. It's true three o' us hev been troubled by Injun bullets, but Jim Hart thar spent his time inventin' a new way o' cookin' rabbits, which will keep him happy for the next five years."

"And he could not spend his spare time in a better way," said Adolphe Drouillard. "Ze man who invents a new wholesome dish ees a blessing to hees country."

"Shake, friend," said Long Jim, holding out a huge hand still dripping with portions of the Ohio, and Adolphe Drouillard, without hesitation, shook.

"Them two shots that hit in the water close to us wuz fired at you, wuzn't they?" asked Thrale.

"Yes, they were aimed at us," replied Henry, "and so was the little volley on the bank, which you must have heard. As you probably know, there's a fort and settlement not many miles on called Fort Prescott. We've warned it, and the garrison has also beaten off all attacks. But all the allied tribes of the north are here, and they expect to catch you, the fort, and everything else, in their net. They are led by all their great chiefs, but Timmendiquas, the White Lightning of the Wyandots, is the soul of the attack. We have seen his vigilance in our effort to reach the river. We were discovered, fired upon by a party, although their bullets missed us in the dark, and then we had to swim for it."

"You must have dry clothing at once," said Adam Colfax.

"We won't mind changin'," said Shif'less Sol, "an' we'd like to dry our rifles an' have 'em reloaded ez soon ez you kin."

"We'll have that done for you," said Adam Colfax, looking at them with admiration.

They resigned their weapons to his men, although they had succeeded in keeping their powder dry in tightly closed horns. Adam Colfax then led the way to his cabin, where dry clothing was brought them, and food and drink were given. Then Henry told to the little, but deeply interested, company the tale of their wanderings and adventures.

"It certainly seems as if Providence were watching over you," said the devout New Englander.

"We have sometimes thought so ourselves," said Paul with the utmost sincerity.

"This Timmendiquas, as you describe him, is a most formidable chief," said Adam Colfax, pondering, "and the renegade, Girty, too, is a very dangerous man. As I see that we shall have to fight them, I would spare this fleet further loss if I could."

"We will have to fight," said Drouillard, "eef not to-night, then to-morrow, and eef not to-morrow, then next week."

"I think he tells a fact, sir," said Henry to Adam Colfax. "But we can rely upon the fort making a powerful defense. Major Braithwaite is a brave and active man, and we must not forget, sir, that Daniel Boone and Simon Kenton are somewhere near in the woods. If they have gathered their forces, we can gather ours, too."

"That is so," said Adam Colfax, as the council and the five returned to the deck of the *Independence*. The council might have been depressed, but the five were not. Warm food and warm clothing restored them physically, and here they were with the fleet once more, meanwhile having done many things well.

"Ain't it fine fur a lazy man like me to be back on a boat," said Shif'less Sol in a low voice to Paul. "Nuthin' to do but set still an' talk, nuthin' to do but eat an' drink what's brought to you, nuthin' to do but sleep when you're sleepy, no Injuns shootin' at you, no havin' to run on your legs 'till you drop. Everything done fur you. It's a life fur me, but I don't git much av it."

Paul laughed at Shif'less Sol's tone of deep satisfaction.

"Yes, it's good, Sol," he rejoined, "but it won't last. We won't have more than a day of it."

The face of the shiftless one took on a look of deep disgust. "Nuthin' good never lasts more'n a day," he said, "an' ef it does last more'n a day you gen'ally git tired o' it."

Adam Colfax resumed his watch of the shores. Like Major Braithwaite, he had a pair of powerful glasses, and he sought with their aid to detach something from the black wall of the southern shore.

"I can make out nothing," he said in disappointing tones, after a long look, "except a bright spot which must be a fire a little distance back in the woods. You have keen eyes, Henry, my boy, see what you can see."

Henry also saw the "bright spot," and he was quite sure that it was a fire. Then he took a look at the heavens, now a solid expanse of cloud behind which the stars twinkled unseen. A slight wind was blowing up the river, and its touch was damp on his face. When the lightning flared, as it still did now and then, he saw that it was not mere heat lightning but the token of something graver.

"I have a suggestion to make to you, sir," he said to Adam Colfax. "Unless I am mistaken, a storm is coming. Is it not so, Tom, and you, Sol?"

"It is," they replied together. "All the signs are sayin' so out loud."

"In an hour it will be here," resumed Henry. "The wind is blowing up river, and I don't think it will change. That favors us. In the darkness and tumult of the storm we ought to force the pass. It is our best chance, sir."

He spoke very earnestly, and the rest of the five nodded their assent. Adam

Colfax was impressed, but he wished to have the endorsement of his lieutenants.

"What do you say, gentlemen?" he asked, turning to them.

"We make zee passage, and we make eet queek to-night, as zee boy says," replied the brave and impulsive Drouillard.

Adam Colfax turned to the Virginian and the Northerners. All nodded in affirmation. Then he turned to the two scouts, Thrale and Lyon.

"It's now or never," they said, looking up at the dark skies.

"Then it shall be done," said Adam Colfax firmly. "We can't afford to delay here any longer, nor can we permit this fort to fall. Our need to hold Kentucky is scarcely less great than our need to help our hard-pressed brethren in the east."

Then he turned to the five, in whose valor, skill and fidelity he had the utmost confidence.

"Do you wish to remain on the *Independence*," he said, "or would you prefer another place in the fleet?"

Shif'less Sol, the talkative and resourceful, looked at Henry. Tom Ross, the man of few words but resourceful, also looked at Henry. The gaze of Long Jim was turned in the same direction, and that of Paul followed. It was an unconscious revelation of the fact that all always looked upon Henry Ware as their leader, despite his youth.

"If you don't mind, sir," said Henry Ware to Adam Colfax, "give us a boat to ourselves, a small one that we can row, and we will advance somewhere near the head of the fleet."

"The boat will be ready for you in five minutes," said Adam Colfax. "Whatever you ask we will always give to you, if we can. Meanwhile, I will get the fleet ready, for I see that the time cometh fast."

He spoke in almost Biblical words. In fact, there was much in Adam Colfax that made for his resemblance to the heroes of the Old Testament, his rigid piety, his absolute integrity, his willingness to fight in what he thought a just cause, his stern joy when the battle was joined, and his belief—perhaps not avowed—in the doctrine of an eye for an eye and a tooth for a tooth.

He quickly summoned a small boat, and the five, refreshed and armed, dropped into it. Then he sent the word throughout the fleet, the *Independence* moved up near the head of the column, and they prepared to force the watery pass.

CHAPTER XIX

THE WATERY PASS

Henry was at the tiller of their boat, and the others pulled on the oars. Their strong arms soon sent it to a point near the head of the fleet. On the way they passed the *Independence* and Adam Colfax. Adolphe Drouillard and the others waved their hands to them. Paul, as he rested one hand from his oar, waved in reply, and then put both hands to the oar again.

All signs were being fulfilled. The darkness was increasing, and it was more than that of the night. Heavy clouds were moving up toward the zenith and joining in one until they covered all the heavens. Save when the lightning flashed, both shores were hidden in the darkness. The voyagers saw only the turbid current of the Ohio, raised into waves now by the wind which was coming stronger and stronger.

"Rough night, but good fur us," said Tom Ross.

"And it will be rougher, also better," said Henry.

The lightning increased, blazing across the skies with dazzling intensity, and heavy thunder rolled all around the half circle of the horizon. The darkness turned into a bluish gray, ghostly and full of threat. Adam Colfax went through his fleet, warning everybody to cover up the stores and to beware of wind and wave.

The men wrapped themselves in their cloaks and protected beneath the same cloaks their rifles and ammunition. But, despite every order, a hum ran through the fleet, and rowers, riflemen, and guides talked in whispers. They recalled the great double battle on the Lower Mississippi, that of the bank and that of the bayou. The crisis now was equally as great, and the surroundings were more ominous. They advanced in the darkness with thunder and lightning about them, and they felt that they were about to face the bravest of all the Indian tribes, led by the greatest of their leaders.

The heat was succeeded by a rushing cold wind, the lightning flared brighter than ever, and the thunder became a slow, monotonous, unbroken roll. Paul, despite his work at the oar, shivered a little.

"She'll be here in a minute," said Tom Ross. "Be shore you fellers keep your powder dry."

It was about midnight, and they were advancing rapidly toward the pass. They saw by the flashes of lightning that the cliffs were rising and the river narrowing.

"The hills on both sides here are jest covered with warriors," said Jim Hart.

"Thar may be a million uv 'em," said Shif'less Sol, "but in the rain an' a black night they can't shoot straight."

The wind began to whistle and its coldness increased. Great cold drops struck the five in the face.

"Here she is!" said Tom Ross.

Then the rain swept down, not in a wild gush but steady, persistent, and full of chill. Lightning and thunder alike ceased. Every boat saw only the outline of the one before it and the rolling current of the Ohio beneath it. Noise had ceased on the fleet at the stern command of Adam Colfax and his lieutenants. The men talked only in whispers, there was no flapping of sail, only the swash of the oars in the water, drowned by the wind. Since the lightning had ceased, both shores were lost permanently in the darkness, and the five, who now knew this part of the river thoroughly, moved up to the head of the line, leading the way. After them came the *Independence* and then the fleet in the same double line formation that it had used before.

"Do you see anything on either side, Henry?" asked Tom Ross, raising his back from the oar.

"Nothing, Tom," replied Henry, "and it seems strange to me. So great a chief as Timmendiquas would foresee such an attempt as this of ours, at such a time."

"We ain't goin' to git through without a fight, rain or no rain, night or no night," said Shif'less Sol in a tone of finality, and Henry silently, but in his heart, agreed with him.

They were going so slowly now, to prevent collision or noise, that only Tom Ross and Long Jim rowed. Henry and Shif'less Sol, near the front of the boat, leaned forward and tried to pierce the darkness with their eyes. The rain was beating heavily upon their backs, and they were wet through and through, but at such a time they did not notice it. Their rifles and their powder were dry under their buckskin hunting shirts, and that was sufficient.

Henry and Shif'less Sol near the prow bent forward, and, shielding their eyes from the rain with their hands, never moved. The blackest darkness even can be pierced in time by a persistent gaze, and, as the channel of the river narrowed still further, Henry thought he saw something blacker upon the black waters. He turned his head a little and met the eyes of Shif'less Sol.

"Do you see it?" he whispered.

"I see it," replied the shiftless one, "an' I take it to be an Indian canoe."

"So do I," rejoined Henry, "and I think I can see another to the right and another to the left."

"Indian sentinels watchin' fur us. The White Lightnin' o' the Wyandots is ez great a chief ez you said he wuz. He ain't asleep."

"I can see three more canoes now," said Henry as they proceeded further. "They must have a line of them across the river. Look, they see us, too!"

They saw an Indian in the canoe nearest them rise suddenly to his knees, fire a rifle in the air, and utter a long warning whoop, which rose high above the rush of the rain. All the Indian canoes disappeared almost instantly, as if they had been swallowed up in the black water. But Henry and his comrades knew very well that they had merely been propelled by swift paddles toward the shore.

"It's the signal," exclaimed Henry. "We are not to pass without a fight."

156

The five stopped their boat, the *Independence* also stopped, and the whole fleet stopped with them. The sound of a rifle shot from the right bank rose above the sweep of the wind and the rain, and then from the left bank came a similar report. The five knew at once that these were signals, although they could not yet surmise what they portended. But the fact was soon disclosed.

A sudden blaze of light appeared on the high south bank, and then, as if in answer to it, another blaze sprang up on the equally high north bank. Both leaped high, and the roar of the flames could be heard mingling with that of the wind and rain.

The effect of this sudden emergence of light from dark was startling. The hills clothed in forest, dripping with water, leaped out, the water turned from black to gray, and the fleet in its two stationary lines could now be seen distinctly.

"What a transformation!" exclaimed Paul. The faces of his comrades were lurid in the light from the two great bonfires, taking on an almost unearthly tinge.

But Henry Ware said:

"It is Timmendiquas! It is his master-stroke! He has built these great bonfires which rain cannot put out in order to place us in the light! On, boys, the faster we go now the better!"

Adam Colfax also understood, and, as he gave the signal, the huge sweeps made the *Independence* leap forward. Behind her the whole fleet advanced rapidly. It was well that they had protected the sides of their boats as much as they could with planks and bales of goods, as a great rifle fire was immediately opened upon them from either bank. Hundreds of bullets splashed the water, buried themselves in the bales or wood, and some struck the rowers.

But the fleet did not stop. It went straight on as fast as the men could send it, and few shots were fired in reply. Yet they could see the forms of warriors outlined in black tracery against the fires. Two other fires, equally large, and opposite each other, leaped up further on. Henry had not underrated the greatness of Timmendiquas as a forest general. Even with all the elements against him, he would devise plans for keeping his enemy from forcing the watery pass.

Paul was appalled. He had been through scenes of terror, but never such another as this. The Indians had begun to shout, as if to encourage one another and to frighten the foe, and the sweep of the wind and the rain mingling with their yelling gave it an effect tremendously weird and terrifying. Nature also helped man. It began to thunder again, and sudden flashes of lightning blazed across the stream.

"Don't fire unless you see something that you can hit," was the order passed down the lines by Adam Colfax, and the fleet pulled steadily on, while the hail of bullets from either shore beat upon it. Many men were wounded, and a few were killed, but the fleet never stopped, going on like a great buffalo with wolves tearing at its flanks, but still strong and dangerous.

157

The smallness of their boat and the fact that it lay so low in the water made for the safety of the five. The glare of the fires threw the bigger vessels into relief, but it was not likely that many of the warriors would notice their own little craft.

There was a blaze of lightning so vivid that it made all of them blink, and with a mighty crash a thunderbolt struck among the trees on the south bank. Paul had a vision of a blasted trunk and rending boughs, and his heart missed a few beats, before he could realize that he himself had not been struck down.

The whole fleet paused an instant as if hurt and terrified, but in another instant it went on again. Then the bullets began to sing and whistle over their heads in increased volume, and Henry looked attentively at the southern shore.

"I think that warriors in canoes are hovering along the bank there and firing upon us. What do you say, Sol?"

"I say you're right," replied the shiftless one.

"Then we'll let the *Independence* take the lead for a while," said Henry, "and burn their faces a little for their impudence."

The boat turned and slid gently away toward the southern shore. The light cast from the fires was brightest in the middle of the stream, and they were soon in half shadow.

"Can you make 'em out clearly, Sol?" asked Henry.

"If I ain't mistook, an' I know I ain't," replied the shiftless one, "thar's a little bunch o' canoes right thar at the overhangin' ledge."

"Sol is shorely right," added Tom Ross, "an' I kin reach the fust canoe with a bullet."

"Then let 'em have it," said Henry.

Silent Tom raised his rifle, and with instant aim fired. An Indian uttered a cry and fell from his canoe into the water. Henry and the shiftless one fired with deadly aim, and Long Jim and Paul followed. There was terror and confusion among the canoes, and the survivors, abandoning them, dashed up the bank and into the darkness.

They reloaded their rifles, scattered some canoes further up, and then swung back to the fleet, which was still going forward at the same steady, even pace under a ceaseless shower of bullets. It was here that Adam Colfax best showed his courage, tenacity, and judgment. Although his men were being slain or wounded, he would not yet let them return the fire, because there was no certainty that they could do any damage among the warriors in the forest. He might have fired the brass twelve pounders, and they would have made a great noise, but it would have been a waste of powder and ball badly needed in the east.

He had run more than one blockade, but this awed even his iron soul. The note of the Indian yell was more like the scream of a savage wild beast than the sound of a human voice, and the mingling of the thunder and lightning with all this noise of battle shook his nerves. But his will made them quiet again, and from the deck of the *Independence* he continually passed back the word: "Push on! push on! But don't reply to their fire."

The two scouts, Thrale and Lyon, with several of the best riflemen, also dropped into a small boat and began to pick off the skirmishers near the water's edge. Two other boats were filled with sharpshooters for the same purpose, and their daring and skill were a great help to the harassed fleet.

The pass was several miles in length, and at such a time the fleet was compelled to move slowly. The boats must not crash into and destroy one another. Above all, it was necessary to preserve the straight and necessary formation of the fleet, as confusion and delay, in all likelihood, would prove fatal.

Adam Colfax calculated that he had passed less than one-third of the length of the narrows, as they had been described to him, and his heart became very heavy. The fire of the Indian hordes was increasing in volume. The great bonfires blazed higher and higher, and every minute the fleet was becoming a more distinct target for the savage sharpshooters. The souls of more good men were taking flight.

"We have not gone more than a third of the distance," he said to Adolphe Drouillard. "At this rate can we last all the way?"

The brave Creole replied: "We have to do it."

But his face looked doubtful. He saw, and Adam Colfax saw, signs of distress in the fleet. Under the persistent and terrible fire of the warriors the two lines of boats were beginning to sag apart. There were some collisions, and, although no boat had yet been sunk, there was danger of it. The apprehensions of Adam Colfax and his lieutenants were many and great, and they were fully justified.

The boat of the five came alongside the *Independence*, and Adam Colfax looked down at it.

"We want to come on board," called out Henry.

The *Independence* slowed just a little, and Henry and Shif'less Sol sprang upon her. The other three remained in the boat. Bullets struck near them as they boarded the *Independence*, but none touched them. It was still raining hard, with the vivid accompaniment of wind, thunder, and lightning. Another thunderbolt had struck close by, but fortunately nobody had been hurt.

"We've a plan to suggest, if you should think good of it, sir," shouted Henry in Adam Colfax's ear—he was compelled to shout just then because of the thunder.

"What is it?" Adam Colfax shouted back.

"How far away would you say that bonfire is?" asked Henry, pointing to one of the great fires on the southern shore.

"Not more than four hundred yards."

159

"Then, sir, we can put it out."

"Put it out?" exclaimed Adam Colfax in amazement. "I would not dare to land men for such a purpose!"

"It is not necessary. We must shoot it out. You've got good gunners, and the cannon can then do it. They might put a lot of the warriors there out of the fight at the same time."

One of the brass twelve pounders was mounted on the *Independence*, and Adam Colfax was taken at once with the idea.

"I should have thought of that before," he said. "I hate to lose any of our cannon balls, but we must spare a few. Uncover the gun and aim at the nearest fire, hitting it at the base if you can."

This to the gunners, who obeyed eagerly. They had been chafing throughout the running of the gantlet as they stood beside their beloved but idle piece.

The tompion was drawn from the gun, the polished brass of which gleamed through the night and the rain. It was a splendid piece, and the chief gunner, as well as Adam Colfax, looked at it with pride.

"You are to shoot that fire out, and at the same time shoot out as much else with it as you can," the leader said to the gunner.

"I can do it," replied the gunner with pride and confidence. "I shall load with grape shot, triple charge."

Adam Colfax nodded. The triple charge of grape was rammed into the mouth of the brass piece. The muzzle was raised, and the gunner took long aim at the base of the blazing pyramid. Henry and the shiftless one stood by, watching eagerly, and the three in the boat at a little distance were also watching eagerly. Every one of them ran water from head to toe, but they no longer thought about rain, thunder, or lightning.

"He'll do it," the shiftless one said in the ear of Henry.

The gun was fired. A great blaze of flame leaped from its muzzle, and the *Independence* shook with the concussion. But the bonfire seemed to spring into the air. It literally went up in a great shower of timber and coals, like fireworks, and when it sank darkness blotted out the space where it had been.

"A hit fa'r an' squar'!" exclaimed Shif'less Sol.

From the fleet came a thunder of applause, which matched the thunder from the heavens, while from the shore rose a fierce yell of rage and execration.

"Well done! Well done!" shouted Adam Colfax to the gunner, who said nothing, but whose smile showed how much he was pleased at this just praise.

"It's likely that some warriors went out with their fire," said Henry. "A lot of them were bound to be around it, feeding it and making it go in all this rain."

"They can be well spared," said Adam Colfax. "God knows I am not a seeker of

160

human life, but I am resolved to do my errand. Now for the opposite bonfire on the northern bank."

The *Independence* swung through the fleet, which parted to let her pass, quickly closing up again. The boat came within seventy or eighty yards of the northern shore, all those aboard her sheltering themselves by one means or another from the Indian bullets, one of which struck upon the brazen muzzle of the twelve pounder, but which did no damage.

The triple load of grape was used again, and the first shot was not successful, but the second seemed to strike fairly at the base of the bonfire, and it was extinguished as the first had been. The two further up were soon put out in the same manner.

The thunder of applause rose in the fleet at every successful shot, and then it swung forward with increased speed. The river at this point sank into darkness, save when the lightning flared across it, and the Indian bullets, which still came like the rain itself, were of necessity fired at random, doing, therefore, little damage.

Shif'less Sol laughed in sheer delight.

"It was a good trick they played on us," he said, "worthy uv a great chief, but we hev met it with another jest ez good. I s'pose it's a new way to put out fires with a cannon, but it's fine when you know how to shoot them big guns straight. A-kill-us an' Hannibal an' Homer an' all them old soldiers Paul talks about wuz never ez smart ez that."

But the battle was not over, nor had they yet forced all the watery pass. The northern Indians were numerous, hardy, and wild for triumph. The great mind and spirit of Timmendiquas, the White Lightning of the Wyandots, urged them on, and they swarmed in hundreds along either shore, standing in the water among the bushes and sending in an incessant rifle fire. Others waded beyond the bushes, and still others darted out in their light canoes, from which they sent bullets at the two dark lines of boats in the middle of the river.

The rain came in gusts, and mingled with it was a wind which shrieked now and then like a human being, as it swept over the forests and the water. The thunder formed a bass note to all these noises, and the lightning at times fairly danced upon the water with dazzling brilliancy. It was a confused and terrible advance, in which the boats were in imminent danger from one another. Every one was compelled to move slowly lest it be sunk by the one behind it, and half the fighting force of the fleet was forced to pay its whole attention to the oars and sweeps and steering gear.

Paul was dazed a little by the tremendous confusion and mingling of sights and sounds. He saw an Indian near the southern bank aiming his rifle at their boat, and he sought to aim his own in return, but the flash of lightning that had disclosed the warrior was gone, and for the moment he looked only into blank darkness. He shut his eyes, rubbed his hands over them, and then opened them again. The darkness was still there. He did not at that time feel fear. It was too

161

unreal, too much like a hideous nightmare, and he did not realize its full import until afterward.

"Shall we ever get through?" he asked, raising his voice above the tumult.

"Some o' us will! most o' us, I hope!" shouted Shif'less Sol in reply. "Jumpin' Jehoshephat, but that bullet was close! I think I got a free shave on my left cheek. Did you ever hear sech a yellin' an' shriekin' an' whizzin' o' bullets!"

"They are certainly making a determined attack," said Henry. "If they had the fires to go by they'd get us yet. Look, there goes a new fire that they've lighted on the southern bank."

A high flame flared among the bushes, but the brass twelve pounder was promptly turned upon it, and after the second shot it disappeared.

"It ain't healthy, lightin' fires to-night," said Long Jim grimly.

The boats swung forward now at a slightly increased pace. On the *Independence*, Adam Colfax, Adolphe Drouillard, Thrale, Lyon and the others half stood, half knelt, looking steadily ahead, their minds attuned as only the minds of men can be concentrated at such a crisis. In this hour of darkness and danger the souls of the New Hampshire Puritan and of the Louisiana Frenchman were the same. One prayed to his Protestant God and the other to his Catholic God with like fervor and devotion, each praying that He would lead them through this danger, not for themselves, but for their suffering country.

The five in their own boat were not less devoted. They, too, felt that a Mighty Presence which was above wind, rain, and fire, alone could save them. Their hands were not on the trigger now. Instead they bent over the oars. Every one of them knew that bullets could do little the rest of the way, and it was for Providence to say whether they should reach the end of the watery pass.

The river narrowed still further. They were now at the point where the high banks came closest together and the danger would be greatest. But there was no flinching. The fire from either shore increased. Thunder and lightning, wind and rain raged about them, but they merely bent a little lower over the oars and sent their boats straight toward the flaming gate.

CHAPTER XX

THE TRUMPET'S PEAL

Major George Augustus Braithwaite, scholar of William and Mary College, man of refinement and experience, commissioned officer who had been in the assault at Ticonderoga, and who had stood victoriously with Wolfe on the Plains of Abraham, leaned upon a bastion at Fort Prescott and watched one of the wildest nights that he had ever seen. He wore his three-cornered military hat, but the rain flowed steadily in a little stream from every corner. He was wrapped in an old military coat, badge of distinguished service, but the rain, too, ran steadily from every fringe of its hem and gathered in puddles about the military boots that enclosed his feet.

He thought nothing of rain, or hat, or cloak, or boots. The puddles grew without his notice. The numerous flashes of lightning disclosed his face, worn and anxious, and with lines that had deepened perceptibly in the last few days. Beside him stood the second in command at Fort Prescott, Gregory Wilmot, a middle-aged man, and the brave scout, Seth Cole. They, too, seemed unconscious of the rain, and looked only at the river that flowed beneath them, a dark and troubled stream.

The storm had gone on long and it showed no signs of abating. It was the fiercest that any of them had ever seen in the Ohio Valley, and the lightning was often so brilliant and so near that they were compelled to shrink back in fear.

"How long has it been since the boy Henry Ware left us?" asked Major Braithwaite.

"A week to-day," replied the scout.

"And the fleet has not yet come," said the Major, as much to himself as to the others. "I've always believed until to-night that it would come. That boy inspired confidence. I had to believe in him. I had no choice."

"Nor I, either," said Gregory Wilmot. "I believed in him, and I do now."

"It's the lack of news that troubles me so much," said the Major sadly. "The leaguer of the fort has grown closer and tighter, and it seems that nothing can get through now."

"I tried to get out last night," said the scout, "but a snake would have had to grease himself to slip by. It's their great chief, Timmendiquas, who is doing it all, and he doesn't mean that we shall know a single thing about what is going on outside."

"He is certainly carrying out his intentions. I give him all credit for his generalship," said Major Braithwaite.

The three relapsed again into silence and stared at the river, now a dark, flowing current, and then molten metal in the dazzling glare of the lightning. The time, the place, and his troubles stirred Major Braithwaite deeply. To-night the wilderness oppressed him with its immensity and its unknown, but none the less deadly, dangers. Things that he had read, scraps of old learning at college, floated through his head.

"*Magna pars fui,*" he murmured, looking at the river and the black forest beyond.

"What did you say, sir?" asked the scout.

"I merely meant," replied the Major, "that we, too, have our part in great events. This, with distance's long view, may seem obscure and small to the great world elsewhere, but it is not obscure and small to us. Could any spectacle be more tremendous than the one we behold to-night?"

"If the fleet does not come it is not likely that we shall behold any more spectacles of any kind," said Gregory Wilmot. "The red men hold their cordon, and in time our food must become exhausted."

"That is so," said the Major. "Some of the women have given up already, and look upon themselves as dead."

"We are not lost," said the scout. "He'll come, that boy, Henry Ware, will. He's only a boy, Major, but he's got a soul like that of the great chief, Timmendiquas. He'll come with the fleet."

Major Braithwaite wished to believe, but it was hard to do it. How could anything come out of that darkness and storm and through the Indian host? A soldier, he recognized the mental grasp and energy of Timmendiquas and the thoroughness of the leaguer of both fort and river. He left the bastion presently and went into one of the log cabins where some of the wounded men lay. He made it a point to visit them and cheer them whenever he could, and he would not neglect it to-night. He spent a half hour with them and then he returned to the bastion.

"What have you seen?" he asked.

"Nothing but the river and the woods and much lightning," replied Gregory Wilmot.

"Nor heard anything?"

"Only the thunder and the wind."

"I am weary of both. Surely they cannot last much longer."

Neither Gregory Wilmot nor the scout replied. Both were soaked with water, but they had forgotten it, and none of the three spoke again for at least ten minutes. Then Major Braithwaite, whose eyes had roved from the river, saw the scout lean forward and press himself against the wooden crest of the bastion. It was as if a sudden quiver had run through him, but his ear was toward the river and he leaned still further forward as if he would get yet nearer to hear. It was only by a flash of lightning that the Major saw this, but it was enough to arouse his interest.

"What is it? Do you hear anything?" he asked.

The lightning flashed again, and the scout raised his hand.

"I don't know yet whether I've heard anything but the thunder an' the wind," he replied, "but I seemed to hear somethin'. It wuz fur away, an' it growled low and threatenin' like thunder. An' it wuzn't eggzackly like thunder, either. I don't quite seem to make it out. Hark! thar she goes ag'in!"

Major Braithwaite and Gregory Wilmot also leaned forward eagerly, but they could hear only the fiendish shrieking of the wind and the sullen mutter of certain thunder.

164

"You believe you heard a sound that was neither the thunder nor the wind?" said the Major.

"Yes," replied the scout, "an' I've heard it twice. Ef it wuzn't fur the second time I wouldn't be so shore. Listen, thar she goes ag'in, like thunder, but not thunder eggzackly."

"Can you make out what it is?"

"I wuz in the big French an' Injun War, too, when I wuz jest a mite uv a boy," replied the scout, "and when I wuz layin' in the woods one day an' one uv them battles wuz goin' on I heard a sound that's like the one I've been hearin' now."

"What was it?" exclaimed the Major eagerly.

"It wuz the fust time I ever heard it. I wuz layin' close in the thicket, a' it wuz at least five miles away. But I've never forgot that sound. It wuz a cur'us thing. It wuz like a voice talkin'. It kep' a-sayin' somethin' like this, 'Look out fur me! Look out fur me!' It wuz a cannon shot, Major, an' it's a cannon shot that I've been hearin' now, once, twice, an' now three times, an' it's sayin' jest ez it did years an' years ago, 'Look out fur me! Look out fur me! Look out! Look out!' an' it's a-sayin' to me at the same time that the fleet's a-comin'."

"Do you really think so?" exclaimed the Major joyfully.

"I shorely do, an' I do more than think, I know. The cannon that them Injuns an' renegades had hez been sunk. Thar ain't any others in all the west except them on the fleet, an' it's them that's been talkin'. Ez shore ez we live, Major, the fleet's buttin' its way through the darkness and the wind an' the thunder an' the lightnin' and the rain an' the Injuns an' the renegades, an' is comin' straight to Fort Prescott."

The scout stood up, and Major Braithwaite saw by the lightning that his face was transfigured. Hope and certainty had replaced fear and uncertainty.

"Thar!" he exclaimed. "The fourth time. Don't you hear it, louder than before?"

A low, deep note which certainly differed from that of the thunder now came to the ears of Major Braithwaite, and his own experience of battle fields told him its nature.

"It is cannon! it is surely cannon!" he exclaimed joyously. "And you are right! It is the fleet coming to our relief! The boy got through!"

Major Braithwaite's face glowed, and so did that of Gregory Wilmot, who was also now sure that they had heard the sound of the white man's great guns. But they kept it to themselves for the present. There must be no false hope, no raising of the garrison into joy merely to let it fall back deeper into gloom. So they waited, and the far note of the cannon did not come again, although they pressed themselves against the wooden bastion and strained ears to hear.

The heart of Major Braithwaite gradually sank again. It might have been an illusion. A heart so eager to hear might have deceived the ear into hearing. The darkness seemed to have closed in thicker and heavier than ever. The flashes of lightning, although as vivid as before, were not so frequent, but the wind rose, and its shrieking got upon the ears of the three.

"I wish it would stop!" said the Major angrily. "I want to hear something else! Was it imagination about the cannon? Could we have deceived ourselves into hearing what we wanted to hear? Is such a thing possible?"

The scout shook his head.

"It wuzn't no deception," he said. "I shorely heard cannon. Mebbe they've quit firin' 'em, an' are comin' on now with the rifles an' the pistols. It must be that. I'm like you, Major, I believe in that boy, Henry Ware, an' he's comin' right now with the fleet to save all them women an' children behind us."

"God grant that you may be right," said Major Braithwaite devoutly.

The three still leaned against the crest of the wooden wall, and the rain yet drove upon them, unnoticed. They listened, with every nerve taut, for a sound that did not come, and whenever the lightning flashed they strained their eyes down the dark reaches of the river to see something that they did not see. Over an hour passed, and they scarcely moved. Then the scout straightened up.

"Now I hear 'em," he said, "Listen! It's not the cannon that's talkin'. It's the rifles. I tell you that fleet, with the boy on it, is comin'. It's shoved its way right through all them nests uv hornets an' wasps. Hear that. Ef that ain't the crack uv rifles, then I'm no livin' man."

Sounds, faint but with a clear distinct note, came to them, and again Major Braithwaite knew that he could not be mistaken. It was like the distant fire of the skirmishers when the Anglo-American army advanced through the woods upon Ticonderoga, and he had heard the same sound in their front when they first stood upon the Plains of Abraham. It was rifle fire, the lashing whip-like crack of the western rifles, and it was a rifle fire that was advancing.

"Glory to God!" he exclaimed in immense exultation and relief. "It's the fleet! The fleet's at hand! There cannot be any doubt now! Take the men to the walls, Wilmot, because it's likely that the Indians will renew the attack upon us when they see that the fleet is coming to our relief."

The face of Major George Augustus Braithwaite, scholar and soldier, was transformed. Both the scout and Gregory Wilmot saw it when the lightning flickered across the sky, but the same joy was pounding at their own hearts. Wilmot, obeying the Major's order, hurried away to see that the walls were manned by riflemen ready to repel any attack, but the scout remained.

"They're comin', they're comin', shore, Major," he said, "but they've had to make a mighty fight uv it. You kin be certain that Timmendiquas did everything to keep them from gittin' by. Listen, thar go the rifles ag'in, an' they're nearer now!"

Good news spreads as fast as bad, and in ten minutes it was known throughout the beleaguered houses of Fort Prescott that a great and glorious event had occurred. They would not be taken by the Indians, they would not be slaughtered or carried into captivity. Relief, many boats and canoes filled with their own warlike country-men, an irresistible force, were at hand, because Major Braithwaite and Gregory Wilmot had heard the welcome sound of their rifles and cannon.

Out into the rain and darkness poured men, women, and children, and they cared for neither rain nor darkness, because the rescue from imminent death was coming, and they would see it.

People gathered around Major Braithwaite and the scout and they did not order them back, because this was a time when all would wish to know, and in the night and darkness they waited patiently and hopefully to see what the fitful flashes of lightning might let them see.

The sound of random shots came from the dripping forest, and the men of Gregory Wilmot at the barrier replied, but Major Braithwaite paid little attention to such a diversion as this. The Indians would not undertake now to storm the fort—they had failed already in several such attempts—and their renewed fire was merely proof that they, too, knew that the fleet had forced the watery passage.

"Thar she goes ag'in!" said the scout. "Ez shore ez I'm a livin' sinner that's the crack uv Kentucky rifles, fifty uv 'em at least!"

"You're right," said Major Braithwaite, "and it cannot come from anything but the fleet. Hark, there's a new sound, and it removes the last doubt!"

Clear above all the other clamor of the night, the wind, the firing, and the rain, rose a long, mellow note, low but distinct, sweet and clear. It was a haunting note, full of music, light, and joy, the peal of a silver trumpet carried by the herald of Adam Colfax. Mellow and clear its echo came back, sweeping over forest and river, and its breath was life and hope.

"The battle trumpet!" exclaimed Major Braithwaite. "The vanguard of the fleet! It is speaking to us! It tells us that friends are near. Here, you men, build up a bonfire! Let them know just where we are and that we are on watch!"

Twenty willing hands brought dry wood, and, despite the rain, a great blaze leaped up within the palisade. It grew and grew. The flames, yellow and red, roared and sprang higher, casting a bright light over the wooden walls, the forest, the cliffs, and the river. Bullets whistled from the forest, but they passed over the heads of the people in the fort, and they let them go by unnoticed.

Higher rose the fires in the face of the rain, and the great yellow light over the river deepened. When the lightning flared it was a mixture of gold and silver, and it was so intense that they could see the very crinkling of the water on its surface.

Again came the mellow note of the silver trumpet, a clear, far cry that died away in little curves and undulations of sound. But it was nearer, undeniably nearer, and once more it breathed life anew into the listeners.

There was a sudden blaze of lightning, more vivid than all that had gone before. The whole surface of the river leaped into the light, and upon that surface, just where the stream curved before flowing into the narrowest passage between the hills, appeared a black dot.

It was more than a black dot, it was a boat, and, despite the distance, the astonishing vividness of the lightning made them see in it five figures, five human figures, clad in the deerskin of the border.

"Tis the boy, Henry Ware and his comrades, ez shore ez I'm a livin' sinner," muttered the scout. He could not see the faces, but he was quite sure that the one who knelt in the prow was Henry Ware.

"It is they! It must be they!" exclaimed Major Braithwaite. "And look, there are other boats behind them turning the curve—one, two, three, four, and more—and look, how their rifles flash to right and left! They beat back the red savages! Nothing can stop them! Build up the fires, my lads, that they may see!"

The trumpet pealed for the third time, and it came from the prow of the *Independence*. A mighty shout rose from the fort in reply, and then from the forest and the cliffs came the long, defiant yell of the red men, who were not yet beaten. The light was now sufficient to show them swarming along the edge of the water, and even venturing far from the bank in canoes. The tide of battle swelled anew. Timmendiquas the Great, Red Eagle, Yellow Panther, and the renegades, Girty, Blackstaffe, Braxton Wyatt and the others, urged them on. But always it was Timmendiquas, the great White Lightning of the Wyandots, who directed.

Major Braithwaite watched with fascinated eyes. The heavens were growing somewhat lighter, and that fact, allied with his bonfire, was now sufficient to disclose much. He saw the fleet, despite all the attempts to hold it, moving steadily forward in two parallel lines; he heard again the mellow notes of the silver trumpet, calling alike to the men of Adam Colfax and to those in the fort. He looked, too, for the boat that he had first seen, the one that had contained the five figures, and he found it, as before, in the very front. The five were still there, and he thought he could see their rifles flashing. The good Major felt a singular throb of relief. Then, as the battle thickened, his courage and military energy leaped up.

"We cannot stand here idle when so great an event, one that means so much to us, is going on," he said to Seth Cole. "If I mistake not, the savages are about to make their supreme effort, and it becomes us to help repel it."

"I reckon you're right, Major," said the scout. "The next ten minutes will say how this thing is goin' to end, an' we ought to be in at the sayin'."

"How many men have we on foot, and fit to fight?"

"'Bout sixty, I reckon, Major."

"Then we'll take thirty, leave the other thirty under Wilmot to hold the fort, and go forth to help our friends who wish to help us."

Action was as prompt as decision. In five minutes the brave borderers were ready, one of the gates was thrown open, to be closed immediately behind them, and with the Major and the scout at their head, they rushed toward the bank.

It was the purpose of Major Braithwaite to lead his men down the stream a little, and as soon as a position of vantage could be reached, open a covering fire that would protect the boats. They crossed the cleared space around the fort unharmed, but directly after they reached the woods beyond, bullets began to whistle about them, and the Indian war whoop rang through the dripping forest. The Major knew that he was attacked in force, and so far from helping the fleet his men must now defend themselves. But he would be an aid, nevertheless, since the attack upon his own party must draw off warriors from the leaguer of the fleet.

His men fell back to the shelter of the tree trunks, and began to fire, every one like a sharpshooter choosing his target. The Major's back was now to the river, and he could hear the rattle of the rifles behind him as well as before him. Two or three minutes of this, and a shout reached his ear. It was not the shrill, high-pitched yell of the Indian, but the deep, full-throated cry of the white man, and the Major knew it. A sudden burst of firing came from a new point, and then the attack seemed to melt away before him.

Meanwhile, the fleet, with the savages hanging on either flank, crept on up the river.

CHAPTER XXI

FORCES MEET

Major George Augustus Braithwaite had judged aright. Henry Ware knelt in the prow of the first boat, as it showed beyond the curve after forcing the watery pass. The shiftless one knelt just behind him, and in the stern was Paul, kneeling, too. The rifles of all three were hot in their hands. Long Jim and Silent Tom were now at the oars.

It all seemed—that last half hour—a dream to Henry and Paul. They had moved in a kind of mist, now red, now black. They had seen the black hills lowering above them, and the innumerable flashes of fire. They had heard the roar of the tempest and the unbroken crackle of hundreds of rifles, and they had fired in reply almost mechanically. Their one object was to press forward, always to press forward, and so long as their boat continued to move they knew that they must be succeeding.

Now they beheld the wider water before them, and upon a high hill upon the southern shore a great fire blazed, by the light of which they saw wooden walls and roofs.

"We are through!" exclaimed Henry. "We have at least come as far as the fort, whether we can land or not!"

"Yes, we are through," said the shiftless one, "but I never run such a gantlet afore, an' I hope never to do it ag'in."

He laid down his rifle a moment, and began to feel himself critically and carefully.

"What are you doing?" asked Henry.

"Me?" replied Sol. "I'm tryin' to see whether I'm all here, or whether most o' me is scattered around in the Ohio. When a million savages are shootin' at a feller, all at the same time, an' keep on doin' it, it's more'n likely that feller will soon be in pieces. No, I ain't hurt. Some o' my huntin' shirt hez been shot away, but the body o' Sol Hyde is sound an' whole, fur which I do give thanks. How are you, Henry?"

"All right. I've been grazed twice but there's no damage."

"An' you, Paul?"

"Nicked on the wrist and scared to death, but nothing more."

"An' you, Tom?"

"Nigh deef, I guess, from sech a racket, but I'm still fit fur work."

"An' you, you onery old Long Jim."

"Mighty tired, an' hungry, too, I guess, though I don't know it, but I kin still shoot, an' I kin hit somethin' too."

"Then we've come through better than we could hev hoped," said the shiftless one joyfully. "'Pears again that Paul was right when he said down thar on the Missip that Providence had chose us fur a task."

"The battle is not over yet," said Henry. "If we help the fort we've got to make a landing, or the Indians can go on with the siege almost as if we were not here. And landing in face of the horde is no easy task."

"Ain't it likely that the people in the fort will help us?" said Shif'less Sol.

"If I know Major Braithwaite, and I think I do," replied Henry, "they will surely help. It was a good thing on their part to build that bonfire as a signal and to show us the way. See how it grows!"

The fire, already great, was obviously rising higher, and its light deepened over the river. The whole fleet was now through the pass, and it swung for a few moments in the middle of the stream like a great bird hovering before it decided on its flight. The light from the bonfire fell upon it and tinged it red. Although the savage attack had not ceased, and some of the white men were still firing, most of them lay for a little while at rest to take fresh breath and strength for the landing. Henry looked back at them, and spontaneously some scene from the old Homeric battles that Paul told about came to his mind. He knew these men as

170

they lay panting against the sides of the boats, the light from the bonfire tinting their faces to crimson hues. This gallant fellow was Hector, and that was Achilles, it was Ajax who sat in the prow there, and the wiry old fellow behind him, with the wary eyes, was even the cunning Ulysses himself.

It was but a fleeting fancy, gone when Adam Colfax hailed them from the deck of the *Independence*. The eyes of the Puritan still burned with zealous fire, and those of Drouillard beside him showed the same spirit.

"What do you think of the landing?" he said to the five collectively. "Can we force it now? What do you think?"

"I think we can," Henry replied for them all, "if the people in the fort help—and listen to that! They are helping now!"

There was a sudden spurt of firing from the undergrowth on the southern bank. Nor was it fitful. It continued rapid and heavy, and they knew that a diversion of some kind had been created. It must be due to the men from the fort, and now was the time to make the landing.

Adam Colfax stood upright on the deck of the *Independence* at the risk of sharpshooter's bullet, and looked eagerly along the Kentucky shore, seeking some low place into which his boats could push their prows. His was a practiced mariner's eye, and he saw it at last, a cove which was the ending of the ravine in the high bank, and he said a few words to his trumpeter. The silver peal rose once more, mellow, clear, and reaching far, and the tired men rose, as usual, to its call. Steady hands held the rifles, and strong arms bent the oars.

The *Independence* and the boat of the five swung in toward the cove, and the whole fleet followed hard at their heels.

The savages uttered a great cry when they saw the movement, and swarmed anew for the attack, firing rapidly from the forest, while their canoes pushed boldly out from the northern shore. But Henry judged that the violence of the attack was less than when they had been in the pass, and he inferred that a considerable part of their force was drawn off by the diversion from the woods. He could mark by the rapid blaze of the rifles in the forest the place where this contest was being waged with the utmost courage and tenacity. His attentive ear noticed a sudden great increase in the firing there, and it all seemed to come from one point.

"Somebody has been reinforced, and heavily, at that," he said to Shif'less Sol.

"It's shorely so," said the shiftless one.

A faint sound, nay, hardly more than an echo, came to their ears. But it was the echo of a deep, full-throated cry, the cry that white men give.

"It's friends," murmured Henry. "I don't know who they are, but they are friends."

"It's shorely so," said the shiftless one.

Their boat and the *Independence* were now not thirty feet from the land, and in a few more moments they struck upon the shelving margin. The five instantly leaped ashore, and after them came the men of the fleet in a torrent. Now they heard that full-throated cheer again, loud, clear, and near. A powerful friend was at hand, and Adam Colfax, Drouillard ever at his side, understood it.

"Forward, men!" he cried in his highest voice. "Clear the red swarm from the bushes!"

With four score brave riflemen he charged through the forest, sweeping away what was left, at that point of the horde, and, as the warriors vanished before them, they met in an open space two other forces, one coming from the east, and the other from the south.

Adam Colfax, the brave Drouillard still at his side, stopped and stood almost face to face with a tall, middle-aged man who wore a uniform and on whose head rested a cocked hat from which the rain had long been pouring in three streams, one at each corner. The man's face bore signs of physical exhaustion, but his spirit showed triumphant. Behind him were about thirty men who leaned panting upon their rifles.

The eyes of Adam Colfax shifted to the second force, the one that had come from the south, the leader of which stood very near, also almost face to face when he turned. The second leader was even more remarkable than the first. Hardly in middle age, and with a figure of uncommon litheness and power, he had a face of extraordinary sweetness and repose. Even now, fresh from the dangers and excitement of deadly conflict, it showed no excitement. The mild eyes gazed placidly at Adam Colfax, and his hands rested unmoving upon the muzzle of his rifle. He was clothed wholly in deerskin, with the usual cap of raccoon skin. By the side of him stood a young man clothed in similar fashion. But his strong face showed all the signs of passion and battle fire. His deep-set eyes fairly flashed. Behind these two were about thirty men, mostly young, every one of them brown as an Indian and in wild garb, true sons of the wilderness.

Henry Ware quickly stepped forward. He alone knew them all.

"Mr. Colfax," he said, nodding toward the head of the first column, "this is Major Braithwaite, the commander of Fort Prescott, and this—"

He turned and paused a moment as he faced the leader of the second band, him with the peaceful eyes. He felt that he was calling the name of a great man, a fit match for any Hector or Achilles that ever lived.

"This is Daniel Boone," he said to Mr. Colfax, "and this, Mr. Boone, is Adam Colfax, the commander of the fleet that has come from New Orleans on its way to Pittsburgh."

"Daniel Boone!" exclaimed Adam Colfax, and stepping forward he took the hand of the great hunter, explorer, and wilderness fighter. It was an impulse which did not seem strange to him that he should leave Major Braithwaite for second place, and it seemed natural, also, to the Major, who did not know until then the name of the man who had come so opportunely with his friends to his relief.

172

"I knew Fort Prescott was pushed hard and would be pushed harder," said Daniel Boone, smiling gently after he had shaken hands with Adam Colfax and Major Braithwaite, "so me an' Simon—this is Simon Kenton—hurried south after some of our friends, hunters an' sech like, an' it 'pears that we've got back in time."

"You certainly have," said Major Braithwaite with deep emphasis. "Never was help more opportune."

"It was a good fight!" exclaimed Simon Kenton, the battle fire not yet dead in his eyes.

Daniel Boone smiled again, that extraordinary smile of sweetness and peace.

"But the one that really brought us all together at the right minute," he said, "was a boy, though he is a mighty big and strong one, and he stands here right now."

He put his hand upon Henry Ware's shoulder, and Henry blushed under his tan in embarrassment.

"No, no!" he cried. "It was everybody working together, and I'm just one of the crowd."

He retreated hastily behind his comrades, and Daniel Boone laughed.

"Don't you think that we'd better go into the fort now, Mr. Boone?" asked Adam Colfax with deference.

"Yes, as soon as we can," replied Daniel Boone, "but we ought to keep a strong line down to the fleet. We can do it with a chain of men. We are not out of the woods yet. We might be, if a common man led the Indians, but Timmendiquas, Timmendiquas the Great, the White Lightning of the Wyandots, is out there, and he does not know what it is to be beat."

"He surely must be a mighty chief," said Major Braithwaite—the way in which everybody spoke of Timmendiquas impressed him. "But come, we will enter the fort."

He led the way, and the triple force, now united, followed close behind. Paul's eyes were chiefly for the hunters who had come with Boone and Kenton, and he read their minds—they did not regard what they were doing as an act of benevolence, one for which they could claim a great reward; they were doing, instead, what they loved to do, and they were grateful for the chance. It was the wildest looking band of white men that he had ever seen, but it was worth a regiment to the fort.

The gate was thrown open again, and the three forces passed in, there to receive the welcome that is given only by those who have been saved from what looked like certain death. The scout and the others who knew him gave Henry Ware the hearty clasp of the hand that means so much, and then the five went to a cabin to eat, rest and sleep.

"We'll need you to-morrow," said Adam Colfax, "but meanwhile you must refresh yourselves."

"That sounds mighty good to a tired man," said Shif'less Sol in his whimsical tone. "I never worked so hard in my life before ez I hev lately, an' I think I need to rest for the next three or four years."

"But we got through, Sol, we got through, don't furgit that," said Long Jim. "I'd rather cook than fight. Uv course, I'm always anxious about the vittles, but I ain't plum' skeered to death over 'em."

"Reminds me I'm hungry," said Shif'less Sol. "Like you, Jim, I furgot about it when I wuz down thar on the river, fightin', but I'm beginnin' to feel it now. Wonder ef they'll give us anything."

Sol's wish was fulfilled as a woman brought them abundant food, corn bread, venison, buffalo meat, and coffee. When it came they sat down in the home-made chairs of the cabin, and all of them uttered great sighs of relief, drawn up from the bottom of their hearts.

"I'm goin' to eat fur two or three hours," said the shiftless one, fastening an eager eye upon a splendid buffalo steak, "an' then I'm goin' to sleep on them robes over thar. Ef anybody wakes me up before the last uv next week he'll hev a mighty good man to whip, I kin tell you."

Eager hand followed eager eye. He lifted the steak and set to, and his four faithful comrades did the same. They ate, also, of the venison and the corn bread with the appetite that only immense exertions give, and they drank with tin cups from a bucket of clear cold water. There was silence for a quarter of an hour, and then Shif'less Sol was the first to break it.

"I didn't think I could ever be so happy ag'in," he said in tones of great content.

"Nor me, either," said Jim Hart, uttering a long, happy sigh. "I declar' to goodness, I'm a new man, plum' made over from the top uv my head to the heels an' toes uv my feet."

"And that's a good deal of a man, six feet four, at least," said Paul.

"It's true," repeated Long Jim. "I'm like one uv them thar Greek demigods Paul tells about. Now an' then I change myself into a new figger, each more bee-yu-ti-ful than the last. Ain't that so, Sol? You know it's the truth."

"You could become more bee-yu-ti-ful a heap o' times an' then be nothin' to brag about," retorted the shiftless one.

"Now let's all go to sleep," said Henry. "It must be past midnight, and you may be sure that there will be plenty of work for us to do to-morrow."

"'Nough said," said Tom Ross. He threw himself upon one of the couches of skins and in three minutes was fast asleep. Sol, Jim, and Paul quickly followed him, and the long, peaceful breathing of the four was the only sound in the room.

Henry looked down at his comrades, and his heart was full of gladness. It seemed wonderful that they had all come with their lives through so many dangers, and silently he returned thanks to the white man's God and the red man's Manitou, who were the same to him.

There was a single window to the cabin, without glass, but closed, when necessary, with a wooden shutter. The shutter was propped back a foot or more now in order to admit air, and Henry looked out. The lightning had ceased to flash, save for a feeble quiver now and then on the far horizon, and it had grown somewhat lighter. But the rain still fell, though gently, with a steady, soft, insistent drip, drip that was musical and conducive to sleep.

Henry saw the dusky outline of buildings and several figures passing back and forth, guns on shoulders. These were riflemen, and he knew that more were at the wooden walls keeping vigilant guard. Once again he was filled with wonder that he and his comrades should have come so far and through so much, and yet be safe and whole.

There was no sound save an occasional light footstep or the clank of a rifle barrel against metal to break the musical beat of the rain. All the firing had ceased, and the wind moaned no longer. Henry let the fresh air play for a while on his face, and then he, too, turned back to a couch of skins. Sleep, heavy, but not dreamless, came soon.

Henry's dream was not a bad one. On the contrary, it was full of cheer and good omen. He lay in the forest, the forest, dry, warm, green, and beautiful, and an unknown voice over his head sang a splendid song in his ears that, note by note, penetrated every fiber of his being and filled him with the most glorious visions. It told him to go on, that all things could be conquered by those who do not fear to try. It was the same song among the leaves that he had heard in his waking hours, but now it was louder and fuller, and it spoke with a clearer voice.

The boy turned on his buffalo robe. There was no light in the cabin now, but his face in the darkness was like that of one inspired. He awoke presently. The voice was gone, but he could still hear it, like a far sweet echo, and, although he knew it to be a dream, he considered it to be fact, nevertheless. Something had spoken to him while he slept, and, confident of the future, he fell into another sleep, this time without dreams.

When Henry awoke the next morning Daniel Boone sat by his couch. His comrades awakened, too, one after another, and as they sat up, Boone, out of the great goodness of his soul, smiled upon them.

"You are woodsmen, fine woodsmen, all of you," he said, "an' I want to talk with you. Do you think the great chief, Timmendiquas, will draw off?"

"Not he!" exclaimed Henry. "He is far from beaten."

"An' that's what I say, too," repeated Boone in his gentle voice. "Adam Colfax and Major Braithwaite think that he has had enough, but I'm warnin' them to be careful. If the warriors could crush the fleet an' the fort together they'd strike a terrible blow against the settlements."

"There is no doubt of it," said Henry. "Timmendiquas, so long as he has a

175

powerful army of the tribes, will never give up such a chance."

"Mr. Colfax thinks they've suffered so much," continued Boone, "that they will retreat into the far north. I know better. Simon Kenton knows better, and we want you and one or two of your comrades to go out with us and prove that the warriors are still in a circle about the fort an' the fleet alike."

"I'm your man for one," said Henry. All the others promptly volunteered, also, but it was arranged that Paul and Long Jim should stay behind to help the garrison, while Henry, Shif'less Sol, and Tom Ross should go with Boone and Kenton. But it was agreed, also, that they should not go forth until night, when the darkness would favor their forest inquiries.

The five had slept very late, and it was past ten o'clock when they went out into the large, open space that lay between the houses and the palisade. All signs of the storm were gone. The forest might give proof of its passage, but here it was as if it had never been. A gentle wind blew, and the boughs moved softly and peacefully before it. The sky, a deep blue, showed not a single cloud, and the river flowed a stream of quivering molten gold. The fleet was drawn up in a long line along the southern bank, and it, too, was at rest. No sweep or paddle stirred, and the men slept or lounged on the decks. Nowhere was an enemy visible. All the storm and strife of the night before had vanished. It seemed, in the face of this peaceful wind and golden sun, that such things could not be. Adam Colfax and Major Braithwaite might well cling to their belief that the warriors, beaten and disheartened, had gone. The women and children shared in this conviction, and the afternoon was a joyous one in Fort Prescott, but when the night had fully come, Boone and Kenton, with Henry, Tom Ross and the shiftless one, went forth to prove a thing that they did not wish to prove, that is, that the Indians were still at hand.

They went first in a southwesterly direction, and they saw many signs of the savages, that is, that they had been there, but these signs also indicated that now they were gone. They curved about toward the northwest, and the result was the same, and then, for the sake of certainty, they came back again toward the southwest. Assured now that the southern woods contained no Indians anywhere near the fort, they stopped in the bushes near the bank of the river and held a little council.

"It 'pears to me that it's turned out just about as all of us thought it would," said Daniel Boone.

"It's so," said Simon Kenton, "but we had to look first an' be sure."

"That is, we all believe that the Indians have gathered on the northern bank," said Henry, "and under the lead of Timmendiquas are planning a grand attack upon us."

"It's so," said Shif'less Sol.

Tom Ross nodded.

"That bein' so," said Daniel Boone, "we must cross an' take a look at them."

All the others nodded. Everyone was anxious for the perilous task.

"We can swim the river," said Henry, "and, also, we can borrow a small boat from the fleet."

"I wouldn't borrow a boat," said Daniel Boone. "The fewer that know about us the better, even the fewer of our friends. It 'pears to me that if we were to stroll down stream a little we might find a canoe that somebody had left there for a time of need."

Henry smiled. He felt sure that the canoe would be found. But he and the others, without another word, followed Boone for a distance until they came to a point where the banks were low. Then Boone forced his way noiselessly into a patch of bushes that grew at the very water's edge, and Simon Kenton followed him. The two reappeared in a minute, carrying a spacious canoe of birch bark.

"Simon an' me took this," explained Boone, "before we went south for our friends, an' we hid it here, knowin' that we'd have a use for it some time or other. We'll crowd it, but it'll hold us all."

They put the canoe upon the water, and the five got in. Boone and Kenton lifted the paddles, but Tom Ross at once reached over and took the paddle from the hand of Daniel Boone.

"It shan't ever be told uv me," he said, "that I set still in a boat, while Dan'l Boone paddled me across the Ohio."

"An' yet I think I can paddle pretty well," said Daniel Boone in a gentle, whimsical tone.

"'Nuff said," said Tom Ross, as he gave the paddle a mighty sweep that sent the canoe shooting far out into the river. Boone smiled again in his winning way, but said nothing. Kenton, also, swung the paddle with a mighty wrist and arm, and in a few moments they were in the middle of the river. Here the light was greatest, and the two paddlers did not cease their efforts until they were well under the shelter of the northern bank, where the darkness lay thick and heavy again.

Here they stopped and examined river, forest, and shores. The fleet at the southern margin blended with the darkness, but they could dimly see, high upon the cliff, the walls of the fort, and also a few lights that twinkled in the blockhouse or the upper stories of cabins.

"They're at peace and happy there now," said Daniel Boone. "It's a pity they can't stay so."

He spoke with so much kindly sympathy that Henry once more regarded this extraordinary man with uncommon interest. Explorer, wilderness fighter, man of a myriad perils, he was yet as gentle in voice and manner as a woman. But Henry understood him. He knew that like nature itself he was at once serene and strong. He, too, had felt the spell.

"They won't be troubled there to-night," continued Boone. "The Indians will not be ready for a new attack, unless it's merely skirmishing, an' Adam Colfax and

Major Braithwaite will keep a good guard against them. Now which way, Simon, do you think the camp of the Indians will be?"

Kenton pointed toward the northeast, a silent but significant gesture.

"There's a little prairie over there about two miles back from the river," he said. "It's sheltered, but safe from ambush, an' it's just the place that Timmendiquas would naturally choose."

"Then," said Boone, "that's the place we'll go to. Now, boys, we'll hide our canoe here among the bushes, 'cause we're likely to need it again. We may come back mighty fast, an' it might be the very thing that we wanted most at that partickler time."

He laughed, and the others laughed, too. The canoe was well hidden among the bushes, and then the five borderers disappeared in the forest.

CHAPTER XXII

THE SPEECH OF TIMMENDIQUAS

A score of Indian chiefs sat in the center of a little, almost circular, prairie, about a half mile across. All these chiefs were men of distinction in their wild forest way, tall, lean, deep-chested, and with black eyes full of courage and pride. They wore deerskin dress, supplemented with blankets of bright blue or red, but deerskin and blankets alike were of finer quality than those worn by the warriors, many hundreds in number, who surrounded the chiefs, but at a respectful distance.

However commanding the chiefs were in presence, all yielded in this particular to one, a young man of great height, magnificent figure, and a singularly bold and open countenance. He was painted much less than the others, and the natural nobility of his features showed. Unconsciously the rest had gathered about him until he was the center of the group, and the eyes of every man, Red Eagle, Yellow Panther, Captain Pipe, and all, were upon him. It was the spontaneous tribute to valor and worth.

Near the group of chiefs, but just a little apart, sat four white men and one white boy, although the boy was as large as the men. They, too, looked over the heads of the others at the young chief in the center, and around both, grouped in a mighty curve, more than fifteen hundred warriors waited, with eyes fixed on the same target to see what the young chief might do or to hear what he might say.

There was an extraordinary quality in this scene, something that the wilderness alone can witness. It was shown in the fierce, eager glance of every brown face, the rapt attention, and the utter silence, save for the multiplied breathing of so many. A crow, wheeling on black wings in the blue overhead, uttered a loud croak, astonished perhaps at the spectacle below, but no one paid any attention to him, and, uttering another croak, he flew away. A rash bear at the edge of the wood was almost overpowered by the human odor that reached his nostrils, but, recovering his senses, he lurched away in the other direction.

It was Yellow Panther, the veteran chief, who at last broke the silence.

"What does the great Timmendiquas, head chief of the Wyandots, think of the things that we have done?" he asked.

Timmendiquas remained silent at least two minutes more, although all eyes were still centered upon him, and then he rose, slowly and with the utmost dignity, to his feet. A deep breath like the sighing of the wind came from the crowd, and then it was still again.

Timmendiquas did not yet speak, nor did he look at any one. His gaze was that of the seer. He looked over and beyond them, and they felt awe. He walked slowly to a little mound, ascended it, and turned his gaze all around the eager and waiting circle. The look out of his eyes had changed abruptly. It was now that of the warrior and chief who would destroy his enemies. Another minute of waiting, and he began to speak in a deep, resonant voice.

"You are here," he cried, "warriors and men of many tribes, Shawnee, Miami, Delaware, Illinois, Ottawa, and Wyandot. All who live in the valley north of the Ohio and east of the Mississippi are here. You are brave men. Sometimes you have fought with one another. In this strife all have won victory and all have suffered defeat. But you lived the life that Manitou made you to live, and you were happy, in your own way, in a great and fair land that is filled with game.

"But a new enemy has come, and, like the buffalo on the far western plains, his numbers are past counting. When one is slain five grow in his place. When Manitou made the white man he planted in his soul the wish to possess all the earth, and he strives night and day to achieve his wish. While he lives he does not turn back, and dead, his bones claim the ground in which they lie. He may be afraid of the forest and the warrior. The growl of the bear and the scream of the panther may make him tremble, but, trembling, he yet comes."

He paused and looked once more around the whole length of the circle. A deep murmur of approval broke forth, but the forest orator quieted it with a single lift of his hand.

"The white man," he resumed, "respects no land but his own. If it does not belong to himself he thinks that it belongs to nobody, and that Manitou merely keeps it in waiting for him. He is here now with his women and children in the land that we and our fathers have owned since the beginning of time. Many of the white men have fallen beneath our bullets and tomahawks. We have burned their new houses and uprooted their corn, but they are more than they were last year, and next year they will be more than they are now."

He paused again and looked over the circle of his auditors. His eyes were flashing, and his great figure seemed to swell and grow. Like so many men of the woods he was a born orator, and practice had increased his eloquence. A deep,

179

angry murmur came from the crowd. The passion in their hearts responded to the passion in his voice. Even the white men, the renegades, black with treason and crime, were moved.

"They will be more next year than they are now," resumed Timmendiquas, "if we do not drive them back. Our best hunting grounds are there beyond the Beautiful River, in the land that we call Kain-tuck-ee, and it is there that the smoke from their cabins lies like a threat across the sky. It is there that they continually come in their wagons across the mountains or in the boats down the river.

"The men of our race are brave, they are warriors, they have not yielded humbly to the coming of the white man. We have fought him many times. Many of the white scalps are in our wigwams. Sometimes Manitou has given to us the victory, and again he has given it to this foe of ours who would eat up our whole country. We were beaten in the attack on the place they call Wareville, we were beaten again in the attack on the great wagon train, and we have failed now in our efforts against the fort and the fleet. Warriors of the allied tribes, is it not so?"

He paused once more, and a deep groan burst from the great circle. He was playing with the utmost skill upon their emotions, and now every face clouded as he recalled their failures and losses to them, failures and losses that they could not afford.

"He is a genius," said Simon Girty to Braxton Wyatt. "I do not like him, but I will say that he is the greatest man in the west."

"Sometimes I'm afraid of him," said Braxton Wyatt.

The face of Timmendiquas was most expressive. When he spoke of their defeats his eyes were sad, his features drooped, and his voice took on a wailing tone. But now he changed suddenly. The head was thrown back, the chin was thrust out fiercely and aggressively, the black eyes became coals of fire, and the voice, challenging and powerful, made every heart in the circle leap up.

"But a true warrior," he said, "never yields. Manitou does not love the coward. He has given the world, its rivers, its lakes, its forests, and its game, to the brave man. Warriors of the allied tribes, are you ready to yield Kain-tuck-ee, over which your fathers have hunted from the beginning of time, to the white man who has just come?"

A roar burst from the crowd, and with a single impulse fifteen hundred voices answered, "No!" Many snatched their tomahawks from their belts and waved them threateningly as if the hated white man already stood within reach of the blade. Even the old veterans, Yellow Panther and Red Eagle, were stirred in every fiber, and shouted "No!" with the others.

"I knew that you would say 'No,'" continued Timmendiquas, "although there are some among you who lost courage, though only for the moment, and wanted to go home, saying that the white man was too strong. When the fleet reached the fort they believed that we had failed, but we have not failed. We are just beginning to tread our greatest war path. The forces of the white men are united; then we will destroy them all at once. Warriors, will you go home like women or stay with your chiefs and fight?"

A tremendous shout burst from the crowd, and the air was filled with the gleam of metal as they waved their tomahawks. Excited men began to beat the war drums, and others began to dance the war dance. But Timmendiquas said no more. He knew when to stop.

He descended slowly and with dignity from the mound, and with the other chiefs and the renegades he walked to a fire, around which they sat, resuming their council. But it was not now a question of fighting, it was merely a question of the best way in which to fight.

"Besides the fleet, Daniel Boone, Simon Kenton, and thirty or forty men like them have come to the relief of the fort," said Girty.

"It is so," said Timmendiquas.

"It would be a great stroke," continued the renegade, "to destroy Boone and Kenton along with the fort and the fleet"—he was as anxious as Timmendiquas to continue the attack.

"That, too, is so," said Timmendiquas gravely. "While it makes our task the greater, it will make our triumph the greater, also. We will watch the fleet, which I do not think will move yet, and when our warriors are rested and restored we will attack again."

"Beyond a doubt you're right," said Girty. "We could never retreat now and leave them to enjoy a victory. It would encourage them too much and discourage our own people too much."

Timmendiquas gave him a lightning glance when he used the phrase "our own people," and Girty for the moment quailed. He knew that the great White Lightning did not like him, and he knew why. Timmendiquas believed that a man should be loyal to his own race, and in his heart he must regard the renegade as what he was—a traitor. But Girty, with all his crimes, was not a coward, and he was cunning, too, with the cunning of both the white man and the red. He recovered his courage and continued:

"The taking of this fleet in particular would be the greatest triumph that we could achieve, and it would be a triumph in a double way. It has vast quantities of powder, lead, cannon, pistols, bayonets, medicines, clothing, and other supplies for the people in the east, who are fighting our friends, the British. If we should take it we'd not only weaken the Americans, but also secure for ourselves the greatest prize ever offered in the west."

The eyes of all the chiefs glistened, and Girty, shrewd and watchful, noticed it. He sought continually to build up his influence among them, and he never neglected any detail. Now he reached under his buckskin hunting shirt and drew forth a soiled piece of paper.

"Braxton Wyatt here, a loyal and devoted friend of ours, has been in the south,"

181

he said. "He was at New Orleans and he knows all about this fleet. He knows how it was formed and he knows what it carries. Listen, Timmendiquas, to what awaits us if we are shrewd enough and brave enough to take it:

"One thousand rifles.

"Six hundred muskets.

"Six hundred best French bayonets.

"Four hundred cavalry sabers.

"Two hundred horse pistols, single-barreled.

"Two hundred horse pistols, double-barreled.

"Three hundred dirks.

"Six brass eighteen-pounder field pieces.

"Four brass twelve-pounder field pieces.

"Two brass six-pounder field pieces.

"Four bronze twelve-pounder field guns.

"Ten thousand rounds of ammunition for the cannon.

"Two hundred barrels of best rifle powder.

"Thirty thousand pounds of bar lead and more than two hundred thousand dollars worth of clothing, provisions, and medicines.

"Wouldn't that make your mouth water? Did any of us ever before have a chance to help at the taking of such a treasure?"

"It is not wonderful that the white men fight so well to keep what they carry," said Timmendiquas.

Then the chief questioned Braxton Wyatt closely about the fleet and the men who were with it. His questions were uncommonly shrewd, and the young leader saw that he was trying to get at the character of the boy. Wyatt was compelled to give minute descriptions of Adam Colfax, Drouillard and the five, Henry Ware, Paul, Shif'less Sol, Tom Ross, and Long Jim.

"We know him whom you call the Ware," said Timmendiquas with a sort of grim humor, "and we have seen his strength and speed. Although but a boy in years, he is already a great warrior. He is the one whom you hate the most, is he not?"

He looked straight into Braxton Wyatt's eyes, and the young renegade had an uncomfortable feeling that the chief was having fun at his expense.

"It is so," he admitted reluctantly. "I have every cause to hate him. He has done me much harm, and I would do the same to him."

"The youth called the Ware fights for his own people," said Timmendiquas gravely.

There was an uncomfortable silence for a minute, but the flexible Girty made the

182

best of it.

"And Braxton, who is a most promising boy, fights for his, too," he said. "He has adopted the red race, he belongs to it, and it is his, as much as if he was born to it."

Timmendiquas shrugged his shoulders, and, rising, walked away. Girty followed him with a bitter and malevolent glance.

"I wish I was strong enough to fight against you, my haughty red friend," was his thought, "but I'm not, and so I suppose it's policy for me to fight for you."

The Indians devoted the rest of that day to recuperation. Despite their losses, perfect concord still existed among the tribes, and, inflamed by their own natural passions and the oratory of Timmendiquas, they were eager to attack again. They had entire confidence in the young Wyandot chief, and when he walked among them old and young alike followed him with looks of admiration.

Hunters were sent northward after game, buffalo, deer, and wild turkeys being plentiful, and the others, after cleaning their rifles, slept on the ground. The renegades still kept to themselves in a large buffalo skin tepee, although they intended to mingle with the warriors later on. They knew, despite the dislike of Timmendiquas, that their influence was great, and that it might increase.

Twilight came over the Indian camp. Many of the warriors, exhausted from the battle and their emotions, still slept, lying like logs upon the ground. Others sat before the fires that rose here and there, and ate greedily of the food that the hunters had brought in. On the outskirts near the woods the sentinels watched, walking up and down on silent feet.

Simon Girty, prince of renegades, sat at the door of the great buffalo skin tepee and calmly smoked a pipe, the bowl of which contained some very good tobacco. His eyes were quiet and contemplative, and his dark features were at rest. In the softening twilight he might have seemed a good man resting at his door step, with the day's work well done.

Nor was Simon Girty unhappy. The fallen, whether white or red, were nothing to him. He need not grieve over a single one of them. Despite the distrust of Timmendiquas, he saw a steady growth of his power and influence among the Indians, and it was already great. He watched the smoke from his pipe curl up above his face, and then he closed his eyes. But the picture that his fancy had drawn filled his vision. He was no obscure woods prowler. He was a great man in the way in which he wished to be great. His name was already a terror over a quarter of a million square miles. Who in the west, white or red, that had not heard of Simon Girty? When he spoke the tribes listened to him, and they listened with respect. He was no beggar among them, seeking their bounty. He brought them knowledge, wisdom, and victory. They were in his debt, not he in theirs. But this was only the beginning. He would organize them and lead them to other and greater victories. He would use this fierce chief, Timmendiquas, for his own purposes, and rise also on his achievements.

183

The soul of Simon Girty was full of guile and cunning and great plans. He opened his eyes, but the vision did not depart. He meant to make it real. Braxton Wyatt came to the door, also, and stood there looking at the Indian horde. Girty regarded him critically, and noted once more that he was tall and strong. He knew, too, that he was bold and skillful.

"Braxton," he said, and his tone was mild and persuasive, "why are you so bitter against this boy Ware and his comrades?"

The young renegade frowned, but after a little hesitation he replied:

"We came over the mountains together and we were at Wareville together, but I never liked him. I don't know why it was in the beginning, but I suppose it was because we were different. Since then, in all the contests between us, he and his friends have succeeded and I have failed. I have been humiliated by him, too, more than once. Are not these causes enough for hatred?"

Girty drew his pipe from his mouth, and blew a ring of smoke that floated slowly above his head.

"They are good enough causes," he replied, "but I've learned this, Braxton: it doesn't pay to have special hatreds, to be trying always to get revenge upon some particular person. It interferes too much with business. I don't like Timmendiquas, because he doesn't like me, doesn't approve of me, and gives me little stabs now and then. But I don't waste any time trying to injure him. I'm going to make use of him."

"I can't make use of Henry Ware and the others," said Braxton Wyatt impatiently.

Girty blew another ring of smoke and laughed.

"No, you can't, and that's the truth," he said, "but what I wanted to tell you was not to be in too great a hurry. You've got talents, Braxton. I've been watching you, and I see that you're worth having with us. Just you stick to me, and I'll make a great man of you. I'm going to consolidate all these tribes and sweep the west clean of every white. I'm going to be a king, I tell you, a woods king, and I'll make you a prince, if you stick to me."

A glow appeared in the eyes of Braxton Wyatt.

"I'll stick to you fast enough," he said.

"Do it," said Girty in a tone of confidence, "and you can have all the revenge you want upon the boy, Ware, his comrades, and all the rest of them. Maybe you won't have to wait long, either."

"That is, if we take the fort," said Wyatt.

"Yes, if we take the fort, and I'm specially anxious to take it now, because Dan'l Boone is in it. I don't hate Boone more than I do others, but he's a mighty good man to have out of our way."

McKee, Eliot, Quarles, and Blackstaffe joined them, and long after the twilight had gone and the night had come they talked of their wicked plans.

CHAPTER XXIII

ON THE OFFENSIVE

Boone, Kenton, Henry, Sol, and Ross were returning in the night through the forest. They had stolen near enough to the Indian camp to see something of what had occurred, and now and then a word of the speech of Timmendiquas had reached them. But they did not need to see everything or to hear everything. They were too familiar with all the signs to make any mistake, and they knew that the savage horde was preparing for another great attack.

"I was hopin'," said Daniel Boone, "that they'd go away, but I didn't have any faith in my hope. They think they've got to hit hard to keep us back, an' they're right. I s'pose these are the finest huntin' grounds in the world, an' I wouldn't want to give them up, either."

"The attack led by Timmendiquas will be most determined," said Henry. "What do you think we ought to do, Mr. Boone?"

"Hit first, an' hit with all our might," said Boone with emphasis. "Mr. Colfax is takin' ammunition to the east, but he's got to use some of it here."

A happy thought occurred to Henry.

"They had cannon, which we sunk," he said, "and of course they've got a lot of ammunition for these guns left. What if we should capture it? It would more than make up for what he will have to expend."

"And why couldn't we raise them guns?" said Shif'less Sol. "It ain't likely that the explosion tore 'em up much, jest sunk 'em, an' even ef they wuz dented about a bit they could be fixed up all right."

"That is certainly worth thinkin' about," said Boone. "We must lay that notion before Adam Colfax and Major Braithwaite. If the guns are raised it ought to be done to-night."

They hurried toward the spot where they had left their canoe, but they did not forget caution. Their message was too important for the messengers to be caught by scouting Indian bands. They trod softly, and stopped at frequent intervals to listen, hearing now and then the hoot of owl or whine of wolf. They knew that the warriors were signaling to one another, but they felt equally sure that these signals had no reference to themselves, and they pressed steadily on until they came to the river.

They found their canoe untouched, and rowed out into the middle of the stream, where they stopped at Daniel Boone's command.

"You know just where them boats were when you sunk 'em?" he said to Henry.

Henry pointed to a spot upon the water.

"It was within three feet of that place," he replied. "I'd stake anything upon it."

"Then it'll 'pear strange to me if they don't belong to us before mornin'," said Boone. "The fleet has all kinds of men, an' some of 'em will know about raisin' things out of water. What do you say, Simon?"

"Why, that them cannon are just as good as ours already," replied Kenton with energy.

Boone laughed softly.

"Always the same Simon," he said. "You see a thing that ought to be done, an' to you it's as good as done. I don't know but that it's well for a man to feel that way. It helps him over a heap of rough places."

The boat resumed the passage, and without interruption reached the further shore, where they hid it again, and then entered the woods on their way to the fort.

"All of us must talk mighty strong about this attack," said Boone. "We must hit while we're all together, an' we must make Adam Colfax and Major Braithwaite feel the truth of what we're sayin'. If the Indians have the biggest force that was ever gathered here, so have we, an' that mustn't be forgot."

Daniel Boone spoke with great emphasis. His usually mild voice rose a little, and his words came forth sharp and strong. Henry felt that he told the truth, a truth most important, and he resolved, boy though he was, to second the famous woodsman's words, with all his power.

They reached the fort without incident, noticing with pleasure that communication between fort and fleet was still sustained by a strong double line of sentinels. Daniel Boone asked at once for a conference with Adam Colfax and Major Braithwaite, and it was held in the chief room of a great, double log house, the largest in the place. Besides the two commanders, the five, Drouillard, Thrale, Lyon, Cole, Wilmot, and several others of importance were present. Boone, as became his experience and fame, was the first spokesman, and he laid before the commanders and their lieutenants all that the party had seen and heard. He urged with great vigor the necessity of attack. He believed that they would have a much greater chance of victory if they struck first instead of standing on the defensive, and he spoke, also, of the cannon in the river, and the ammunition for them in the Indian camp. If they were successful, the ammunition taken from the Indians would more than fill the place of that used by the fleet in the battle. The eyes of Adam Colfax glowed appreciatively at the mention of the cannon.

"It would be a great thing for us," he said, "if we could arrive at Pittsburgh with more cannon than we started with at New Orleans. We've got divers and the best of boatmen in our fleet, and I'm in favor of going out at once to salvage those guns."

186

"An' do we attack?" asked Boone persistently. "Remember there is a great treasure in the Indian camp, the ammunition they brought for the guns, which you can take with you to Pittsburgh. The harder we strike now the better it will be for us hereafter."

The stern face of Adam Colfax began to work. The battle light came into his eyes.

"I'm a good member of the church," he said, "and I'm a man of peace, that is, I want to be, though it seems to me that Providence has often set my feet in other ways, and I believe that what you tell us, Mr. Boone, is true. If we don't strike hard at this chief Timmendiquas and his men, they will strike hard at us. I shall put it to the men in my fleet; if they favor it we will go. What do you say about yours, Major?"

Major George Augustus Braithwaite looked at the men about him, and the battle light came into his eyes, also.

"It shan't be said, Mr. Colfax, that my men stayed behind when yours were willing to go. I shall take the vote, and if they say fight—and they certainly will say it—we go with you."

Messengers hurried forth and polled the two camps. An overwhelming majority were in favor of making the attack. In the fleet the men, used to danger and loving it as the breath of their nostrils, were practically unanimous. But Adam Colfax and Major Braithwaite agreed to drag first for the cannon.

At three in the morning a dozen boats went forth upon the river. They contained the two commanders, Boone, Kenton, Henry, and others, besides the divers and the men with grappling hooks. It was a dark night, and, in addition, Simon Kenton and a dozen good men went upon the northern shore to search the woods for a watching enemy.

Henry and Seth Cole were in the boat with Adam Colfax and Major Braithwaite, and the two sought to mark the exact spot upon the water at which the cannon had been sunk. This might seem a most difficult task, but the last detail of that eventful night had been photographed upon Henry's mind. It seemed to him that he could remember, within a foot, the exact spot at which the guns had gone beneath the current of the Ohio.

"It is here," he said to Adam Colfax, and the scout nodded. All the boats anchored, and the divers dropped silently into the muddy stream. Henry watched eagerly, and in a minute or so they came up sputtering. Their hands had touched nothing but the bottom. Adam Colfax and Major Braithwaite looked disappointed, but both Henry and the scout insisted that it was the right place.

"Try again," said Adam Colfax, and the divers went down a second time. The last of them to come up looked over the side of their boat, and when he wiped the water from his eyes, triumph showed there.

"They are here," he said. "I touched one of them. It is sunk in the mud, but we can raise it."

187

They uttered a little suppressed cry of triumph, and presently the divers touched the other, also. The grappling hooks were sent down, and those in the boats watched eagerly to see if the cannon could be raised. Every big gun was precious in those early days of war, and if Adam Colfax could add two such prizes to those he already had on the fleet he would be repaid for much that they had suffered on their great voyage.

The hooks at last took hold. The gun was lifted two or three feet, but it slipped from their grasp and buried itself deeper than ever in the mud. A second trial was made with a like result, but the third was more successful, and the gun was lifted from the water. It came, muzzle first, presenting a grinning mouth like some sea monster, but the suppressed little cry of triumph broke forth again as the cannon was loaded, with toil and perspiration, upon one of the larger boats. Their joy increased when they saw that it was practically unharmed, and that it would be indeed a valuable addition to their armament.

Salvage was also made of the second gun, which was damaged somewhat, but not so much that the armorers of the fleet could not put it in perfect condition within a week. Fortunately they were not interrupted in their task, and when Kenton and the scouts rejoined them, and they started back to Fort Prescott, Adam Colfax and Major Braithwaite shook hands in mutual congratulation.

"I never expected to pick up two good guns in this manner," said Adam Colfax. "Suppose you mount them upon your own walls until we are ready to go."

Henry, Ross, and Shif'less Sol, after sleeping through the morning hours, were joined by Paul and Long Jim, and spent the afternoon in scouting. They crossed the Ohio in a canoe some distance below the fort, and once more entered the deep woods, bearing back in a northeasterly direction toward the Indian camp. Here Henry and the shiftless one went forward alone, leaving the others to wait for them.

They did not dare approach near enough to the camp to observe with minuteness what was going on, but they saw that a great stir was in progress. Fresh detachments of warriors from the Shawnees and Miamis had arrived, but the Wyandots, the least numerous of them all, still held the first place. The palm for courage, energy, and ability was yet conceded to them and their great chief, Timmendiquas, by all the rest.

"I don't think they'll be ready to move against us again for about two days," said the shiftless one.

"And we'll strike before then," said Henry. "They won't be suspecting such a movement by us, for one reason, because a river is between."

"That's so," said Sol, "an' they've been doin' so much attackin' themselves that they won't think about our takin' the job from 'em."

They returned with their news, and at midnight the white army started forth on its great but hazardous attempt. The night was fairly clear, with a good moon and many stars, and the departure from the fort was in silence, save for the sobbing of the women and children over those whom they might never see again.

It was a formidable little army that issued from the southern gate of the fort, the one away from the river, perhaps the strongest that had yet been gathered in the west, and composed of many diverse elements, the Kentuckians who had been Kentuckians only a year or two, the wild hunters of Boone and Kenton, the rivermen, a few New Englanders, French and Spanish creoles, and men from different parts of Europe. It was a picturesque group without much semblance of military discipline, but with great skill, courage, and willingness in forest warfare.

Every man carried a long-barreled rifle, and they were armed in addition with pistols, tomahawks, and knives. The cannon were left behind as too unwieldy for their purpose. Adam Colfax, Major Braithwaite, Gregory Wilmot, Thrale, Lyon, Cole, Drouillard, and the other lieutenants were at the head of the little army, and Boone, Kenton, the five, and at least fifteen more were in advance or on the flanks as scouts and skirmishers. The five, as usual, were close together.

The army marched southward about a half mile, and then, turning, marched parallel with the river about two miles, in order to hide their movements from lurking Indian scouts. The fleet, meanwhile, dropped down the Ohio, clinging closely to the shadows of the western shore.

The five were rather grave as they walked ahead of the army, examining every tree and bush for sign of a foe. None knew better than they the dangers to which they were about to be exposed, and none knew better than they the wilderness greatness of Timmendiquas.

"A lazy man always hez the most trouble," said Shif'less Sol in a whisper to the others. "Mebbe ef he wuzn't so lazy he'd be lively 'nough to git out o' the way o' trouble. I'm always takin' good resolutions, resolvin' to mind my own business, which ain't large, an' which wouldn't take much time, an' never keepin' 'em. I might be five hundred miles from here, trappin' beaver an' peacefully takin' the lives of buffalo, without much risk to my own, but here I am, trampin' through the woods in the night an' kinder doubtful whether I'll ever see the sun rise ag'in."

"Sol," said Long Jim, "I sometimes think you're the biggest liar the world hez ever produced, an' that's sayin' a heap, when you think uv all them history tales Paul hez told. You know you don't want to be off five hundred miles from here trappin' innocent beaver an' shootin' the unprincipled buffaler. You know you want to be right here with the rest uv us, trappin' the Injuns, an' shootin' the renegades ef the chance comes."

"Wa'al, I reckon you're right," said the shiftless one slowly, "but I do wish it would come easier. Ef I could rest comf'table on my bed an' hev 'em driv up to me, I wouldn't mind it so much."

The march down the river was attended by little noise, considering the number of men who made it, and at the appointed place they found the fleet ready to take them on board. The scouts reported that the enemy had not been seen, and they believed that the advance was still a secret. But the crossing of the river would be a critical venture, and all undertook it with anxious hearts.

They had come back to one of the narrowest parts of the pass that had cost them so much, but no enemy was here now, and silently they embarked. All the five, as usual, were in one boat. It had turned somewhat darker, and they could not distinctly see the farther shore. Their eyes were able to make out there only the black loom of the forest and the cliffs. Their boat had oars, at which Tom Ross and Jim Hart were pulling, while the others watched, and, being scouts, they were well ahead of the rest of the fleet.

"S'pose," said Shif'less Sol, "them woods should be full o' warriors, every one o' them waitin' to take a shot at us ez soon ez we came in range? Wouldn't that be hurryin' to meet trouble a leetle too fast?"

"But I don't think the warriors are there," said Henry. "It was good tactics to come down the river before crossing, and if Indian scouts were out they must have been fooled."

"I'm hopin' with every breath I draw that what you say is true," said Shif'less Sol.

Henry, as he spoke, kept his eyes on the dark loom of forest and shore. He did not believe that an Indian band would be waiting for them there, but he could not know. At any time a sheet of rifle fire might burst from the woods, and the boat of the five would be the first to receive it. But he would not show this feeling to his comrade. He sat rigidly erect, his rifle across his knees, and nothing escaped his eyes, now used to the darkness.

Henry looked back once and saw the great fleet following a little distance behind and in ordered column, making no noise save for the plash of oar, sweep, and paddle, and the occasional rattle of arms. Talking had been forbidden, and no one attempted to break the rule.

They came closer and closer to the shore, and Henry searched the forest with straining eyes. Nothing moved there. The night was windless, and the branches did not stir. Nor did he hear any of the slight sounds which a numerous party, despite its caution, must make.

"They ain't waitin' for us," said Shif'less Sol.

"We've give them the slip."

"You must be right, Sol," said Henry. "We're within range if they are there, and they'd have fired before this time."

Ross and Jim sent the boat toward a little cove, and it struck upon the narrow beach, with the woods still silent and no enemy appearing. Henry leaped ashore, and was quickly followed by the others. Then they slipped into the woods, reconnoitered carefully for a little while, finding nothing hostile, and returned to the river.

The landing of the whole force destined for the attack was made rapidly, and with but little noise. The boats, all with skeleton crews, swung back into the

190

stream, where they anchored, ready to receive the army if it should be driven back.

Then the white force, led by Adam Colfax and Major Braithwaite, the scouts going on ahead, plunged with high courage and great hopes into the woods.

CHAPTER XXIV

THE DECISIVE BATTLE

The white army was soon hidden in the forest. It was, beyond a fact, the largest force of its kind that had yet assembled in this region, but it disappeared as completely as if it had ceased to be at all. A mile from the river it stopped, and the two commanders held a short conference with Boone and Kenton. The manner and great reputation of Boone inspired the utmost confidence, and they were very anxious not only to hear what he said, but also to do what he suggested. The council was short, and it was held in the darkness with the soldiers all about.

"Send Henry Ware and his comrades forward to see if the way is open," said Boone, "an' if it is, we should rush their camp with all our might. A night attack is usually risky, but it won't be long until day now, an' if we can get a start on 'em it will be worth a heap to us."

Adam Colfax and Major Braithwaite agreed with him, and Henry and his comrades set forth again ahead of the army. Simon Kenton went with them.

The six stole forward. They were quite sure that Timmendiquas would have out sentinels, but neither he, the other chiefs, nor the renegades would anticipate so swift a counter stroke.

The country was rough, but they made good progress, flitting forward in a silent file. Cry of wolf and hoot of owl came now and then to their ears, but they did not believe that they meant anything save the announcement from warrior to warrior that all was well.

They managed to come without detection, within several hundred yards of the camp, where they ascended a little hill and could see the low flare of light from the fires.

"I don't think we should try to get any closer," said Kenton. "We might run into a nest of 'em an' never get back. We've seen enough to know that the army can get up pretty close, an' at least attack before the savages are wholly ready. S'pose we start back."

Paul rose in obedience to the suggestion, but Henry at once pulled him down again.

"Somebody's coming," he whispered, and the six lay still in the bushes.

191

They heard light footsteps, and three men, or rather two men and a boy, emerged from the shadows. The three were seeking the easiest path, and they marked where the trees and bushes were scarcest. It was with a shivering feeling of repugnance and anger that Henry recognized them, and the same feeling animated his comrades. They were Simon Girty, Blackstaffe, and Braxton Wyatt, and the three were talking, not loudly, but in tones that the hidden six could hear distinctly.

"The attack will be begun again to-morrow night," Girty was saying, "an' it's going to be a success. Whatever you may say about him, Timmendiquas is a general, and I never before saw the Indians worked up to such a pitch. They were singing and dancing for hours to-day, an' I believe they'd now go through a lake of fire an' brimstone to get at that fleet."

"We'll let the Wyandots lead the way," said Blackstaffe.

"We certainly will," said Girty.

Then the two older men looked at each other and laughed, a low horrible laugh that made the flesh of Henry and Paul creep.

"Yes," said Girty, "we'll let the Wyandots lead, and then the Shawnees and Miamis and the others. We'll take our part, but I think some of these warriors can be spared more readily than we can."

Braxton Wyatt laughed, too, when he understood.

"That's good policy it seems to me," he said. "We plan, while the warriors do most of the fighting."

"Stick to that, an' you'll be a great man," said Girty.

The king of the renegades stood in a little opening, and the moonlight fell full upon his face. They could see it distorted into a malicious grin of cruelty and self-satisfaction. Slowly the rifle barrel of Shif'less Sol, in the bushes, was raised to a level, and it was pointed straight at a spot between the cruel, grinning eyes. An infallible eye looked down the sight, and a steady finger approached the trigger.

Never, until his last day came, in very truth, was Simon Girty, the renegade, nearer death. But Henry put out his hand, and softly pressed down the rifle barrel.

"I don't blame you, Sol," he whispered. "It would be getting rid of a monster and saving many good lives, but you can't do it now. It would break up our whole plan of attack."

It was one of the greatest griefs in the life of Solomon Hyde, called the shiftless one, that he was compelled to yield to Henry's advice. He had held Simon Girty, the arch criminal, under his rifle, and he had picked out the spot where he knew he could make his bullet hit, and then he must put down his rifle and pass over the opportunity just as if it had never been.

"You're right," he whispered back in reluctant words, and lowered his rifle. The three renegades continued to talk of the projected attack, but they passed on, and soon their words could be heard no longer. Then their figures became indistinct and were lost to sight. Shif'less Sol uttered a low cry, so full of bitterness that Henry was forced to laugh, knowing as he did its cause.

"I never had sech a chance afore," said Shif'less Sol, "an' I'll never hev it ag'in."

"Henry was right," said Simon Kenton. "'Twould never have done to have given an alarm now. We must hurry back, bring up the army, and strike before the dawn."

There could be no difference of opinion on such a subject, and they rapidly retraced their footsteps. In three-quarters of an hour they rejoined the army, and told that the way was clear. The leaders heard the report with great satisfaction and promptly arranged the plan of battle. The chief thing that they sought to guard against was the confusion so often arising from darkness, when friend might fire into friend.

"They mustn't get too much excited, and they must look before they shoot," said Boone. "It will be only two hours to daylight, an' if we can hold together till then we can beat 'em."

The army, although kept in a body, was numbered in detachments. Adam Colfax took the lead of one, Major Braithwaite another, Boone another, while Drouillard, Thrale, and all the other prominent men also had commands. The five, Kenton, and the scouts led the advance.

Once more they took up their progress through the woods, and pressed swiftly on toward the Indian camp. It was one of those darkest hours before the dawn, and so many men marching at a rapid pace, could not keep from making considerable noise. Bushes rustled, arms rattled, and dry sticks broke with a snap beneath heavy feet.

"On, men! on!" cried Adam Colfax. "We can't be slow now!"

A dog howled, and then another. An Indian sentinel fired his rifle, and then a second and a third did the same. The white vanguard replied, and then with a great shout the army rushed toward the Indian force.

But Timmendiquas was not wholly surprised. His men, posted in a circle around the camp, gave the alarm as they fell back, firing their rifles, and uttering the long Indian yell. Hundreds of throats took it up, and the savages, seizing their weapons, sprang forth to the conflict. In a moment, the woods were filled with sparkling flames, and the bullets whistled in showers. There were shouts and cries and a rain of twigs cut off by the bullets in the darkness.

The five and Kenton fell back upon the main body and then rushed on with them, keeping in the front line.

"Let's keep together! Whatever happens, let's keep together!" cried Shif'less Sol, and the others in reply shouted their assent. They were compelled to shout now, because hundreds of rifles were cracking, and the roar was swelling fast.

193

Innumerable flashes lit up the forest, and a cloud of fine gray powder rose, stinging the nostrils of the combatants, and, like an exciting narcotic, urging them on to action.

The first rush of the white army bore all before it. The Indian sentinels and the others who constituted the fringe of their band were rapidly driven in on the main body, and many of the soldiers and hunters began to shout in triumph as they reached the edge of the prairie and saw their foe, huddled in dark masses beyond. But as they came into the open they met a strong core of resistance that soon hardened and spread.

The great chief, Timmendiquas, although partly surprised by the swift attack of the whites, did not lose either his presence of mind or his courage. He showed on that morning all the qualities of a great general. He rallied the warriors and posted them in bands here and there. Hundreds threw themselves upon the ground, and from that less exposed position sent their bullets into the charging force. Timmendiquas himself stood near the center with the veterans, Red Eagle and Yellow Panther, on either side of him. He scorned to seek cover, but remained, at his full height, where all could see him, shouting his orders and directing the battle. Behind him were the renegades firing their rifles, but protecting themselves, with the caution upon which they had resolved.

Henry and his comrades kept their place in the front of the charge, and, according to their plan, close together. The darkness was now lighted up so much by the incessant firing that the boy could see very well not only the long line of his friends, but the black masses of the enemy as well. He felt the resistance harden as they came into the prairie, and he knew that the Indians had been rallied. He thought he heard the voice of Timmendiquas calling to them, and then he believed that it was only his fancy. Because he knew that Timmendiquas would do it, his active brain made a picture of him doing it.

He was suddenly seized and pulled down by the strong arms of Tom Ross. All his comrades were already stretched flat upon the earth. The next instant a great volley was fired by the Indians. The bullets from hundreds of rifles swept over their heads, and many struck true behind them. Some men fell, and others staggered back, wounded. There were cries and groans.

The Indian yell, poured from many throats, arose. It was long, high-pitched, and it seemed to Henry that it had in it a triumphant note. They had stopped the white advance, and they were exulting. But the little army, rising up, rushed forward again, and then threw itself flat upon its face once more to escape the withering fire of the Indians. From their own recumbent position the white men replied, sending in the bullets fast.

It was a confused and terrible scene in the intermittent light and darkness, white men and red men shouting together in their deadly struggle. The front of the conflict lengthened, and the clouds of smoke drifted all through the forest. It entered the throats and lungs of the combatants, and they coughed without knowing it.

Henry lay long on the ground, pushing forward a few feet at a time, loading and firing his rifle until it grew hot to his hands. He was not conscious of the passage of time. His brain burned as if with a fever. He felt now and then a great throb of exultation, because the white army was always advancing, only a little, it was true, but still it was an advance, and never a retreat. But the throb of exultation presently became a throb of rage. The advance of a sudden ceased entirely. The Indians were gathered in such heavy masses in front that they could not be driven back. Their front was one continuous blaze of fire, and the whistling of the bullets was like the steady flowing of a stream. Timmendiquas, despite his disadvantage, had marshaled his forces well, and Henry knew it.

The boy began to have a great fear that they would be driven back, that they would be defeated. Was so much blood to be shed, so much suffering to be endured for nothing? His thoughts went back a moment to Fort Prescott and the women and the children there. Theirs would be the worst fate. He put one hand to his face and felt that it was wet. He was seized with a furious desire to rise up and rush directly into the flame and smoke before him. He longed for the power to win the victory with his single arm.

A lull of a few moments in the firing came presently, and the darkness instantly closed in again. A long, triumphant yell came from the Indians, and the white men replied with a shout, also triumphant. Henry was conscious then that his eyes were smarting from the smoke, and he coughed once or twice. He half rose to a sitting position, and a hand fell upon his shoulder.

"Come, my boy," said a voice in his ear. "We want you and your comrades for a new movement. We've got to take 'em in the flank."

Henry looked up and saw the mild face of Boone, mild even now in the midst of the battle. He sprang to his feet, and, with a sort of wonder, he saw his four comrades rise around him, unhurt, save for scratches. It did not seem possible to him that they could have come so well through all that fire. He did not think of himself.

"Come," said Boone, and the five went back a little space, until they came to a clump of trees beneath which Adam Colfax, Major Braithwaite, Drouillard, Simon Kenton, and few others were talking.

"I hate to risk so many good men," said Adam Colfax.

"It must be done," said Major Braithwaite. "It's our only chance, and we must take it while the darkness lasts. The day will break in a half hour."

"You're right," said Adam Colfax, flinging away his last fear. "Take two hundred of our best men, and may God go with you!"

In five minutes the two hundred were on their way with Major Braithwaite, the five, Boone, and Kenton at their head. It was their object to curve about in the woods and then fall suddenly upon the Indian flank, relying upon weight and surprise. They trod lightly and soon passed beyond the area of smoke. Behind them the firing was renewed with great violence and energy. Adam Colfax was

195

pressing the attack afresh. "Good!" Henry heard Major Braithwaite murmur. "They won't suspect that we are coming."

Fifteen minutes of marching, and they were at another segment in the circle of the prairie. The crackle of the firing was now further away, but when they came to the edge of the open they saw the flash of the rifles and heard again the repeated whoops of the Indians.

"Now!" exclaimed Daniel Boone. "This is their exposed side, and we must rush upon them!"

"Come!" exclaimed Major Braithwaite, raising his cocked hat upon the point of his sword and running into the open prairie. The two hundred and fifty followed him with a wild shout, and they hurled themselves upon the Indian flank. At the same time Adam Colfax and his whole force rushed forward anew.

The two divisions closed down like the clamps of a vise. The charge of the flanking force was made with such immense courage and vigor that nothing could withstand it. Major Braithwaite continually shouted and continually waved his sword. The cocked hat fell off, and was trampled out of shape by the men behind him, but he did not know it, and he never regretted it. Henry was conscious, in that wild rush, of the friendly faces about him, and of the red horde before him, but he felt little else, save an immense desire to strike quickly and hard.

The red men fight best from ambush and by means of craft and surprise. Struck so suddenly and with such energy on the flank, they gave way. Superstition increased their fears. The face of Manitou was turned from them, and many of them ran for the forest.

Timmendiquas raged back and forth. Now and then he struck fleeing warriors with the flat of his tomahawk and shouted to them to stay, but all of his efforts were without avail. The jaws of the vise were coming closer and closer together. The renegades, considering the battle lost, were already seeking the refuge of the woods. Yet Timmendiquas would not go. With the Wyandots and the bravest of the Shawnees and Miamis he still held the ground where a group of tepees stood, and many men fell dead or wounded before them.

Adam Colfax and Major Braithwaite met in the prairie, and in their excitement and joy wrung each other's hands.

"A glorious triumph!" exclaimed the Major.

"Yes, but we must push it home!" said the stern Puritan, his face a red glow, as he pointed toward the tepee where Timmendiquas and the flower of the warriors still fought.

Henry was near them and heard them. He saw, also, a gray light shooting down, and he knew the dawn was at hand.

The Major raised his sword once more. Adam Colfax took his hat in his hand and waved it. Then the whole white force, uttering a simultaneous shout, rushed upon the group around Timmendiquas. Henry and his comrades, shouting with them, were in the front of the attack.

The Indian band was swept away, and, with the battle smoke in his nostrils, Henry followed the survivors into the forest. The day was coming, but it was still dark within the shadow of the trees. Henry marked the dusky form of a tall warrior, and he followed him with every ounce of energy that he could command.

The warrior ran rapidly and soon the prairie was left behind. The noise and confusion of the dying battle sank away, but Henry did not notice it. The fury of the conflict was still in his veins, and he thought of nothing but to overtake the fleeing warrior, who was not far before him.

The gloom in the forest deepened. Thickets grew all about them, and the last light from the firing was shut out. Then the tall warrior turned abruptly and fired at his pursuer. The bullet whistled by Henry's ear, and he would have fired in return, but it was too late. The warrior was rushing upon him, and his own impetus carried him forward to meet the Indian. They were locked the next instant in a desperate grasp, as they writhed and struggled over the leaves and grass, each putting forth his utmost strength.

It was too dark in the forest for Henry to see his opponent, but he knew that he had never before been seized by anyone so powerful. He was only a boy in years himself, but boys, in his time in the west, developed fast under a strenuous life, and few men were as tall and strong as he. Moreover, he knew some of the tricks of wrestling, and the Indians are not wrestlers. He used all his knowledge now, trying the shoulder hold and the waist hold and to trip, but every attempt failed. The immense strength and agility of the Indian always enabled him to recover himself, and then the struggle was begun anew.

The beads of sweat stood out on Henry's forehead, and he believed that he could hear his sinews and those of his opponent crack as they put forth prodigious efforts. Both fell to the ground and rolled over and over. Then they were back on their feet again, without ever releasing their hold. Henry tried to reach the knife in his belt, and the Indian sought his, too. Both failed, and then, Henry, crouching a little, suddenly put his shoulder against his antagonist's chest, and pushed with all his might. At the same time he hooked his right foot around the Indian's ankle and pulled with a mighty jerk.

It was a trick, the device of a wrestler, and the great Indian, losing his balance, went down heavily upon his back. Henry fell with his full weight upon him. The Indian uttered a gasp, and his grasp relaxed. Henry in an instant sprang to his feet. He snatched up his rifle that he had dropped in the bushes, and when the fallen man rose the muzzle of a loaded rifle, held by steady hands, confronted him.

Henry looked down the sights straight into the face of the Indian, and beheld Timmendiquas, the great White Lightning of the Wyandots. Timmendiquas saw the flash of recognition on the boy's face and smiled faintly.

"Shoot," he said. "You have won the chance."

Conflicting emotions filled the soul of Henry Ware. If he spared Timmendiquas it would cost the border many lives. The Wyandot chief could never be anything but the implacable foe of those who were invading the red man's hunting grounds. But Henry remembered that this man had saved his life. He had spared him when he was compelled to run the gantlet. The boy could not shoot.

"Go!" he said, lowering his rifle. "You gave me my life, and I give you yours."

A sudden light glowed in the eyes of the young chief. There was something akin in the souls of these two, and perhaps Timmendiquas alone knew it. He raised one hand, gave a salute in the white man's fashion, and said four words.

"I shall not forget."

Then he was gone in the forest, and Henry went back to the battle field, where the firing had now wholly ceased. The white victory was complete. Many Indians had fallen. Their losses here and at the river had been so great that it would be long before they could be brought into action again. But the renegades had made good their escape. They did not find the body of a single one of them, and it was certain that they were living to do more mischief.

Henry sought his friends at once, and his joy was very great when he discovered them to be without wounds save those of the slightest nature. The leaders, too, had escaped with their lives, and they were exultant because they had captured a thousand rounds of ammunition for the two cannon and four hundred good muskets from the Canadian posts, which would be taken with the other supplies to Pittsburgh.

"It was worth stopping and fighting for these," said Adam Colfax.

A week later the five sat in a little glade about a mile south of the Ohio, but far beyond the mouth of the Licking. They had left the fleet that morning as it was moving peacefully up the "Beautiful River," and they meant to pass the present night in the woods.

Twilight was already coming. A beautiful golden sun had just set, and there were bars of red in the west to mark where it had gone.

Jim Hart was cooking by a small fire. Paul lay at ease on the grass, dreaming with eyes wide open. Tom Ross was cleaning his rifle, and he was wholly immersed in his task. Henry and Shif'less Sol sat together near the edge of the glade.

"Henry," said the shiftless one, "when that battle wuz about over I thought I saw you runnin' into the woods after a big warrior who looked like a chief."

"You really saw me," said Henry, "and the Indian was a chief, a great one. It was Timmendiquas, although I did not know it then."

"Did you overtake him?"

"I did, and we had a fight in the dark. Luck was with me, and at the end of the struggle I held him at the muzzle of my rifle."

"Did you shoot?"

"No, I could not. He had saved my life, and I had to pay the debt."

The shiftless one reached out his hand and touched Henry's lightly.

"I'm glad you didn't shoot," he said. "I'd have done the same that you did."

An hour later they were all asleep but Tom Ross, who watched at the edge of the glade, and Henry, who lay on his back in the grass, gazing at the stars that flashed and danced in the blue sky.

Sleep came to the boy slowly, but his eyelids drooped at last, and a wonderful peace came over him. The wind rose, and out of the forest floated a song, soothing and peaceful. It told him that success, the reward of the brave, had come, and, as his eyelids drooped lower, he slept without dreams.

THE END

8387691R00109

Made in the USA
San Bernardino, CA
08 February 2014